Praise for the novels of

ROBIN D. OWENS

"RITA® Award-winner Owens offers a world strongly imbued with a sense of magic in this contemporary fantasy series launch.... Romance and fantasy fans will enjoy Jenni's preparation to enter a new world of compromise between the Folk, humans, and technology."
—*Publishers Weekly,* starred review, on *Enchanted No More*

"A multi-faceted, fast-paced gem of a book."
—*The Best Reviews* on *Guardian of Honor*

"This book will enchant readers who enjoy strong heroines."
—*RT Book Reviews* on *Sorceress of Flight*

"Fans of Anne McCaffrey and Mercedes Lackey will appreciate the novel's honorable protagonists and their lively animal companions."
—*Publishers Weekly* on *Protector of the Flight*

"Strong characterization combined with deadly danger make this story vibrate with emotional resonance. Stay tuned as events accelerate toward the final battle."
—*RT Book Reviews* on *Keepers of the Flame*

"A glorious end to the series."
—*Wild on Books* on *Echoes in the Dark*

Also available from

ROBIN D. OWENS

and LUNA Books

THE SUMMONING SERIES

Guardian of Honor
Sorceress of Faith
Protector of the Flight
Keepers of the Flame
Echoes in the Dark

and the digital prequel
"Song of Marwey"

MYSTIC CIRCLE

Enchanted No More

Enchanted Again

ROBIN D. OWENS

LUNA™

LUNA™

Recycling programs
for this product may
not exist in your area.

ENCHANTED AGAIN

ISBN-13: 978-0-373-80341-5

www.Harlequin.com

Printed in U.S.A.

To all my friends, online and off; to my critique buddies
and beta readers, word warriors and other LUNA authors.
I couldn't do this without your continued support.

And to my mom and my new stepdad.

Enchanted Again

CHAPTER 1

March
Denver, Colorado

IF SHE'D AGED NATURALLY, AMBER SARGA would have been twenty-six. But her gift for curse breaking cost her days, weeks, months…years.

She'd found another gray hair today. Gray hair on a gray day.

Amber was taking a break from her home genealogical business to prepare a flower bed. Halfheartedly she stuck the big trowel into the dirt. An odd scent drifted to her and she straightened. There was something in the air….

When her yellow Labrador puppies, Baxt and Zor, went into a barking frenzy, she turned. And saw a small brown being in her garden. Her mouth fell open.

He was plucking a bloom from the heavy mass of her violets and dropping the flower into a jar.

He was nothing human. Small, under three feet, thin, triangular face and large triangular ears, he was definitely magic. Over the past few years, living in Mystic Circle's cul-de-sac, Amber had gradually become aware that there was true magic in the world, and magical people.

Although they tried, the puppies couldn't get near him. They bounced off some sort of force field. He wore boots and sturdy pants and a shirt. All brown.

Amber swallowed. "What are you?"

"I'm a brownie," he grumbled.

She had a brownie in her garden. She swallowed again. "And you are, uh, harvesting violet blooms?"

His brown slit-pupil gaze fixed on her trowel, he gave a short nod. "You have good stuff here." He sniffed. "Much better than Jenni's few plants."

He must mean Jenni Weavers, her neighbor to the south. With enough spit to speak again, Amber said, "Thank you. And you need the blooms for...?"

"Going to crystallize them as a candied accent."

"Ah." Amber nodded. It didn't seem strange that a magical being would eat violets. "I have a chocolate pie recipe with crystallized violets."

The brownie's large eyes grew huge, seeming to take up more space on his face. "Chocolate pie," he breathed, clutching his jar. Then he offered it to her. "Chocolate pie." The tips of his ears quivered.

Ah, so he *loved* chocolate.

"I could make a chocolate pie for you. And maybe you could help me with my magical gift."

His mouth pursed as he scanned her from top to toe. "One of the Cumulustre human offspring. Gypsy strain?"

"Huh? I'm Amber Sarga."

He scrinched his boney shoulders together and kept his mouth shut.

The puppies' yips increased in volume. With a flick of his fingers and a guttural mutter, the brownie cast *something* fine and silky at the pups. They abruptly collapsed into snoring sleep. Then he glanced at her from the corner of his eyes and bent down to caress another violet bloom. "I can candy them for you...for the chocolate pie."

"Of course."

"When will you make it?"

Amber raised her brows. "I'll shop for the ingredients today and the chocolate pie will be done tomorrow afternoon." Every time she said *chocolate pie* the brownie's catlike pupils dilated a little more.

Again with the mournful eyes. He was better with the appealing look even than the puppies.

He said, "All the chocolate in Jenni's house disappeared."

Into a round brownie tummy, Amber figured.

A shiver ran along the ground under Amber's soles. Her ears popped as a female brownie appeared. "What are you doing here, Pred?" She put her hands on her hips and tapped a tiny foot on the yellow grass. Her flexible triangular ears rolled close to her skull and up again. She glared at the man. "You *knew* she has enough magic to see you, and that she believes in magic. Why didn't you turn invisible?"

The guy threw out his chest. "She's Jenni's friend and our neighbor. If she can see magic, better that she sees me than violets being plucked and vanishing."

With a huff of breath the woman shook her head. "We agreed that we wouldn't contact her. You know the consequences."

"What consequences?" asked Amber.

The female brownie sniffed lustily in Amber's direction. "As we thought. A descendant of the air-elf Cumulustre family." The tiny woman frowned. "Cadet branch. Strain of Romani blood."

"Not enough for the gypsies to claim me," Amber said, barely able to speak for the words buzzing in her brain: Descendant. Elf. Cumulustre. *Elf!*

"Now we've met her, we can't ignore her," the little woman continued, staring at Pred. "*You* will have to inform the great brownie Tiro that he is not free. His geas to serve the human branch of the Cumulustre family is still in effect."

The guy cringed, shoulders up, ears down. "Tiro will be angry."

"Were the violets worth it?" the woman asked.

Standing tall—nearly three feet—the guy hissed, "Yesss. She is going to make us *chocolate* pie with the violets. Anything else is not our problem."

"Chocolate pie." The woman stilled. Weakly she said, "Well, I suppose the damage is done." She took the jar from the guy's limp fingers, sprinkled fizzing *magic* on it and the violets candied.

"This enough?" asked the man.

"Yes," Amber said automatically.

The brownie woman sighed. "Maybe, if we are careful, we won't have to say anything to Tiro for a while." She put the jar on the ground, linked elbows with the man, muttered, "Cumulustre" and they both vanished. Probably to next door. Amber's next-door neighbor, Jenni Weavers, was not quite human. Amber wasn't exactly sure what Jenni was, but the woman had a way with fire.

Amber sat down hard, and the puppies, now released from the sleep spell, bolted over to her and tumbled into her lap, licking her face.

Rafe winced as his friend's fist hit the top of his car. No way to treat a Tesla. Rafe said nothing. Conrad had just watched his wife divorce him and the judge give custody of his son to his ex.

Not to mention the fact that former wife, infant son and her attorneys vanished as soon as they'd left the courtroom. No sign of them, hide nor hair.

Rafe dreaded the words Conrad would say pretty damn soon.

"It's the curse," Conrad said.

Those words. Everything in Rafe stilled. Or maybe his muscles froze and his blood pumped hot. One of the strange things that had brought them together in college, the fact that they both came from "cursed" families. Weird in the modern world.

Conrad fumbled his key chain. Rafe jostled Conrad, snagging the door opener when it dropped from his fingers. "You're riding. I'm driving."

Grumbling, Conrad shambled to the passenger side. As soon as he was strapped in, he repeated, "It's the curse."

Rafe stopped checking the rearview for the progress of the huge SUV inching out into the lane behind him. He looked at Conrad, who was as pale as the white shirt he wore with his gray suit. "You can't believe a guy you saw once," Rafe said.

"The guy was my father, and he was right. We Cymblers love and lose. Lose our sons, too. Soon after we find the kid again as an adult, we die. Has been happening for generations. He left a family tree. You saw it."

"You shouldn't believe an alcoholic."

"That's brutal, Rafe. You're just in denial of your own damn deadly curse."

Rafe started the car. "I'll get you home and we'll check in with the private investigative firm I hired to keep track of your wife."

"Wait. Rafe, just wait a damn minute." Conrad sounded drunk. He hadn't been sleeping well, Rafe knew that, and Conrad was probably hanging on to the last shred of his control. Hell, the man was desperate.

Rafe flexed his fingers on the steering wheel. Nice machine. He preferred Italian, but this electric vehicle was excellent. "What?"

Conrad said, "I'm thinking we need to try more unusual avenues to get rid of our curses."

"What are you talking about?" The SUV was finally gone. Rafe reversed.

"I've got the name of a curse breaker." Conrad tapped the nav and a map showed up. "That's the way."

Snorting before he grimaced, Rafe said, "This is stupid."

"Humor me." Conrad's voice cracked.

"Yeah, right." Rafe waited a beat. Conrad said nothing more. Rafe could understand pride. "Okay." He scrolled the map so he could see the whole thing, then back at the route. Rafe hadn't been in Denver for a while, but he was good with maps.

A lot of cops were in the vicinity and they eyed the hot red Tesla roadster. Rafe drove carefully to the street.

Before he could say anything, his cell rang with a familiar tone. "That's my detective. Pocket of my jacket. Put it on speaker." A cop was tailing him, watching. He'd mind his manners.

Conrad snatched the phone, thumbed it on. Through the static, Rafe heard, "Davail, this is Herrera at Ace Investigations."

"Yeah?" Rafe asked.

"We lost them," reported the private detective Rafe had hired…just in case.

"Find them. Money is no object." He jerked his head at Conrad, who turned off the phone. Then Rafe accelerated on northbound Speer and kept to the posted, low speed limit on the elevated bridge.

Conrad said, "Thanks, bro. I'll pay you back." He rolled his shoulders. "Now it begins, the search—" he waved "—everything else. At least I know I'll live until I see him again. Not like *your* family death curse. You really think you're going to last eight months to your thirty-third birthday?"

Rafe ignored the fast clench of his gut. "For sure. Don't worry about Marta and Dougie. We'll find them. This P.I. firm's the best."

Conrad shook his head again.

A few minutes later they'd pulled up and parked in front of a brick Victorian house, complete with turret. The place was tucked away in a quiet cul-de-sac.

"This is such a stupid idea," Rafe said.

Conrad said stiffly, "She's the real deal, a gypsy and a curse breaker. I got her name a while back from a Romani psychic."

Conrad had always believed more in the "curses" than Rafe. Believed enough to research them a little, visit a psychic or three, line up experts, "keep his options open." Rafe had ignored his friend's quirk then. Now it was a real pain in the ass. More, Rafe was worried that some wacko would latch onto Conrad's hurt and fear and milk it for all he was worth. Which was considerably less than it had been since Marta had wanted a lump sum settlement and Conrad had paid it.

But Conrad still had a couple of million to attract leeches of the worst sort.

Conrad closed his door, glanced around. He rolled

his shoulders. "Don't need to lock the Tesla. Lots of good energy."

Rafe winced, but Conrad loved his car. Seemed to Rafe that was a good sign they wouldn't be staying long. The sooner he got Conrad back to the home he'd inherited from his mother, the better.

"I'll know if the woman's a fake. I always know," Conrad said.

Rafe shrugged. Conrad had always said that, Rafe had always doubted the whole thing.

"There's a certain something about a woman with psi." His mouth twisted. "Marta had it, a strong gift." Conrad cocked his head. "Do you hear voices?"

"Kids," Rafe said. The tones had been high and piping, but were lost now in wild puppy barks. Reluctantly he followed Conrad as the man ignored the front concrete sidewalk and went around the south side of the house to a six-foot iron-post gate.

"Hello, Amber Sarga!" Conrad called.

Two young golden Labs raced from the back to jump on the other side of the gate. A frowning woman appeared a few instants later, not looking anything like the image Rafe had imagined. He'd visualized long dark and curly hair, and her wearing gypsy garb like he'd seen in films.

Instead he thought of honey. Her skin was a natural tan, her eyes slightly tilted and golden brown. Her shoulder-length hair was a mixture of honey-and-maple-syrup-colored shades. And her lips were full and a dark rose. She wore blue jeans and two layered sweaters. The bottom one was white, a nice contrast against her skin, the top a dark turquoise.

"Ms. Sarga." Conrad actually grabbed the gate and rattled it. "I need to speak to you immediately. It's an emergency."

Amber stared at the pair of handsome guys. About her physical age of early thirties, older than her true age of twenty-six.

The dark, sophisticated-looking one appeared sweating and desperate. The guy with blond hair was scowling. If the clothes they wore and the car they drove was any indication, they were rich.

None of that mattered as much as the fact that her fingers were tingling like they did when her gift stirred. She was in the presence of a strong curse. Then a *wave* of air rippled toward her and she revised her thought. Two strong curses.

"Hsssst!"

She glanced back and saw the male brownie just around the corner of her house.

"Come back here! Don't go near them! Don't use your magic!" A stream of hushed words shot from the small man.

"Please, Ms. Sarga," the dark guy pleaded.

A lump of aching emotion formed in her chest. She didn't want to refuse someone who needed help. She hated doing that.

A desperate man. A desperate curse. A decade of aging.

"Baxt, Zor, go to the yard." She used a hand signal but didn't think the pups would have obeyed her if they hadn't spotted the brownie.

Slowly Amber walked to the gate. It wasn't padlocked, so the men could have entered, good that they hadn't.

"I'm sorry." She made her voice as soothing and gentle as she could. "My workload is full right now." A lie, she could use a good client or two—but not this one. "I can recommend—"

"Please, Ms. Sarga. I must speak with you immediately."

"Sir, genealogy is not a business that has emergencies." She couldn't help him now—maybe never—but not now, when she might be able to learn more about her magic from the brownies and how to use it better.

There was a long pause. His voice cracked. "My wife has vanished, along with my year-old son."

A shudder passed through her. She wanted to ask what his curse was—but that would be revealing too much.

"I'm sorry." She forced the words from her throat.

The man jerked hard on the gate and she stepped back.

"Conrad, take it easy." The blond guy put his hand on the dark one's shoulder.

"Conrad?" asked Amber, then felt a surge of anger at herself. Don't ask names. Don't get involved. Her gift didn't age *only* her. And she'd given up her magic as too dangerous months ago, gotten the puppies to ensure she wouldn't waver.

The blond man weighed her with a hard stare.

Words tumbled from Conrad. "I'm Conrad Tyne-Cymbler. My curse has already happened. I'm worried for my son." He drew in a ragged breath. "I don't want him to grow up without a father like I did."

She flinched at the pain in Conrad's voice. "I'm sor—"

"Please help me. You're a genealogist. I have a family tree. I can hire you to work on that as well. I'll pay you whatever."

"I can't find your son—"

"I have private investigators," Conrad said at the same time the blond man said, "We're working that situation."

Conrad continued, "I'm desperate. Please help me."

Amber blinked again, this time against stupidly stinging eyes. She couldn't refuse a direct and desperate request for help. At least she could listen, maybe trace the original curse so the guy could break it himself. That could happen. Maybe.

"All right." Her voice was thick, dammit! She didn't want the man to know how weak she was.

"Can we come in?"

She said the first thing that came to mind. "Do you have your family tree?"

"I...uh...no."

She looked at the blond, who had angled his body as if to protect his friend from her. "Do you?"

He snorted. "No."

She widened her hands. "I need to prepare. Come back tomorrow."

"You promise you'll listen?" persisted Conrad.

Amber hesitated.

"I need you," he pressed.

Again she couldn't say no. A problem most of the women of her family had had. They were all dead now. "All right. Tomorrow. Nine a.m. at my office on Hayward and Oak. You have the address?"

Conrad nodded. "Thank you."

"This is crap," said the blond.

She sucked in a breath. "Do you have a card?"

"Card?" Conrad asked blankly.

After another narrow-eyed stare at her, Conrad's friend dipped a hand in the pocket of Conrad's fine gray suit jacket and pulled out a piece of pasteboard. Scowling, the man shoved it though the spears of the gate.

Amber had to go closer to get it and as she did, the hair on the back of her neck rose. This man's curse was even worse than the other's. He didn't appear to care.

She took the card, avoiding his fingers.

"I'll see you tomorrow." She turned and walked to her backyard. Pred, the brownie, was still there.

They stared at each other silently until the roar of the engine announced that the men were gone. The brownie looked up at her with big, sad eyes, his ears rolled down to his head. "Too late now. I will have to tell Tiro about you. He will be angry." The small being shook his head. "It is not good to live with an angry brownie."

"Live! What?"

With a shake of his head, Pred said, "And that is not the worst. Your magic hurts you when you use it. I am sorry for you."

But not as sorry as Amber was…

CHAPTER
2

RAFE HAD BEEN DRIVING FOR SEVERAL minutes when he had to say it. "That was one of the stupidest things I've ever seen you do."

"I'm dealing with my curse and the aftermath," Conrad snapped, not opening his eyes. "Unlike you. And you've made a career of being stupid. Rock-climbing, glacier snowboarding, extreme sports. Like you're tempting death to take you before you're thirty-three."

"Like I'm living every moment of my life to the fullest," Rafe said evenly, an old argument.

"I really love Marta and my son." Conrad veered back to the most important topic.

"I know you do," Rafe said. He threaded through the traffic on Speer, muscles moving as he used the clutch and gearshift. He was better with action.

Conrad said, "You told the P.I. team to check out flights to Eastern Europe, right?"

"Of course. And did you do a run on her?" Rafe asked.

"Marta ran," Conrad answered.

"I meant, did you have someone investigate the sexy genealogist?"

Conrad cracked an eye, the side of his mouth near Rafe kicked up. "Sexy, huh?" He closed his eyes. "She did have a good body. Looked like her name…Amber. Yeah, I had someone research her background."

"When?" Rafe asked.

"When?" Conrad's tones were getting slow and foggy. "When I got her name. 'Bout a year and a half ago, I guess."

"You still have the file?"

"Sh-sure." Conrad fell asleep.

Rafe took the exit for Conrad's mansion in Cherry Creek. Since Rafe only had a small, dusty apartment in Manhattan that he hit from time to time between adventures, he was bunking with Conrad.

At a stoplight, he punched the in-car phone for his investigators.

"Mr. Davail," the detective's assistant said politely. "We will call you with any updates."

"Got another job for you."

"Oh. Yes?"

"Name is Amber Sarga, gypsy genealogist, age in the early thirties, brown hair and eyes, about five feet seven inches, a hundred and thirty pounds." He still thought of the woman as honeyed, much warmer and more vital than amber. Not stony to him. "She lives at number seven Mystic Circle in Denver." He paused, mouth turning down, decided to say the words anyway. "Supposed to be—" but he couldn't get "a curse breaker" out of his mouth "—psychic."

"We'll get right on that," the assistant assured him.

"It's urgent. Got a meeting with her tomorrow morning."

"We'll have a report to you by the end of the day."

"Thanks." He disconnected the call and wondered what the hell he was getting into. Conrad twitched and moaned.

A fleeting curiosity about his own family tree—and all those first sons who died before thirty-three—wisped through Rafe's mind.

Maybe he'd call his younger brother. Gabe was the practical one, running the family corporations, salt of the earth. He'd said something about a family tree a long while back. Rafe would bet his helicopter that Gabe had a chart or two Rafe could slap down in front of the honeyed Ms. Sarga.

Not that it would change anything. A tendril of fear began to whip acid inside his gut. Conrad's curse had come true.

Would his?

Amber played with the pups, enough to tire them for a few minutes, then went to her downstairs office and initiated a computer search for Conrad Tyne-Cymbler.

He didn't have any social network pages, but her

online investigation program showed his home—inherited—at a pricey address in Cherry Creek. His worth was recently downgraded due to a prospective divorce settlement. Amber winced, recalling the hurt that had emanated from the man. A quick search of public court files showed that the divorce hearing had been set for this morning.

She did an online query about his wife, Marta Dimir. Nothing showed up...except a quick ice-cube quiver sliding through Amber. Her minor magic that she used in genealogy, a certain past-time-sense, warned her that if she explored Marta Dimir's background she would find violence, despair, darkness.

Amber shook off the feeling. Let Tyne-Cymbler's investigators take care of the wife angle. The man had spoken of his son, and Amber noted that the boy was nearly a year old. But that wasn't what snagged her interest. Tyne-Cymbler obviously felt that the curse that affected him would also impact his son.

A father-to-son curse.

She brought up the professional genealogical database she used most often. The Colorado Tynes had a family tree available online, about five years out of date. The chart listed Conrad's father, deceased, and Conrad, but named no other Cymblers. It didn't show the Cymbler line.

There were some pics in the family albums and one of them showed the blond guy, an old college roommate of Conrad—Rafe Davail. Very uncommon surname.

Very good-looking guy who lived in Manhattan.

Without thought her fingers typed in his name on the ancestry site and got a hit. She stared at the chart.

Davail had a father-son curse, too. Anxiety tightened her throat as her eyes tracked the graph. For the past three hundred years, the first Davail son had died before he'd turned thirty-three. Rafe's father was gone, so was his grandfather and great-grandfather. There was a great-uncle who was a second son, and Rafe had a younger brother.

That wasn't good.

The only item of value Amber had in the world from her family was a gypsy ancestress's journal. A far too sketchy journal when it came to talking about curses.

But she knew what she was seeing.

Rafe Davail was very cursed.

Thumps and bumps woke Amber in the night. Her heart pounded—home invaders! The pups sprang from her bed and shot down the hall, barking. She snatched at the phone, pressed 911, started shouting over the dispatcher. "This is number seven—"

The ceiling light flicked on and a brownie appeared on the end of her bed. The phone slipped from her grip.

He wasn't Pred from next door. This one wasn't as skinny, though he was still thin. His face was more wrinkled, with lines of bad humor. His head between his large triangular ears was black. "Go ahead," the brownie said. "Let's see some fun." He went transparent.

Amber fumbled for the phone. "Never mind," she panted into it. "False alarm. My… A friend came in."

"Are you sure you're all right?" asked the dispatcher.

"Fine. Fine," Amber said.

"We have a fix on your phone and will send a squad car by."

The brownie opened and closed his hands, fingers stiff, mumbling something. Again her phone dropped.

"Changed the signal. They'll go to the wrong address, blocks away from Mystic Circle," he sneered.

"Who are you and what do you want?" Amber asked.

His features drew together and darkened with anger. His large triangular ears shook, probably with fury. She felt at a disadvantage in bed so she hopped out. "Who are—"

"I heard you the first time. Tiro. I gotta live with you." He jumped from the bed, making gargley noises that might be brownie cursing.

"Tiro?" Amber asked.

"My name, human." The brownie stalked over and walked around her. She turned in place to keep an eye on him. He opened his mouth and curled his tongue… like a cat using a sixth sense.

"The Mistweaver brownies were right. A wretched Cumulustre descendant. I thought your whole line had died out from stupidity four generations ago."

Amber crossed her arms. The March night was cold since she kept the heat low. Her nightgown was flannel, but her feet were bare. "I beg your pardon," she said in a voice as chilly as her feet.

She heard the grinding of his teeth, then he flung his head back. "And you look as stupid as all the rest. Smell like it, too. A curse breaker, right? And when you 'help' someone, you age? And your body is nearly a decade older than your true age?"

He knew her magic. He knew her family. What else did he know and what could she learn from him?

She sighed. "Yes."

Tiro stomped to the middle of the room. "If you human women of the Cumulustre bloodline had learned your lesson, I wouldn't be here. Bound to watch over you and serve you—those're my ancient orders from the elf." Stomp. "Can't contact Cumulustre without permission. Those damn Mistweaver brownies won't talk to him, either. Stuck." A hard jump on her floor.

"Watch over me why?"

He shot a finger at her. "'Cause you're a curse breaker and you age when you do magic. Cumulustre wants you watched until all of you are gone."

Amber opened her mouth.

"Stop pestering me," he snapped, whiskery eyebrows dipping.

She took a different angle. "So are you going to fall down and froth at the mouth?"

"No." But he stomped again. "But you're going to press your luck and break curses and age and die before your time, 'helping others,' like all of your ilk. Damn women."

Now ice chilled her insides as well as the late winter air wrapping around her. She was afraid he was right.

"Never saw a curse you didn't want to break. Have

to *help*." He barked a laugh and the puppies yipped louder, pushing against him. He rubbed each of their heads and didn't move an inch when they bumped against him. "Stupid," he repeated, staring with a considering eye. "You look softer than most. You'll probably go fast."

"I don't think so." She cleared her throat, knowing she shouldn't ask, but couldn't help herself. "You can't help me with my gift?"

Tiro smiled with all his pointy teeth and Amber took a step back. He looked more than happy, positively gleeful. "Give me permission and I can contact Cumulustre and all your problems will be over."

Grue slithered along her spine as if she'd stepped into a horror movie. One where you made a bad choice or a bad wish and suddenly you were running for your life or tortured or dead. She could hear her now-rapid pulse in her temples. "No, thank you. You can take the guest room."

His lip curled. "I *want* your office. Ground floor, view of the gardens, round window." He leered a bit. "Closer to the elemental energy balancer's house and the best magic."

"Huh?"

"Jin-des-farne Mist-wea-ver." His so-precise enunciation was to intimidate.

Her eyes narrowed. "Fine. Tonight you move everything in my office to the room above it, place things *exactly* as they are below. If you can do that, you can have the office as your room. If I find anything out of place, you immediately move everything back to the room on the ground floor and you get a cubicle area in the basement." She didn't know the brownie's magical powers, and from his widened eyes and a hint of respect, she thought the job might press him a little.

She kept her gaze steady and widened her own smile to show teeth, even though they weren't as sharp as his. "And you do that without the rude thumping noises that woke the puppies and me."

The dogs were drooling on his feet and he didn't seem to notice.

Tiro clapped his hands. "Done!" He vanished, and the pups looked at the dark square of the hallway beyond her open door. Then their heads swiveled back to their baskets on the floor and her comforter on the bed. Baxt plopped onto his rump and scratched his ear, then hopped back onto the bed. Zor circled around where Tiro had stood, sniffing deeply. He ambled to the door, sniffed again, then joined Baxt on the bed. They stared at Amber with big brown eyes and thwapped their tails on the bed and her chest loosened. Tiro was not the new object of adoration.

Settling back into bed and turning the light off, she considered the information she'd gleaned. Jenni Weavers's real name was Jindesfarne Mistweaver. Sounded magical to Amber.

The brownies that Amber had met that morning were now called "Mistweaver" brownies. Were they bound to Jenni like the unhappy Tiro was to Amber? So many questions.

But with every conversation Amber learned a little more. Jenni was an elemental energy balancer and Tiro wanted a room closest to Jenni's house. Amber could draw deductions from that. The old elements—earth, air, fire, water—Jenni could equalize, which, in turn, probably made the magic better somehow. Amber had always liked the feel of Mystic Circle and Jenni's magic might be the reason why.

As Amber let her eyelids drift shut, she listened for sounds. Nothing more than the dogs' breathing, the hum of the furnace turning on. Nothing from Tiro. Was he a dream? Perhaps. Dream or not, would he still be here in the morning?

She didn't know. She snuggled deeper into the pillow-top on her mattress. She'd learn more about magic from him, she was sure. A smile curved her lips.

Meanwhile he was moving all her bookcases and books and maps and charts and the huge desk and credenzas up to the second-story room at the end of the hall. She'd known after she'd furnished the office downstairs that she'd made a mistake and should have used the upstairs room that got more sunlight during the year. Now that was being fixed.

Perfect.

When sun glistened on the faint coating of mist on her windows, Amber woke again—a little late as the puppies weren't bouncing around on her bed. She figured the brownie was taking care of them as she heard playful barks from the backyard. Stretching languorously, she wondered at her changed circumstances.

Brownies in her garden, then a very grumpy one in her house. Just how nasty could he be? He wasn't happy to be here, that was for sure, but if he'd moved her office, she'd cut him a break until he went on his way.

She slid from bed and noticed her door was shut. She liked the wiggling warmth of the puppies' bodies, but waking to dog breath wasn't always great. And if the brownie decided to stay—and she'd surmised that the brownies at Jenni's house were responsible for a lot of the changes next door in the past couple of months— she'd prefer nominal privacy from him. She considered herself an outgoing and laid-back person but Tiro had been sour.

After showering and dressing, she went to the door at the back of the house that had been an exercise room.

Tiro appeared before the closed door, now painted a rich vanilla color. Apparently what she'd thought was a part of his head was a skull cap...and he was twisting it in his hands.

He was nervous. Good. She'd need to keep the up-per hand in this relationship.

Stepping by him, she turned the knob, swung the door open, entered the room...and stood in shock. It was no longer the drab gray that she'd been mean-ing to paint. It was creamy beige like her office. She hadn't meant... But other than the fact that the room was slightly smaller than the one below, everything looked precisely as she'd left it. She stared for a good minute at the shelves against the walls, the U-shaped desk facing the windows, the credenzas stacked with her current open files.

Amazing. But it wouldn't do to be approving. She went to a bookshelf and lifted a cracked maroon mug that held pencils. Sure enough, her lucky penny was there. Slowly she walked into the *U* of her desk. A few pages of paper were on her desk, covered with notes on the Smart-Gortel job. She picked up the pen angled on the paper. It was blue.

She didn't think she'd used a blue pen yesterday. She glanced at her engagement calendar/journal to her left. The ink noting her progress yesterday—a few hours of work, she'd have to step it up—was green.

Were brownies color-blind? Was Tiro?

She picked up the pen, turned to look at Tiro, who stood in the doorway. "This is wrong," she said as coolly as she could. Her wits were still scattered from the amount of work he'd done—the *magic* that had happened when she'd slept.

His small shoulders tensed. She rolled one of her own, let her gaze scan the rest of the room.... "I'm sure there are other flaws. But the job is...acceptable.... You may stay in the downstairs room that was an office. Where did you put the exercise equipment?"

"In the basement. I painted the ceiling here."

She glanced up. It was a wonderful trompe l'oeil, three-dimensional paint job, and it seemed like she was looking up into the round blue dome of the sky... with clouds.

"You like?"

Amber looked back at the brownie. She didn't doubt that his disposition was grumpy, but there was a vulnerability in his eyes that softened her and she couldn't crush his spirits. "Wonderful. Absolutely wonderful."

He plunked his cap back on his head, turned and thumped from the room down the hallway and the stairs. "I'm going to *my* room. If I must stay here…" His grumbling tapered off.

So far, so good. Somehow she'd convince Tiro to help her, and if not him, the Mistweaver brownies. She'd figure out how to make the curse breaking work without such a huge downside. There must be a way.

Rafe got up early and ran the streets of Cherry Creek for exercise. He'd looked in on Conrad and found the man sweaty and moaning in his bed. Guy wasn't going to have much good sleep again. They'd heard nothing from the private investigative firm that was supposed to be tracking and finding Marta and Dougie.

Ace Investigations *had* reported on Amber Sarga. There was no evidence that she practiced as a psychic. She had a sole-proprietorship genealogical firm called Heritage that she marketed to expectant parents in upscale neighborhoods. She was a model citizen except for one speeding ticket on the elevated bridge on Speer Boulevard. That item made Rafe smile. The one anomaly was that although Rafe thought she was in her early thirties, her birth certificate said she was twenty-six.

Three years younger than Rafe's brother, Gabe. Rafe had called Gabe.

His brother had been impatient when Rafe had

called. A pang had gone through him. He'd once been the adored older brother. Not anymore, not for several years. He'd "played" and left Gabe to work at the family businesses. More, Rafe barely made time to see his family at holidays…what little family he had. Gabe was twenty-nine and hadn't married, so there was only him and Uncle Richard. Rafe missed the closeness he'd had with Gabe, but they had little in common anymore. Rafe got the idea that his brother was counting the days until Rafe's thirty-third birthday.

Just as he had been trying to ignore the image of an hourglass with sand zooming from a small amount at the top to a large pile in the bottom.

As his feet hit the sidewalk and force pounded through his legs and body, his thoughts segued to his curse, much as he didn't want to think about it. How could he believe in something like that?

He'd asked Gabe, and his brother had replied the same as Conrad had. How could he afford not to?

Rafe still didn't have any answer. But he knew one thing. If he were going to act, it would have to be soon.

And how did you act to stop a curse?

Curse breaker. Could there be such a thing?

He'd find out soon. And if she screwed with Conrad, he'd break *her*.

CHAPTER
3

AMBER HAD BRIBED THE BROWNIES INTO attending the morning meeting with Conrad Tyne-Cymbler. The bribe had been chocolate cake and cocoa with whipped cream.

She needed all the information on curses and her gift that the small magical beings could give her.

The Mistweaver brownies had sensed that Tiro had arrived and had dropped in to check on her. Amber got the feeling that with Jenni gone, they were bored. And curious. Tiro appeared truculently curious himself.

The only difficult part was that the shared office space she rented was down a few blocks in the small neighborhood business district. Apparently only the cul-de-sac was completely magical, and though the brownies could go anywhere, the cul-de-sac was "protected" against evil. So the brownies would be on the watch for any adverse magics. Since time was growing short, Amber didn't ask about that.

She wondered if Rafe Davail would be with his friend and decided that he would...no matter how stupid he thought the whole situation was. He struck her as a man who looked out for his friends.

After a chat with the receptionist, Amber confirmed that the shared conference room was free and set up there. The brownies perched—invisible, she thought, though she could see them—on a corner cabinet, full of chocolate cake. The huge mug of cocoa they shared was between them. It seemed to waver between opaque and invisible if she stared.

She put the remainder of the cake on the table along with plates and forks, and had urns of coffee and tea prepared on one of the credenzas.

The sound of a high-performance car stopping and parking came. She twitched a lace curtain to look out the front window.

Yes, there were the men. Wearing casual clothes today, high-end jeans and raw silk shirts, Conrad in dark teal under a black bomber jacket. Rafe wore a long-sleeved navy shirt under a black motorcycle jacket. Conrad Tyne-Cymbler looked worse than yesterday. Rafe Davail appeared fiercely determined.

Her pulse beat faster. If she let it, the sound of her own blood pumping would magnify her anxiety. She could always turn down Conrad.

The front door creaked open, and the receptionist greeted the men.

Amber's hands began to tingle and as she watched a

faint pinkish-purple haze rose from her fingertips. She froze.

Tiro scowled, gestured his long-fingered hand at the mist. "You are stup— Not smart to break curses." Another sniff. "But the more you age, the sooner I can leave."

The more she aged, the sooner she would die, for sure.

And two cursed ones had just entered the building. Double whammy.

"The men are here." Hartha, the female brownie, opened the door a crack, then stepped back and put her hands on the small bumps of her hips and her foot—shod in a pointed-toe shoe of purple suede—tapped. "I think humans would consider them attractive. Elves would think them very ugly."

Amber poured out a mug of hot black coffee and took a sip. Lovely. Yes, she found both of them attractive. She could guess what elves looked like from myths and movies. No doubt most humans looked ugly in comparison. To her, the brownies appeared a lot like wet cats. Who knew if these brownies were considered comely or not? Tiro's features were more squashed than Hartha's or Pred's. Was that generational, or due to place of origin?

"The dark-haired one is staring at me and blinking, but I do not think he sees me. His face is pale and strained." Hartha sniffed and Amber couldn't decide whether it was in punctuation or she was scenting him. "He has a fair amount of magic for a human, but has suppressed it until it erupts in pulses. His magic is golden and orange with a touch of pale pink-violet." The little brownie woman turned her head to Amber as if to prompt a response.

Amber had no clue what the colors meant.

"Earth and fire and air," Pred said and smiled under a whipped-cream moustache.

"Air is elf," Amber murmured.

"Earth is dwarf, fire is djinn," said Pred.

Tiro grunted. "We don't need to teach the girl."

"She gave us chocolate cake and hot chocolate with whipped cream and is making us chocolate pie," Hartha said as Pred slurped his cocoa. "It is difficult for minor folk such as we to obtain chocolate. You've had more than your share."

"Earth is dwarf and fire is djinn," Amber repeated. "Djinn like a genie. My neighbor Jenni Weavers—you call her Jindesfarne Mistweaver—is good with fire. She must be djinn."

"Jenni is one quarter djinn and one quarter air and half human," Hartha said, still looking out the door.

Fascinating. Amber continued her line of reasoning, slid her gaze to Pred to watch for any reaction that her next words were right. "Elves and dwarves and djinn are…ah…not minor elementals."

"Greater Lightfolk," Pred said. "Dwarf, djinn, elf, mer."

"Mer…mermaid…merfolk?" Amber asked.

"Yes." Pred came over to stand with Hartha, stared through the crack. "The dark-haired one is looking at us and is uncomfortable. The blond man is leaning on the desk and flirting with the human woman."

Trying to get information about Amber from the receptionist, no doubt. Since Amber had rented the office space for several years and the receptionist appreciated well-built and well-heeled men, Rafe was probably getting several earfuls.

Pred made faces, then giggled. "The dark one—"

"Conrad," Amber supplied.

"Conrad can *almost* see us. Maybe." Pred wiggled his nose, stuck out his tongue. "He has much, much human blood."

Amber returned to learning mode. "Conrad has no, um, minor Lightfolk in his bloodline?"

Pred chuckled like gravel skittering down the sidewalk. "We are too small to mate with normal-size humans. Especially air and fire sprites. And you are ugly."

Hartha hissed and hopped a full yard back from the door. "The other! The fair-haired one!"

"Rafe," Amber corrected.

"He has turned toward us. He does not see us, but I feel his magic and his curse."

"What?" asked Pred and Amber.

"Death curse."

Amber shuddered. The thread of hope she'd held that she was wrong died. One of the main things the journal of her ancestress warned of was to never— *never*—attempt to lift a death curse.

She didn't know what happened, but it would be

really bad, probably kill her and everyone she was emotionally linked with.

Hartha continued to speak as she sidled away from the entrance and back to the far corner cabinet. "Rafe's colors are white-violet and blue-green, gold with a tiny hint of orange." She reached for the large mug, wrapped her long-fingered hands around it as if they were cold.

Pred's eyes protruded and he gasped. "Four elements? *Four!*"

Amber had thought that was good. "That isn't an asset?"

Hartha's face was hidden as she drank from the hot chocolate mug. She set it down and her gaze sharpened. "He has great magic, but carries a major glyph of green sealing most of his power."

The door opened and the bad magic enveloping the men expanded to hit Amber in a huge wave. She wanted to run. She glanced wildly at the brownies. Conrad was too desperate, Rafe too attractive. She'd made a bad mistake.

No way out. She had to be strong. She had to say "no" and mean it.

Tiro stared at her. His upper lip lifted in scary amusement. "How old is this fair-haired fellow called Rafe?"

Hartha lifted and dropped her shoulder. "Young. Not too much more than his third decade."

"His uncursed life span could be sixty more human years." Tiro rubbed his hands. "I will gain my independence much sooner than I thought. She will lift the curse and die."

★ ★ ★

There was a terrible high-pitched buzz in the room that would drive Rafe crazy if he had to work here. The back of his neck prickled as if someone were watching him. He glanced out the main window, saw the Tesla and other parked cars, and no one on the street. The spot between his shoulder blades tingled—and that was his main warning signal.

He wanted out of the room, out of the building, hell, out of the States. He could be snowboarding in Vancouver. Nah, he was ready for spring. But *somewhere else.*

He wanted Conrad out of the place, too.

Amber was paler than yesterday, as if she'd had a shock. Not his problem.

Rafe shifted his shoulders, rubbed the back of his neck, and followed Conrad's stare to a corner of the room that seemed to blur. No. Of course not.

Conrad swallowed, but then his mouth hung open. Rafe took a step and jostled him. No man should look so clueless in front of a threat. And despite her truly excellent figure showcased in a red knit dress, Amber Sarga was a threat.

"I'm sorry," she said. "I can't help you—"

Conrad choked and crumpled, panting. Rafe grabbed him and steered him toward one of the chairs that he half fell into.

Amber poured a cup of black coffee and put it on the table in front of him. Conrad plunked the mailing tube he was carrying onto the table. "I...brought... my...family...tree," he panted.

"I can't." But Amber's voice wavered. She looked at the strange blurry corner. Conrad rubbed his eyes and his temples, scrubbed his face. Rafe blinked to clear his vision. Nothing there.

"Please, we know you're a curse breaker. I'm begging you, I need your help. If not for me, for my son."

"What kind of curse is it?" Her voice was low and gravelly, full of satisfaction. Rafe shook his head. It hadn't been her speaking.

Of course it had been.

"Like I said yesterday, in the Cymbler family, soon after we have a son, he disappears. We don't meet him again until he is an adult. Shortly after that meeting, we die and it goes on and on and on and on and—"

Rafe put his hand on Conrad's shoulder, squeezed it. "Drink your coffee." He lifted his hand, moved to put himself between Conrad and Amber's pitying gaze.

But she didn't look as if she were pitying Conrad because of his delusional ramblings. She appeared terrified. No golden tan like Rafe had admired yesterday. She was unnaturally white.

Almost as if she believed in curses, too.

"I met m' father. He told me of the curse." Conrad hunched over the drink, lifted it trembling in his hands. Droplets of coffee dribbled down his cup, hit the table.

No, they didn't. There was no wetness on the table. There had to be. Rafe better get his eyes checked.

Conrad gulped from the mug. His hand found a paper napkin and he wiped his mouth, plunked his cup down and looked around Rafe to stare at Amber.

"You know," Conrad said quietly. "You know there are such things as curses, and you know how to break them."

Amber stood, gazing at Conrad, still too pale. "You don't know what you ask."

Straightening, Conrad reached for the tube. "This is the Cymbler family tree. It's five years out of date. Study it. You can see that what I said is true." He glanced up at Rafe. "Rafe's is there, too." He jerked his head, indicating Rafe. "This is my friend, Rafe Davail. He's cursed, too."

Amber's light pink lips moved. "I know." Rafe didn't actually hear the words.

"More coffee?" Conrad lifted his cup.

Amber moved to a side cabinet and reached toward a carafe. Rafe intercepted her. "I'd like some. I'll do it."

She stiffened and her body nearly brushed his. He could catch her scent and he recognized it, knew he'd never forget. Naturally it was the fragrance of crumbling amber. Dark. Musky. Dangerous.

Rafe poured himself a cup of coffee, stepped over and filled Conrad's cup. Nope, not a drop of liquid on that table. He put the pitcher back.

Conrad drank, then cleared his throat. "I know there are rules to curses. Some sort of release or unbinding must be built into a major curse when it is invoked." Conrad smiled but it wasn't in amusement. He really believed this stuff.

Rafe strove not to.

Amber looked startled. She wet her lips. Color

was coming back to her face, her lips were rosy now. "Yes?" she asked.

"The least you can do is follow my family tree back, see when the curse might have begun. I know you're an excellent genealogist, can work back farther than others. I know you…have a special touch."

Her whole body went stiff. It didn't look good on her, she should always be supple. "I strive to give my clients satisfaction," she said flatly.

"I've seen some of your reports," Conrad said. "Incredible research and stories." His eyes narrowed, and he drank more coffee. "Almost as if you were there." His face went hard and Rafe was glad to see it. Conrad continued, "I'll pay whatever you want for you to remove the curse on my son."

"Conrad!" Rafe protested.

"And Rafe will pay whatever you want to remove the curse on me, even though he doesn't believe in it."

"I can't do that," Amber said.

"Then you look at my family tree and use your psychic gift to tune into the past and find out how I can break it."

Rafe stared.

His cell rang and he pulled it from his pocket. "Ace Investigations." He thumbed the speaker on.

"This is Herrera of Ace." The prime investigator sounded tired. "We've found Marta Dimir and Dougie Tyne-Cymbler in Bakir Zagora."

Conrad shot to his feet. Years dropped off him. "I'm outta here. I'll be in Bakir Zagora by this evening."

"Black Stream Hotel," said Herrera.

"Wait!" Rafe said, blocking the door. Conrad shoved him away and ran through the lobby to the front door. Rafe knew he'd have to take the guy down to stop him.

"Rafe, take care of this business for me. Please."

Rafe strode to catch up. "You can't mean…"

Conrad grabbed Rafe's shirt. "Look. I need all the help I can get." He swallowed hard. "I feel like I'm in a war. I gotta go."

"I understand that, but—"

"Never asked much from you, Rafe, but you need to fight for me on this front. Please."

CHAPTER

4

RAFE LOCKED GAZES WITH CONRAD. RAFE didn't know what to say, but time seemed to slow down and a chill touched his spine like the winter wind of mortality. Conrad was his best friend. Rafe had been hard on friends. Not even his brother wanted to be with him. Too bad, so sad.

And while he stood, Conrad shot out the door, into the Tesla and was gone. The way he was driving, he'd better watch for cops.

"Davail, you there?" That was shouted from his phone.

"Yeah, yeah," he said. "Keep an eye on Marta and Dougie. Conrad's on his way."

Herrera said, "I'll need another man or two here in Bakir Zagora."

"Money's no object," Rafe said.

"Right. Later." The P.I. hung up.

When Rafe went back into the conference room, Amber had her arms crossed over her very fine breasts. Her expression was cool. "There are some things money can't buy."

Rafe shut the door hard behind him. He should go after Conrad.

But his friend had asked him to help him here. "Are we talking about 'curse breaking'?"

"That's right," she said. "No amount of money on the face of the earth—"

Rafe waved. "Yeah, yeah." He didn't believe her. People always had a price. And he usually solved problems by throwing money at them. Money he'd inherited and which his brother invested very well, as he'd been told acidly the night before.

He ran his hand through his hair. His scalp was sweaty and he hadn't noticed. "What about genealogy?"

"What about it?"

"Money can buy a good trace of family trees. We're very good clients, Ms. Sarga." He rubbed his neck, squeezed his shoulder blades. "Look, can we discuss this somewhere else? The buzz from the lighting here is really giving me a headache."

Her brows rose. "Buzz from the lighting."

"That's right. And I'll need to get a taxi or rent a car, or buy one."

She sighed. "There's a good coffeehouse around the corner, the Sensitive New Age Bean."

"That where you got the drinks?" He gestured to the carafes on the sideboard.

"Yes."

"Sold," he said.

"You go ahead. I'll meet you there. I need to tidy up here."

Nodding, he opened the door and walked out, leaving the tube with the family trees on the table.

Amber moved to the credenza, and all three brownies were there before her. Hartha cleaned up and Pred claimed the cocoa carafe. She scowled at Tiro. "You had no right to answer as if you were me, asking what kind of curse it was. I won't have that."

He sneered, shrugged. "Humans and their rights." His upper lip lifted. "You can't do anything to me."

"I can give all the chocolate pie I'm making to Hartha and Pred."

Pred snorted with laughter. Tiro growled and the younger, smaller brownieman disappeared.

Amber walked over to the table and looked at the tube. Her palms tingled and wisps of pink-purple emanated from them as she touched it.

"Tell me, Tiro, did any of my, uh, forebears ask you to help them?"

His face darkened and looked like it became the consistency of rock. Amber stepped back. His big eyes turned down briefly as if sad, then he shrugged again. "They always thought they could fix curses. Every one of them. They all died young."

Like Amber's mother and aunt had. They'd cut all emotional connections with her and sent her away to relatives when she was six, where she'd been cared for but never really loved. Looking back, she thought they had decided to do a major curse breaking and had failed. She didn't know for sure, though.

They hadn't taught her about curses. She only had that one journal—obviously a middle volume of a set. She'd never thought to trace a bloodline back to witness the beginning of a curse. Usually she'd just felt the hideous shroud of the curse and broken it.

"Was Conrad right about there being rules for curses? That a release or unbinding is built at the time of the original curse?"

"What of it?" Tiro asked. "The curse lasts and the requirements for the unbinding gets lost and that's the end of it."

Possibilities surged through Amber, enough to make her light-headed and lean against the wall. "But I am proficient in finding information in the past. Maybe this is another way…"

"Occasionally there are witnesses to the curse or it's recorded," Hartha encouraged.

"I have a smaller magical gift that might help," Amber said.

Tiro grunted. "You women are always hopeful. You always try. You always die."

Hartha finished inspecting the surface of the mahogany table. Somehow she'd stopped coffee from splashing on it from Conrad's cup.

"All right?" Amber asked, pushing away from the wall.

"Yes." Hartha lifted her chin with pride in her work. Her gaze scanned the room. "All is tidy."

"Thank you," Amber said.

Hartha nodded. "Your chocolate cake was very good." The tips of her ears quivered. "And we will have chocolate pie with candied violets for tea this afternoon."

"Yes," Amber said.

Hartha vanished with the cake and Amber was left with Tiro. He stumped around the room, then cackled. "Buzz of the lighting," he said, mocking Rafe Davail's words.

"Not very courteous of you," Amber said. She picked up the tube. Magic ran from it to her hand, sank into her skin. She wished Jenni were here to ask about things. One last glance and she said, "We are all bound together for a while." As she said that, she knew it was the truth. She didn't know how or why, but they were bound together. "Rafe Davail and me and you."

"You'll die soon."

"Maybe I will." She didn't want to. There must be ways to mitigate the consequences of curse breaking; she should be able to find them. She was sure her ancestors didn't have *three* brownies to help them. She opened her hands and flicked her fingers at him. "I thank you for moving my office, but I release you. Go back where you came from, I sure don't need you in my life."

"*I can't.*" Tiro didn't roar loudly, but affected the air pressure so that her ears popped. He hopped onto the table so they were eye-to-eye. "The great elf Cumulustre put a binding on me to serve your line until there were no more of you stupid curse-breaking women." He stomped back and forth on the conference table, and Amber swore she could hear wood splintering, but the top was smooth and polished, not even a trace of small brownie footprints.

Magic.

"I thought you were all gone. All dead. The main line and all its branches."

"So you have to live with me, huh?" Amber asked. "Keep an eye on me? Is that all? Can't you help me? I can see you. I can see the other brownies. Jenni is a djinn. I could have a lot of help."

"Not enough, not ever enough."

Amber shrugged a shoulder. "Well, wherever you've been, and however you've spent your time since you were last with humans, it sure has made you grumpy. Not even regular infusions of chocolate would sweeten you." She turned and walked from the room, leaving the door open.

"I was very happy by myself in my cottage!" he shouted.

She didn't look back. By the time she crossed the foyer to the outer door, waving to the receptionist, Tiro was gone and the conference room was empty.

The wind had come up and whipped her hair around her and she'd wished she'd buttoned up her raincoat. But the Sensitive New Age Bean was only around the block, so she wouldn't be in the spring cold for long. She tucked the long tube under her arm and hurried. As she did so, she noticed the...flatness...of the scent of the air, and when the wind kissed her lips, the flavor wasn't tasty. And she knew what was missing. The fragrance and savor of magic.

She pushed the door open to the coffee shop. Instead of magic there was the rich smell of espresso, and the slight sweetness of baked goods.

The place was crowded as usual. Amber was not the only one doing business at the Bean. People worked on laptops, spoke quietly on cells, spread papers or textbooks on the tables. There were a few meetings, too. A local Realtor, a financial planner, one of the architects from the firm on the corner—all were deep in discussion with one or more clients.

Rafe Davail had chosen a small table for two in the back room. The round table was painted with fluffy Chinese clouds with a dragon peeking out, chasing a shiny gray pearl. Rafe lounged in a low-backed chair, his arm along the top rung, his legs showing long muscles in his faded jeans, his leather jacket open. She was sure it was outrageously expensive. She'd never thought a blond could look darkly brooding, but he managed.

As she passed the threshold of the front room to the back, he glanced up, then stood. He gestured to two cups in front of him. "Seemed like a day for hot chocolate."

Tiro perched on the high shelf of the back bookcase, and had his gaze fixed on the drinks as if he hadn't tasted the treat in millennia. Was chocolate addicting to brownies? She'd better ask.

Meanwhile, Rafe had slipped the large tube from her grasp and set it on the table, then touched her shoulders and she realized he was going to take her coat. She hadn't expected such manners from him, then recalled he'd been brought up in wealth and figured he'd had etiquette drummed into him. The feel of more than a curse zinged through her. Magic, power, something. And desire. That was bad.

He folded her coat over her chair, waited until she was seated and sat. Then he pushed the mug of cocoa to her, and got his brood back on.

"Just so you know, I don't want to be doing this."

"I never would have guessed," she said.

One side of his mouth lifted. "Pretty evident, huh?"

"Yes."

He rubbed the back of his neck, shook his head. "I thought my headache would get better here. Doesn't seem to be happening."

"Just a minute," she said. He didn't look up as she stood.

She sauntered back to the bookcase. "What are you doing here, and why are you bothering Mr. Davail?"

"I am bothering no one. He can feel magic, but he doesn't believe, so he can't see me. Can be irritating."

"I'm sure you can tamp down your magic and be a little less intrusive and odd. It will be so much easier to talk to him if you aren't bothering him."

"You're the one who's talking to a bookcase," Tiro said.

Amber gritted her teeth, glanced over her shoulder and saw Rafe staring at her. Had he heard her? The espresso machine had been going and she'd kept her voice down. Still...

Amber glared up at Tiro. "I'm only a duty to you. Go sulk in your room and leave us be."

"He is attracted to you."

"I'm an attractive woman."

"And he is handsome for a human, this I know." Tiro began shaking his head slowly.

"I don't want to hear anything more about how I'll die. Just *go*."

"I will keep my magic close to me." Tiro said. "Not let it spread through the room." He crossed his arms. It seemed his only concession. Amber wondered if it were a good or bad sign that he was interested in Rafe Davail. But in the next few seconds, she *did* feel a thinning of magic in the atmosphere. Well, she had a business to run. She spun on her heel, quickly enough to see that Rafe's gaze had been aimed at her butt.

Too bad he had a death curse, she really would have liked to spend some time with him. She plucked down one of the notebooks with blank paper that was kept for the patrons and walked back to the table, keeping her smile easy. "I'm sorry, I didn't bring any supplies with me." She reached into her purse and a pen slipped into her fingers. The way her hand felt, that was another minor magic. Maybe hanging around the brownies was increasing that, too. She hoped so.

She opened the tube and pulled out rolled charts. One was older, the other smelled like it had been copied at a shop with a blueprint machine that morning. She glanced at that one and saw the Davail line. Once again several entries jumped out at her…all men who had died before they were thirty-three. She glanced at Rafe as she set it aside—he was in the last months of his thirty-second year.

Then she unrolled the Cymbler family tree. The last entry, "Douglas Dimir Tyne-Cymbler," was printed in ballpoint ink. No doubt Conrad's addition. She let that end of the paper curl up as she scrolled to the beginning of the large sheet and the thirteenth century. She couldn't tell just by looking whether Conrad's curse had been in effect then. Surely if it had happened later, there would have been documentation.

"Do you know anything about the Cymbler curse?" she asked absently.

There was a creak as Rafe tilted his chair back on two legs. His gaze met hers over his cup as he sipped. "I vaguely recall Conrad's ramblings after he met his father. We were in college…roommates. You and Conrad. Puzzle solvers." Rafe shrugged, this time a regular-type shrug. "I'm more into action."

"Sports." She recalled some of the pics online she'd seen, he wasn't sitting in one of them.

"That's right."

Amber kept her hands flat on the roll. "Mr. Davail, just what do you expect of me?"

His chair came down with a clunk. "I expect you to research Conrad's family tree. Check out whether there really is some sort of…bad luck."

"Does he have any histories, stories, notes?" Amber asked.

"Not that I know of. He would have brought them to you if he had them."

"How far back do you want me to go?"

Rafe waved a hand. "As far back as it takes, as long as it takes." He leaned forward, blue gaze steady. "Charge your usual rates and keep track of your time and expenses."

Anger surged through her. "You don't seem to get it, Mr. Davail. I didn't contact Mr. Tyne-Cymbler or you. I did not come to your home and ask for your help. I have absolutely no intention of taking monetary advantage of Mr. Tyne-Cymbler in the state he's in." She drew in a breath, checked around, but no one was paying much attention to them. Keeping her voice low, she continued. "I'm not promising to break his curse. I'm contracting to do genealogy for him. That's all."

"He said something about special stories."

Amber glanced away. How could she have known that those little bits of magic she did during her historical work would lead to such problems? "Now and then I can…find certain family moments or two that my clients are unaware of. I include them in my reports."

"Psychic?" Rafe asked, his voice laden with disbelief.

She blinked but didn't meet his gaze, shrugged herself. "Extrapolation." Now she looked him in the eyes. "But there's usually documentation for the stories." She thought that's how her minor magic functioned, only showing what was recorded somewhere. She just had to find it.

Rafe reached into his jacket pocket. "Do you need a retainer?"

"No."

"I want you to work on this as hard as you can."

"I do have other clients."

He nodded. "All right, I agree."

"What?"

"Bump up your price until you can work only for us."

"No. I have other clients."

"Finish 'em up first, then give us all your time."

She stared at him. "You don't believe in curses."

"Of course not."

She glanced up to Tiro. He whistled and Rafe flinched. Rafe was magic whether he knew it or not, whether he believed or not. "But somewhere inside you, you don't think that Conrad will find his wife and child, do you? That's why you're authorizing such a push on my part."

"Just do it." He narrowed his eyes. "And let's hope one of your stories you find during your little psychic episodes is the event that Conrad wants to hear about."

"You are a very irritating person," she said. "Very arrogant."

"Deal?" He put out his hand, palm up. Amber had studied palmistry briefly. She couldn't help but notice that his life line had a dark bar and a break when he was a relatively young man. The line faded after that.

Her heart gave a hard thump. But there was a square near, indicating protection. And another curved line nearly parallel. Again, showing he could have help. That meant his life *could* go on.

"Deal?" he repeated, impatiently.

CHAPTER

5

SHE PUT HER HAND IN HIS AND HE TURNED his hand over and clasped her fingers. More intimate than a handshake. Again she felt the curse, the magic, the sizzle of desire.

His body heat seemed enormous, as if he were living life fast and hard. He withdrew and finished his hot chocolate, nodded to her own. "That's getting cold."

She sat and drank it, felt the cool melting of whipped cream on her upper lip and sucked it off. Wonderful. "What can you tell me about Mr. Tyne-Cymbler?"

"Call him Conrad, and call me Rafe."

Now his posture was more casual, his long legs stretched out. He stared into the bottom of a cup that had to be near empty, then looked up. "He's my best friend. He has been since we met freshman year in college. He's loyal." Rafe jerked a shoulder. "He's solid, will keep his word. He loves Marta and Dougie and

"Sorry. And Conrad dumped me, and there's something about this place that feels funny. No offense."

She stared at Tiro. "None taken, though you were uncomfortable in my office, too."

"Okay, I get it. It's me." He rubbed the back of his neck. "This whole damn thing has made me twitchier than usual." He managed a smile at her. "And Conrad left me flat. I'd just as soon wait near your place—"

"Mystic Circle?" She leaned on the words.

Rafe winced, nodded. "Yes, Mystic Circle. Please. Wait." He hesitated. "Not quite done with this discussion."

Amber heaved a put-upon sigh, but stayed while he charmed—and tipped—the barista for putting his drink in a to-go cup. Rafe was old money and big city and it showed.

But she was Mystic Circle. Magic. Brownies. Right now she was hiding that fact, but it warmed her insides. And she'd match that as an exclusive club against any other Rafe might belong to: winners of extreme sports, old money wealth, Manhattan home owner.

Death cursed.

Yes, that might be very exclusive, too, but not a group anyone would want to belong to. And she should remind herself that whether he believed in curses or not, most of his male forebears had died before they were thirty-three. He was thirty-two.

That would certainly weigh heavily on her. Almost as heavily as Tiro's doomsaying.

They left the coffeehouse in silence and began walking back to Mystic Circle. They were away from the

he was too good for her. She was a schemer from the beginning."

Amber recalled the feeling of darkness that had made her uneasy when she looked at Marta Dimir's name. She shook her head slightly.

"What?" asked Rafe.

"I looked you two up on the Net."

"Of course you did."

"And on the main database I use." But not all the databases. There were others, more obscure. If there were information on Conrad and his family curse, she'd find it. "The Tyne family tree is online."

Rafe grunted. "Bunch of tight asses."

"But the Cymbler family tree isn't."

He didn't look at her, but said, "You were going to make a comment about Marta?"

"It seemed to me that she was more...used...than a schemer herself."

Rafe sat up. "What?"

"I just got that feeling."

"Yeah, feelings." He frowned, then stood and walked back to the counter, placed his mug in the dirty dish bin, then leaned on the bar and asked for a hot black espresso. He drummed his fingers and looked out the main window to the street. Amber thought he was considering her words.

He was still here, because of his friend. Conrad wasn't the only one who was loyal and solid.

Then Rafe yanked his phone from his pocket, called. Scowled. He left a message, then made another call and words shot from him in what she already knew were orders.

She drank her own cocoa. He was an interesting man. The barista shot Amber a grin as she placed Rafe's mug on the counter before him. Oh, yeah, Amber's gaze had wandered along his body. It was evident that he was in prime shape from all those sports of his.

All those extreme, risky sports. One of which could kill him in the next few months. Would that be fate or free will?

Heavy questions she'd never really wanted to contemplate.

Rafe nodded to the server as he laid down a bill, flashed her a smile that Amber hadn't been given. Then he prowled back toward her, stood over her with narrowed eyes, drank from his cup. "You have a *feeling* that Marta is being used."

"Yes."

He sat back down in the chair opposite, his entire attention focused on her in a way he hadn't done before. "If Marta is being used, then someone tougher than her might be after Conrad, and now he's going to their playing field. I called him and Ace Investigations."

Again Rafe glanced aside. This part of the coffeehouse didn't have windows and she believed that bothered him since he spent so much time outdoors. Thinking back, there hadn't been a free table in the front room—except the table saved for group and community events, and he hadn't encroached on that.

There were a lot of things to like about Rafe Davail.

"Conrad also believes in psychic crap." Rafe drank

more, didn't look at her. His expression turned to one of scorn. "Nothing I could say could talk him out of spending money on those fakers. He claimed Marta was psychic, was fascinated with her because of that. She hosed him good. Now I've got to deal with another woman with *feelings*."

And there was a lot to dislike about Rafe, too. "Like I said before, I didn't seek you two out." She stood and rolled the charts, stuck them in the tube and picked it up. "I'll get right to work." The smile she aimed at him was cool. "You'll be pleased to know that I *do* work on weekends."

"Marta married Conrad, broke his heart, took his money and his kid," Rafe said. He stood, too. "I can see that I should have gotten this to go. Wait for me."

"Why? You hired me to do a job for a friend of yours. You don't like me. You don't respect me."

"I'll walk you home," he said.

"That's not necessary," she said.

He moved his shoulders, not quite a shrug, more like an itch in his back. Amber looked at Tiro. He was glowering, as usual. At Rafe.

"I'd rather you let me walk you home," Rafe said.

She cleared her throat. "You have a hunch or something?"

"No," he snapped. Then he grimaced, ran a hand through his hair. "Sorry. It's been a very long couple days. Probably shouldn't have hinted that your feelings make you a bad person."

"No. You shouldn't have done that." She waited his rationalization.

storefronts and into the residential area before he spoke again. "Aren't you going to ask me about my curse?" His smile was sharp.

"No."

"It was a gypsy woman—"

She lifted her brows. "Really?"

"That's the story. Really common story, isn't it? What else would someone say if you talked about such a crazy thing? Hell, who else did curses? But we don't have much in the way of histories, stories or notes. Too many deaths in the family." His expression was shadowed again, dim with brooding. "I was five when my dad died. He and Mom were estranged." Another quick smile, this one humorless. "Though they got together a few months before he died—long enough to make my brother, Gabe."

"I'm sorry. How did he die?"

"Hit-and-run car accident."

"Even worse."

"Yeah. It was bad. Lived with my great uncle after that." Rafe glanced at her. "'Til my teens. Then he and Mom decided I'd be better off in an academy. That wasn't too bad. It was European and we were all into sports." He chuckled. "I'm not too bad of a polo player."

"Uh-huh. Is your mother still living?"

His athletic stride became stiffer, she didn't think he'd noticed. "Yes. She's not in our lives. Never really wanted to be. What of your own parents?"

Well, she'd asked him. But she was the genealogist and interested in families. She didn't know why he'd ask about hers except it was small talk people did when they were attracted to each other. Though she couldn't gauge how much he was interested in her. He might like looking at her, but she wasn't in his league—any of his leagues—and didn't think she'd care to be. Didn't guys like him date supermodels or minor European royalty?

"I never knew my father. My mother and aunt died when I was about six, and I was brought up by distant cousins." Well-paid relatives who hadn't loved her, not as much as she sensed his uncle and brother loved Rafe.

"Huh. Something we have in common."

"I guess so," she said. They stopped at the sidewalk leading up to her house. She gestured with the tube. "I'll start work on Conrad's lineage tomorrow. I have another job I need to finish first." Rafe was looking down at her with intent eyes, as if, for the first time, he was seeing *her* instead of some gypsy psychic woman taking advantage of his desperate friend.

She wasn't sure that she liked him looking at her as if he were interested. She should definitely not get too close to this guy and his curse. "Due to the circumstances, I won't be putting Conrad's family tree online, unless you notify me that he—or you—want it public to try to garner additional information." Rafe was still staring at her. "Your family tree is already online and public, but the living are masked except on my pro databases. Do you want me to add information and comments to the public database, or not?"

That query clunked a bit as they stared at each other. Would he still be living in eight months?

He took a step back and his expression became more guarded, his smile casual with a lack of sincerity, a flash of hurt in his eyes. "I'm sure my brother and uncle would appreciate that." Rafe nodded toward the tube. "Gabe sent that to me."

She nodded. "And maybe, since Conrad is soon to be out of the country, I could have your contact information? Since you want reports and all. If your brother didn't provide you with an account name and password for the database, I can do that for you, too."

He ran his hand through his hair, his smile turned lopsided. "I did bring a tablet computer. I was staying with Conrad. Don't know that I'll remain there. He wouldn't mind, but it's a cold place." He shifted his balance, as if uneasy, something she didn't think he usually did. "I should be windsurfing in Tarifa, not here."

"Up to you. Think about it and email me or call." She handed him her card and started up the sidewalk to home. It looked good, a sanctuary from scariness. Death curses, lost children…men who'd been lost children. "I'll have your first report in about three days. Then we can update weekly. Naturally, the farther back we go, the slower it gets. I'll let you know if I have to travel on site anywhere." A quick business smile and she slipped in the door, shut it behind her with a sigh and leaned back against it, closing her eyes.

"You gonna break his curse and die?" Tiro said.

She jumped, clapped a hand to her chest. Talk about scary weirdness.

Tiro said, "You shouldn't even associate with him. Just going to lead to trouble. I tell you that right now."

"Where are the puppies? I prefer their greeting."

"They wanted out," he said. "Nice pups. You know if you break a big curse while you're emotionally attached to them, they'll die, too. Dogs age even faster than humans."

That made her insides clench and hurt. "I know." She could feel blood drain from her face as memories of dying pets stabbed her. She glared at Tiro. "I learned that the hard way. It would have been nice to have someone around to let me know such consequences."

"I thought Tshilaba left journals. She'd worked on them long enough."

"Journals! Plural? I only have one, and it doesn't tell me very much."

Tiro whistled and the back door slammed open and the puppies raced in. For the first time, the morning tilted into balance as she hugged and scratched them. This is what mattered—loving, being loved.

Helping mattered, too, but not at the cost of loving.

"So," Tiro said. "Can I help you with the chocolate pie?"

"Can you help me with my magic?"

He scowled and shuffled his feet. "I helped in the beginning for the first five women. Didn't work, no matter how I tried. I've a binding to serve you. Can help or not. But you don't *learn,* none of you." He pounded his chest and it was like an echo against rock, then he pointed a four-jointed finger—the brownies all had four-jointed fingers—at her.

"You have a binding, too. Your elf Cumulustre blood gives you magic, but being human limits it. You drain yourself for others. That isn't healthy. That's your great lesson. And none of you women have learned it." He threw up his hands. "Why are you all so stupid?" With a last glower, he disappeared.

Shaken, Amber let the puppies knock her on her rump, accepted doggie kisses. She let emotion storm through her, past regrets…and current fears.

She decided to focus on current hopes. Being around the brownies seemed to have boosted her magic. She would concentrate on her minor magic, the visions of past events as she worked on family trees. She needed to check her ancestress's journal to see what it said about the solution of a curse given at the same time the original curse was laid. But Amber was sure she'd have remembered that if it had been there.

Curses. Bindings.

They were much alike.

Rafe watched the very-easy-on-the-eyes Ms. Amber Sarga shut her house door firmly behind her.

He turned and looked at the round park in the middle of the circle, finished his drink and noted an empty trash can. He crossed and dropped in his cup. The park smelled nice, like winter passing.

The place had a good mixture of full evergreens and tall, budding deciduous trees. When the bushes leafed out and the flower beds were full of blossoms, the park would be as pretty as any in Denver; the garden as good as any at Conrad's house.

Not that he would be here to see them. Winter sports were done, and he was looking forward to the summer season—beaches and waves, at least in the Northern Hemisphere.

It had been one odd morning. All the back-and-forth with the gypsy Sarga. The unaccustomed headaches and irritation. Conrad had acted strange even before he'd dumped and abandoned Rafe. He was pretty cool with that, he understood why Conrad ran, but it still left Rafe stranded. He pulled out his phone and called a limo service owned by another mutual friend.

"Brilliant Limousines," the female dispatcher said in a throaty voice.

"Yes, I need a pickup at Mystic Circle."

"Mystic Circle?"

"Yeah, you know, in northwest Denver?"

He heard rapid key tapping. "Oh. Yes. Mystic Circle. Where are you going?"

He had to pick up his stuff from Conrad's, but he sure wouldn't be staying there. "One hundred South Gilpin."

More tapping. "Right. Would you like to charge that now?"

"I have an account." He rarely used it. "Rafe Davail."

"We'll have a car there in half an hour."

"That's fine."

"And you'll be at what house address on Mystic Circle?"

"I'm on the street. It's a cul-de-sac, find me."

"Yes, sir."

He hung up.

Birds warbled in the trees. Someone was baking something that smelled really good. Nice day.

Conrad had been right about the neighborhood. The area was charming. It felt…safe. Rafe shrugged off the word. He hadn't spent his life feeling safe.

Maybe because he'd never known "safe." His parents had argued since he could remember, which had made living with them tense as a small child, a fact he'd forgotten until Amber had asked about his upbringing.

Safe. An odd word, and maybe that wasn't what he was feeling. Maybe it was the simple lack of pressure to do the next competition, to be what acquaintances and the press believed him to be, to… Hell, he didn't know. He only knew he had a half hour to burn and walking around the cul-de-sac was a good way to do it.

Mystic Circle. He snorted. How lame could you get? As if there were really woo-woo in the world. Magic.

Curses.

Did he really believe Conrad would find Marta and Dougie? Deep down? No.

Did he really believe he, himself, would be alive at the end of the year? Deep down?

CHAPTER

6

DEEP DOWN IN THE DARK INSIDE HIM, something was screaming like a bloody animal caught in a trap.

He shoved that thought firmly aside. He didn't think about it. Ever.

The circle was a good-size neighborhood, the houses not too close together. The first division of their family business had been real estate and Rafe knew enough about that to appreciate the area. Like many Denver neighborhoods, it was a mixture of styles. A brace of craftsman bungalows, the smallest of the houses, sat at each side of the entrance of the cul-de-sac. The street was only wide enough for two lanes—and two lanes the size of regular cars. Forget SUVs here.

Amber's southern neighbor was a Denver square, two-storied of deep redbrick, and round windows on the second level that almost looked like eyes. When he and Amber had passed it, it had seemed to waver so he'd continue around. Amber's place was a Victorian with a turret and a round window or two.

Next was a Tudor English-manor-type place that wouldn't look out of place in the Berkshires. Then came a four-storied castle with round turrets on each side. The land rose a little and there was a stone wall topped with iron spikes before that place. Rafe paused before the gate. The house looked empty, but was obviously the most expensive lot in the neighborhood, and well-cared-for.

The following house wasn't a style he knew. Wide at the bottom with a large porch consisting of many-paned windows. He liked the look of it. Redbrick, white trim. Solid. Three stories. It made him think of sea captains.

In Denver, right.

He kept on going to see a Spanish-style place with a red-tiled roof. Next was a house of angles, square towers, round windows again. Oddly charming though it was pink. A little plate on the gate read The Fanciful House. Then he reached the last bungalow and was at the street entrance and he still had fifteen minutes.

And he was getting hungry. There was an Irish pub in the business district. He'd call Brilliant Limos and direct them to O'Hearn's. But he was reluctant to leave the cul-de-sac; it offered a quiet peace. He'd often thought that peace was overrated, but he liked it here.

His stomach grumbled and decided for him.

Within the minute, he'd asked the limo service to divert to O'Hearn's and was informed that his friend

Don was driving a black BMW sedan. He told the dispatcher that he'd treat Don to lunch and got an affirmative. Everything was set. He was a block from the business area and crossing the street to the corner pub when they dive-bombed him.

Huge crows. No! Shadowy bats.

He flung his arms up to cover his head, beat the things off. Could've sworn their beaks pierced his skin at his wrist. Were *sucking*.

His hand grasped something—feathers? Oily fluff, leather. But he felt a neck in his fingers, the thing struggled madly. More things hit his head, his shoulders. Too much force for birds or bats. Like he'd been caught in a shot of forced air.

He fell. Hard on the pavement. Heard the neck snap. The bird went limp.

Brakes squealed and a big, black Beemer stopped inches before hitting him. The door flew open and a man got out, yelling, "Hell, Rafe, what the hell are you doing in the middle of the street!"

Rafe let the thing go, sat up and rubbed his head. It hurt, but he didn't think he'd hit it on the tarmac. One of the bat things had thudded into his temple, hard.

No. Of course not. "You see any bats?"

"Bats!" Don sounded incredulous. He set a beefy hand under Rafe's elbow and boosted. "On a sunny day? In Denver?"

"No, I didn't think so," Rafe said. Blinking, he looked around. There were pigeons on the phone lines, but not even one crow. Damn.

"Geez." Don, a stocky man a decade older than

Rafe, manhandled him into the back of the car. "I'd'a never heard the end of it if I'd hit you. You need a doc? Should I take you to an emergency room?"

"No." Rafe rubbed his temples. Liquid trickled along his left arm from his wrist. Tears in his shirt, scuffs on his jacket that he couldn't determine came from sliding along gravel or a claw or two.

He used Don's word. "Hell."

Don pulled over to the curb, looked at Rafe over the seat. "A walk-in clinic's close."

Rafe worked his jaw, then smiled. That hurt. "No, I'm good. Had worse problems from a fall or two."

Don grunted. "Better you than me. You still want to eat at O'Hearn's or go to Conrad's?"

"Conrad's first. I want a hot shower."

"Heard his divorce went through."

"Yes."

"Damn shame."

"Yes."

"Strap in, buddy," Don ordered and kept his gaze in the rearview until Rafe did, then he checked for traffic—none—and pulled back into the street.

"You know any good hotels in the area?" The words were out of Rafe's mouth before he knew he was going to say them. He *didn't* know why. Except he liked the looks of Mystic Circle. And maybe he wanted to keep an eye on Sarga.

"There's a good bed-and-breakfast a few blocks away. Big old Victorian place."

"Girly?" Rafe asked.

"Nah, not so much. Also, an apartment place that might have something open."

"I'll take the B and B," Rafe decided.

"Not staying at Conrad's?"

"No. He's going out of town, and I like the looks of this area. We can pick up my duffel, then come back to O'Hearn's."

"Sounds good. Steak is good at O'Hearn's," Don said.

"Right." Rafe leaned back against the leather seat. The morning was catching up with him. He felt more battered than he should have, weaker. A glance at his left wrist showed blood crusting his blue cuff. He pushed the cuff back and saw bruising around the puncture.

Unaccustomed to being attacked from the air, he'd landed poorly. The left side of his face was scraped, and the fact that he'd gotten it from pavement when he wasn't riding a bike and having fun pissed him off. His head ached and he figured he had a nice lump coming up above his temple. His left knee throbbed.

He talked basketball teams with Don and wondered about bats and crows and headaches and gypsy curses.

Rafe and Don never made it to O'Hearn's. Instead Rafe showered and changed at Conrad's and they ate food that had been prepared for Conrad and Rafe. He found a quick text from Conrad that he'd gotten Rafe's message about Marta being used, and would be wary. Conrad had hired a plane to fly to Bakir Zagora.

That reminded Rafe to call a car leasing company and rent a car. He settled for a Jag.

After lunch, Rafe informed the dour housekeeper he'd be staying at a bed-and-breakfast and saw relief in her eyes. He left her the number in case of any emergency.

When the Jag arrived, Don insisted on following Rafe to Juno's Inn. The limo owner kept a shrewd gaze on him as Rafe took the steps. He ached, he didn't deny that. At the porch, he turned and jerked his thumb for Don to go away. The BMW drove slowly, and Rafe figured he'd be hearing from Don the next day—just in case he was in worse shape than he admitted.

The middle-age woman who admitted him also noted his scraped face and limp and assured him that his room had a spa tub. Rafe nodded. He gritted his teeth up another flight of stairs. The place was too fussy for him, and he wondered how Amber Sarga decorated her Victorian.

Then he made it to the bed and decided to lie down for a couple of minutes. As sleep swirled around him, he saw shadows dive-bomb him again, felt the peck and stab of beaks…and the thing's bone crack as its neck broke.

It took longer for Amber to wrap up Cissy Smart Gortel's family tree and report than anticipated. But by the time Amber had, she was feeling better.

After she'd finished the family tree, she'd spread it out on her large worktable. Even before she touched the large chart, pink-purple magic swirled from her fingers. Surely it was a good sign that her minor magic came quicker now?

She knew, then, that she'd be able to include a story. Darkness had swirled around her and she'd observed a scene in the Smarts' past. A wonderful, hopeful scene. Cissy's forebears had been part of the underground railroad and helped slaves escape. A couple of hours later, Amber had found documentation of the event from several stories of ex-slaves compiled after the Civil War.

Smiling, Amber rolled up the chart and the report and put them in a tube and attached the proper postage. Before she left the room, her gaze was drawn to the tube that Conrad had given her.

No, it should wait for another day. Or at least after chocolate pie.

At the bottom of the stairs Tiro stood, scowling and with his arms crossed. For an instant he looked like an odd garden statue and she had to choke back a laugh.

"I'm ready for my pie," he grumbled. He glanced at the mantel clock in the living room. "It's almost tea time."

"Chocolate pie takes twenty minutes to make at the most." She had some frozen crusts.

He grunted. Amber shrugged and headed into the kitchen.

Time with the other brownies mellowed Tiro slightly. He was downright gleeful when he learned another brownie at Jenni's place was indentured to a *cat*. And Tiro was pleased to be asked to help with Pred's excavation projects.

Pred finished his piece quickly and said, "I will extend the tunnel from the common meeting area under the center of the cul-de-sac to your basement." He glanced at Tiro. "You can help."

Tiro's eyes gleamed. "Digging!"

"See what you miss when you live by yourself?" Hartha said.

Pred tilted his head. "Open the tunnel from Jenni's basement to yours. Put in a door."

Amber stared, thought of the sunroom that had appeared nearly overnight on the back of Jenni's house. "Where's Jenni? She's been gone a month."

Jenni's brownies appeared unhappy, even with rings of chocolate around their mouths and on their lips. "Jindesfarne is on a dangerous mission," Pred said.

Hartha looked toward the south, where the street of the cul-de-sac led to other human byways. "Change is coming, for sure." Her thin shoulders shivered. She stared at Tiro. "And sometimes it isn't good. Mystic Circle is a special place. And great evil Dark ones know of it." She frowned at Tiro. "Now we have this brownieman here, and someday he will bring Cumulustre. That is not something to anticipate, either."

"What's a Dark one?" asked Amber.

"Pure evil with power you can't imagine. Only four remain," Tiro said. "Of course this place would draw them. We'll run if we need to."

Amber didn't think he meant her. Sounded like she might be sacrificed one way or the other.

CHAPTER
7

RAFE AWOKE WHEN THE LIGHT CHANGED, the last yellow slant of the sun angling from the windows. Sitting up, he groaned. Damn, he felt like an old man, stiff and sore. But the short sleep had cleared his mind. He knew what he needed to do. He was going back to the business district near Mystic Circle and find that dead crow. Maybe then he'd get a clue about what was going on.

Ignoring his aches and pains, Rafe headed into the diminishing day. Once he was in the car, the purring motor and the sweet vibration soothed him. It was a short drive to the place where he fell. He had a good geographic sense and was sure he could find one bird corpse.

The street had many more cars parked along it than before. He found a spot near where he had fallen and began checking the street and curb. Absolutely no feathers. An odd porous-looking hollow stick of grayish-white caught his eye. Hunkering down, he picked it up. It was light and felt…slimy. There hadn't been snow in Denver for days, and nothing else was damp.

He looked closer at his prize and the back of his throat coated as a nasty scent rose from it. Definitely a bone. But clean. Like something had eaten whatever the bone belonged to. Standing, his gaze ran along the gutter and bumped at another gray bone. This looked roundish…with, maybe, a tooth?

Again he squatted. This time he didn't touch the thing, didn't even want to nudge it with his foot. God knows what crap it would leave on his shoe. He found a stick and stirred at the mess of old leaves and gravel and a shoddy leather patch.

For an instant he thought he saw a skull. And not a regular bird skull. Something out of his childhood playtime when he had dinosaur action figures. He shook his head. No, of course not. He looked closer. He'd been wrong. Now it looked birdlike. He poked it with a stick and the whole damn thing fell into dust. Must have been there a long time. Not just today.

Then there was a last shaft of light through purple velvet clouds and he glanced up to see a bloody sun. He dropped the stick.

The whole day had unsettled him. His head ached. He must have banged it harder than he'd thought.

He damn well wanted a drink, and O'Hearn's would be the place to get it.

Green paper shamrocks decorated the pub's windows, reminding Rafe that St. Pat's holiday was soon. Walking through the canvas-and-plastic outdoor porch toward the door, he opened it to the smell of good pub food and excellent beer.

The long room was floored in dark wood, with cushy-sided booths all along the walls. Since it was a little early for the office-job slaves, he had a pick of tables and seated himself in the corner. He ordered chips and salsa and the best imported beer they had and desultorily watched the TV over the bar, where silent talking heads were imposed in front of a basketball game.

Damn Conrad for getting him into this. God-awful strange stuff had been happening to him all damn day.

A tall man with gleaming silver hair, wearing a long, caped-shoulder trench coat that swirled around him, strode up to Rafe and slipped into the opposite seat. Rafe eyed him but wasn't inclined to protest. There was something about that man…

The dude was…well, not pretty, 'cuz he was masculine enough… Aw, too handsome. But he carried the same brand of beer Rafe was drinking. Stretching out long legs covered with smooth, dark brown leather, the man looked toward the door, didn't meet Rafe's eyes. It seemed more like he was being courteous than cowardly. Rafe guessed it was the way he moved—like a guy who could take care of himself and wipe the floor with you.

Someone turned the TV volume up and sports stats spewed from it, drowning out all other sound. The man said clearly, "So, Rafael Barakiel Davail, how would you like to learn how to live past your thirty-third birthday?"

Rafe choked on his beer. Spewed. Oh, that was couth. Worse, his bottle fell from his limp fingers and hit the table and tipped over, chugging out beer. Liquid went on his hands and the table and his pants and dripped onto the floor. He stared at the gathering puddle, not wanting to look at the guy. Maybe he wasn't really there. Maybe this was all a hallucination.

Despite himself, his gaze slid to the man's long, elegant fingers. He moved his forefinger in an arc of no more than a half inch. The pungent scent of spilled beer vanished. So did the amber liquid Rafe had been looking at. So did the stickiness on his fingers, the dampness on his knee. The wooden table shone as if another layer of poly had just been added, and two full glasses of beer with light froth stood on the table.

"I prefer draught porter, don't you?" the man asked.

Rafe just closed his eyes and thunked back into the corner.

"Rough day?" asked the guy.

"Somehow I think you know," Rafe said. He cracked his eyelids and saw a concerned expression on the man's face. And ears as pointed as a movie elf's.

Damn. It. To. Hell.

Rafe looked away and when he glanced back there were no pointed ears. The man studied him quizzically.

"You said something about my birthday?"

A corner of the man's mouth lifted, but his eyes grew hooded. "Cautious? Being so stubborn isn't wise." He shifted a trifle, as did his coat, and Rafe thought he saw a weapon strapped to the guy's hip. Then the man lifted his drink and drank, and his expression grew pleased. When he looked back at Rafe, his smile faded. "What I could tell you is a long and convoluted story. Which I see that you would not believe. And not believing, it would fade from your mind within hours, particularly the details that are vital."

He met Rafe's gaze and Rafe was caught. The blue of the man's eyes became all there was in the universe. Dimly, Rafe knew he was in trouble, tried to twitch, do *anything* to break the man's mental hold, couldn't. No fear came, only the wish to please this one.

Then the guy looked away and Rafe's gut churned. He should get up, leave. Hell, he should kick the chair out from under the man and head out the back door. He didn't think he'd get far.

Once again the dude kept his gaze aside and Rafe appreciated that.

"Rafael Barakiel Davail," he said softly. So softly that Rafe shouldn't have been able to hear him over the loud TV.

Rafe drank his beer. Unusual taste. He let it sit on his tongue while he considered if it actually came from this place. Helluva thing to think. "That's my name," Rafe said.

"Indeed. But the addition of the name of the angel of fortune will not keep you from death from the curse."

Now the man's voice was all too deadly.

Rafe took another swallow. "You here to kill me?"

"No. And I did not set the shadleeches on you."

All the fine hair on Rafe's body ruffled. Shadleeches. The image of the bird-not-bird skull came, the hollow gray bone.

"The sooner your life ends, the sooner some will rejoice." The man cut his gaze to Rafe, then back. Rafe felt the power of him, knew he could have snagged him again.

"So there are things that you *can* hear. Such as discussion of your curse."

Rafe kept his flinch inward, didn't think doing that hid it from the man's sight.

"Shadleeches," the guy said.

"What are shadleeches?"

"Will you remember if I tell you?" the elf mused. "They are the evil things that attacked you, born from dark magic in the last half decade. Dark ones— greater magical beings whom we Lightfolk fight—use shadleeches to attack and weaken people with magic." The elf paused two beats. "Like you."

Rafe's mind grappled with the notion. His mouth was dry and he drank more ale, swallowed. "What do they look like?"

"Rather like airborne stingrays but with defined heads." Another few seconds of silence, then the guy repeated, "Shadleeches."

Rafe shuddered.

"That's a good sign. We may be able to save you."

"We?"

"I. A friend. Yourself. You are not as blind as you

might be, and your hearing is better than your sight. I advise you to *listen* to that around you."

"My birthday," Rafe persisted.

"That is the complicated story that you can't hear yet. But you might hear and remember this—I can offer to ensure you are where you must be on your thirty-third birthday."

Damned if the man's voice didn't lilt in an almost musical way, and the light caught the silver of his hair and his ears were back to being pointed...then round.

"M'father, all my forefathers..." Rafe lifted his hand in a helpless gesture. "One'a them must have listened to you." That came out bitter. If they had listened, he wouldn't be here listening to one strange dude.

"I couldn't make this offer to your father, or any of your forebears. But in the last few months there have been developments." He smiled and Rafe felt uncomfortably stunned. Like he was slowly being wrapped up in a silken spiderweb.

"I can see I disconcerted you." The elf...no, the *man* stood. "We can talk later, after you give up trying to convince yourself that you have brain damage, are mad, or hallucinating. When you accept the truth." He stood looking down on Rafe and every breath he took was hard, as if the air wouldn't be sucked into his lungs. "I'm not sure it is a good thing that you are attracted to Amber Sarga. That's bound to cause complications." There was a shrug and the guy's cape... coat...whatever...rippled. His nod was regal. "Don't wait too long, Rafe Barakiel, or it will be too late."

Then he was gone and Rafe's nose twitched and he thought he smelled ozone after a hard rain.

He studied the beer, then decided to drink it anyway. As he reached for it, he saw a business card. It was pale green. One word was in script. *Pavan.* The rest read Eight Corp, and gave an address in downtown Denver.

He drank his beer and threw down a twenty, decided to leave the Jag and walk to Juno's Inn. His steps took him to Mystic Circle and he stared. There was a For Sale sign in front of number two, the fanciful pink house. Fumbling in his pocket for his phone, he snapped a pic, texted his financial agent "buy now."

Then he jogged to the inn, every step making his head ache, sloshing the beer in his belly. And he felt as if the shadow of a beast of prey fell over him.

Amber couldn't help herself. After dinner she went up to her office and opened Conrad's tube and took out the family tree charts.

Rafe's chart felt odd and slick and yet had an undertone that she liked, that called to her.

More than just a curse needing to be broken called to her.

She leaned Rafe's roll against a bookcase next to the window. Conrad's she spread out on her worktable. Handling the paper had magic gathering in her hands, flowing through her body. Her own minor magic that let her experience moments of the past.

This magic she'd discovered by accident. The gypsy journal made no mention of it.

She placed her hands on the middle of the family tree. The connection wasn't as good because the paper wasn't hers, nor was the work. But her hands stuck, so there was something there. Many scenes, perhaps. And, maybe, far back in the past, the vital scene.

Amber drew in a long breath.

Pink-purple sparks rose from her fingers to circle her head. As she fell through the well of blue-black, her ears rang. Her magic adjusted first to any change of language. The fall was short, but the abrupt stop was hard.

Not far back, then, a few decades. Amber blinked the dark fog away to settle into the vision.

The colors of the world had faded as usual to black and white.

Two men were sitting on a park bench, they both had features in common with Conrad Tyne-Cymbler. Both were wearing sixties clothes, the older man, who was in his late thirties, had on a suit and tie. The younger lounged, arms crossed and legs stretched, in jeans and sneakers and a white sweatshirt, scowling as he drew short puffs on a cigarette he held between thumb and two fingers.

"Son, I'm sorry we didn't meet before."

"Yeah, right." He blew out a stream of smoke.

Amber could hear the conversation clearly, but no other ambient noise.

The older man shook his head. "I was afraid."

The younger laughed, cut off as he saw his father dab at his face with a handkerchief.

"Afraid I'd die. We have this bad family thing going on. Some say it's a curse."

"Come on, man...." The one in jeans glanced around, saw a bottle and dropped his cigarette precisely into it, glowing end first.

The bottle exploded.

Older Cymbler's yell cut short as a fragment slashed his jugular, ripped it open. A terrible dark flow painted his throat, widened into a spurt. Younger Cymbler's mouth opened in a scream that echoed through the years. He clapped his hand on his opposite arm, which had more glass poking out of it.

He stared and stared at his father's body as it slumped off the bench and rolled to the grass.

Horror. Terror. Grief. The huge flash of feeling, of tearing emotions, slammed into Amber, plummeting her back to reality and the now. She always experienced this fall and the distortion of her senses to understand the past event, then the blow of emotions from those in the scene shocking her back to her own time and body.

This time she didn't have to sort the emotions, replay the words to extrapolate what had happened.

It had been all too hideously clear. Almost as bad as battle scenes.

She'd slipped and lay on the floor. There was movement from the threshold and her heart stuttered. Who?

Tiro watched her.

Gingerly Amber sat up, holding her head. Her eyes focused slowly from the dimness and dreary colors of the past to the eye-hurting color of the backs of her reference books—maroon, hunter-green, navy. The reason she kept her walls a creamy beige in this room. Easy on her eyes when she transitioned from the then to the now.

Tiro clomped over, each footfall seeming like an ogre's instead of a brownie's. He stood looking down at her, shaking his head. Then he drew in a long, sniffing breath. "Ah. At least this magic doesn't age you or your pups. Bad on your eyes and ears, though." He narrowed his eyes. "Somewhere in *your* branch there is more than elf magic. Hard to determine. A touch of lesser water-naiad or naiader." Again he snorted. "And Treefolk—maybe a different Treefolk-elf mix. Huh." He turned and stomped away.

Head throbbing, she was too late to ask what on earth the Treefolk were and how her magic might be affected.

Moving muscle by muscle, she pushed from the thick carpet—this wasn't the first time she'd landed on the floor—and back into her office chair. She stared at her own family tree on the wall. She'd become fascinated with genealogy when she'd wanted to trace back her gift to discover if there were any additional journals that would help her with the aging thing.

She'd lost her line in the fourteenth century when a small city had been wiped out by the Black Death. She certainly hadn't made it back to an elf named Cumulustre.

Nor had she experienced any past moments that showed an elf. Mostly the visions of her own bloodline showed women aging and dying as they broke a curse.

All her life she'd yearned to understand her talent, to mitigate or circumvent the consequences of it, the aging, studying each word of the journal...experimenting with small curses, ill will cast by children with magic at each other.

The past few years she'd lived at Mystic Circle, she'd come to believe in magic and had even more hope that somehow she'd discover how to help people and not pay the high cost.

But today her mind scrabbled to understand this new world and find her way among concepts she didn't understand, to glean what could work for her.

She took some aspirin from her drawer, tossed them down with cold coffee. Then she went to work on her computer. Sure enough, the freak accident had happened, Conrad's grandfather had died—and Conrad's father had an injured arm that had never quite healed. That curse wasn't quite a death curse. Apparently if the men didn't meet, the elder could live until old age and die of natural causes. Very strange.

Next she searched for more journals of her ancestress. It had been several years since she'd done that and online resources were so much better now. She sent some requests to antiquarian dealers.

Branches tapped on the window, the wind was rising. Rafe's chart fell down. Steps slow, Amber went over to it, picked it up. As always she was hit with the slick evil of the curse, the tingle of magic—stuff she was sensing more and clearly all the time—and something about the man and the family tugged at her.

Drawing in a good breath, she rolled the chart out on the worktable, too.

She shouldn't care what happened to the man. But like she'd done on the database, she traced the Davail line back and back and back, and the sense of the curse and the magic was all along the chain of lives. To the beginning of the chart, three hundred years before.

Too tired and sad to want to experience another vision, she went to her chair and swiveled in it, thinking about curse breaking. Nothing in the journal said that a major curse, one that would last generations because the curser knew what he or she was doing, had a release, too. Amber's eyes went to the top notebook on her bookshelf. The black one detailing the curse that had cost her the most—five years and her old cat, Jasmine. Hurt and guilt still twisted inside her at that. She hadn't realized until then that she paid the price for fixing curses. Probably why her mother and her aunt had cut all ties with her when she was a child.

Even then she'd *felt* when their love had dropped away from her, when they'd abandoned her to relatives who only valued the pay they got to raise her.

She shivered. She'd felt cold and wondered what her aunt and mother felt. She'd believed her mother and aunt had loved her. Had they? She'd always question that.

Swinging back and forth, she stared at the black notebook. She'd been twenty-three at the time and new to her business...and already passing for older than she was due to various small curses broken over the years. Roger Tremont's daughter had had the curse, an ill-health thing that would shorten her life.

Amber hadn't been able to resist—she never had, much—and had done the preparations as noted in the journal. She'd asked Roger and his daughter over for their last genealogical meeting and took the girl's hand while Roger was reviewing his family tree. Amber *pulled,* drawing out a fine net of gray magic. It shattered as it hit the air, but had also drained Amber. She'd collapsed, fallen and seen her cat go into convulsions and die.

Roger had helped her up and she'd gotten him out of the house. Over the next minutes, she had aged and some of the obscure language in her ancestress's journal that she'd never understood about consequences had become obvious. Later, she figured she'd lost five years. How many years she'd given Roger's daughter, she didn't know.

Another result of that action was that her perception of curses became more sensitive, and the images of what they were doing to their victims grew worse. And the need to break them and help became difficult to ignore.

Slowly she stood and took down the notebook. But as she recalled, the curse hadn't been going on long. Roger had consulted her to discover if there were any genetic reason for his daughter's sickness.

Putting the book on her desk, she didn't open it. Not tonight. But if there was someplace to start looking for a curse that might have had an unbinding built in when it was cast, that was the case.

She turned and left the room, flicking off the lights and closing the door behind her.

Already too late for her, and her cat, they'd paid the price and that was still harsh and bitter in her blood.

She walked by a glowering Tiro, who lurked in the hall and drank a mug of hot cocoa.

Neither of them said anything.

The blue eyes followed Rafe into sleep. They stared, then the eyelids closed and Rafe saw that they were fringed with silver. Not white lashes, not gray. Silver. Like the elf's hair.

In the dream he knew the man was not a man, but an elf.

In the dream he was not alone. There were men behind him, many of them. He could feel them, like many shadows at his back. Yes, the sun was before him, and the bright blue eyes had vanished into the bright blue sky. With clouds edged with silver from the sun.

Rafe shuddered. He knew this dream now. The one he'd had as a child. The yearning one.

The first yearning had been for a father, a man who would love him. Hell, a man who would spend a few minutes of time with him, even a damn weekend morning that some of his friends had with their fathers who'd been divorced from their mothers.

Next came the yearning for the dagger.

A couple of the shadows had been with him then.

During the hot, sexual dreams of puberty, he'd yearned for a girl. Some specific girl. He didn't know her, but figured he'd know her if he saw her. Or touched her. Or plunged his body into hers.

And the dagger dreams had increased.

More shadows had been at his back, then.

He'd banished the dream after college. When he knew that he wouldn't have a special woman. Not with his family history. No wife or son for him. He'd known then, too, that the blade was an unattainable magic he didn't believe in.

And he knew that he'd become a gray shadow behind another boy and man.

CHAPTER
8

THE ELF HAD BROUGHT THE DREAM BACK
to Rafe.

No. In the way of dreams and his unconscious that
formed them, he knew the crow-bat-evil-things had
brought the dream back. That had started the countdown to his death.

He wouldn't be able to outrun it, or speed away by
cycle or car or boat.

And the dagger was back.

It floated before him horizontally, blue-steel and
glittery as if there were an enamel coating on it with
silver and gold sparkles embedded in it.

Or maybe those were stars.

His heart thumped hard. He wanted that blade. The
shape of the weapon was more triangular than a regular sword blade and the length was less than a sword

but more than a long dagger. The simple grip was a silver wire-wrapped handle.

He'd forgotten how the need for that blade…and maybe the girl…swallowed him, an ache that filled him, the dream, the universe.

As much as the longing to live, not for three more months, but until he passed away in his sleep from old age. After seeing his children, his sons—first and second and however many more—and daughters grown.

He wanted *life* with a passion that others couldn't understand. He wanted the woman and he wanted the children.

But the elf's eyes in the dream opened again and glittered like the blade and Rafe knew in his core that if he wanted to live and love, he must find the dagger.

Rafael Barakiel Davail, the elf said and Rafe woke up in a cold sweat.

Hell! What a dream. He rubbed his eyes, his face. And found that he had dried perspiration on his skin.

Flinging the sheets and heavy comforter aside he went to the bathroom and the mirror. His left wrist burned. The light was soft but didn't make him look any better. His eyes appeared sunken, the skin on his face white and tight. When he looked down at the inside of his left arm, the veins looked black, not blue.

The sight caught at his throat, closed it. Fear shot through him. The type of fear that he clamped down on hard, refused to acknowledge, buried beneath other physical fears.

Three o'clock in the morning, of course, and it was time for the hardest question.

Did he believe that he would die before he reached thirty-three?

He tried to put the question off, but it throbbed in his brain like a splinter. How could he believe in something so irrational as a curse?

Conrad's curse had come true.

Rafe didn't have to look at the family tree file on his computer pad to know that every first son in his family had died before thirty-three for generations, and the family name had gone to a younger son or a nephew. That was beyond weird. What were the odds?

Could he afford to *not* believe in the curse? Face it. His life was on the line and there were no stakes higher. His eyes narrowed and he shifted from foot to foot, thinking that that was wrong. But what could be higher stakes to him than his own life?

That of his brother's.

But his brother was safe. Gabe's firstborn son wouldn't be, a tragedy to come, that Rafe wouldn't be around to suffer.

Conrad was safe, too. Rafe had gotten a short text from him. He was still hurting, but determined to find Marta.

Curses.

Just too much to believe in. Because if he believed in curses he'd have to rethink his whole life…and believe in other stuff, too. Like creatures that weren't birds or bats but nasty, oily something-elses with hollow bones that disintegrated. And believing in blue-eyed elves that could snare you with a direct gaze. And dreams of magical blades and women.

And death in under eight months.

Nope. He just couldn't believe. Not now, not even in a Victorian bathroom with cream-colored paper and lights in colored glass that looked like flowers that seemed more fantasy than real.

If he believed in the curse, he would have to *act* in some way to forestall it. And he didn't know what to do, and from the past, all the other men in his family had been helpless to change their fate.

He couldn't be helpless.

Since he wouldn't be able to go back to sleep, he decided to do a little research of his own and pulled out his computer notepad.

The man-elfman had known his full name. Rafe turned on his tablet and pulled up search engines, keyed in his full name. Nothing. Not much under Rafael Davail or Rafe Davail, either. His wins, that made him smile. A few pics of him on the slopes or in the wind or waves, and that was good, too. Some with a lady or two on his arm. No special woman.

He recalled the name of the man—Pavan—and searched for that. Nothing that referred to a male individual who might have pointed ears. Definitely no social pages.

Then there was Eight Corp. Also very low-key. A closely and privately held corporation based in Denver and doing something in the energy sector. Which could mean about anything.

The low-battery icon on his screen flashed and Rafe swore. He hadn't been quite ready to quit. Rolling off the bed, he crossed to his duffel and pulled out the cord, attached it to his computer, hunkered down to plug in the thing.

Shock sizzled up his fingers, flung him back into the middle of the room.

The lights went out.

His limbs flopped. Wha'?! Shaking his head, he levered himself up. He *knew* he hadn't touched the prongs of the plug, or the outlet.

But he'd been shocked, for sure. If he *had* been closer to the outlet, touched it or the metal of the plug, he'd be dead.

His nerves still quivered under his skin. He lifted his hand and sniffed. Didn't smell burned and that was a relief. He rubbed his fingertips together. Still working, still could feel them. Also good.

Moonlight from the large window pasted a pale square of light on the rug, but the lamps he'd had on were dark. He staggered to his feet and pulled the lamp chain, then tried a wall switch. Nothing.

Glancing out the window toward the corner, he saw that streetlights were on.

Again he shook his head and considered going to the lobby. He opened the door, no light in the hallway except from the skylights. Tiptoeing to the staircase, he listened. Nothing, no commotion. Which, if they hadn't already noticed the electricity was off, must mean everyone else was in bed and probably asleep. So he went back to his room.

A rectangular red light blinked at him from the bed. His tablet. The screen looked like it was covered in blood spatter. Frowning, he picked it up. The screen went from red to black with dripping scarlet letters. *Time has run out. The bomb exploded. You die.*

Swallowing hard, he touched the pad. The end logo of the game, "Fly or Die," scrolled down for a few seconds before the computer turned off.

Shaken, he sat on the bed in the dark. Yeah, of course he had the app "Fly or Die." He'd played it a few times.

He'd never lost.

He shoved the tablet onto the bedside table, squinted. Something else was luminous.

It was the pale green business card he'd gotten that evening. Odd. He picked it up again, eyes widening when he saw a new word on it. "Pavan," it said, then below, "Troubleshooter."

Rafe began to think that he'd need someone to help him shoot the trouble in his life.

He crawled under the covers. It was a cold night. He waited to hear the heat turn on, but it didn't. The old-fashioned wind-up mantel clock ticked the seconds away.

In the morning he was awakened by an apologetic host, informing him that the inn would have to close. There had been a freak accident that had blown the electrical system.

Rafe nodded, dressed and paid his shot and took off in the Jag to Mystic Circle. He wondered if Amber would like to go out for breakfast, then noted it was late, about 10:00 a.m.

He didn't want to be anywhere except the cul-de-sac.

Amber and the house he was interested in were good rationalizations to go back. Not just because he felt safer there for some unknown reason.

His cell lilted with the orchestral tune of his financial advisor. Since the Jag was a stick shift, he didn't answer. As soon as he pulled into Mystic Circle, tension eased from him. He stopped before number two, the one he wanted to buy. The For Sale sign was gone. His heart gave a solid thump of disappointment. Had someone—say a dude with silver hair and pointed ears—snapped up the house before Rafe? And would it appeal to such a guy?

More hard thoughts about curses that worked when there should be no such thing. Of tall men who could look at you and have you sitting still to do whatever they wanted. Of disappearing beer and appearing lager.

He closed his eyes, replayed his conversation with Pavan and the implications. He'd followed his hunches most of his life, all except the deepest ones. Decision time.

His phone rang again and he answered his financial advisor's call. "Hey, Cynthia. I'm sitting in front of number two Mystic Circle right now."

"It's very odd," said Cynthia. "They won't close without proof that you'll be alive at the end of the year. I've never heard anything like it. Who can give proof of such a thing? I can forward some medical records if you want…"

"That wouldn't work," Rafe said. "Will they take earnest money to keep the house off the listings?"

"Yes…but, you know, it didn't *get* listed." Her tone was disapproving at the inefficiency.

"Who's the owner?"

"Oh. It's a firm there in Denver, *not* a regular real estate firm, though they have holdings…. Eight Corp."

Rafe wasn't really surprised. "All right then. Give them the earnest money."

A pause. "The amount is such that I'll have to notify your brother, Gabriel."

Rafe didn't say that she could tell Gabe the next time they were in bed—he was slightly less rude. "When's the wedding?"

"He won't make plans until next year."

Probably because he thought he'd be mourning a brother. Gabe hadn't told Cynthia the family secret, then. Tough on a good guy to inform a beloved that their first son might die because of a curse. Too many ways a discussion like that could go wrong.

"Tell Gabe that he'd like the house, and the area. Anything in the block is worth snapping up. And let him know my will is up to date."

"You aren't doing anything dangerous, are you?"

"I'm not participating in any competitions right now." No sports at least, though an idea was forming in his head that he'd be going on a quest. Which would be the most dangerous thing he'd ever done in his life.

But have the biggest and the best payoff.

Amber was double-checking the information listed on the Cymbler family tree. As she worked on the computer database and the hard-copy roll, she noted when her magic flared. Times that might show scenes of the past.

But she was unaccustomedly pessimistic. She didn't think that any of those scenes would lead her to the truth of how to break Conrad's curse.

Both his and Rafe's curses were ancient things, and the farther she went in the past, the less able she was to interpret her visions correctly. And the more energy it took.

Her hand went to the aged leather of her gypsy ancestress's journal and she stroked it. Time to reread it again in the light of the new information she had. Brownies. Elves. Dwarves. Mers and…djinns. Yes. Jenni was a djinn.

She missed her neighbor. Jenni must be aware of magic, since she was the one making the cul-de-sac especially magical. She would be able to answer a lot of questions for Amber.

Jenni was only half human. That's what the brownies had said. A little thrill went through Amber. She figured she must be human herself except for a sliver… but she had this power because an elf had given it to her family line and it stuck.

She liked her magic. Loved helping. She didn't like the consequences. The black notebook recording the worst curse she'd broken squatted on her desk. She'd look at it later today. After a piece of chocolate pie.

Her email pinged and she opened the program to see that she'd gotten a notification from one of the online search services she used to scan for a gypsy diary—Tshilaba's. Fingers trembling with excitement, she opened the message to see that a used bookstore in Chicago had some original journals for a ridiculously low price. Reading the descriptions, and comparing it to the volume she had in front of her, she decided to order them on the off chance they were what she wanted. She didn't want to ask questions that might alert the seller to the fact that Amber might empty her savings account to buy the books.

As soon as she hit "buy," the knocker on her front door sounded.

"That man is here, the walking dead one," Tiro growled.

Downstairs, she looked through the peephole and there was Rafe Davail. He appeared to have had a rough night, was unshaven and his jaw was tight with strain.

Feelings stirred in her. She opened the door. He offered his hand, and even knowing it was a mistake, she took it. Yes, she felt the slimy death curse first, then all too delicious attraction that shot straight to her sex. If she were a different kind of person she wouldn't equate sex with love. But she did. She was in bad trouble.

"You are in bad trouble," said Tiro.

Rafe squinted, cocked his head, as if he were almost hearing the brownie. Then he shook his head. "If you don't help me, I'll die," he said brutally.

She removed her fingers from his grasp.

His gaze was on hers now, serious. "Since I've met you I've been attacked by…things, nearly run over by a car and almost shocked to death."

"What! I had nothing to do—"

"I don't think you did. But maybe consulting with a curse breaker is making someone…nervous."

"Don't let him in. Who knows what ill he brings with him?" Tiro said.

Again Rafe turned his head toward the brownie standing behind her.

"But, you know, all of this happened to me outside of Mystic Circle. Inside this area…I get a feeling of safety." Rafe smiled.

"All of the magics here won't stop death from coming to him. Will only stop minor accidents, not fierce intent at murder," Tiro said, clumping away, waving a hand. "Go ahead, let him in. Let him stay. I'm going down to the basement to dig. At least I'll accomplish something while I'm here."

"The bed-and-breakfast I've been staying in has had their electrical system shorted out," Rafe said, still listing the disasters. Amber was scrambling to keep up.

"You've been lucky," she said. Her breath was stuck in her chest, making her sound stupid. Pinwheels spun before her eyes in bright fluorescent gel-ink colors showing that she was going to do something equally, incredibly stupid. But Tiro's word—*murder*—had stabbed with visceral power.

"You have a nice big house," Rafe said, leaning against the doorjamb, a not-so-innocent smile on his face.

She cleared her throat. "I have a guest room."

"Good."

"No, no, no, don't!" Now both Hartha and Pred

were in the entry room, scowling. Hartha actually had an apron on with a smudge of dirt and was holding a steaming china teapot. Pred had a shovel. Amber thought they might have been in the basement.

"I'm sorry," she said, meaning her words for the brownies. But Rafe's face hardened, he pushed away from the door.

"I've got a bid on the house across the circle, number two." He grimaced. "Paid a lot of earnest money to Eight Corp to hold it for me 'til the end of the year. Maybe I can rent it until then—"

"You can stay here," Amber said.

The brownies moaned and disappeared.

"Did you hear that?" Rafe asked. He strained to listen. Ever since Amber had opened the door, he'd been hearing odd sounds, almost like high-pitched talking.

Her face went bland but there was challenging amusement in her eyes and her raised brows. "What?"

"Kids." Had to be kids.

"I'm not married and I don't have children." Her smile widened. "Guess again."

That damned itchy feeling between his shoulder blades was back. He glanced behind him, thought he saw a tall man with silver hair in the cul-de-sac's park. No.

Maybe.

What he didn't see was the iron trash can that he'd thrown his coffee mug into the day before. Little things, all adding up to a nearly unbelievable conclusion.

"Guess again, what?" he asked.

"What else could the sound be?" Amber challenged.

"Singing chipmunks?" he asked.

She laughed, then shook her head. "No." Now she stared coolly at him, evaluating him, and something about her stare had him remembering the words of the guy the night before. *You are not as blind as you might be, and your hearing is better than your sight. I advise you to listen to that around you.*

"You can stay here if you can tell me what the sound is. Otherwise you can take your chance with Eight Corp," she amended.

She probably thought she was being tough. He knew she was too damn soft. Once more he looked at the park in the middle of the cul-de-sac. There were shadows that could hold a man. Or an elf. Rafe inhaled all the way to the bottom of his gut. "Then the sounds could be…magic."

Three small beings popped into existence behind Amber. Rafe reeled against the threshold. Grabbed it to steady himself.

"This is not good," said the littlest guy with big ears, who didn't look human at all.

"I'm inclined to agree with you," said a musical voice from behind Rafe.

Slowly he turned and saw a beautiful being who was also not human, but whom he'd met before.

CHAPTER 9

THE MAN-ELF JOINED RAFE AT THE DOOR. Rafe hadn't seen him move. "May I enter?"

Amber stared at them and opened the door wide. "You're welcome." She gasped, more than once. Rafe whirled and caught her as her eyes rolled back and her knees gave out. She was lighter than he'd expected as he swung her up in his arms.

"Well, well," said the mean-looking creature, some male thing, bigger than the other male critter. "Come in then."

Rafe didn't like the gloating of his tone, but Amber was dressed for a warm house, not for a spring day with a brisk wind. She wore a cream-colored blouse, dark jeans and a light blue sweater, but was barefoot.

He took her to the closest piece of furniture, a long couch of a fancy blue-and-teal pattern with carved wooden trim back and arm ends. As he set her down, she was coming around. She put her hand to her head as she stared at the silver-headed dude. The guy wasn't frowning but Rafe got the idea he disapproved of Amber.

Pavan closed the door behind himself and the entry hall and living room got dimmer.

Amber straightened and watched the guy. She licked her lips in a nervous mannerism that Rafe hadn't noticed before. It seemed to him that if she were okay with three little magical creatures, she could deal with an elf.

Then he recalled how the elf had captured him with his gaze and Rafe would have done anything the guy asked him. Not to mention that as Pavan's coat swirled, Rafe saw he was armed with blades on his thighs. And the man—elf—exuded competence. The kind of aura a guy has when he knows he's the best at what he does. Since Rafe could act that way now and again due to his sports wins, and hung out with others at the top of their games, he knew the attitude.

He sat down on the couch, too, but there was room enough for all three of the small people between them. Those three had moved away to the opening between the living room and dining room with half walls that held pocket doors.

"You aren't Cumulustre?" Amber asked. She seemed a little dazed.

"Pavan," the elf said. Now he was close and the light was dimmer and Rafe saw his ears *were* pointed and his hair true silver and he had a pale whitish glow about him.

Amber's gaze slid to the tallest creature, the guy. The other two had linked hands and stood like an old married couple.

"Cumulustre is not a happy individual," Pavan said.

The grumpy creature jerked. His triangular ears rolled down to his head so fast they sounded like shades snapping up. He bowed to the elf and whispered, "I know, great Pavan."

Pavan lifted a brow then studied Amber. Rafe noted that the lady did not meet his eyes. "You'll be helping Rafael Barakiel," Pavan said.

Amber sat tall, her shoulders straightened. Her glance ran along the elf's face, then away. "Yes."

"I'm sorry to say this," the elf said and there was a slight vibration in his tone that had Rafe abandoning his casual lounge.

Pavan's next words were very soft and gentle, but the meaning sliced. "But in this quest, saving Rafael's life is essential, and I don't think you could contribute much."

And whether Amber lived or died wasn't important to the elf. She got that before Rafe did.

"Told you so," said the grumpy little guy.

The shock that there *was* a quest ricocheted through Rafe's mind and kept him frozen before he processed the rest of the elf's sentence.

Rafe stood. "No. Amber isn't helping me."

"Mystic Circle is the safest place for you," Pavan said. "But I am sure that Eight Corp will not allow you to rent number two. This house would be a good place for you to board."

Rafe grimaced. The elf had put his request to stay with Amber on a financial basis. That would have been all right yesterday, when he'd thought she was a greedy fraud and only her time was involved…but with lives on the line, no. Not okay.

"I'll look somewhere else," Rafe said.

Amber lifted her chin. "If Rafe's life is so significant, you should speak to Eight Corp about letting him have number two."

Again, the elf's face muscles didn't move, but he emanated a glacial dissatisfaction. He focused his gaze on Rafe and Rafe concentrated on projecting his own I-can-handle-it attitude.

"Rafe's life is more significant after he's completed a quest and is trained. If he were trained he could be an asset in the situation we face in another place…." Pavan shook his head. "But he's not." One side of his mouth twitched in a faint curl. "He barely believes in magic. No one would trust him, and we don't want a death curse in number two Mystic Circle." Pavan's shoulders lifted and fell the merest fraction. "We are all very busy now with other events and cannot spare any time except for this visit."

Pavan's glance swept over Amber and the three small creatures and Rafe had the idea that the elf had catalogued them to their last molecules. The little ones leaned toward each other, ears tight against their heads.

"Then maybe you should get on with your business," Rafe said, his voice raspier than he'd intended, but the dude's manner was wearing on him. He sat again, nodded to Amber to let her know that they'd talk about living space after the elf was done. "Tell the story of my curse." Rafe angled his head toward Amber. "I'm listening and she can take notes and beat the facts into me later if I forget."

There was a rumble like foot-scuffed rocks from the grumpy creature who scowled at Rafe.

"Maybe I can be introduced to you?" Rafe raised his brows to the trio.

Amber said, "Tiro is a brownieman staying with me because of a binding of his own."

Nearly a growl from the guy.

"Pred and Hartha live next door with Jenni Weavers."

"Brownieman," Rafe repeated with no inflection.

"Brownieman and browniefem. In plural, brownies," Amber said.

"I see." He did. He was looking at *brownies*. And if he turned his head, he would see an elf. And not a cheerful little being, either. A guy who could probably break him in two with minimal effort.

But all of them had wavy air around them...if he let himself see it. Brownish for the brownies. Ha ha. White for the elf.

Pavan sank into a large wing chair slanted toward the couch and considered Rafe. He felt the elf's gaze penetrate, as if the man weighed every strand of muscle he had, every last ounce of determination, every iota of Rafe's will to live. Rafe would have liked to have met the elf's eyes, but had already learned he couldn't.

"It wasn't supposed to be this hard for you Davail men," Pavan said in a quietly musing tone.

His eyes cooled as he glanced at Amber. "Unlike the Cumulustre women, this problem was not of your own making. We did not foresee some of the consequences of our actions."

"What are you talking about?" Amber asked.

Stretching his legs, Pavan said, "The first Davails worked with us—the Lightfolk—and accepted the change in their blood so their line would become warriors against the Dark."

"I'm not a warrior," Rafe said.

"No." The elf tapped his fingers together. "It is not a profession often chosen in this time and place if a man has sufficient funds. And modern techniques of warfare don't always work against the Dark."

Rafe's gaze went to Pavan's hip. He was sure the man was carrying a dagger or two. Or a short sword and dagger. Weapons, anyway.

"There are Dark ones after him?" Amber asked shakily.

"The great Dark ones have become aware of Mystic Circle and are active around it," Pavan said. "I found signs of shadleech activity."

All three of the brownies shivered and quietly drew forward and hopped onto a love seat set in the curve of the turret. Though Pavan didn't look at them, Rafe was sure he saw the rim of the elf's ear quiver.

"What are shadleeches?" asked Amber.

"They are magical evil beings that were born in the last few years. Rather batlike or like a manta ray with a long beak. Not wholly physical." Pavan glanced at

Rafe's left wrist. "They can drain magic and life from a person."

All three of the brownies stared at him. The little male, Pred, sniffed lustily. His eyes got even larger and more protuberant. "They attacked him. The Davail first-son."

"Rafe," Rafe said automatically. This wasn't good.

Pavan stared at him directly. Rafe looked at his sculpted nose. "The Davail bloodline was specifically modified by us Lightfolk to fight great Dark ones more than a millennia ago. The firstborn sons of your line would prove that they were strong enough to fight the Darkfolk by finding and claiming a specific dagger. They were honorable men whose land had been confiscated and families tortured and killed by a great Dark one." Pavan's jaw flexed. "Standard procedure for evil—whether Darkfolk or human. We gave them better reflexes, more strength especially after their quests and training…and magic, then, too. We gave them special weapons." His silver brows caught the light as they arched. "You do dream of a dagger?"

Rafe cleared his throat, coughed. "Yeah." He thought a few seconds, scowled and ran his fingers through his hair. "Hell, I'm going to have to give back my trophies, aren't I?" Ticked him off.

Pavan's smile was swift and amused. "Not necessarily. Your physical attributes are currently within the realm of other high-achieving humans. You have to work to win…after your magic is freed and you train, though…"

Rafe couldn't prevent a grumble. The brownie

woman vanished from the settee in an unnerving way. Before Rafe could blink, she was standing before him holding a small tray with tall, thin-walled china mugs full of coffee. His was just the way he liked it. The back of his neck tightened and his ears buzzed as she tsked at him when his hand trembled as he bobbled the drink. A tiny bit sloshed over the rim but no droplets hit the floor.

The brownies had been at Amber's office the day before! And Conrad…what had Conrad seen and heard? No wonder Rafe's friend had behaved so oddly. Rafe was glad he was sitting down.

The brownie woman—browniefem—had glided over to Amber with the tray. Rafe stared at the little woman's feet under her long dress. She had shoes that curled up at the toes.

Of course.

Amber blinked at the mug being offered to her, took it and whispered, "Thank you, Hartha."

"You dream of the dagger," the elf reminded gently.

"Yeah, I do. Blue and silver and white, starbursts, triangular blade," Rafe said. He drank too quickly but the coffee wasn't hot enough to burn his tongue.

Pavan nodded. "After he found the dagger, the Davail son would arrive at one of the Lightfolk palaces on his thirty-third birthday, with the weapon. We would know that he'd been tested and was ready for advanced training. When you appeared at a Lightfolk palace, you would be taught how to fight to defeat Dark ones."

"Sounds like a story," Rafe said, but his mouth remained dry. He drank more coffee.

Pavan's shoulders rippled, too graceful to be called a shrug. "Plenty of stories about us." He waved a hand. "Legends, myths. This happens to be the truth of your line. And so the men of Davail fulfilled their purpose for generations. Dark minions fell to you."

The guy just said *minions?*

"For a while we lost track of your line. Magic faded in this world. That was a greater threat than the Darkfolk and we turned our attention to surviving. When your family crossed our path again, we discovered you had been cursed. Now you face this curse. Your brother is not a man who is suited to be a warrior, and your cousin—"

"I don't have a cousin."

Pavan looked down his nose, glanced at Amber. "A distant branch. That cousin, too, labors under the curse, though it will not strike him until next year if you fail to survive."

Rafe's mind whirled and his breath locked in his chest. "Not just my life on the line if I don't break the curse. Not just any son Gabriel has."

"No."

Amber had stiffened at the end of the couch and he knew she was thinking the same thing. If he persuaded her to lift the curse on his family, which seemed essential, it wouldn't only be him.

"Two," she said in a thready voice. "I can't."

"You can't do one, let alone two," Tiro the brownie said.

Pavan stared at Amber as if she were less than smart. "Currently the curse is concentrated upon Rafe, so only Rafe's life would be applicable to the breaking. Once broken, of course, all others would be free of it. But I strongly discourage the woman from interfering in the curse. She has her own lesson to learn. You did not contact her to lift your curse?"

So there were things that the elf didn't know, and that was a damn relief. "No," he said.

"It does not reflect well on a warrior to ask another to put herself in peril for him."

"Not Davail," Tiro sneered. "Cymbler."

The elf closed his eyes. "Those lives are entangled again? Cymbler and Davail?"

Tiro snorted, then cackled. "Humans who fight Darkfolk tend to gravitate together. You Lightfolk can't control fate. Not even you, Pavan."

Amber said, "Tell us about the Davail death curse. Who cursed him? What are the conditions of the release of the curse? I've learned that there must be a loophole."

"Indeed, there must," Pavan said coolly, his smile as sharp as a knife. "But in this case the 'loophole' requires what Rafe must do to live."

"And that is?" He should have been terrified, and the whole thing yanked on his nervous system, but there was relief bubbling through him, too. He wasn't helpless.

He might go down fighting but at least there was something he *could* fight. As his determination flamed up, he felt like a warrior.

Pavan's lips curved. "The person who cursed your line is currently called Bilachoe, a human originally apprenticed to a Dark one who has always had ambitions of becoming greatly powerful. He knew the Davail line was created to kill evil and knew of the requirement that a Davail must appear at a Lightfolk palace on his thirty-third birthday. Thus Bilachoe cursed you all to die before then."

"How's that work?" Rafe asked.

"First you will draw risky circumstances into your life. If you manage to evade a stream of bad luck that has surrounded the first Davail son for nearly a millennia, the curse acting upon you, Bilachoe will no doubt send others to kill you."

"Minions," Rafe said. The cup was too delicate to really wrap his hands around. He took another sip of coffee. "My father died in a hit-and-run accident."

"That could have been the curse working, drawing him to the wrong place at the wrong time."

"Or it could have been murder by Bilachoe."

"I doubt he drives," Pavan said drily. "We don't."

Amber frowned. "Surely there must be a weakness to Bilachoe, too. He must be affected by the curse in some way. Shouldn't he have an Achilles' heel or fatal flaw we can exploit?"

"None I know of. Bilachoe has kept to places on the planet where misery and hopelessness have soaked into the earth for centuries. None of the Lightfolk, major or minor, visit such areas. We would be espied immediately and bound or killed more easily there than anywhere else."

"Would any mortal weakness engendered in Bilachoe at the time of the curse be evident at that time?" Amber asked.

"This is not the computer game that Jenni wrote. I know of no mortal weakness, or if there might even be one," Pavan said with an edge to his patience.

Amber lifted her chin. "And the loophole?"

"The firstborn Davail son must kill Bilachoe. Who has grown in power since the curse."

"But you don't know whether he has a limitation?" Tiro asked.

"Do not question me, brownieman," the elf said in a dark, low voice that had the brownie shivering back into the seat cushion of the love seat.

"When was the curse?" Amber persisted.

"Approximately eight hundred and twenty years ago," Pavan said.

Rafe went a little dizzy. "This dude's been, uh, accruing power for over eight hundred years?"

"That's right." Pavan looked at Rafe's cup of coffee. Rafe drank.

"That's 1197 A.D. Your chart only goes back to 1712," Amber observed.

"I doubt Bilachoe has been practicing warrior skills, though," Pavan said.

"Good to know," Rafe said. He finished the coffee, set his back teeth. He wasn't helpless. Something wouldn't just sneak up on him. He was gaining enough knowledge to protect himself. He'd get more. "If I get this dagger, will that help against Bilachoe?"

"The dagger was forged to kill great Dark ones?" Amber asked.

Pavan appeared surprised at her intelligent question. "Yes."

"So it should work on Bilachoe, too." A line still showed between Amber's brows. "He's not a great Dark one?"

"Not quite," Tiro said.

The elf looked toward the brownie, who crossed his arms and stuck out his chin. "Lived near Bilachoe's area of influence."

"The curse must have worked on Bilachoe, too. Given him some fatal weakness." Amber breathed deeply to steady herself and shot Pavan a look. The elf was utterly gorgeous and completely unhuman in her point of view. "The best magic is balanced magic. I think good strives to balance with evil and vice versa. Bilachoe must have a flaw."

"Faulty assumptions," Pavan said.

He definitely didn't like her for some reason. That wouldn't stop her. He had such a glamour about him that she guessed matching gazes with him could be disastrous. She stared at his eyebrows. They were as beautiful as the rest of him. Not too thick or thin, elegantly arched and silver.

"I have some minor magic and can see specific visions of the past." Eight hundred and twenty-five years would be tricky, but she would give it her all. Davail sounded French. France eight hundred and twenty-five years ago and "warriors" might mean the Third Crusade.

Journeying into the past at the moment of the curse was a better alternative than trying to break the curse by drawing it from Rafe. Tiro was probably right that that would kill her.

She glanced at Rafe. He was looking better than since she'd first met him. Then he'd had a deeply buried air of worn despair and recklessness. Now he simply appeared honed like a man being tested.

As if being told he was a warrior had brought that steel within him to the forefront.

She could do no less, intended to match that courage and strength.

There was a slight thump, an alteration of air pressure. Amber tilted her head. She was becoming more accustomed to the small modifications in her home—the sounds, the rippling of magic as beings appeared or vanished. Another large change in the magic had occurred. As strong as Pavan's but…denser.

Squeals of excitement came from the brownies and they vanished. A minute later there was a rumbling voice, speaking a harsh language that was all edges to Amber's ears. Then she heard the bustle of Hartha in the kitchen and the scent of hot chocolate rose. "They are in the living room, sir. I will bring you hot cocoa and cookies."

Amber was a cookieholic. She didn't keep cookies in the house.

She waited, became aware that Pavan was waiting, too. He smiled and it was ravishing, of course, and the first lighthearted thing that he'd done since he'd entered her home.

"I wasn't offered cookies," Pavan said.

"You're an elf," a deep, rumbly voice replied, "and the brownies know that you disapprove of Amber, here."

Amber stared. Now she had an elf, three brownies and a dwarf in her living room.

CHAPTER 10

HE WAS SHORT AND HUSKY, HIS FACE weathered and bearded. But he moved lithely and had a sword strapped to his back.

"My friend, you are taking too long to brief the Davail. I am here to remind you that we have a meeting with the Eight within the hour and must leave soon," the dwarf said.

Small sounds of protest from the brownies.

One side of the dwarf's mouth kicked up. "I s'pose I can settle a few minutes to eat some cookies." He glanced around. "Nice place." Walking up to her, the dwarf offered his hand. When she held hers out, he took it and bowed over it. "Thank you for your hospitality, Mistress Amber."

"You're quite welcome."

He was a good foot taller than the brownies and much broader. He glanced at them. The brownies had gathered around him as if he was the sun and they were satellite planets. "You have treated the brownies well and I thank you for amusing them in Jindesfarne Mistweaver's absence."

"They are easy to be with," Amber said. She smiled. "Though I think I will watch their chocolate intake."

"Chocolate," the dwarf said reverently.

"I have a drink made with real milk and cream and chocolate," Hartha offered. "Please sit down, great sir, and I will serve it to you, along with the sugar cookies."

Amber's mouth watered at the thought of sugar cookies. She would resist. Really.

The dwarf crossed to a large blue velvet hassock. He wore brown leather that looked like armor to Amber. Immediately Hartha was before him with a pottery mug in a glaze about the same color as his clothes, with whipped cream floating on top and steam rising from it. A small inlaid wooden occasional table holding a plate stacked with cookies scooted to the dwarf's right hand.

"I'd like some hot chocolate, too," the elf said mildly.

Hartha sniffed, slid a quick glance to him and away. "You do not treat Amber with courtesy. What kind of a being is rude to one's own host?" She vanished.

After a squee of horror Pred disappeared, too. So did Tiro.

They hadn't gone far. Amber could still sense them in the kitchen. Since Pavan was gazing thoughtfully in that direction, he could, too.

The dwarf was hooting and coughing. A small spray of white crumbs dusted the floor and his footstool.

Pavan stood and walked over to Amber. He inclined his body in a stiff bow, but didn't offer his hand. "My apologies for my discourtesy."

Amber nodded. "You're forgiven."

"Thank you."

"Would you like cocoa and cookies?" Amber rose from the couch and walked toward the kitchen, but Hartha was back, bustling and staring at the elf, gesturing for him to reseat himself. The browniefem gave him a small teacup of cocoa made of nearly translucent china and an equally small plate with two cookies.

Amber returned to her seat on the couch, noticing Rafe was strained around the eyes, appearing a little shell-shocked.

"Thank you, Mistress Amber and Mistress Hartha," the elf said.

Rafe moved restlessly, studying the dwarf. "I guess you're friends with Pavan and work for Eight Corp, as a troubleshooter, too."

The dwarf grinned, showing pointed red teeth that took Amber aback, and answered, "I prefer to hack at trouble or skewer it, myself, lad."

Clearing his throat, Rafe said, "Do you have a card?"

The dwarf's brows rose until they nearly reached his brown-threaded-with-gray hairline. "A card," he repeated as if he rarely said the word. He studied the cookie, which appeared perfect to Amber—just a little brown at the edges.

Of course she wouldn't ask for one.

A piece of gold-colored cardstock appeared near the dwarf, then it separated into two. One floated toward Amber, the other to Rafe. He snatched it out of the air as if magic still bothered him and she took hers. "Thanks," she said. The card read Vikos, Eight Corp, Troublehacker.

She laughed.

Vikos put the whole cookie in his mouth and crunched, winking at her.

Pavan finished his mug of cocoa and his delicate china cup and the plate that had held two cookies disappeared.

Hartha sniffed again.

Rafe said, "Could I have more—"

But Hartha was there taking his mug, vanishing and returning, handing his refill back to him.

The scent of coffee overwhelmed the fragrance of cocoa, in contrast to the magical beings overwhelming the humans in the room. Pred and Tiro were back on opposite sides of the love seat, drinking mugs of hot chocolate.

"Thank you…Hartha," Rafe said.

"You're welcome," she said. Then she was sitting with her own mug and a cookie between the male brownies.

"So you can help me if I get the dagger," Rafe said.

"That's right," Pavan replied. "Before then you are considered being tested for your fate and must prevail without our aid."

"How can you help me later?"

"I can give you hints to where the Lightfolk palaces are located and how to get there…later."

Pred opened his mouth. Hartha elbowed him in the ribs.

"How do I find this magic knife?"

Pavan's arched and silver brows rose. "You manifest it into your life. Call it to you."

Rafe's eyes narrowed and his face flushed. Amber felt the heat of his irritation.

"I'm not a warrior and magic has been part of my mindset for about—" he looked at his watch "—half an hour."

Pavan stared at him. Naturally Amber couldn't read the elf, but she thought he was running rapidly through options, faster and with more experience than she would ever have.

"Perhaps a construct." Pavan snapped his fingers and a tablet computer spun above the couch several times before dropping with a slight swish of air between Amber and Rafe.

Standing, Pavan said, "Now we must go help Jenni. We have no more time to spend with you."

Rafe stood, too, so Amber rose.

"A big battle is coming!" squeaked Pred.

Pavan inclined his head, his gaze glanced over Rafe. "It's a pity that you aren't a warrior against the Darkfolk already. We could use you."

Rafe stood solid, of course, but Amber felt all the nerves in her body give a cold quiver.

"When is this bad time? Will Jenni be all right?" Pred pressed.

"The spring equinox," Pavan said.

Again there was a sweep of the elf's glance up and down Rafe. "It's barely possible that you might find the dagger before then. If so, contact Eight Corp." Pavan hesitated. "If we should fall, ask for Cloudsylph."

Hartha gasped. "The air royals."

Pavan nodded. "The King and Queen of Air are aware of this situation." A smile, this one unamused, twitched on and off his lips. "I doubt that they will perish."

Vikos grunted. He stood, too. "Don't know what we'll face from the Darkfolk, but doubt any of the royals will die." He shouldered the elf's thigh, but the elf didn't move. "And we're damn good warriors." Now his gaze studied Rafe. He nodded slowly. "You compare well to your forebears."

Rafe seemed to freeze beside her, he mouthed, "Thank you," but his voice was so low that Amber didn't hear him.

"'Welcome," Vikos said.

"What about Conrad?" Rafe asked.

"Who?" Pavan and Vikos said in unison.

"My friend, Conrad Tyne-Cymbler."

"That is for another time and place," Pavan replied evenly. "We must go."

Then the elf was gone.

Vikos burped and glanced around. "This is a good place." The dwarf bowed to her and Rafe, nodded toward each of the brownies. Then he moved to the middle of the living room, into the center of the circular floral rug, and began stamping and turning.

Amber began to feel a deepening of the atmosphere. Was it being infused with magical energy? Earth magic energy? She thought so.

The dwarf started a low, raspy chant, turned in place. Amber's ears popped.

As if they couldn't contain themselves, the brownies hopped from their perches and began to circle him, chanting, too.

And there were four—a man even littler than Pred and scruffier than Amber would have thought a brownie to be.

And a fat calico cat who sat smiling and purred loudly. Jenni's cat.

Amber watched, openmouthed. Rafe had leaned back in his seat and crossed his arms.

The house started vibrating as if the air inside moved like it was a huge drum. Sound slid up and down through the space of roof and basement and walls. Small tinkles like china chimes, then the ringing of bells, little bells like the brownies had on their shoes and the sleigh bells on one of Amber's side doors, to a last, huge *bong* of a great church bell.

Then silence, one final sentence in dwarven that sounded a little lower than her hearing would go, and Vikos bowed again, his face sober. "Blessings upon this house."

Amber let out a breath that had been compressed in her chest. "Thank you." She bowed back to him, wondering why she'd deserved such a blessing.

The cat and the smallest brownie disappeared.

Vikos nodded once again at Amber and dematerialized, too.

"The *guardians* were here." Pred breathed heavily through his nose with little snorts. *"The guardians."*

"We saw 'em," Tiro grumbled, but he'd turned toward the west as if he continued to sense Pavan and Vikos.

"Why do you call them the guardians?" Amber asked.

"They are older than the royals, the Eight," Hartha said, whisking away the crumbs around Vikos's seat. "They didn't leave Earth when most of the great Lightfolk did, in what you humans call the fifth century. They stayed to keep watch on the newly elevated royals."

"Uh-huh," Rafe said in a tone bordering on disbelief.

"Eight royals?" Amber asked. "Earth, air, fire and water?"

Hartha nodded. "A mated couple for each."

"But only two guardians?" Amber asked.

Hartha frowned. "I think there were always only two. Not many wanted to stay on Earth where magic was thinning."

Rafe made a noncommittal noise and Amber found herself nodding her head. A lot of this was escaping her, too. Not very logical. Not very believable. But very real.

"And *we saw them,* the *guardians!*" Pred wrapped his arms around himself, his ears rolled down and up a couple of times. *"We took part in a great Lightfolk's blessing!* That should help with the death curse energy."

Rafe shook his head, rubbed the back of his neck. Then he picked up his computer tablet. "I left this in my duffel in the Jag, which is parked outside." He stared intently at Amber.

She shrugged. "Magic."

He turned the small computer on. "It's fully charged," he said.

"Yes?" Amber commented.

He shook his head. "It was really low when it went into hibernation early this morning. Another story." He frowned. "The dude didn't even touch it."

"No, he didn't," Amber agreed.

"It's the meld," Hartha said.

"What's that?" asked Amber.

"The Lightfolk royals…Eight Corp…are working with human technology and magic to meld energy."

Amber stared at the browniefem and thought Rafe was doing the same. "Okay, that's completely lost me. Can't take any more."

"We have been blessed." Hartha flicked her fingers in what Amber thought was her own brownie blessing. She liked it better when Hartha had been lecturing the elf on discourtesy.

The browniefem came to stand before Rafe, head tilted as she scrutinized him. She nodded. "You have magic. Warrior magic, but most of it is bound by that green glyph. The sign of an elf spell."

"To be freed after his thirty-third birthday?" Amber asked.

"Yes," Hartha said. "But enough magic to see and hear us if he believes."

"And to manifest his dagger," Amber said.

The brownie woman shrugged. "We will go home now." She let out a deep sigh, put a thin hand over her small breasts. "I am feeling better about Jenni if the guardians are helping her."

"She will be all right." Pred smiled. His gaze slid to Amber. "But if she isn't we get the house. She gave you a paper?"

Amber dragged her mind back from pondering sigils binding magic.

"Yes."

"It is not good to inherit a house due to violent death." He raised his nose as he looked at Tiro. "Amber will not give you *her* house when she dies."

Amber choked.

"Don't need her house. Got my own." Tiro vanished.

"In some light-and-magic sucking place ruled by Bilachoe," Pred continued pointedly. "Not like here in Mystic Circle in Denver, where the meld will happen and good magic will flow again *first*."

"Come along, Pred," Hartha said. She grabbed his arm and they disappeared, too.

Amber wandered into the kitchen to see if there might be any remaining cookies to pop into her mouth as she banished the thought of her own death. The brownies weren't optimistic that she'd be able to refuse Rafe.

She had to.

One glance at the spotless kitchen showed a lack of cookies. She was still hungry, and Rafe had followed her.

"Want a sandwich?" Amber asked.

"Yeah." He moved his shoulders around, as if he needed to release tension.

"The neighborhood's nice to jog in," she said, going to the refrigerator and pulling out the variety of deli meats and cheeses that she had, stacking a loaf of bread on top of them, and carrying mustard and mayonnaise.

He snorted. "I've nearly been killed twice in this neighborhood."

The packages slipped from her hands to the center island, and she thought back to the long conversation full of staggering information. "Those shadleeches?"

"Yeah. Nasty things. Then nearly duplicated my father's death, hit by a car." He set down his tablet on the shelf of the corner cabinet and moved back to the island. He opened the bread bag and took out some slices, began layering meat and cheese.

Amber's spirits began to sink. An awful tension at the base of her skull told her she was going to make a mistake. "You truly almost died?"

Rafe hesitated.

"I don't think you've lied to me since we've met. You've been upfront about your feelings and every-thing. Don't start lying to me now." She picked up a knife and slathered on too much mustard, slapped on thin slices of ham and thicker ones of sharp cheddar.

He tossed the bag of lettuce he'd taken from the fridge to the island and leaned against the appliance.

"Yeah, three times. First an attack by those shadleech things." He pushed up his left sweater sleeve and she saw nasty red and shiny scars that looked like bites.

Amber felt her eyes widen. She swallowed hard. Her mouth was too dry to eat her sandwich now. She went to the refrigerator and got out the pitcher of iced tea. "Then you almost got run down?"

One side of his mouth lifted in a grimace. "Yeah, by a friend of mine, even. Don Brilliant of Brilliant Limos picked me up yesterday after our meeting when Conrad bailed on me."

Glug, glug, glug. The tea gurgled darkly as it filled her glass.

She sipped the tea. She'd brewed it too long and it was bitter. Hell. She met Rafe's blue gaze. "And the third?"

"This morning." He jerked his head toward his computer tablet. "Like I said, it was low. Went to plug it in and got shocked across the room."

Amber coughed. "Rea-really?" she gasped.

"Yeah. I didn't touch the metal prongs of the plug *or* the outlet. Screwed up the inn's electricity, too."

"Wow." She took the time to put her sandwich on a plate and carry that and her glass to the polished dining room table, where she set them on a place mat. Again, Rafe followed.

They ate awhile in silence before he said, "I didn't mean to lay the guilt on you."

"Yes, you did. But you're reconsidering."

"Yeah."

She took a big breath. "There's a guest suite on the

third floor. It was the attic and is just one big room with a small bathroom. Shower, no tub. The ceiling is finished." She eyed him. "You should fit under most of it."

He looked around. "How many bedrooms do you have?"

"I had my office down here, but Tiro's made a bedroom of it." She waved a hand. "Long story. So one bedroom upstairs is my office now. There are two others on the second floor, mine is the big one facing the street, and, like I said, the suite on the third floor. Two full baths on the second floor and a half bath down here, and the one on the third floor."

He grunted as he chewed his sandwich. When he was done, he said, "I don't think number two has as much space."

"No, but it's charming."

"What of your basement?"

She wiggled her brows. "I haven't looked down there since Pred and Tiro started messing with it."

At that moment the air changed again and dog barks sounded as the puppies shot through the back door Tiro must have opened for them. They went straight to their spot in the butler's pantry and sounds of crunching and slurping came.

Rafe smiled and she smiled back. He stood and took his plate and glass of water to the sink, rinsed them.

Amber said, "The dogs need to be walked. Tiro will play with them in the backyard, but they need to get out. They might be a little protection. At least they bark at strangers."

Rafe slanted her a look. "You'd trust them with me, doomed to death?"

She didn't show her inward quiver. "Sure."

"You're going to let me stay here, aren't you?"

She sighed. "Yes."

He inclined his head and for a moment looked as noble as the elf. "Thank you."

The dogs came over to her. She petted them fiercely.

She praised their beauty lavishly, ran her hands over their young bodies. No, she would never jeopardize their lives. Never.

They accepted only a few minutes of attention before nosing Rafe and getting pets from him, then sniffing at the chair where Pavan had sat and the hassock Vikos had used, then collapsing on their beds in the living room.

Amber finished her meal and did the dishes while Rafe got his duffel from his rental car. She was looking across the kitchen at the corner cupboard at Rafe's tablet when he came back in the kitchen. "Any coffee?"

"Sure." She'd just made a pot and gestured to him to pour a cup.

"What do you think this 'construct' business is?" he asked.

Amber had a vague idea. Pavan seemed to know Jenni well and had mentioned her game. Jenni worked as a story writer for a software gaming company that produced one of the most popular massively multiplayer online games, Fairies and Dragons. Amber didn't want to say that to Rafe, though. She reckoned that all his games were real life and physically challenging.

"Maybe we can determine that." She nodded to his tablet.

He picked it up reluctantly and they settled back on the couch.

When he turned it on, the app icons showed onscreen. There weren't a lot, certainly not as many as Amber had on her pocket computer.

She pointed to a new icon of a fairy astride a dragon's long neck. It was the last program in a row, next to one called "Fly or Die."

"A construct." Rafe scowled. "I don't like the sound of that." He snorted again. "*Manifesting* the damn dagger." He touched the icon.

The world around them fell away.

CHAPTER
11

"THIS CAN'T BE REAL," RAFE SAID, DENYING
the circle of standing stones and the towering forest
around him.

"It's a game," Amber said, too cheerfully because
the rain dripping down the collar of whatever he was
wearing was sure cold and wet.

She looked younger and was wearing some sort of
silvery scale armor that conformed to her torso and
shaped her breasts really nicely. Her pants were black
leather and gored for easy movement and her boots
were tall and black and cuffed. She had a silver tiara
around her brow.

"That's an excellent look for you." She smiled.

Rafe glanced down at himself. He wore armor, too.
Not a good sign as far as he was concerned. His gear
wasn't metal, more like layers of stuff, maybe leather
and silk and something else, padded where he might

need it most. It glowed a dark green. He'd probably be near invisible in this forest. He shifted and realized he wore a groin guard. When he moved some more, he discovered it was the most comfortable guard he'd ever had, but he still didn't like it or the implications.

He shrugged and a long cape—looking a little too much like the elf's for his peace of mind—moved around him in a glow that matched his armor. *Magic*.

"What is this crap?" he said. "Where the hell are we?"

"You've never played Fairies and Dragons?"

"No. I'm into sports."

Amber turned slowly. Her hand had gone to her hip, where it looked like a wand was stowed. On her other thigh she wore a fantasy pistol made of ceramic or something. "Looks like the Standing Stones Sanctuary in the forest of Lin to me. We're in the beginning zone of Fairies and Dragons. It's a safe area. Players can only log off in a safe area." She tilted her chin down a path. "The city of Van should be down that way. It has weapon shops, maybe your dagger…"

Rafe grunted. "What will stop us?"

"Oh, plenty of things will try, I imagine."

Rafe didn't want to imagine anything. "Do I look like myself?" He crossed his arms and found heavy metal-studded gauntlets on his hands.

Amber nodded. "Yes. Longer hair." Then her lips curved. "You have elf ears." She was grinning.

"What!" Red outrage hazed his vision. He lifted his hands, but his gloves were too thick to really feel any curves or points. He became aware of something very, very wrong. "I have no weapons."

Her brows lowered. "You should. You're a Red Dragonfly Knight."

"What?"

"Heavy-fighter with a hint of magic. You have wings under that cloak, red, signifying an offensive fighter. As for weapons, you should have a knife and sword..."

"How do you know that?"

She shrugged. "I looked at your player profile. I can see it as a scroll over your head if I concentrate."

He stared.

"I looked at mine, too," she said. "I don't have a real character with these attributes in my game."

"Fairies and Dragons?"

"Yes. Jenni Weavers writes the game. Everyone in Mystic Circle plays. Sometimes we even all log on at the same time."

They were all crazy.

Frowning, Amber said, "All right, think *profile*. Maybe you'll see—"

"Profile," he said. Before his eyes a ragged scroll of paper appeared. His name: Rafe Barakiel; weapons: claymore, main gauche. Secondary magic: wind defense.

"Help me, help me!" cried a high voice.

Rafe's profile faded.

Skidding to a stop on the path before them was a tiny round man in green with a tall hat. He bounced up and down. "I need help to rescue my pots of gold from my evil twin!"

"Oh, the leprechaun storyline that Jenni wrote is live now!" Amber said. She sounded thrilled.

"This blows," Rafe said. "I'm outta here." He pounded a fist against a slab and discovered himself back on the couch, hitting the padded arm with his fist.

"Well," Amber said, brows raised. "That was interesting."

"That was damn crazy." Rafe stood and went to his duffel. "I'll put away my stuff." He stopped. "You play that game, Fairies and Dragons."

"I have it on my secondary laptop." She paused. "The password is 'changeling.'"

"Right. Thanks for letting me stay."

Her quiet tone stopped him at the bottom of the stairs. "Magic, Rafe. We're involved in it." He heard her deep inhalation. "And that was fantasy and fun. You'll remember that I can catch glimpses of the past."

He hadn't. He looked at her. She was pale under her tanned skin tone.

"That's real," she said, "and part of my life."

He gave the idea a little thought and approved of it. "That can be helpful." Conrad had felt so and as much as Rafe was reluctant to think of the curse, it seemed the answers lay in the past. "Later."

She stood, her expression closed. "I have work. I'll be in my office."

Of course the first thing she did was hit her heavy-duty work computer with searches. Bilachoe for one.

After she'd typed in "Billacho" the search engine asked: "Do you mean Bilachoe?"

She did, and looked at that. There were only a half-dozen entries of scanty information.

"Eastern European folk tales and mythology, a fiery demon who delights in the misery of others."

Amber considered that. No doubt those folk who saw and talked and wrote about Bilachoe didn't know what else to call him except "demon." An evil being. None of the definitions mentioned any weaknesses. Which meant she'd have to talk to Tiro.

She shut her computer and went to the open door... just as Rafe stepped up to it. They stood there close, no more than five inches apart, and she caught his scent. A fragrance that included an undertone of magic, something she didn't think that she'd have smelled last week. So she stood there, inhaling him. The magic was wispy, but what she caught of it smelled like a mountaintop in the autumn wind. Fresh with a hint of cold, summer gone.

Her stomach pitched as she realized that this might be Rafe's last spring and summer...he might only live until the next winter. His birthday was in late November.

Then there was the earthy smell of virility, faint sweat. She looked up and was caught by his blue gaze and pupils dilating. He liked what he saw of her—how she smelled?—too.

His left arm came around her waist, drew her against him and he had the hardest body, the most muscles, she'd ever felt and that was as dizzyingly attractive as his scent of magic.

"Amber..." He rumbled her name huskily enough to cause a thrill to vibrate through her.

The fingers of his other hand traced her jawline, then he bent to kiss her and everything inside her clenched at the touch of his lips. It had been so long since she'd had sex, had found any man attractive enough to want to go to bed with. But Rafe Davail stirred all her senses.

He moved closer, one strong leg between her own and that felt exquisite. Then he opened his mouth and his tongue dueled with hers and he tasted of curse.

Dark, deep curse...

She shouldn't have found that tempting, but she did, as if he opened the universe for her, showing the possibilities beyond this life.

Now *that* thought was scary.

One last nibble at his bottom lip, fuller than it looked, and she drew back. His arms cradling her fell away.

Before she could say anything, the dogs were yipping and pushing around them, between them. Another pace back, taking her body thrumming with need from the man she knew could satisfy her in the most sensual and intimate ways.

She bent and petted the dogs, letting her hair veil her flushed face. Murmuring nonsense to her pets because that was all she could think of.

Rafe leaned on the doorjamb, crossed his arms, his

gaze going to her desk and her computer. "What did you learn?"

"The first mention of Bilachoe was later than what Pavan told us. I postulate that he gained stature after your curse." She grimaced. "He's nasty. Likes strife and war and pestilence."

"Huh."

"And is a fire demon."

"So we need intel on Bilachoe," Rafe said. A side of his mouth quirked. "Maybe we can mine Tiro the brownieman for data."

"From what I understand of Tiro, he'll charge for it."

Rafe shrugged. "I can handle the freight."

She figured he could.

"Just a matter of finding out what he might like." Rafe looked down at the dogs. "Wanna go for a walk?"

Baxt and Zor erupted into excited barking.

"They okay off leash here in the circle?" he asked.

"Of course not." Amber slipped past Rafe and went down the stairs to the entryway and the hooks on the wall, pulling down two leashes.

The puppies skidded to a stop before her, jostling. Not jumping, so they were remembering their training.

"What element is brownie?" Rafe asked.

"Oh, that's right, you don't know. The four ancient elements—earth, air, fire, water—all have major and minor Lightfolk."

"Got it. Earth is brownie and dwarf."

"Right," she said.

His brows dipped. "The elf. Fire?" Then Rafe shook his head. "No. Air?"

"Yes. The brownies say there are airsprites and fire-sprites. I haven't seen any. Don't know that any are here in Mystic Circle."

Rafe grunted. "What's the major race for fire?"

"Djinn. You know, genies."

He blinked. "Seriously?"

"Yes. But I don't know that they look like the cartoon characters. My neighbor, Jenni—" she waved toward Jenni's house "—is supposedly, um, quarter djinn. She has auburn hair but otherwise doesn't look like any fire being that I'd imagine."

"Uh-huh. A lot to consider." Rafe took the leashes and clipped them on Baxt and Zor, looking with revulsion at the neon pink one attached to Zor's collar. "Dude, this is just wrong."

"It glows in the dark," Amber said.

"It glows in the light, too." He leaned down to rub the dogs. "I'll go get you some new ones later." His lips firmed and he cast her a glance. "I can't stay cooped up in Mystic Circle all the time."

"There's a pet store close, at the east end of the block with the Sensitive New Age Bean."

"Then we'll head there." He shook his head. "My next task is to manifest the dagger. If that don't beat all." He shook his head and winked at her, jingled the leashes. "We'll walk around to number two, maybe explore." Shrugging, he said, "Of all the houses in the cul-de-sac that's the one that looks the most girly. Wouldn't be my first choice."

Amber got irritated. "It's a pretty house, a lot of interesting angles."

"Would look better if it weren't pink."

"It's peach."

"Yeah, yeah." With a last wave he went out the door accompanied by joyful dog yips, controlling their lunges easily.

Amber was afraid he was fitting into her life too quickly and far too nicely.

Just as she knew Tiro would continue to be an irritant. Nerving herself, she crossed through the rooms on the first floor to the kitchen and the basement and hesitated. Tiro was down there. She strained to sense if he was alone, wondering whether she'd like to speak with Pred and Hartha, too.

She hadn't been down in the basement since the brownies had been working on it…maybe more than that, a week or so. The furnace was fine, she hadn't needed to store anything or get anything from down there.

The basement itself was three-quarters of the house, with a crawl space in the front, facing the park in the middle of Mystic Circle. The walls were brick and the floor concrete, except the crawl space was dirt.

With a sigh, she trudged to the door. She wasn't looking forward to talking with Tiro again. He'd say the same thing and she'd say her bit and their discussion would clash and there would be no consensus.

She first noted that the twisty stairs were *clean*. She

washed the stairs about once a year during the height of summer. They also seemed sturdier under her feet. Just exactly how much would she owe the brownies for upgrading her house?

Better not look as if she were happy about whatever they were doing.

And when she got down and turned toward the noise, it wasn't hard to be completely shocked.

There was no crawl space. The basement was one large room. Previously it had been bisected with a lathe and plaster wall. The new multicolored brick walls were tuck-pointed and in perfect condition. The floor was paved in flagstones that nearly matched the brick.

Three gorgeous wooden doors were set in the walls, all larger than a human, each unique. One to the south and Jenni's house, one to the north and Tamara's, and a third in the east, the front, toward the center of the cul-de-sac and the park.

"Huh," she said, blinking. There were more than a couple of lights hanging by a string, too. Recessed lighting. Just how good were brownies with electricity?

She cleared her throat. Pred glanced at her, a scared expression passing over his face, and ran. She thought she actually saw him run *through* the door to Jenni's property.

Tiro stood, arms on his hips, chin jutted, slit-eyed. "Under the house is much better now."

"It certainly is different," Amber said.

Flicking a hand in a gesture too fast for Amber to

follow, Tiro said, "Humans have too many rules about building and such."

"Um. I suppose you know what you're doing."

Tiro just sneered. He turned his back and marched over to the south door, framed in oak, pulled out a cloth and polished. "Jenni gave Pred permission to play under her house, and run a path to under the park and make a new common room there."

"A. Common. Room. Under. The. Park."

"For community events," Tiro said.

Amber squared her shoulders. "I doubt Jenni had any idea of exactly what Pred was doing."

"She wanted the sunroom, said Pred could play in the basement."

"Uh-huh. And she gave me some papers. Guess I should actually look at them."

"Humans." Tiro spat on the door and rubbed it away with the cloth. Just what qualities did brownie spit have? No, she wouldn't get distracted.

"I've come to ask about Bilachoe."

"I knew it! You fell for a pretty face and a sad story, just like all the others of your type." He didn't look at her. "You will break the curse and die. The puppies will die."

"I won't let that happen. I'll cut all the emotional bonds between myself and them. And if I'm linked to you, you'll age, too, won't you?"

He turned and hopped up and down in fury. "You think I care about *that*!"

"I don't know what you care about. Nothing, as far as I can see."

"What's the use of caring about you, who will drain power from a death curse and grow old in minutes and die? Or caring about puppies who are short-lived? Or a cursed human mortal who has no chance against Bilachoe? Bilachoe, a thing who is close to becoming a great Dark one himself?" Tiro gave the door a huge swipe with his rag, top to bottom, levitating in the process. Amber kept her focus on his words.

"He's powerful."

"I said so, didn't I? A few more hundred deaths of torture and pain to swell his power and he will be a great Dark one."

"Oh," Amber said, looking around for a chair to sink into. Despite the clean tidiness of the basement, there was still no chair. She swallowed. "I'm sorry that you cared for my predecessors and they hurt you. I'm sorry that you think you will care for me and I will hurt you." She found her hands twisting together, a bad habit she'd broken herself of when she was nine.

"You just want to help," he sneered.

"Yes, what's so wrong about that? I want to help others. I *believe* that I was given this gift to help others."

"Your line was given this gift by Cumulustre to learn a lesson, because his lover was too soft and her girl-children were too soft. And, still, after centuries you *are too soft!*"

"I believe that helping others is the most important thing in the world."

"But you will drain yourself, hurt yourself to help others. Is that a good thing?"

She couldn't answer, her throat had tightened.

Now he stared at her with flinty brown eyes. "How did you feel when your mother and her sister cut their emotional bonds to you and left you to break the curse of someone else? And never returned? You think that was noble?"

She remembered her mother and aunt leaving. She'd been young, just six, but she remembered. She recalled that she'd felt completely alone. Grudgingly accepted by her relatives, no love from her mother or aunt. No tenderness had remained. She'd never had a bond as loving since. She swallowed again and realized tears were leaking from her eyes and flowing down her cheeks.

Stopping halfway up the stairs, she made one last point. "Some people are cursed. If we don't help them, who can? Who will?"

CHAPTER
12

SHE TRUDGED UP THE STAIRS TO THE kitchen, looked in the fridge. There was no chocolate, of course. She was sure there would be no chocolate in the house that the brownies couldn't sniff out. Plenty of chocolate a few blocks down in the business district—restaurants, a deli. The Sensitive New Age Bean was sure to have chocolate cake.

Amber settled for cinnamon-sugar toast and Earl Grey tea, an old comfort food treat from when she'd been dating her first boyfriend.

Love hadn't stuck then, either.

And this pity party had already gone on too long. She had work to do.

Back upstairs she took a moment to soak in the fact that she loved her office, that it was *just right,* and that it was getting sunlight that Tiro's room downstairs wasn't. Warm, golden spring sunlight. Cheerful. She *would* be cheerful.

After one last bite of the toast, she logged on to the Fairies and Dragons game forums, ready to do a search for Bilachoe there, too. Just in case Jenni had known about him and incorporated him into the game.

The forum showed two blinking hot topics. One was on the fun and funny storyline of the leprechauns. Jenni had written another hit with a few unusual twists...apparently there was a slide down a rainbow... and that made Amber smile. She wouldn't think of danger right now—not to Jenni and the guardians, Rafe, or herself.

The second issue was a rampant rumor that the original game company that had created Fairies and Dragons was being acquired by a company called Melding Myths. Amber blinked at the name, something about it...she continued to read and found that the developers were staying on and storylines by Jenni Weavers would be highlighted. Which most people thought was excellent. Amber wondered if Jenni knew about this.

Digging a little deeper, Amber discovered that Melding Myths was a new software company that was a subsidiary of Eight Corp, based in Denver, Colorado.

Amber's fingers froze on the keys.

Eight Corp, the company that had an elfin troubleshooter and a dwarven troublehacker...and the discussion of Eight Corp with Pavan and the brownies had led to information that there were four elemental magical couples, *royal* couples. The eight most powerful Lightfolk. Just how much did this Eight Corp have to do with the royal couples and magic?

Another place to go for information. She noted it on her pocket computer, then stood.

Now that she'd been reminded of the elf and the dwarf, her hands itched for Rafe's tablet computer and the very strange, very real game she'd experienced. Instead, she left her desk and hauled out the secondary laptop that she used for gaming. Since Jenni hadn't been around for a month, Amber hadn't played a lot. Still, she could build that character she'd been— though she didn't think much of it. A Silver Fairy Webspinner was a weak toon—character—and more defensive than she cared for. Hard to do solo missions.

She supposed she should be grateful that Pavan had included her in Rafe's game at all. That he had made her character weak was evidence of how he viewed her.

Building Rafe's character would be fun. The standard faces didn't give her much to work with, but she'd see what she could do to make one look close to Rafe. The body types were better...and his costume had been in line with what was available in the game.

When Rafe and the dogs returned, she called to him from the room on the ground floor that she'd fitted as a consultation room for clients before she'd rented office space. The dogs trotted over to her, obviously having enough exercise for the day. They licked her hands and did the whine thing, telling her that they wanted their spoonfuls of wet food.

"This is my computer with Fairies and Dragons on

it," she said. She turned her computer so Rafe could see his character standing in the stone circle where they'd been earlier. He looked at it, glanced away.

"I think I got all your attributes right, and your name is Rafe Barakiel." She tried a quick smile. "Maybe you'd like to check the game out in an easier atmosphere than what Pavan put on your tablet."

He grunted.

All right, he was not thrilled. "Any incidents?" she asked.

He smirked. "The counter woman at the pet store hit on me."

"Of course."

He raised his brows, a sly smile curved his lips. "Of course?"

"You're eminently hittable."

"Glad you think so." He made a point of leering at her butt as she turned and bent to pet the dogs some more and went to the kitchen to feed them.

Tiro was there, sitting at a miniature café set that he'd stuck in a corner, drinking coffee. Scowling as usual, but he let his mug float as he murmured and petted the pups. He might not care for anything else, but he'd bonded with them.

She spooned out the dogs' food and poured more kibble in their dishes, along with emptying the old water and putting out new. They drank sloppily and she cleaned up, then they exited out the dog door to the backyard and she saw them flop in the sun on a patch of violets.

"No threats on your walk?" Amber asked when Rafe came in.

"No." Rafe rolled his shoulders. "Mystic Circle felt great, so we went around a couple of times. Then we walked down to the store." He smiled. "Plenty of other people and dogs out there. Maybe the curse is letting up a little. You know, try three times—" He mimicked punching. "Then wait, then try again. What do you think, Tiro?"

Amber frowned. She hadn't told Rafe about her discussion with Tiro.

The brownie scrutinized Rafe. "You are going to fight Bilachoe?"

All humor vanished from Rafe's expression. "That's the plan. Better to go down fighting than just hanging around waiting for death."

Tiro gave a slow nod. "And how are you going to fight the evil one?"

To Amber's surprise there was no scorn in Tiro's voice. Progress? Or was it as Pavan said, the Davail line had heroically been altered to fight great Dark ones and Bilachoe had cursed them, and Tiro believed Rafe might have a chance?

Rafe looked through the kitchen until he found cheese and crackers and made himself a snack, answering the brownie. "I'll find a fencing teacher and learn how to handle a knife." Rafe's jaw hardened and his teeth snapped into the cracker. "I'll...manifest...the dagger, somehow."

"I have an idea about that," Amber said. "You felt the magical energy in the cul-de-sac?"

Rafe winced, set his shoulders and nodded. "Yeah."

"All right, that can help with manifestation."

Drilling Tiro with his gaze, Rafe said, "You have any ideas about Bilachoe?"

Tiro glanced at Amber. "I told her that Bilachoe is close to becoming a great Dark one himself. A being of immense and evil power." The brownie's words thudded into the air like sharp-edged rocks. He stared back at Rafe.

Again Rafe shrugged, finished another cracker. "Like I said, planning and going down fighting is better than just walking around with doom over my head about to strike." A quick, vicious smile. "Who knows, maybe I can weaken Bilachoe so my distant cousin can beat him next year."

"Being rather fatalistic, aren't you?" Amber murmured.

Rafe gestured to himself. "Give me a race to run and win—snowboarding, sailing, skiing. Hell, cycling, car or plane. That I can do. Fighting? Not so much." He made another batch of cheese and crackers. "Reminds me that I need to talk to my brother about this cousin, maybe Gabe can find him."

Amber clicked her tongue. "Genealogist here."

"You can find him for me," Rafe said.

"Sure."

"Done. Anyway, I can do the best job I can on Bilachoe, maybe help out this other guy with the Davail curse." This time Rafe's shoulders twitched and for a moment, even sagged. He shook his head. "I hate the idea of Gabe's son going through this. And Gabe watching it." Rafe's mouth turned down. "Since I denied the curse, I could deny the hurt to others."

"I'm sure your brother is hurting," Amber said.

Rafe munched on a couple of crackers. "Not much, I pushed him away. He thinks—like many people think—that I've wasted my life with extreme sports."

"Those who think that haven't walked in your shoes."

"Nope." Rafe lifted his last cracker and held it like a salute to Tiro. "We who are about to die, salute you."

Admiration appeared in Tiro's eyes. "The brick walls of the basement need another application of sealant." For a small creature he sure could thump his footsteps. He walked to the door, angled his chin at Rafe. "Bila-choe fears a dagger, but he also fears a shield." The stairs groaned behind Tiro.

Rafe threw his last half-eaten cracker in the trash. "A shield! How am I supposed to tell a fencing master that I want to train with a knife and a shield!"

Amber walked up to him and put her arms around him, held him. His arms went loosely around her. While scanning the Net, she'd seen him with a lot of supermodels on his arm, so he'd likely had a good amount of sex, but what about caring? And tenderness? Those things that she'd spoken of to Tiro?

Rafe had pushed his family away, understandably. He'd had a good friend in Conrad Cymbler, but guys didn't hold each other, and Conrad was desperate himself.

Just how lonely was Rafe? She tightened her grip around him, made nonsensical, comforting sounds.

Their bodies lined up well together. She liked his muscularity, his vitality, felt cushy and smaller against him. His heartbeat was even and solid. He deserved comforting and tenderness and...loving.

He sighed, then rubbed his cheek on her hair. "I'm nothing but a spoiled rich guy."

"No. You're strong. You've lived with your curse all your life, lived a full life and tried to spare your loved ones."

He snorted. "Yeah, that's me, all right. Sounds more like you."

"My magic isn't a curse."

"No? It costs to break curses, doesn't it?"

She slipped away, tidied up the cracker crumbs on the counter. She'd just held him, tried to give him comfort. She didn't want to brutally tell him that breaking his curse could cost her life. Didn't want to deny hope to him, or herself. Not right now. "I don't want to talk about that now."

After a few seconds of hesitation, he shrugged once more and it appeared like he was shrugging on a manner, an attitude that was "Rafe Davail," instead of the glimpse of the true self she thought she'd seen.

Tilting her head, she studied him. "You meant what you said to Tiro. You're going to fight Bilachoe."

Rafe nodded. "Going to do my best. Learn to fight. Manifest what I can manifest." He waved a hand but still made the word sound dirty. "Make Bilachoe send minions, come himself."

"All right."

"And you'll help me?"

"Yes."

"What about Conrad's stuff? How are you doing on that?"

Heat flowed to her cheeks. "I've been distracted." She grimaced. "I think his curse will be as far in the past as yours."

He said, "So you can *see* moments of the past."

Even after all he'd experienced in the last two days, he didn't sound as if he believed her. Or maybe that faint uncertainty she'd noted was because he wanted to believe her. She hunched a shoulder. "Sure." Then she breathed deeply, a long inhale, a sifting exhale. "Let's try something, magic man."

"Magic man," he repeated blankly.

"You have magic. Trapped, but there." Was having trapped magic better than life-draining magic? Yes. "And you have magic in all four elements."

"Is that good?"

"Supposed to be. I'm learning just like you." She held out her hand and when he took it, the feel of him surprised her. His hand was larger, warmer and more calloused than she'd expected. He was used to holding ropes for climbing and sailing, wasn't he?

"Learning?"

"The brownies came into my life a few hours before we met."

He grunted and she knew why. Destiny?

She led him to her office and to the worktable under the windows, and searched for a sense of his magic. An image came of a bright sunburst of white light, and heat. More than the heat of his body along with a tang along her tongue of tart apple. She didn't know what it meant. She did know that she liked touching him, holding hands with him, far too much. Attraction shimmered through her with promising temptation that she must deny.

When they reached the table he used his free index finger to trace back the Cymbler family tree. Pink-violet sparkles rose within her, swirled until they were thick mist around them both.

"Huh," he said, but it didn't stop her from falling into the dark pit of the past. She squeezed his hand and wondered if she took him with her.

The tones were gray and black and white, the costumes of the 1920s and she felt as if she'd fallen into an old movie.

"What's going on?" Rafe asked, voice echoing tinnily.

"Watch." Hard to form the word on her cold lips, to move her mouth and emit the sound.

A small spotlight was on a trumpet player that she couldn't hear. Her attention focused on two men at a round table away from the stage. She floated, pulling Rafe behind her like a balloon caught in the wind. The men leaned toward each other, heads slick, one blond, one dark, with features similar to Rafe and Conrad but looking thicker, not as refined. Conrad's ancestor seemed a good decade older than Rafe's, in his early forties.

"Find your son?" asked Davail. He wasn't looking at Cymbler, his gaze was restless.

"Yeah." The dark guy tossed down a short tumbler-ful of liquid.

Now Rafe's forebear met the man's eyes. "Going to talk with him?"

"Nope. These are dang'rous times. He deserves better'n me as a dad. Gotta good step-pop, so he's set." The man raised his hand, palm out. "I decided. Don't try'n talk me outta it. Did you find the sticker you was lookin' for?"

"It's close." Davail lowered his eyelids but didn't quite shut his eyes. "Here in Chi-town for sure. Think I pulled it with me when I came here, maybe. Now I'll search."

Doors slammed open, machine guns chittered. Davail jerked and the new stain on his light suit jacket turned terribly black. Cymbler lunged under a table and lived.

Moaning yanked Amber from the scene and she realized she wasn't holding on to Rafe's hand anymore. Just as well. She found herself folded over the table, the edge digging into her stomach. Something was hard against her legs. Rafe, on the floor.

"Holy crud," he said groggily.

CHAPTER 13

SHE HAD ONLY ENOUGH ENERGY TO LEVER herself away from the table and onto her feet and stagger to her desk chair. "Oh, my God." She wiped her face. It was damp with sweat. By the time she looked over at Rafe, he was sitting with knees upraised, head lowered.

"Geez," he said. "Did I just see one of my guys die?"

"Probably." Feeling shaky, Amber swiveled in her chair and hit a few keys on her keyboard, pulling up Rafe's chart. A small sweep of the mouse showed the entry. She checked the information then logged on to the internet, searched the time. Found the place and the incident. Jase Davail was the only one killed, though there were injuries.

She smelled Rafe before his shadow fell over her— he'd sweated, too.

"Poor jerk," Rafe said. "Wrong place, wrong time again."

Amber swung around to look up at him. He was haggard, shaken and trying to make light of his death curse.

"How old was he?" Rafe asked.

Amber flicked back to the family tree. "Just thirty. He already had two sons and a daughter."

Rafe winced. He pulled his collar away from the back of his neck, met her eyes. "That's some trick you have there, lady."

"My minor magic," she murmured.

His eyes widened and his forehead creased. "Minor?"

"The curse breaking is major."

"That wasn't curse breaking?"

"No."

"Damn, Conrad was right. About every fricking thing." Rafe went back to the table, looked at the scroll and shook his head, then turned and leaned against it, crossing his arms. He met her eyes and she could see that his pupils were still expanded. Then he looked out the window to the backyard that was in the wall at a right angle to him. "Jase said he'd found the knife. In Chicago."

"That was nearly a century ago," Amber pointed out.

Rafe pushed away from the table. "Well, it ain't eight hundred years." His smile was crooked. "So that's an upside. If you don't mind, I want to take a shower."

She wanted to comfort him somehow, hold him again, but his body was closed off, so she only said, "Go ahead."

"Thanks." Without another word he walked from the room. There was still a hint of a swagger in his step, so he wasn't as shocked as she was.

She'd made another mistake. The first was inviting him to stay, and she was getting too close to him, too fast. Too many mistakes could lead to disaster.

And death that was all too present and all too real.

The brownies provided the meal that evening and ate with her and Rafe, but talked mostly about Jenni and how they'd arrived to keep her house. They enthused about the house itself, including the new additions they'd made, like the sunroom. Amber reassured them that should anything happen to Jenni, she would file the papers that transferred the house to "Mr. and Mrs. Brownly" at the city and county building.

At dusk Amber took the dogs for another walk around the neighborhood and they all sniffed the air. She'd lived in Denver long enough to know that March snowstorms could be the worst of the year, but it appeared that the unusually warm and early spring was going to hold. She'd feel better when March was done, though. Her heart gave a little jerk when she realized she was wishing time away.

Time was precious. She'd already lost years.

And she was wishing away the days of Rafe's life, too.

She and the dogs reached the opening of the cul-de-sac to the neighborhood beyond and she stopped and tried to *feel* the magic. Sensed there was a cloud of doom beyond. The puppies showed no inclination to run outside of the circle, which was unusual, but maybe they'd had enough earlier that day. And though Rafe had said there hadn't been any incidents, perhaps the dogs had sensed something more threatening than he.

When she returned to the house, it seemed that it was nearly as empty as it was a week ago. She, too, would retreat to her separate space. From what she could sense of Tiro, he was in and out of the tunnels that the brownies were making in the cul-de-sac. The way they were going, it would soon be a wheel underground. She wondered if they'd spoken with Rafe about number two Mystic Circle.

Occasionally she could hear thumps overhead, and sounds that puzzled her until she realized that some of her exercise equipment must have been moved to the third floor. Rafe was working out with steady dedication. He had the body to prove that physical exercise was a priority to him.

He might not be a fighter yet, but he was in prime condition. And it was all too easy for her to imagine him bare-chested and in shorts, sheened in perspiration—and with that dark and deadly curse clinging to him like a black mist.

All she'd had to do was say "no." Amber sat curled up in bed, her chin on her knees and watched the puppies tumble around, coming up for snuggles or doggy kisses, running her hands through their fur or brushing them. Feeling the warmth of them around her. More than pets, her reminders not to use her curse-breaking powers. They'd age and dogs' lives were so much shorter than humans.

But she hadn't said no to Rafe.

He'd told her baldly that he would die if she didn't let him stay, and she'd believed him. Understood that he was now believing in his own curse. That whatever effect it had had in his life before then, it was definitely drawing fatal circumstances into his life now.

He could die at anytime. She'd discreetly checked the dates of his forebears' deaths and found that most died between their thirtieth and thirty-first year. Those who'd lived the longest had married late and had a child on the way. Her mouth curled wryly. She wondered if fate was stayed in this matter to have the first Davail son procreate. Only a few of the first sons had died without children, and the line had passed to their brothers or nephews.

And Rafe had drawn more magic, a real elf, into her life! True, Pavan seemed deeply disapproving of her and she hadn't had the nerve to confront that issue and ask why. But he was fascinating to observe.

The elf hadn't looked like movie elves. More glamorous, completely *different* from humans in the underlying bone structure of his face. A narrower, finer structure with higher cheeks, not to mention his ears.

He'd added—and left—some of his magic in her home. Just by visiting he'd changed the atmosphere.

As had the dwarf. She'd liked him a lot better since he'd been more sympathetic. Vikos had gone beyond

Pavan in that he'd blessed the house. That spun more magic through it, and the brownies had hummed in pleasure since it was earth elemental magic. It seemed that had grounded Amber more.

Though she still had asked Rafe to stay. Right now he'd be safe. Both dwarf and elf had assured them of that. The magic was strong in Mystic Circle and not good for evil beings.

Great Dark ones, and the new, awful shadleeches that Pavan had described, could not enter the cul-de-sac.

They were safe. Trapped, but safe. For now.

He couldn't breathe! Rafe jerked to sit, his lungs pumped heavily. Disoriented, he couldn't think where he was—the hotel in Toronto? No, Conrad's place in Denver...but his room there had big windows. Shouldn't there be a streetlight? Nope, that was Juno's Inn last night.

He shook his head, his whole sweat-beaded torso, trying to pull some sense into his life, continuing to pant. Slow the breath. Smothering, yeah, he'd felt that. His death curse that he'd always denied. Should have expected strange sleep after he finally admitted it. Not to mention brownies and elves and dwarves, and a trip to the past and seeing the curse in action. He stretched, making sure he extended each muscle.

Maybe a run around the cul-de-sac would be good. Ice spit at the windows. Hell. March in Denver had always been weird. There might be a dusting of snow on the ground when he woke up, to be gone by mid-morning.

A different kind of light caught his attention. His computer tablet was glowing again, this time the screen was dark red and the numbers on it a bright white. The figures said 7, 2, 3, 19:42 and were counting down. He stared at it a couple of minutes before understanding jolted through him sickly. Seven months, two weeks...et cetera until his thirty-third birthday.

Since he couldn't bear the light he got up and picked up the tablet. The screen went to a forest. "Loading *REAL* Fairies and Dragons by Pavan" scrolled across in gold. He turned the computer off.

Damned if he'd play at night, when he'd had a full day, wasn't at his best.

Though he pummeled his feather pillows into a good shape and pulled the high thread-count sheets over his body, fifteen minutes later he was still awake.

The few minutes he'd been in the game rolled through his mind again and again like film in an infinite loop. He also recalled the small warrior on Amber's laptop who had moved jerkily.

Manifest the knife, Pavan had said as he'd plopped the computer next to Rafe. How the hell was Rafe supposed to manifest the knife?

He got out of bed and pulled on shorts and socks, threw on a long dress shirt. The house got cooler as he descended the stairs. Even as he thought he was doing something stupid, he continued to the room where Amber had left her laptop. He sat in the comfortable desk chair, powered up the computer and opened Fairies and Dragons.

Amber had four characters. One was a level one Silver Fairy Webspinner, dressed as she had been when he'd triggered the game on his computer, though the character's features weren't nearly as pretty as Amber's own, and the eyes were an eerie silver. Her highest character was a Green Wasp Ranger.

None of the terms were familiar in the slightest from the few months he'd played a fantasy card game as a kid.

Instead of the Red Dragonfly Knight or whatever Pavan had made him, Rafe created a tough-looking dude, a Golden Hornet Knight.

He died three times within a half hour. The game didn't actually call it "dying," but "defeated." He damn well knew what it meant when he was unmoving and facedown eating dirt with ghoolies partying on his limp form. Then he'd push a key and be whisked to a safe place—the plush "Fairy Dome." There were a couple of other high-level players talking about the fun leprechaun mission who ignored Rafe, fine with him.

He hated the leprechaun. But not as much as he hated the leprechaun's evil twin.

Rafe manifested nothing, and dragged up to bed more frustrated than when he'd gotten out of it. His tablet remained dark as he slipped into the sheets, but when he closed his eyes, he saw hideous monster faces coming close, ready to clobber him. The images still beat the countdown to his birthday…and the last second to his death.

He woke late again—after nine—and felt like he'd been up all night. His eyes hurt from the strain of looking at the computer in the dark, and his shoulders and back and mouse-holding wrist hurt from hunching over the damn piece of electronics. This was no way to treat his body. He should be up in the mountains skiing or snowboarding. Being *active*. Which reminded him that if he faced this Bilachoe, he'd be fighting with a dagger.

He had some self-defense and karate training. He'd preferred less hand-to-hand competitive stuff. People out to kill him was different than pitting himself against the elements. Glancing at his phone, he saw that Conrad had called. A twinge went through Rafe. He'd been concentrating more on himself—and having Amber focus on *his* curse, rather than Conrad's. Rafe glanced at the clock, it would be something like six to eight hours later, depending on where his friend was. Late afternoon. He swiped his thumb across the number.

"Tyne-Cymbler," Conrad said. He didn't sound good.

"Anything I can do?" Rafe asked.

"No. We see Marta, then we don't. You already helped, a lot, when you told me she might be controlled by someone else. I think that's the case."

Of course Conrad would prefer that.

"Good, that's good." It wasn't, but that's what Conrad wanted to hear and all Rafe could give him at this time. He hoped to hell Conrad didn't want him to come to Eastern Europe. Rafe *needed* to stay here.

"You got an update on the curse breaker?" Conrad asked.

"She knows her stuff," Rafe said. "She's, uh, looking into the past when your curse was."

Conrad's response was a small, relieved sigh and Rafe felt even more guilty. But he wasn't about to tell Conrad that he'd seen their ancestors in a Chicago speakeasy. Conrad wouldn't believe Rafe's turnaround anyway.

"Wanted to ask if you know any good fencers in Denver," Rafe asked.

Conrad snorted, and didn't mistake Rafe's question. "Yeah, there's the Denver Fencing Lyceum and a couple of clubs."

"Lyceum," Rafe muttered, unsure if he knew how to spell the word.

"That's right. Good people. We've got a local Olympic champion in sabre."

Rafe hesitated, then asked, "Have you seen Dougie?"

There was a long pause. "No. Only Marta. I think she needs help." Rafe had never felt the distance between himself and his friend more—emotionally, the man loved the woman desperately; physically, Conrad was across the world; mentally, Rafe still didn't believe that Marta was telling the truth, or good enough for Conrad.

After another pause, Conrad asked, "How're you getting along with the curse breaker?"

Well, Rafe wasn't going to say he was living with Amber. He considered talking about brownies and magic, then decided against it. What came out of his mouth was, "You ever play Fairies and Dragons?"

"Sure."

Why had Rafe needed to ask?

Conrad said, "Thing you gotta remember about that game is that strategy pays. Figure out your moves in advance, choose your setting and your battles. Running and bashing doesn't pan out."

Rafe could have told him that.

Once again Conrad hesitated, but the man could read Rafe better than Rafe read him. "You don't like virtual action, but if you're going to play the game and don't want to lay out the monthly fee because you think it's stupid, my call-name is Tyrex2020, and my password is the first three digits of my social and the middle name of my son." There was a shout in the distance.

"Gotta go. Oh, and try the Purple Dragonfly Knight, I think he'd suit you. Let me know what the curse breaker says. Later."

Before Rafe could respond, Conrad had cut their call.

Rafe called the Denver Fencing Lyceum and made an appointment for private coaching. The first time available was that afternoon and he tried not to think of the figures on his computer counting down.

He showered, scrubbing. Yeah, the body felt like he was getting out of shape. He needed action, and better that it be fencing, he guessed. Energetic sex would be good, too. As he thought of Amber rolling around with him, his body agreed.

He also had to ask Amber about those trips to the past of hers and whether she thought she'd find anything hopeful for Conrad.

It added insult to Rafe's dragging steps down the staircase to hear the joyful chimes and bells of a character achieving the next level in Fairies and Dragons. He'd made it to level three.

And why would Amber be playing this early? She had work. Two cases, at least. Had he actually hired her? He wasn't sure.

The minute he walked into the room, she said with a gleam in her eyes, "I see you played the game last night. Fun, isn't it?"

"No."

"Oh, I guess you fell down into Pretard's Pit."

He had. Four times. "How'd you know?"

"Everyone new does." Her smile wasn't as smirky as before, but he still didn't like it.

"Is that like 'everyone gets a speeding ticket on the elevated portion of Speer Boulevard.'"

Her spine snapped straight and her eyes cooled. "No, only unobservant people in a hurry get tickets there."

He smelled food, so he wandered out of the room with the desk and entered the kitchen and saw a warming dish and lifted the lid. It was an omelet with good stuff spilling out of it—bacon, cheese, mushrooms, green peppers. "Hartha make this?"

"I did," Amber said.

"Thanks, looks great." He slid it onto the plate waiting next to it and took that and silverware to the dining room.

Amber joined him with a cup of coffee. She gazed at him with serious eyes. "I have some information on Bilachoe for you. As you know, the 'release' of the curse is to kill him." She swallowed. Rafe figured she wasn't used to speaking of killing things. Too damn soft. For that matter, he wasn't accustomed to thinking about killing things, either. Though if it came down to some evil fiery demon or himself, he'd give the action his best shot. Meantime, he ate the omelet. It was as good as it had looked.

"I haven't gotten far enough back on your bloodline to find where the curse started. Your chart starts at 1712 and the elf said the curse was about 520 years before that. I'm continuing to trace back. I still think Bilachoe must have a weakness. A detriment due to the curse."

Rafe sorted out what he wanted to say—Amber's take versus Pavan's. "You think that casting a bad curse like that must affect the person in some way."

Her chin lifted. "An evil curse should cost the curse maker, yes."

"Because the universe is fair and good and evil should be balanced?" He tried to keep his voice even, but she glared at him.

"That's right."

"Entropy...and crap...happens," Rafe pointed out.

Automatic logging off of Fairies and Dragons and defeat of character in one minute, said the computer in the other room.

Amber stood. "I need to get that. My character, Sylvant, isn't in a safe place to log off."

"This isn't a game," Rafe said.

"You think I don't know that! Why the hell would I be playing such a squishy character if I had the choice? But Pavan made that character for me and if I have to play it for real, I'd better know her strengths and weaknesses."

"Squishy?" Rafe asked.

"Easily killed…ah, defeated."

"I could die in this real life." He'd only finished three-quarters of the omelet but his appetite had gone.

"Rafe, so could I."

CHAPTER 14

"NO, YOUR LIFE *CAN'T* BE ON THE LINE." Couldn't be true. He stood and followed her.

"Don't be more of a jerk than you are. You think Bilachoe and his minions wouldn't take out someone who could remove that curse from you at any time?"

He stopped. "You could do that?" His heart thumped so hard he didn't hear her character's footsteps as she ran or the opening door of a tavern. Or the tinkling music of the game ending. Noted absently that Sylvant, the Silver Fairy Webspinner, was level nine.

But Amber wasn't the one who answered. Tiro the brownie was there by the table, glowering at her, before he turned his angry stare on Rafe.

"Magic costs, human," Tiro snapped, then looked at Rafe, snorted. "Entropy. What about 'every action has an equal and opposite reaction.' How much do you think it would cost Amber to break that *death curse* of yours?"

"I don't know," Rafe said blankly.

"You aren't going to tell him?" Tiro demanded of Amber.

She punched the off button on her computer, shut the lid. She grimaced. "I'd probably die."

The hope that had leaped within him died, followed by a chaser of guilt that he'd wanted someone else to fix his problems. He'd been on his own with this damn curse his whole life, carried the burden within him. No need to think of an option that didn't appear to be available. "Sorry," he said.

She dragged in a breath and her breasts lifted and distracted him. She did have lovely breasts. He liked the looks of her legs in her old jeans, too. "I have some ideas."

"Seeing the past."

She nodded. "Eight hundred and twenty years ago was the Third Crusade. I don't usually go that far back in my visions, but I should be able to do that if I prepare."

"Mmm-hmm."

She raised a brow. "Is believing in my visions more or less difficult than believing Pavan's game is real?"

"Hard to say."

"All right."

The television came on in the living room. Loud. "…and in developing news, the fire engulfing several Cherry Creek homes is under control…"

"What!" she said at the same time Rafe did.

They hurried into the room and stood looking at the way-too-small screen. Must have been only twenty inches. How did the woman live like that? And that was a distraction from the sick feeling of looking at one side of Conrad's charred house.

"...freak lightning in the storm that rolled in last night and this morning..." said a serious-faced newswoman.

Rafe winced. His death curse in action, no doubt. He thought it stuck to him, but maybe it drew bad stuff to wherever he was. But Mystic Circle was protected.

Conrad hadn't known, and Rafe didn't want to be the one to tell him. His cell rang and he pulled it from his jeans pocket. It was Conrad.

"Sorry," Rafe said.

"How bad is it?"

"Just heard, got the TV on now. Will snap a shot. Though pics might be all over the Net shortly." Rafe angled his phone at the TV, waited for another view of Conrad's home, shot and sent.

Some seconds later, Conrad said, "Marta and Dougie's rooms. Wonder what she might have left there for me. If she left something for me to find."

"Hell." Rafe hadn't thought of that. He manned up. "Could be my curse, too."

"What a sorry couple of dudes we are," Conrad snorted. "Could you drop by...no. I'll have one of the P.I.'s go over and sort through the whole damn mess. If Marta left me something, a pro might find it. Otherwise my attorney will handle it and find a place for the housekeeper, send her on vacation, maybe. Don't worry about it, man."

"Okay," Rafe said reluctantly.

"I never liked the place, anyway. Mom rebuilt when I was a kid and it's too modern."

"Mystic Circle is really nice," Rafe said.

"Yeah?" Conrad almost sounded as if he perked up. "You seeing a lot of the sexy Sarga, then?"

Rafe looked at Amber. "Yeah."

Conrad whistled. "Good job."

"You sound more cheerful," Rafe said.

"Marta slipped a note to the P.I. to give me. She said she loved me and I had to leave her alone, pleaded with me to go."

"Hmm," Rafe said.

"So I'm sticking," Conrad said.

"Of course you are."

"Folks can handle the business back in Denver," Conrad said.

"Tell me you don't want to move to Bakir Zagora."

"I don't want to move to Bakir Zagora."

"Okay."

"Later," Conrad said.

On the TV another stream of water inundated Conrad's house. Rafe shook his head. "I'd hate to be the one searching that place after the firefighters and insurance people are done with it." He went to the circular tower windows and looked out. The day had stayed gray, though the snow was gone and the newscaster had said it was forty degrees.

"I need to get out of here," Rafe said.

Amber knew that without being informed. He'd been stuck in the neighborhood for a full day. Jogging with the dogs wasn't enough.

"I'm surprised you lasted as long as you have confined to Mystic Circle and the neighborhood," she said calmly. "What are your plans?"

"There's still a lot of snow in the mountains."

"For sure. Snowboarding or skiing?"

He walked to the door, put his hand on the knob and she saw his shoulders tense. "I can't do it." Turning back to her, every line in his face showed frustration. "I can't mess around with sports anymore. I have to *do* something. But it has to be something that will break my curse." His escaping breath hissed. "My fencing lessons don't start until this afternoon."

"And you need activity now."

"Yeah."

"And you don't want to play the game on your tablet."

He cut the air with the flat of his hand. "That's a construct for me to…" He shrugged. "The hell I know."

"Learn how to manifest the dagger."

"What's this manifesting? I looked it up online and only got New Age garbage."

"I believe Pavan means that you should—" she paused and wetted her lips, knowing he wouldn't like what she said next "—try drawing the dagger to you magically."

He snorted. "Oh. Yeah. That's easy. That's going to happen. Not."

"I have an idea," she said. She went and got an L-shaped stick and handed it to him.

"What's this?"

"A dowsing rod."

"What!"

"Maybe if you try to *feel*—"

"Water?"

"Energies. The four elemental magical energies. Mystic Circle is good for that, and the neighborhood, too."

He held the wooden handle…his eyes narrowed wickedly and the rod slowly rose to point at her middle. "Oh, yeah, energy." He raised his brows. "Sexual energy."

She lifted her own brows, smiled slowly, canted a hip, called his bluff. "For sure. What are you going to do about it?"

A fleeting expression of yearning crossed his face, his eyes seemed to deepen with need for more than sex. Then he sent her a cocky smile. "Later. We will definitely do something about manifesting our own energies, combining them, later."

"Does that feel okay in your hand? Or would you like something different? I borrowed these from a friend." She gestured to the love seat in the turret that held more sticks.

He glanced at her, then the array of rods.

The stick didn't feel as strange in his hand as it should have, since he'd always believed dowsing was a load of crap. Rafe studied the selection of L-shaped sticks and handles, clueless.

Tiro strode in. He glanced at the TV and lowered the volume, then stared at the dowsing rod Rafe held and sneered. Tiro said, "The death-cursed needs a better tool."

Amber removed a silver chain from a drawer handle and gave him a chocolate frosted donut, then locked the drawer with the chain again. "So, Tiro," Amber said, "you can feel the magical energies of the cul-de-sac."

Tiro's lip, dotted with brown crumbs, curled. "A'course."

"And you'd know how the sidewalk and the park in the middle and each house feels, magically?" Amber asked.

The brownie nodded.

"Good." She stared at Rafe. "That's what I want you to try to feel through the dowsing rod."

"Will need a better tool than those," Tiro grunted. "Might get him one." He stared at the drawer and Amber gave him another donut.

"A real magical tool," Amber breathed.

"It will be brownie-made, not dwarven-made," Tiro said.

"That's fine," Amber said.

"Sure," Rafe said. "Should get used to magical tools. I'll have a magical dagger when I face Bilachoe," Rafe pointed out. "Probably not forged by brownies."

"The dagger contains all magics forged by dwarves of metal bespelled by elves, in spellfire provided by djinns, and cooled by mers with their water."

"Truly special." Amber nodded, though Rafe guessed she had no idea how impressive that might be, just like he didn't. Probably amazingly awesome, though.

"But if you know what the magical energies of the circle are, you can double-check what he feels," Amber said.

"I can do that." The tips of his ears quivered, folded over a little like he was interested. He piled up several donuts. "Going to my cottage. To freeze these for treats when this ends badly and is all over. Got a real nice dowsing rod at home. Centuries old." He shot Rafe a look from under lowered brows. "You keep it if you live. I get it back if you die."

Rafe cleared his throat and nodded. "Deal."

Another snort and Tiro vanished. Rafe looked at Amber. "How long do you think he'll—"

And Tiro was back, smelling of other places. He placed a stick on the table in front of Rafe. It was a real stick, made of a wood that Rafe couldn't determine, two inches thick and heavily carved with a colorful angular pattern and stained in primary colors. Oh, yeah, like he wouldn't stand out holding this thing—it was forked for two hands.

He met Tiro's simmering look, then gazed at Amber. Her eyes widened, but her return stare was challenging. The tip of the stick appeared to be pointed and encased in copper. Rafe stood and bowed to Tiro. "A work of art. Thank you."

"Ready to start?" Amber asked.

While they'd been talking, the clouds had cleared. It would still be cold, but the sun was out. A tendril of hope deep in his being began to grow. "Sure." He picked up the dowsing rod, meaning to twirl it, and got a sizzle through him down to his soles, tweaking his balls on the way. He sucked in a breath.

Amber was right there, a concerned expression on her face, her fingers on his forearm. "Will you be able to use it?"

"Only one way to find out," Rafe forced through his lips. He felt…felt like some of his insides had been seared and sloughed away, leaving him rawly cleansed and *vital*. Like that one moment of anticipation before a race…with a feeling that he was going to win this one.

"All right, let's start with the house, particularly the basement," Amber said. Down they went. The basement was one large space, though Rafe saw where walls had been. The room had finished brick walls that gleamed, a flagstoned floor and polished wooden doors, taller than a person and each very individual, in each wall.

Tiro stood, feet-planted and cross-armed at the door toward the front of the house and the cul-de-sac park.

Rafe nodded and said, "Cool."

"It's a lot different than it was last week," Amber said drily.

"Uh-huh," Rafe said. The dowser was stirring in his hands, quivering and pointing toward Tiro. As he got closer to the brownie, the stick dipped and held steady about an inch above the ground…which the brownie mostly felt like. Ground, dirt, earth. Heavy, slow energy trick…ling…through…him…slow…ing… his…thoughts.

CHAPTER
15

"SNAP OUT OF IT!" TIRO SAID AND STEPPED on Rafe's toes.

"Ouch!" The brownie looked light, but Rafe's toes ached.

Smiling and showing pointed teeth, which Rafe had forgotten about and hadn't wanted to be reminded of, Tiro said, "The rod is a tool to be used."

Rafe got it. The tool wasn't supposed to be using him. "Brownie is earth."

"That's right," Amber said. "Minor earth race."

Lifting his lip in a sneer—again with the pointed teeth—Tiro said, "If you'd pointed that at a dwarf and the tool used you, your mind would have been trapped in earth."

Rafe nodded, just to make sure his neck and head worked. "Thank you, again."

Tiro pushed the rod aside, and when the brownie

connected with the rod, and to Rafe, he felt the grief and anger and dread that filled the smaller being. The brownie had already been charmed by Amber and thought that she would perish when she broke Rafe's curse. Rafe stared. Tiro scowled ferociously.

"Go check out other energies. You *can* feel other elements, can't you, death-cursed?"

Rafe uncurled his left fingers from around the rod, shook out his hand. Took the time to shake out his arms and legs, too. Lifting his feet from the flagstones eased him the most.

"You broke your grounding," Amber murmured.

She was right, something he'd remembered from his martial arts training and had used in his sports. Would his fencing coach mention grounding? He was sure of it.

He turned, shook his left hand again and grasped the left fork. The stick pointed at Amber. Once more energy moved up the stick in waves. This gave him a little buzz, was much lighter, made him smile. Unlike the brownie's energy, this wasn't just one type of solid flow. It felt tangled. Light and buzzy and jumbled. "Sort of...frothy..." Rafe said.

Tiro snorted.

"Squishy," Rafe and Tiro said at the same time.

"Ha, ha," Amber said.

Rafe nodded. *Soft and essence-of-woman and sexy* were better terms, but squishy would do. The woman wasn't tough-minded. A soft risk-taker. He hadn't run into many of those. They didn't last long on the sports circuit. Usually fell for some sad story and got screwed.

He swept the rod from the pile of Amber's stuff toward the south wall. Immediately his hands heated. His palms began to sweat, the rod dipped and rose faster. When he reached the door in the wall, the stick lowered with brownie energy. One step to the south and he caught his breath. The dowser seemed to nearly float in his hands. His mind was centered and clear. His balance seemed perfect.

Here he could feel swirls of energy, four types, all nearly equal. He strove to memorize them. The heat and quickness of fire, the extreme lightness of air, the slick dampness of water, the heavy earth. Each had its own sensation, each a different rhythmic pulse. He could almost grasp the innate pattern.

Amber and Tiro came to stand beside him. Amber sighed and Rafe sensed that she felt something, but not like he did. And that was weird.

Tiro said quietly, "Got a pocket of balanced energy here because of Jenni Weavers, the elemental balancer." He wrapped long fingers around Rafe's wrist and pulled him back. "We oughta keep it that way as long as we can."

Rafe stepped back into the basement and it was as if he'd left fresh air behind. Sounds jangled, the stick oscillated. This time he took his right hand off that fork.

"You progress," Tiro said flatly, pointed a finger at the stairs. "Take your experiment outside so I can continue my work."

"I didn't ask you—" Amber began.

"Yes, of course I do this to please myself." Tiro's lip curled. "Go."

With a huff of breath, Amber turned and started up the stairs. She had a fine ass, Rafe noted once more as he followed.

A few minutes later they were out in the sunlight. He wore his leather jacket and Amber a bright blue windbreaker.

Outside there was more distraction. Now he felt the energy of plants and trees, different from the other four elements, mostly comprised of earth and water and sun and green. That energy was *alive* in some way that the other elemental energies weren't.

Rafe pointed the rod at the Tudor house north of Amber's—number six—and sorted out the energies. "The woman who lives here is half human. Her magical heritage is three-quarters air-elf, and one-quarter dwarf."

"Wow," Amber said.

He was all too aware of the sexual attraction. Yeah, he liked that buzz. Amber was a serious woman, but these were serious times and he wasn't feeling too lighthearted about the whole situation, either.

She was incredibly easy to be with. Soft, female, sexy. Squishy. He didn't want to squish her.

So he turned toward the top of the cul-de-sac and the castle. He went all the way up to the iron gate and stuck the dowsing rod through the bars.

And had to do some fancy footwork to stay on his feet and not get knocked to his ass.

Amber coughed. He knew she was covering laughing, but didn't care.

"Wow," he said.

"What?" she asked.

"Everything. Just…" He wiped his palms on his jeans, one hand after the other. "Everything, and strong!"

"Like?"

"Like shades of the energy Pavan the elf and Vikos the dwarf left in your living room."

He braced himself, settled into his balance as he slowly pushed the stick through the bars. The end of the rod began to give off sparks and his hands shook from the force. "Strong magic," he said between his teeth. He felt himself rock back and forth. "Individuals. Not balanced." And the taste of it was rich cream on his tongue, the scent a mixture of tempting smells: deep, mysterious forests that could hold golden chests of magic; air so pure and effervescent that it slid into him and lifted his spirit; the gentle warmth of fire removing any chill from the air, cradling him in comfort; the taste of clear and potent water with the vitality of the essence of life. Rich.

The sparks died and he fell to his heels, realizing that he'd been on tiptoe. He staggered a step back.

Amber was there, wrapping her arms around him, holding and steadying him. Power rushed through his veins and he eyed the park in the middle of the cul-de-sac. Though the brush was thick, Amber's blue windbreaker and pale linen slacks would be seen if they made love in the park.

He forced the thought of her damp and welcoming body, of plunging into her, from his head. But he wanted that.

The scent of her was better than any magic. Amber and woman.

He couldn't prevent a rub of his groin against her softness.

She stepped back, but he was pleased to see that she was flushed, and not just from the spring breeze. If he looked hard, he could see her nipples pebbled under her clothes. Another surge of lust went through him and he banished the thought again.

"Interesting reaction," she said.

"Not around you. Happens all the time," he said thickly.

She laughed and her cheeks flushed a deeper pink under her golden skin, beautiful.

"Not *that*," she said. She waved to the house. "Your rod." She screwed her eyes shut and turned red, then when he laughed, she did, too.

After biting her lip, she said, "The reaction of the dowsing rod to the castle."

"Who lives there?"

"We don't know." A cloud crossed her expression. "No, I don't know. Jenni or Tamara might. People... beings, I guess?" She shot Rafe a questioning look.

He swallowed, he could still taste the cream. "Yeah, beings. All of 'em, dwarves, elves, mers and...djinns." He couldn't quite get his head wrapped around a djinn, a genie. Figured they must have feet.

Frowning, he considered all the waves of energy that

had pummeled him, or slid through him, or whatever the hell had happened. There had been lighter, wispier currents. One had been brownie. "Probably all the minor folk, too." He didn't remember all of those.

"Oh." Amber gazed at the castle. "Like I was saying, people come and go. There are lights and a feeling of movement." Her hands opened and closed as if elusive things escaped her grasp. She smiled. "I'd say it was haunted but it doesn't feel like that. No despair or anger."

He ignored that comment, not even saying that he'd felt none, either.

The rest of the circle was less interesting, a mix of human and Lightfolk. Amber knew everyone and had stories. She'd also given him a tip on acquiring more property in the Circle. He figured the real estate would be better in his human hands than bought by Eight Corp.

"Next we have number two, the Fanciful House," Amber said.

"Mine," Rafe said, but thought he meant the woman more than the house. Didn't matter, Mystic Circle and Amber were all mixed up in his yearnings, along with the sheer will to live. He fully intended to have them both.

CHAPTER 16

"YOU THINK THE FANCIFUL HOUSE IS YOURS?"
Amber asked as they sauntered down the sidewalk.

"Yeah, I'm hoping so. I put an outrageous sum of money down on it to hold it for me...until."

"Ah." She squeezed his arm against her and he liked it. Liked the connection. Didn't know when that had last happened with a woman.

"What do you think you and your divining rod will find?"

He stopped. "Divining rod?"

"The guy I borrowed the dowsers from reminded me that it was sometimes called that...to find lost silver and gold in the forest maybe."

The rod hauled his hands to the curb and he looked down to see what Amber had spotted. "Or coins in the street?" he asked.

"Or that." Her smile *was* fey, three-cornered.

He nudged the silver in the street, got a fizz of magic energy. "Magic coins?"

Amber let his arm go and scooped them up. Two silver dollars lay on her hand. "Real silver, anyway. The Lightfolk are sensitive to silver. It can harm them."

"Oh," he said.

She tucked them in his front pocket and his body liked that a lot. Then she took his arm and male satisfaction flared.

They stopped at the corner of Mystic Circle and the small street leading to it, Linden. Amber started to cross, and Rafe trapped her arm against his side.

"I want to take this out of the neighborhood and down to the business district."

She looked at the colorful stick—now some of the patterns on it showed silver and gold—and back at him.

He stood straight. "Think I'm not cool enough to carry this off?"

"You sure are," she said. "But why?"

"I want to check out the neighborhood." He still felt a little stupid with the colorful stick in his hands... obviously a dowsing rod. "I want to see where the magical energies fade."

She nodded. "Good idea."

He also wanted to go to the place the shadleeches had dive-bombed him and determine whether there was any lingering magic that he could feel. The elf had said the shadleeches were evil. As far as he could tell, he hadn't felt "good" or "evil" with the rod. He didn't think the stick was really made that way, to find human or Lightfolk good and evil.

But it might react to Dark ones. He needed to know if that were true and whether he had something that might warn him of evil in the future.

And wasn't it a kick in the ass that he could actually think of that without believing he'd gone crazy.

As they walked down the street, Amber commented on people in one house or another. After the first cross street, he angled, trying to recall the geographic features of what was around him when he'd been attacked and fell.

With so much that had happened since, it seemed years ago. He didn't have to press his memory. Nearly a half block from where he'd fallen, small shocks ran down the stick to his hands. Amber gasped and withdrew her arm from his, shaking out her own fingers. "What's that?"

He glanced at her, gritted his teeth and pressed onward. "If I'm right, it's remnants of the shadleech bombing."

"Oh," she said faintly.

"When I first checked—" his throat tightened "—there were bits of hollow bone and a scrap of what I thought was leather." He shrugged. "Whatever shadleeches are made of. Might still be there. I don't know how fast they decompose."

She made a face. "Eeew." But she stepped off the sidewalk and scuffed her cross-trainers down the gutter. Old leaves and twigs, dust and bits of paper tumbled. Then she sucked in a harsh breath, stooped and stared, stood up and moved her foot more gently. "Objects such as these?" she asked.

Since the rod was nearly bucking in his hands and an oiliness seemed to mix from the rod with the sweat on his palms, he was sure she was right. By the time he reached her, she'd separated a few brown-and-ivory-looking bits and a patch of fur-feather.

"Ick," she said.

As he swung the dowsing rod toward it, the stick jammed his hands into his abdomen. Rafe moved back. "I think that's an identification of evil."

Amber buried the things again with her shoe. "Not sure what we should do about these? Do you sense any, um, active threat?"

He shook out his feet, wiped his palms on his jeans again, shifted his shoulders and eased into a grounded stance. Again he got a humming vibration, this one with a nasty tickle on his palms.

Atavistic fear shuddered from the prickling hair on his skin inward. "What's that smell?"

"Something smells…" Amber said at the same time. She saw Rafe's eyes go wide, his nostrils flare. His face set as he swung the dowsing rod up, pointing above the houses.

She frowned, there was a waver in the air—crows. No! Something different, three flying stingray-things, just like the elf told her.

"Shadleeches!" Rafe muttered.

He pointed the rod like a weapon, grimaced.

Amber saw a tiny stream push from it. But the things were moving too fast. Dark and flapping, gray and black and fangs. Then the shadleeches dove.

She dragged in a breath—rotten meat and dust—

and doubled over coughing. Felt the scrape of claws against her scalp, the sting. Then one flapped, caught in her hair with its leathery wings. She grabbed at it, her fingernails bit into the soft leather and stuff oozed under them. The shadleech screamed.

So did she.

She ripped it from her hair and flung it aside, knew she couldn't put her burning fingertips into her mouth to soothe them.

Rafe was grinning…and swearing, beating the two shadleeches who'd attacked him with his rod. All three were smoking, but she saw no blood from him.

He stabbed at the shadleech that fluttered near her with the divining rod and it screeched high, hurting Amber's ears.

Flipping the stick in his hands, he whacked at the shadleeches like he held a baseball bat and killed them all.

Amber gulped air, thin magic pulsed around her. A movement caught her eye and she lifted a trembling finger, squeaked, "Look!" The gray cloud broke apart into a fleet of shadleeches.

Rafe grabbed her hand. "Run!"

She winced as his hand closed over hers, and took off with him, knowing he was keeping his pace to hers.

The minute they turned into Mystic Circle, the stinging on her hands eased—as if the magic in the venom vanished. She tugged from him, stared at her fingers. The tops of her nails were burned black to the quick, her fingertips red but not blistered.

Rafe winced. "Nasty."

"Yes." She stared at the dowsing rod. Part of the tip was gone, ending in charred jags. One side of it had the paint singed off.

"Uh-oh," Rafe said.

As soon as they reached her front door, Tiro opened it. His brows gnarled as he looked at the dowsing rod and pain sped over his face.

"Tell me how I can help you mend this," Rafe said, offering him the rod.

Tiro lifted his gaze to Rafe. "You fought with it?"

"Shadleeches."

A quiver passed through Tiro. "You won?"

"All three died."

Tiro nodded, glanced at Amber's fingers. "You saved Amber?"

A corner of Rafe's mouth lifted. "I helped."

"Then you used the stick well." The brownie's chest expanded with a breath. "There is enough magic here in the Circle, and enough materials here and at number two to repair the divining rod." He huffed out a sigh. "I'll have it back to you in a couple of hours." Tiro whisked it from Rafe and was gone.

Amber went into the kitchen and washed her hands. The water stung a bit more, but seemed to help her hands. Rafe helped her put antiseptic cream on her fingers.

"You were great," he said.

"So were you, though I think we should have run in the first place."

He grunted.

She shouldn't have expected him to agree.

"The rod might come in handy if it warns of evil."

"Yeah." Then he proceeded to stretch his entire body. She admired how he moved.

He caught her watching and he smiled and her heart thumped hard.

He shook his head. "Whole situation is incredible."

"Yes," she said. "But you aren't in this alone."

"Thank God."

He picked up her hands and looked at them, lifted each to his mouth and brushed a kiss on the back. "We aren't in this alone."

"No."

"Good."

Several hours later Amber had taken care of business, including contacting three new clients that she thought wouldn't take her too long to work, but keep her referrals going. She'd meet with one of the couples here in the consulting room when Rafe went to his fencing lesson.

She'd set up the files on her laptop when the alarm they'd set for Rafe rang. She walked to the entryway to see Rafe in loose jeans and sweatshirt with a workout bag standing by the front door. He was smiling.

No need to tell her that he was itching to get out of the house.

"Be careful," she couldn't help saying. "Things can go wrong with even play swords."

His expression turned sober and he nodded, raised a palm as if taking a vow. "I'll be careful."

"And be careful driving." She couldn't stop the warnings from spurting from her. "That's the worse."

He nodded. "Very careful driving."

She sighed. "At least the place is close and it isn't rush hour."

"I'll go by the backstreets. It's only six miles."

"Famous last words."

"You going somewhere, too?" He stared at her dress.

"Meeting a client." She added gently, "Rafe, you don't live in Denver, and Conrad isn't here. I don't know when he'll return from Eastern Europe. I need a referral flow."

He scowled. "We're paying you plenty—"

"Yes, you are. But both your and Conrad's cases are going to be very challenging, and take me a long time back in the past. I want to balance that with something easier." She smiled. "What, did you always go from one huge competition to another?"

His mouth twitched. "Yeah, yeah. Okay, I get it." He opened one side of his black leather jacket and his smile broadened.

"What's that?" Amber asked. It was a little stick in his inner pocket.

"Tiro made it for me." He pulled out something that looked like a cocktail stirrer but was metal. "A miniature dowsing rod. I can figure out whether humans or human-Lightfolk mixes or Lightfolk are near. Still needs to be this shape, though. As I get better, I might be able to use something symbolic, like a pin and tack." Rafe pointed it at her. "Still frothy."

"So you'll be able to judge your coach at the Lyceum."

Rafe nodded. "Him, too. He squeezed me in between another private lesson and a class. I'll be able to practice with this little rod on everyone." He tucked the thing back into his pocket. "It might even work on a dark minion or two."

"You're sure?"

"I know what humans and humans with magic or curses feel like. I know what half humans and half Lightfolk feel like, and brownies." He patted the outside of his jacket over the pocket. "The stick likes them, there's an attraction." He slid a sly grin toward her and raised his brows. "Especially to froth." Then his face sobered. "But there should be a repulsion to the Dark, like when the dowsing rod reacted to the dead shadleeches. Warning, maybe."

"Good."

He smiled wryly. "I hope so." His glance went to the front door. "Can't stay in the neighborhood forever."

She looked at the door, too. The claw marks of the puppies no longer showed. The jamb and door itself had been refurbished by Tiro. Before she had time to consider the fact, Rafe set an arm around her waist and pulled her to him.

Her gaze went to his face and his intent blue eyes.

"I wouldn't have survived without you," he said. His lips lowered and his tongue nibbled at her bottom lip and she let him in, tasted him. The apple tang was stronger—his magic? Then she quit thinking as her body arched against his, found him ready for sex, and her own core dampened and she emitted a soft and needy moan. Too much. She slid from his grasp and took a couple of steps.

She was panting. Actually panting after a man. No, after a kiss from a dangerously seductive man.

His eyes were gleaming bright with want. "Yeah, I better get going. Sure want some physical release." He winked and she wondered how many of the coaches were female and whether his was. He turned the knob, then frowned.

"What?" she asked.

"Nothing." He yanked and a whoosh of air pushed in.

"Darn, the wind has come up."

"Yeah," he growled. "Nothing I hate more than wind unless I'm sailing. Later."

The door slammed behind him.

Two hours later, Amber was getting increasingly restless and unable to concentrate on her work when Rafe called.

"Uh, Amber, can you come and pick me up? And maybe bring a friend?"

"Are you all right?"

"Yeah, I'm fine," he said.

She strove to *feel* whether that was the truth or not and couldn't tell.

"A friend?" she asked.

"A chocolate-loving friend."

She hesitated, wondering how much this would cost her with the brownies. The expense didn't matter. "Sure, you're at the Denver Fencing Lyceum?"

"Yeah. The Jag's squashed."

Her breath simply stopped. "Squashed."

"Big branch hit it. I ducked. I'm fine, a couple of scrapes."

"Oh." She inhaled slowly. "No shadleeches?"

"Not this time." His voice was even as he said, "Mark, my coach, says that rotten tree has been waiting to come down for years. Tough luck for the rental company, though. Think I'll get a Hummer next."

A Hummer would tempt him into the mountains for sure. Amber bit her lip. "I'll be right there."

She called Hartha and Pred and explained the situation. "Rafe thinks that one of you being in the car might help keep him safe. We'll stop at a store and get whatever kind of chocolate you want."

"Hate human vehicles!" Hartha and Pred said in unison.

Amber stiffened her spine. "All right. I asked. Thank you anyway."

The brownies looked at each other and Pred whimpered. "I will meet you there. Show me on a map where it is. I read human maps."

"Fine. And you'll ride back with us? It's only six miles."

He hissed but nodded. "Want solid dark chocolate bars. Big." He crossed his arms.

"Done," Amber said. Pred trailed her into the downstairs study and looked at the map on the laptop. He hissed again, ears rolling tight against his head, and disappeared with an audible pop that she thought was disapproval for the whole enterprise.

All three of them made it back with no incident.

Pred had refused to talk no matter how hard Amber and Rafe tried, and just huddled on the floor behind Rafe's seat. As soon as they parked, he snatched his chocolate and ran to Jenni's house and straight through the steps up to her porch.

Rafe looked fine. He leaned against the kitchen counter as Amber made dinner and enthused for an hour about the fencing class. He'd signed up for daily personal lessons and classes with others. He also had found a dojo to practice his rusty hand-to-hand skills.

"Okay," Amber said, knowing she'd miss having him around the house. "Your idea about using Pred as a bodyguard was right. Nothing happened."

Rafe frowned. "A bodyguard would be good, but I don't think a human, even an extraordinarily trained human, would work."

"But we know somewhere we might be able to hire others."

"What?"

She inhaled to the bottom of her lungs. "I think we should call or visit Eight Corp."

"It's an energy company," Rafe said.

"*Magical* energy. And it's a software company, Melding Myths. Who knows what else it is? Or who and what might be there? They might have someone who's interested in doing bodyguard duty for you. They are certainly aware of you."

"We'll pay them a surprise visit tomorrow," Rafe said. "Better lay in a big supply of chocolate."

CHAPTER
17

THE NEXT MORNING THEY DROVE THROUGH downtown Denver. Eight Corp's building didn't have an underground parking area—the dwarves and the brownies had other uses for that space?—so Rafe circled until he found a lot. He came around the vehicle and opened the door for her, held out his hand.

She took it and left her fingers in his, and they walked hand in hand. She liked that, the small zips of attraction between them. Nothing wrong with appreciating a man who appreciated her.

The concrete still held the chill of the winter and they hurried up the stairs to the street and out into the sunshine, where they strolled. Rafe didn't seem in any more of a hurry to check out Eight Corp than she.

Here, in the sheltered warmth of the tall buildings, the trees had large buds. Soon she and Rafe reached the Sixteenth Street Mall, with no vehicle traffic other than the free shuttle. "Not my quiet neighborhood," she said, then frowned. "Something's different down here."

Rafe grunted, his head came up like a hunter's. Even after only one session and a class with the fencers, he was less casual about people. He'd already picked up prowling like a predator instead of gliding in an easy sort of way like an athlete. Amber was sorry to see that change in him, but thought it was more of a natural talent being revealed than learned behavior. His bloodline had been designed to kill the Dark, after all.

"There's *magic* here, a lot of it," he said.

Amber stopped and he did, too. She lifted her head. That's what she'd been sensing, but she hadn't figured it out. Rafe had. He was learning rapidly in other areas, too. And he had more magic than she. Envy twinged within her and was dismissed. This was not a competition, this was a joint project.

To save him.

Tensing, she scanned the street. There were a couple of homeless people who looked weird, but, on the whole, everyone appeared normal. No one threatening.

"And the magic seems a little familiar." Rafe's mouth flattened. "Like the game."

"Jenni Weavers's magic," Amber said.

His shoulders relaxed. "Maybe that's it."

"She's not pure Lightfolk, she's human like us."

He squinted up at the sky between the buildings. "Definitely magic here. And, I think, it's circulating, like a pump."

"Hartha said something about a meld between magic and human energy sources."

Rafe shook his head. "Too deep for me, but whatever they're doing, it's working."

Now that he'd pointed it out, she could feel magic sinking into her as if tiny motes slipped into her pores. Would everyone feel that, even people with no trace of magic?

She was more curious than before about Eight Corp. Would whoever was there help them?

Rafe began walking and she kept up. The skyscraper that Eight Corp was in had a dry fountain, still too early to set it going, even if there was no drought this year.

She and Rafe touched door handles together. Magic smacked a spark on her palm like static electricity. Rafe grunted. They pulled the doors open. To the left was a state-of-the-art security console. Would they even make it to Eight Corp? Maybe they should have called ahead.

And been refused on the phone.

"Security," she whispered.

"Now if you were an elf would you worry about security?" he murmured back.

Rafe dropped her hand and walked with more of a businessman's stride. He wore expensive slacks and a jacket, the same outfit she'd first seen him in. She wore a tailored suit she'd bought last year.

The security guard was a heavy older man. "IDs, please," he asked gruffly, not holding out his hand for them.

Rafe passed his driver's license over and the guard swiped the magnetic stripe across a panel. Rafe got his back and Amber handed the man hers.

"We're here for Eight Corp," Rafe said easily, looking at the banks of elevators.

"You have an appointment?"

"No," Rafe said.

"You can go on up to the thirty-second floor, but I have to call the receptionist."

"Fine," Rafe said. He took Amber's arm as she put her license back in her bag, and led her over to the elevator. Not businesslike but she enjoyed his touch.

At the elevator bay, when she breathed in, she breathed in magic.

"Nice," Rafe said.

She waited until the doors closed before she replied, "I wonder what we'll find."

"I don't think it will be a troubleshooter and a troublehacker," Rafe said.

Amber could feel his anticipation. "I agree," she said. "They made a point that they and the—" she cleared her throat "—royals were busy elsewhere."

"With a big battle upcoming," Rafe said grimly. "This place is probably staffed with underlings, then."

The elevator door opened and they stepped onto thick carpet.

"It's not a rug," Rafe said. "Magic."

Amber looked down to see moss.

Rafe crossed over to a huge granite desk that was set against a slab of grayish marble. Amber didn't think the woman who sat behind the desk could reach the floor with her feet.

The small woman, surely a dwarf, stared at them then opened her mouth a little and curled her tongue.

Rafe stiffened. "What?"

Amber said, "I've seen the brownies do that. I think she's testing magic."

There was a sound like cracking and falling scree, the woman put her hands flat on the desk. "I am not a *brownie!*"

"Dwarf," Rafe said matter-of-factly. He bowed.

Amber saw the receptionist's nameplate. "How do you do, Mrs. Daurfin."

"Humans!"

Rafe snorted. "Some reception."

The female dwarf—dwarfem?—hopped over her desk and thunked to the ground, came closer and sniffed loudly. Her eyes widened and she backpedaled to her desk.

"Stupid Cumulustre child and a cursed one." Her fingers fluttered.

Rafe strolled forward, pulled two green cards from his pocket. "Pavan and Vikos paid me a visit."

"The guardians. Get away from me." The woman hurried back behind the barrier of her desk.

Rafe laughed. "I'd like to talk to someone about that cursed business, for sure."

"I can't help you. No one here can. You pollute this space. Go away."

"Why are you here if you can't help us?" Amber asked.

"This is the Meld Project. I am here because dwarves are gatekeepers," the woman muttered.

"Maybe you could tell someone else that we're here?" Amber suggested.

When Rafe pulled his miniature divining stick from his jacket pocket it began quivering wildly in his fingers. "Plenty of magic here—magical beings, too."

The thing pointed toward Mrs. Daurfin.

"Pardon me," Rafe said, then angled his whole body toward the left side of a corridor off the lobby. His brows lowered. "A whole lot of energies I haven't defined yet. Minor elemental energies, but no brownies."

"Go. Now, humans. No one here is interested in speaking with humans." She wrinkled the small blob of her nose. "I don't like the smell of you."

"We would like to speak to someone about hiring a bodyguard for Rafe. A minor elemental will do."

"And there are plenty of them to talk to. We'll wait," Rafe said, and slid onto one of the leather couches. His gaze was fixed on the crack of a door that had seemed part of the wall.

Any other receptionist who wanted them gone would be calling security, but apparently the dwarf woman didn't think to do that.

Amber pulled the largest chocolate candy bar she'd been able to find from her purse and peeled back the corner. The scent of cocoa wasn't much to her nose, but the dwarf woman's nostrils flared.

"We'll pay in chocolate." Amber put the candy on Mrs. Daurfin's desk. "This is for you." She hadn't ever bribed a person before.

The dwarf had big, round ears set against her head. Amber thought that if she'd been a brownie they'd be tightly rolled.

"I smell chocolate," boomed a voice. A man with reddish skin, smaller than his deep and resonant voice indicated, appeared in the room. He was shorter than Rafe by several inches and thinner.

"If you will take these two to the street, I will give you half of this!" The dwarfem waved the chocolate bar.

His eyes fired, literally, little flames danced in the pupils. Amber watched, riveted.

"Payment first, dwarf." He opened his mouth and it stretched into a maw.

Mrs. Daurfin huffed, broke the chocolate into halves and tossed one piece straight into the man's—djinn's, surely he must be a djinn—mouth, wrapping and all.

"Mmm." A little dribble of chocolate, like syrup, came from the corner of his mouth.

Then he was there, wrapping his hand around Amber's upper arm. They were at the couch and he raised Rafe to his feet, closed his other hand around Rafe's biceps, and they were down in front of the building.

Before Amber could grab another bribe from her purse, the djinn was gone, leaving a slight heat haze in his wake.

Weirded out, Amber turned in place, but no one seemed to have noticed.

"Dammit, he ruined my jacket." Rafe frowned at his arm, there were scorch marks in the shape of a hand with flames as fingers.

She studied her own jacket, equally burned. Since it was a light wool weave, it gave off a stench…or maybe… "I think he burnt my arm," she said weakly.

"What! Let's look at that." Rafe stood behind her, gently pushed her jacket down. Her silk blouse was ruined, too. "Hell," Rafe said, putting an arm around her. "You know of a nearby clinic?"

"No," Amber said. She would not let her voice tremble. She couldn't be that badly hurt, could she? But fear nearly overwhelmed the pain as her imagination kicked into gear and she thought of flame eating flesh to the bone. She refused to give in to panic. "There's a drugstore clinic close to Mystic Circle."

"And I bet the brownies would know how to handle this."

The sweet cool rush of relief washed through her. "Of course they will."

Rafe went to her good side and put his arm around her waist. "Let's get home."

That statement made her a little dizzy, too. He was considering her house his home? Or maybe just Mystic Circle. But it seemed like a tempting path to a relationship had just opened before her.

They had terrible problems to overcome, but if they could do that…an incredible future beckoned.

She must be light-headed. No way was this going to work out. And she realized Rafe was helping her into the Hummer and muttering about Eight Corp.

"That went well," she said.

A few minutes later Hartha brownie-chanted over their wounds. Amber's was worse than Rafe's, and whatever degree burns they had been, they were well on the way to healing now. She'd gratefully given the brownie woman the other two chocolate bars in her purse.

Amber was sitting on the couch in her downstairs study and Hartha was standing beside her. One of the dogs was lying on Amber's feet, one of them was near Rafe. He was at her laptop, grumbling and fuming. "Okay, the corporate documents list an Alex Akasha as the CEO of Eight Corp. No telephone number except the one to the receptionist who won't ever talk to us again. We didn't even talk to anyone important. Dammit, she took our chocolate and *hurt* us."

Tiro, who'd opened all the doors of the first floor that connected to each other, was stalking around. His snort was huge and disdainful. "Not some stupid human name. The King of Air is the head of Eight Corp—Cloudsylph."

Rafe's spine snapped straight from his hunch over the computer. "The King of Air," he repeated, loading the phrase with wonder. The man was really becoming interested in magic. Not surprising when Amber sensed some of his own was wisping out from under the sigil that was supposed to contain it. If the man had believed in magic for a while, how much would he have to command? Too late to ask now.

"Eight Corp is the four magical royal couples," Hartha reminded them, wrapping a bandage around Amber's arm. "The Cloudsylphs of Air and the Emberdrakes of Fire are new to their thrones, only fifteen years. Also, human technology is becoming close to magic, so finally a meld is possible. Soon more magic will be in the world. That's part of Jenni's quest." Then the brownie woman pressed her lips together, as if unwilling to speak more about Lightfolk dealings, or danger to Jenni.

Rafe opened his mouth, then shut it, squelching a comment.

"We probably should have asked one of you to go to Eight Corp for us," Amber said, then exclaimed as Hartha pulled the bandage too tight, hurting her for the first time.

"Sorry, sorry!" Hartha said.

"You've been wonderful," Amber soothed.

Pred's ears didn't even roll, but flattened. "Dwarves and others would not talk to brownies. Brownies like and live with humans so we are lowest status."

"Oh. Well, I think you are quite wonderful. Furthermore, I believe I'll make more chocolate pie today," Amber said.

"They've got more than one email addy," Rafe said with a hard gleam in his eye. "No troubleshooter or troublehacker, but I'll send a message to every single one. Telling them that Pavan and Vikos gave us cards, what we wanted to discuss and the results. Ask for compensation for our damage." He grinned. "Maybe tell them that the Davail lawyers will speak with their's."

"Don't think they have lawyers," Tiro grumbled.

"Everyone has lawyers," Rafe said.

"They have magic," Amber said faintly, thinking of the papers she'd file for Jenni if the woman didn't come back, of Jenni's sunroom that had gone up over-night in February.

Rafe's lip curled. "Well, we'll see what happens when I mention attorneys."

Amber glanced at him. Her right arm had been burned, his left had. "You're going to your fencing lesson today?" She already knew the answer, but wanted to hear it aloud. He'd loved fencing.

"Yeah, it's only my shield arm," he replied absently, slowly plinking at the keyboard.

Tiro grunted, probably pleased that Rafe believed the brownie's words about there being a shield to match his dagger.

"I don't think we should ask any of the brownies to go with you," Amber said.

"Nope."

Even Tiro shivered with relief.

Rafe looked over at her. "I'll do my best to stay safe." His smile was strained. "I'm on red alert."

Amber pampered her arm for the next three days, working on her new genealogical cases. It was a relief to do them and she sent two out in record time. She'd included a couple of "extras," little, nearly innocuous dips into the past that showed no death.

She studied Conrad's and Rafe's charts name by name, again noting when she got a pinch that there would be a scene in the past, and keeping track of anything she sensed about those incidents in her work journal.

In long time lines like these, she was more often

than not drawn to a moment of death. Not something she ever cared to experience, but sometimes necessary to glean information. She put that off until she could be better prepared.

Neither chart went to the twelfth century and she began sifting through records farther back.

She reread the one volume of her ancestress's journal and noted the small mentions of magic. And wrote down the warnings about death curses—*avoid at all costs unless you plan to die and the money you get will be enough to fund many generations to come. Do* not *fall in love with a death-cursed.*

Cursed ones are attractive, like flowers to bees. Beware!

A shivery feeling in Amber's bones told her it might be too late. She ignored that.

The other journals hadn't arrived. Despite the fact she'd paid for overnight shipping, the seller had sent them by media mail. Amber knew from experience that could take a month. She got her money back but that didn't help speed the books.

She'd also reviewed the case which had cost her the most years, and found that the release on that one wouldn't have helped. The person who'd cursed her client had died and not been available for a groveling apology. She didn't think her client would have done the squirm-on-your-stomach-to-my-feet anyway. It did sour her, though, to think that she'd cleaned up the man's mistakes. But he'd been a good man when he'd come to her.

The brownies, even Tiro, stayed out of sight. She thought they were deeply uncomfortable that she and

Rafe had brought themselves to the attention of the unpredictable Lightfolk at Eight Corp.

As for Rafe...there were touches between him and her. And kisses. And groping hugs. But they hadn't taken that last step. She knew what was holding her back—fear of falling for a man and lifting a curse that would age her—and everyone to whom she was emotionally attached—many years. Falling for a doomed man who was already touching her heart. She couldn't take the step into sex.

She didn't know what was holding him back.

It only took three days of fencing lessons for Rafe to bond with his coach and the other students at the Denver Fencing Lyceum...and agree to spend the night of St. Patrick's celebrating with them.

He'd told her that he'd been pronounced a "natural," which didn't surprise her, and that he was also learning old-fashioned swordwork. She'd bitten her tongue to stop asking about the shield.

Of course he'd be more interested in athletic men—and women—than her. He would never have sought her out. That had been Conrad.

If she were jealous of Rafe's new friends, that was her problem. And to be honest, it was good to have the man and his death-curse energy out of the house.

He was driven to and from his lessons and activities at the Lyceum by a bodyguard in an armored car from Brilliant Limos, with a nervous Pred on board. There hadn't been any situations...yet.

That evening Tiro had disappeared after a lofty remark about celebrating the holiday with Irish brownies. Why magical folk, some of them no doubt older than St. Patrick himself, would celebrate a Christian saint's day was a mystery to Amber. But maybe brownies just liked to party. She'd noted that the chocolate milk she'd bought earlier in the week had also disappeared from the refrigerator and thought that if that was Tiro's contribution, he would be a hit.

She tried not to be anxious about Rafe. He'd be fine. These were people who valued their bodies and practiced control. None of them would get drunk. And they all knew how to fight. He'd promised not to be alone that night except in Mystic Circle.

Usually she'd go with Jenni and Tamara to O'Hearn's but not this year. Amber had spoken to Tamara and her friend had been more reserved than usual. Amber got the feeling that Tamara knew what was going on with Jenni and worrying. Tamara had told Amber that she was busy baking shamrock and four-leaf-clover cakes. Green cakes. They'd shared a moment of laughter, then decided to get together *when* Jenni got back.

Amber felt stupid staying up and waiting for Rafe, but she did it all the same. The weather was still cool enough for her to light a fire in the living room and watch the flames. That in itself was more than usually interesting. It seemed as if the flames had flickers and auras and afterimages of magic—greeny-blue for water energy, usually problematic in Denver; deep gold with hints of brown for earth; flashes of white for air; and tints of yellows and oranges and reds that she'd never seen before in fire.

She wore a T-shirt and jeans with an open ancient flannel plaid shirt that was several sizes too large.

Her couch was comfortable and the puppies were settled down on their beds and Amber was dozing when something thunked hard against the door. The dogs growled, then jerked her into wakefulness with riotous barking. Their tone told her Rafe had returned. There was scratching at the lock as he tried to insert his key. Rafe had little to no Celtic blood, nor had she, but that hadn't stopped either of them from wearing green, and it hadn't stopped him from drinking more beer than was wise, either, she guessed.

Since she hadn't heard a car, she thought that he'd been dropped off here. Too late to meet one of his new friends.

Still, she looked through the peephole before she opened the door. It *was* Rafe, with a wicked grin and a cut by his mouth and a black eye.

She opened the door and stood back. "What happened to you?"

The dogs were circling, sniffing lustily. There was a scent of yeasty alcohol wafting from him, as well as some blood. She narrowed her eyes. It seemed his suppressed aura of magic, and the binding glyph, was brighter. More questions. Because he was drunkish? Because of his companions? Or because of the slight taint of *other darkness* he brought with him, as if he'd tangled with death once again.

CHAPTER
18

HE TILTED BACK HIS HEAD AND LAUGHED. "Bar fight."

She blinked. "There really are such things?" Then she frowned. "I thought you were going to a respectable bar."

He nodded enthusiastically. "A real Irish bar. With real Irish men. Who took exception to Freddie Armathwaite and his foil." Rafe pruned his lips. "Only English-descended sissy-boys use thin swords like foils and not good solid fists." Rafe dropped his arm around her shoulders and she saw that though he wasn't near sober, he was still steady on his feet.

He continued, "Did I tell you that Freddie is a brown belt in karate?"

"Oh."

"Not one of us has to pay for the damage," Rafe announced as if that were unique. "The Irish guys have to. Tommy Corbin, the owner, said so."

"That's good. Ah. Why don't you come over here and sit down on the couch?" she said. His arm dropped from her shoulders to curl around her waist and give her butt a nice squeeze.

"The couch sounds ex–cell–ent." He nibbled at her earlobe. "You smell great."

"Thanks." She pulled him down to the cushions and when it appeared that he wanted to be more horizontal than she was ready for, she slapped him lightly. "Listen up, Rafe." She pushed him back into a sitting position. "You smell like minions."

He blinked, scowled. "What?"

She turned on the Tiffany lamp at the end of the couch, winced as she saw the red-scrape, purple-bruise side of his face. A lumpy cut seemed dangerously close to his eye. She touched it.

"Ouch!"

"Sorry. You sure you shouldn't go to an E.R.?"

"Cho was there, he's a doctor. He said not. I'm okay." Rafe frowned. "I'm pretty much the worst, everyone else fights better."

"Or the minions concentrated on you."

He shifted to take off his coat, pulled the stick from his inside pocket. Easy enough for them both to see that it was greasily black along the tip.

"Uh-oh. Minions. Dark." He flopped back and closed his eyes. "I think it vibrated. Should have paid attention. Didn't."

"Not good."

He opened his bad eye to squint at her. "They didn't get me, though."

"Not this time."

Nodding, he said, "Was a good idea to stay with the Lyceum group."

"I agree. I'm going to get a cold compress for you. Maybe some herbal tea, too."

"Blech."

Amber went to the kitchen and got an old and softly worn dishtowel, pulled an ice pack from the fridge and wrapped it up and put hot water on.

By the time she returned, Rafe was polishing his stick on the lining of his jacket, which was doing it no good, then stroking and sniffing the jacket itself. After a deep breath, he looked up at her, his expression serious. "Definitely minions. I can smell 'em." He handed her the jacket and she took it and narrowed her eyes. She couldn't tell how many or what sort they were and that bothered her.

Rafe rubbed his neck. "I think there were some professional toughs in there. Guys who hire out to beat other guys up."

"Not part of my worldview," Amber said.

Rafe grunted. He shifted and the stick that he'd been holding lightly between his fingers fell. It flashed silver, but didn't make it to the floor. Instead it angled toward the coffee table and lit with a slight clink on the glass atop the wood. Pointing at Rafe's tablet computer.

He stared at the device and so did Amber. When

she raised her gaze, his stare met hers. Angry and laced with despair.

"Another attempt on my life," he said roughly.

"Looks like."

"But they couldn't get to me because of the Lyceum fighters." Rafe stood and stretched. "I put more people in jeopardy with me."

"Despite the injuries and damages, nothing major was hurt?"

"Nothing major." His jaw flexed. Now when his eyes met hers, they were dark, and seemed to have sunk into his sockets. She didn't like how the shadows of the room painted his face. Almost like a skull. No. Not if she could help.

"Pavan said that he'd given you a construct to help you learn how to manifest the dagger. The game."

"Yeah, and you've been wanting me to do it, and I've avoided it." He shrugged. "Stupid game."

"I know it's not physical—at least the regular game isn't. But Pavan also strikes me as a very physical male, and his app says *REAL*. If he thought this would help…"

"Yeah, yeah, I'll do it. Now." A side of his mouth twisted. "When I'm still a little sloshed and won't feel so stupid about it."

"All right." She picked up the tablet and handed it to him. The kettle whistled.

Rafe's nostrils flared. "Go get the tea. I can probably use that, too."

She made it strong, a good head-clearing tisane, added a touch of honey and poured it into two mugs, a delicate floral one for her and a good solid pottery one for Rafe.

Once again Rafe had evaded curse-brought danger. They were being smart. But how long before their luck gave out?

And to get the dagger he would have to "manifest" it, use magic to bring it into his life, or use his new skill of seeing energies to find it. If it was a real knife in the real world. She didn't know enough.

Neither of them did.

She handed Rafe the mug. He made a face at the flowery scent, but drank it.

He sat in the middle of the couch, so she took a place to his left. His tablet computer was on his lap.

"Guess I'll see if I can 'manifest' stuff in the game."

"A lot of virtual learning going on."

"Don't think I'd like learning to fight that way." He shifted restlessly. His upper lip lifted. "Though if we could reduce Bilachoe to a character and slay him that way, once and for all, fine with me."

"Mmm-hmm." Amber drank the tea, let the smell swirl up her nose. She put the cup down with a decisive clink.

Rafe frowned and swiped his thumb against the icon.

The room and the night transformed into a stony hilltop and a day with bright blue sky and white attenuated clouds.

"What's the day-night cycle?" Rafe asked, brows still down.

"About twenty minutes. I've never timed it, and if there's a mission limit, it's measured in real time."

"Uh-huh." He'd sunk into his balance and moved carefully around, looking at the waves of hills, more woods down below and the odd greeny-yellow patches that Amber knew was swamp.

"Where are we?"

"The Star Diagram safe spot in the Baldy Hills."

Rafe snorted. "Appropriate."

"Yes."

"You're wearing armor," Amber said.

Yeah, his clothes felt different, not as heavy. His body felt…safer.

"It's dragon armor. That means you've grown as a fighter and a magic user."

Rafe touched his chest—the padding and coat were gone. As he glanced down at his arms, he saw his new armor was a deep red. It wasn't cloth or leather, not ceramic or metallic. He flicked a fingernail against it, but the sound gave him no clue as to the material.

"Chitin," Amber said.

If he were a dragonfly, he supposed that was reasonable. His back felt odd. He flexed his shoulders. Two pairs of wings whirred, working the muscles of his back. Translucent with rims of red. He closed his eyes in disgust.

"They're very beautiful," Amber said. She stepped back, as if to scan the whole of him. She looked just like she had the time before. Had she grown in fighting prowess as he had? Rafe thought the situation had changed her, too. But maybe Pavan's game wasn't measuring her, only him.

Her brows raised and she hummed in her throat. "Ve-ry nice. You look buff and tough."

He glanced down, his armor was formfitting. There was a sword strapped to his left thigh, too long to be the manifested dagger. Pulling it out, he found a sabre. With red-flame runes engraved on the blade. Yeah, this was a game for sure. Still, he narrowed his eyes. There was something about those runes, he could almost...not *read* them...but sense what they said. They had energy. In fact, as he gripped the sword and carefully turned in place, he realized that it was more responsive to energies than his dowsing rods. There... in that direction in about a mile was a river. He didn't recall seeing a river in his journeys in the game.

Different place for higher level characters, he supposed. Another turn and his sword swept up, pointing to the pinkish purple sky and the huge moon. "Air energy, what's there?" he asked Amber, even as his wings lifted him to hover off the ground. He felt a pull to it.

"It's the Cloud Castle in the air," she said.

An echo of Pavan's voice sounded in Rafe's memory. *Present yourself at a Lightfolk palace on your thirty-third birthday to be trained.* He wondered if the Cloud Castle of the game was like any real Lightfolk palaces. His heart thumped hard in his chest, his wings whirred, his palm sweated a little around the hilt of his sword. This did not feel like a game.

Clearing his throat, he said, "Profile." Before his

mind's eye he saw a picture of his face...complete with elf ears and a damn long ponytail, along with the notation that he was level twenty-two, had six powers of sword and six of wind and the skills that went with them. Nice. He *had* been working on his sword-fighting skills, and if you counted the practicing with the dowsing rod as magical skill, he'd been developing and flexing that muscle, too.

His accomplishment badges included: air racer max extraordinaire, waterskim racer extraordinaire, sportsman max extraordinaire with a bonus in fast reflexes.

"Nice," he said.

Amber nodded. "Yes, your profile is good." Her eyes were warm. "Reflecting your recent accomplishments." Her brows dipped. "Mine isn't so good. I'm a level eight. And I'm still squishy." She glanced around. "This is the forest of Zent. Too high for me. Any monsters here like shamblers or banshees can defeat me, and I can't touch them unless I use extra powers and get really lucky."

Rafe linked arms with her. "Stick with me, babe. I'll protect you."

"Mmm-hmm," she said absently. "Inviting you to team."

A rock thunked near his toes, broke apart to spell *Sylvant has invited you to team with her. Do you accept?*

"Yes."

"Very cool," Amber said as she watched the pieces of the rock turn back into a lump.

"That stupid leprechaun isn't going to show, is he? Or his equally stupid twin?" Rafe asked.

"They're only in the beginner's forest area. We're in the Baldy Hills."

"Huh."

"Check your mission list."

He found that his hand automatically went to his belt and he pulled out a square of paper. It said, *Find dagger.*

His heart jolted and his breath came fast. He handed the sheet to Amber.

"Wow," she said. She drew herself up, handed him back his paper. She was close, but no longer touching him, and he missed that. "And you know what to do next, right?"

He frowned.

"Check your compass. It should show you where the dagger is."

Rafe swallowed. "Yeah?" Without thought the brass compass was in his free hand. It showed no location. "Nada." He folded it.

"Oh. That's too bad." She got her own list. "I don't have anything at all." Glancing up, her gaze narrowed. "Wait, there's something on the back of your list."

He flipped it open, saw fancy dark blue handwriting. Amber leaned close and he held it so she could see, too. *To find the dagger, follow the energy stream, then manifest it.*

"Yeah, like that's helpful," Rafe said. Same old, same old. "Where's the energy stream?"

But Amber was shaking her head. "I don't know of any energy stream in the game. I don't know to what this refers."

"Okay." Rafe pulled his sword. "Really good dowsing rod."

Her eyes got large. She shrugged. "All right, you lead the way."

"Energy stream," Rafe muttered as he tucked the list back into his belt. "Outside the game there are four elemental magics."

"Not here," Amber said.

Realizing he hovered a few inches from the ground, he stopped his wings, plunked back onto too-solid-for-his-peace-of-mind earth. With a click, his wings folded into a protective casing against his back and sides.

"Cool," Amber said.

"We're walking, not flying. That's slow."

"Yes, but what do you feel with your sabre?"

He looked into the sky and made a face. "That castle is still the greatest pull."

She shook her head. "They don't let you in the Cloud Castle until—"

"What?" he prompted.

Her breath puffed out and she met his eyes and it was a little shock to see that hers were truly a gleaming silver and not the Amber he was used to. She still looked young, but her coloring had changed and he didn't like it. She was now all pale skin with a hint of glitter and short silvery hair. He much preferred the real Amber. All honey and golden and luscious.

"They don't let you in the castle until you're level thirty-five."

"Oh." That sent a trickle of cold fear down his spine.

Construct or not, this was a game, and real life and real magic and real death faced him outside of it.

"Guess I'd better find the dagger."

"I'd imagine it would be worth a fantastic amount of experience points," she said lightly, but he figured she was all too aware of reality, too.

He set his feet down and tried to clear his mind, concentrate on what he could feel in the sword. Energy. River-water energy—but that wasn't important in the game.

Breathing deeply, he visualized the dagger and felt his lips curve as it materialized before him. He snatched at it with his free hand and his fingers passed through it.

"Do you see that?" he whispered.

"No."

He nodded and continued to scrutinize it, see it clearer than he ever had before. Pavan had called it a dagger, so had the Davail who'd died in the dream, but to Rafe it was more like a short sword, the length of his forearm. Cutting edges and a good, sharp point. The whole thing was a dark royal blue, almost as if it were enamel instead of metal. Just like in his dreams, white and golden starbursts appeared and vanished, like little exploding suns.

Since it dazzled his eyes as he continued to stare at it, he closed his eyelids and tried to feel its essence as if it hung before him. Metal? Yes. Cool with zipping snaps of heat. Sound…a few tinkling, lilting, sparkling notes as if part of a melody that Rafe could only partially hear.

What of his other senses? He knew what it looked like, sounded like, smell—? He drew in a lungful of air. Rock…the Baldy Hills, woman-but-not-quite-Amber so he dismissed that scent, and…deepness. That was the only word that occurred to him, a sharp tang darker than citrus. Like deep space. Could it really be reflecting *space?* Like the universe? "Cosmos," he said, and his sword jerked his arm to the right, hard. "The Cosmos Dagger."

That rang in his head like the last clang of the hammer that had forged it.

"The Cosmos Dagger," said the woman who wasn't quite Amber, some squishy character not as strong or as intelligent as the real one. He opened his eyes to see her. She'd been frowning, but twitched her lips up when she saw he was looking at her.

"The Cosmos Dagger." He nodded. "You'll write that down in case—for my cousin, right?"

"If necessary. But let's go find it."

Now that sounded like her. Cheerful. Optimistic.

He realized he liked that about her more than any other feature of her personality. More than he liked the looks of her breasts in the scale armor, or how her pants tightened over her butt as she walked in the direction his sword was pointing.

Tightening his grip on the sword, he commanded, "Lead me to the Cosmos Dagger!" Sure enough, he got a strong pull of direction from it. His breath filtered out of his chest in motes of relief. He would find the knife. He would damn well *manifest* it, and then he would see about destroying the evil being who'd caused so much death and grief to his family. Oh, yes, Bilachoe had a lot to pay for, and Rafe Davail would do his best to call Bilachoe's account due. Rafe swished his sabre up and down in a quick salute. "My name is Rafael Barakiel Davail, prepare to die." More than bitter fear lay on his tongue now. The hot spice of anger and vengeance.

Amber looked back at him, her brows knotted, concerned.

And game monsters—banshees—attacked.

Three dropped from the trees, white wraiths, misty tatters, claw-fingers outstretched. Amber screamed and fell to the ground, rolled, hopped back to her feet, cursing. She flung out her hands. "Cocoon!" Silvery strands shot from her fingertips and encased him, then her in silvery web armor.

The noise was horrendous, his sword sang and the red runes sizzled as they slashed through the wisp beings, vanquishing two of the three. The last one touched him, cold penetrated and his fingers dropped his sabre. "Spellfire!" Amber whirled a whipping web of fire, cast it on the banshee. A ululating wail and it splintered into sparks.

Harsh breaths sounded in the air and Rafe understood it was Amber and him.

"Did that feel too real to you?" he asked.

She nodded. "Yes." Putting a hand between her breasts, she said, "My heart's beating hard and rapidly, and I'm pretty sure I had a good adrenaline surge."

"Ditto." He could hear his own breathing, unlike in the game. His wings flicked out and he rose a few inches. "Dragonflies," he muttered. Though the feeling of hovering was cool, he was pretty sure he didn't like the fussy wings. They didn't look strong enough to really haul ass, and he was afraid for them.

"Fairies," Amber corrected. "We're fairies. Dragonflies and webspinners and all the others."

"God."

He slipped over the countryside and realized the reason his wings had deployed was because there was swamp. Amber flew beside him. Her wings were shaped differently. More like moth or butterfly wings, he supposed. Or regular fairy wings.

He still didn't believe he was doing this. The bar fight earlier that evening was much more his thing, part of his world, understandable. This was just... freakish.

Like magic.

And curses.

And a knife called the Cosmos Dagger.

Then shamblers rose from the ground and lumbered toward them. Large, gross, rotting moss-green monsters with lumplike heads. Burning green eyes showed through the plant-encrusted things.

Unlike the computer game, they smelled. A stench of decomposition rose with each of their steps.

CHAPTER
19

AMBER WENT PALER. THAT DIDN'T HAPPEN
in the game, either, characters changing colors from
fear. Skin color could be anything. Characters could
turn other colors from magic use, yes…fear, no. Made
Rafe feel that hearts—and blood—might actually be
involved here and that wasn't good. What happened
if they died in here?

Only Tiro was in the house with them. Would they
have to depend on *Tiro?*

"Out! Game over! Off!" he shouted. Nothing happened.

"We can't exit. We aren't in a safe zone," Amber
said.

She got that right.

"Shamblers," Amber said, flexing her fingers. "Hard
to kill."

Rafe drew his sword. "Is it better to be on the ground or hovering like this?"

"I don't know."

"You're teamed with me," Rafe said. "That means you're at my level."

"But I don't have twelve powers. I only have four."

"Uh-oh. Can we fly away?"

"They're worse in the air and we don't dare go over the Many Mouths Swamp. The shamblers have these sticky tendrils that will pull you into the mouth of the swamp. Being eaten's worse than being beaten."

Rafe winced. "They're slow."

"They're *here!*"

And Amber flung a spell and they fought. The noises of blows, the fight, was as he'd experienced in the game. But the vibration of the sword up his arm as it struck the shambler in the chest was all too real. Ichor spurted.

And, yeah, there was blood on his part. Blood never appeared in the game. A whiplike stem cut his cheek. He bled. Then a ruffly tendril wrapped around his arm, jerked. He yanked back and ripped the limb from the monster. It yelled. More gore, and the ground was getting slippery. His wings had closed.

He lunged, got the shambler in the chest, the thing fell. He spun...and this time it was a game-body-move, virtual teaching, and he sliced another one.

Then he was hit, bad. He felt the blow cave in a rib, knock his senses silly with pain. He gasped and his sword dropped from his hand. Two monsters jumped on him and nausea jagged through him as they fell to the marshy ground.

"Webcast explode!" shouted Amber.

The bodies atop him were flung away, came down somewhere else with rattling thumps and groans.

He saw huge studded boots with huge wicked rowels aiming for his face. Fear—and need—punched through him. He *reached,* found something, raised his left arm and the foot hit a round glassy thing and the beast yowled in pain.

His right hand closed around a hilt. He thrust, saw a blue blade, heard a terrible scream.

Heavy, thudding footfalls announced backup. Not for them.

"Ambush by greenspurs, five levels higher than us! We can't win," Amber cried. She rushed to his side, grabbed his biceps. "Flee!" She yelled a spell and smoke puffed around them.

And they weren't in the swamp.

They were somewhere else bright with soothing light that filtered through him and healed him. His bruises vanished, as did the sting on his cheek. He rubbed it and encrusted blood flaked under his fingers, but he felt no scar.

He opened his eyes and knew he was in the recovery area of the Fairy Dome, a place of safety and healing. He was propped against a large stuffed bolster in a small circular depression, carpeted with patterned rugs and pillows around the rim.

A small moan as a body crumpled beside his. Amber. He blinked. She was literally white, pallid with blue lips. The circular brooch on her chest that indicated her health showed black with only a thin line of silver. She'd used all her power to save them—to save him.

Good thing this was a game.

He was shaken and panting anyway. He looked down at his own brooch. Full power, full health.

When he glanced back at her, the brooch showed she was regaining health and power slowly. Frowning, he stared at her profile. Under "Flee" power it said, *Save team, drain yourself.* He didn't like that, but done was done and he sure hadn't known how to save them.

Meanwhile, he felt great. He rolled and sat, stroking her hair back from her head. It was wet with sweat, though all he could smell in here was...elves. Honeyed air energy.

No other players were in the dome with them.

As her color returned and her breathing eased, he drew her up against a big pillow, cradled her in his arm. "Thanks."

"No problem," she whispered. "Not sure what would really have happened."

"Me, either." The wounds had been real. So had the healing.

She leaned against him, and he liked it, but couldn't feel her body well because of his armor. He wasn't sure how he could take it off. *If* he could take it off. His body was reacting to her, though not as much as if she'd had her true scent or appearance.

They were quiet and he decided to savor the moment. What were the rules of this screwy game of

Pavan's? Could he have sex with Amber? Who would know? Was someone watching them? Monitoring?

Yeah, another thing he really hated about this game. He didn't know the rules.

"I'm all right," Amber finally said, but she didn't move from his arms.

"Good."

"But, Rafe—" she gestured to a big blue shield beside him that appeared enameled, with starbursts flaring and fading "—where did you get that?"

He stared at it, recalled that it had appeared on his arm and saved him from a face-crunching kick. Automatically his hand reached for it, stroked it. "It's not mine."

"Of course it is." She thumped his chest lightly with her hand as if for emphasis. "It's listed as a power in your profile." She frowned. "You should check your profile yourself, it shows you more than it does me."

Since he was feeling pretty damn good and liked holding her, he closed his eyelids. A couple of seconds later his profile swam before his eyes. Fancy red lettering scrolled at the top: *Latest accomplishment, complete manifestation of the Cosmos Shield.* His eyes popped wide and energy coursed through him.

"Manifested," he said, and again he was panting as if he'd run a long race. "I *manifested* it. Shit."

She slanted him a look. "That's the first I've heard you curse."

"Yeah, yeah, old idiosyncrasy, not cussing. Don't want to send or receive any more curses."

She raised her brows. He didn't want to talk about

that minor thing. Again he stroked the shield, then he fisted his hand and whacked it hard. "It's real." He paused. "Or as real as anything else in the game."

"And it looks like a companion for the dagger?"

"Yeah." He frowned. "Did I have the dagger?" His long sabre was sheathed on his hip. He shook his head as he stared at the beautiful disk. More beautiful than ever because it had saved them. "I don't know *how* I manifested it."

"Think back to the fight."

"Think! Who was thinking?"

"Maybe that's a clue. Not thinking, feeling."

He made a disgusted noise.

"Well, you *have* been 'feeling' energies when you are dowsing. I'm sure you *feel* other things, like how much to angle your board or skis or sails or whatever, whether the snow or water or wind is good or bad." She waved a hand. "You know."

The hell of it was, he thought he did.

A group of other people showed up on the opposite side of the dome and began some lame role-playing. "Let's get out of here."

Light faded into dimness, there came the snores and whuffles of puppies. And he was leaning along the back of the couch on his side, with Amber in his arms.

His Amber. Not some fake silvery being.

She smelled right, and she felt incredible.

His body hardened.

He stared into her beautiful amber-colored eyes, set in her tanned face and framed by her streaked brown hair. Beautiful. Desirable. "Okay," he said, loving her softness pressed to him, how she fit him. He wanted to rip her clothes off and plunge into her.

"Okay?" she whispered.

"You haven't been ready. Time to make up your mind, Amber. Yes or no?" He ached like he hadn't ached for a woman since high school. They'd come all too easily. Not Amber, and she mattered a whole lot more than any woman had for a long time. He hadn't allowed himself relationships.

The scent of her dizzied him, her magic as much as anything else. Her magic was honey and floral and old, rich, crumbling amber. "Amber," he groaned, arching against her.

Her eyes widened, pupils dark and dilated and showing her desire.

She could see only Rafe, feel only Rafe, and he looked and felt so *good*. Real. So many things were strange but real in her life now.

He was lying in just the right spot to stimulate her, but there was longing in his eyes, a longing that she believed meant this would be more than just sex for him. "Yes," she said, and put her hands on the back of his neck, stroked him. He shuddered. She brought his mouth to his, tasted beer and excitement, recalled how he looked in Fairies and Dragons, as if his true warrior nature was revealed. Was that how Pavan saw him?

"Must be doing something wrong if you're thinking," he said. He smiled and she caught the warning of it too late as his fingers went to the neckline of her shirt and ripped downward. She gasped and felt his hands on her breasts and arched and shifted until he rose and she scooted under him, wrapped her legs around him and grabbed his shirt and pulled him down.

Like his, her hands explored and yanked and freed, and soon enough they were flesh-to-flesh and traveling to the heat and light of ecstasy together and shattering into fireworks of pleasure.

They lay panting together. His head was in the curve of her shoulder and she was stroking his hair, something she hadn't been aware of until she took stock.

"God, that was good," he said thickly. Then his arms clamped her tighter to him. "Is. *Is* good."

She wet her lips. "After can be good."

He lifted his head and brushed a kiss on her lips. His face was flushed. Standing and arranging his clothing, he said, "Yeah. What say we take this to the bedroom?"

"Again, I say 'yes.' Your room, since the dogs will head for my bed."

"That's real good. Remember that word—*yes*." He took a step and tripped, fell with little grace.

"Wha—? My God." Instead of rising he rolled to his butt and stared.

Amber stood and arranged the remnants of her clothes. Then looked at what he'd tripped over. She lost her breath. "It's the shield," she croaked. The three-foot crystalline structure was dark enough to blend into the shadows, but the golden suns and galaxies still moved just under its surface.

"Yeah." He stared at it. The last log on the fire collapsed and he flinched. He touched the shield, then stood and lifted it. "No heavier than a Frisbee." He flicked a fingernail against it and the tone rang sweetly. "Not sure what it is, but it stopped the kick of a giant linebacker greenspur."

"It's magic," Amber said. His attention had switched from her to the shield. She shouldn't be irritated at that, should she? Whether or not she should have been, she was.

"I manifested the shield. Good to hold, like it belongs to me, like I could do anything I wanted with it. Let's see...." He flipped it, his hands blurred and then the large disk spun on his finger. "Did stuff like this in college."

"Very impressive," Amber said.

He winked.

Another pop came from the fire. This time a flame flew out. Amber yelped and tried to catch it before it lodged in the rug or the couch.

The dogs woke and surged to their paws, barking. They raced around, circling the flame that had resolved into a small flickering being about five inches high. Orange and red, it stayed just out of the dogs' leaping reach.

"Settle down or you go to your crates!" Amber ordered.

The pups looked at Amber. The firesprite hopped up to one of the fat candles on the mantel, lit it and stood on the wick, close enough to leave a smoky mark on the marble backboard.

A few more short barks came as the dogs looked for the little fire being and sniffed the round rug, then sat and stared at the now-lit candle.

The firesprite flickered in a taunting way. Though it had no obvious sex, Amber got the impression that it was female.

"I am Sizzitt of the Csynder clan. I heard a sstory from kin about your vissit to Eight Corp and your of-fer. My name iss tainted. I will guard your body." She angled long like a flame toward Rafe, then snapped back to the candle wick. "For payment, I will take one of thosse large chocolate barss a day they ssay you gave the sstupid dwarfem. What elsse can you give me? I musst have good pay to attract a mate and make a sspark. Alsso, I do not asssocsiate with browniess. They bore me."

Tiro appeared, smelling like a distillery. He was smiling and that was scary. His feet seemed to dig into the floor and the rest of him swayed. "And you are too flighty for me." He wiggled a four-jointed hand. "Remember that I'm bigger than you. I can *put you out*."

A crackle of anger came from the firesprite. "And I can *burn* your preciouss thingss."

"Not in this house!" Amber said. "Or you can take your fiery self right up the chimney."

Rafe walked over and stood next to Amber. "Any damage to the house will be deducted from your pay."

Sizzitt sat down on the top of a candle, melting runnels of wax as they ran down and overflowed the candlestick.

"Starting with that—" He nodded to the wax.

"Oh, I don't think—" Amber said.

"Amber, you'll have to replace the candle and it will take some time to clean up the wax."

The firesprite flamed blue and there was a high whistle and the wax on the mantel separated itself from the wood and flowed back up to become part of the candle. Sizzitt smiled. Like a djinn, her mouth stretched wider than a human's. Her teeth were pointed flames. Impressive.

"Hey, Tiro." Rafe actually touched the brownie's shoulder with a couple of fingers. "Guess what." There was a rush, then the shield *flew* toward them and hung vertically before Tiro, spinning slightly.

Rafe did that? Did *magic!* Amber guessed that he was getting the hang of manifesting an object.

Tiro belched, then nodded slowly and touched it with his index finger. The disk itself stopped spinning, but the starbursts still wheeled.

The brownie nodded so slowly that his chin rested on his chest, then lifted. "You manifested the Cosmos Shield. Good." He looked blearily up at Rafe, still gently weaving. "If you survive the fight with Bilachoe, I will live with you. Talked a lot with the Irish brownies, sensible chaps. It is not good for brownies to live alone and not with humans." He burped again. Then his gaze switched to Amber. "I will miss you, but I will be nicer now. One can love a short-lived being and let it go."

That was so hopeful to hear. Not.

Tiro wrapped an arm around Rafe's leg and had

Rafe's brows shooting up. "We will care for the dogs for you, Amber."

Her throat closed. Fear surged back and she squelched it. "Thank you. A fun time with the Irish brownies, then."

Again a slow nod. "Yup. They are good company and have good advice." He looked up at the firesprite. "Not like firesprites."

"What of Hartha and Pred?" Amber asked.

"They are dull."

"Boring brownies," Sizzitt said. There was a high hissing crackle that Amber thought was fire-laughter. Sizzitt danced on the wick. "And your clothes ssmell like liquor and would burn sso nicely!" She looked at Rafe. "I will guard you."

Tiro smiled back at her. "He has been attacked by shadleeches."

The firesprite sputtered wildly in yellow and orange, losing her humanoid form.

"You can still back out," Rafe said.

Amber headed to the kitchen and returned with her largest fondue pot. She held it up to the firesprite. If Sizzitt couldn't swim in it, she could sure dunk. "As well as the daily chocolate bars, you get melted chocolate in this once..." What would be good? As usual, she made a generous offer. "Once a week."

Sizzitt went long and bright, then compacted into a molten red ball. "Yess. Yess. Yess. Need to mate and sspark."

"Don' come in m'room," Tiro said, unwound himself from Rafe and popped away.

"My stove is gas and has pilot lights for the burners and oven…" Amber said.

"I will sstay there." Sizzitt left the candle to hover near Rafe's shoulder. The smell of crisping hair came. "Needed to tasste you." Then the firesprite streaked like lightning toward the kitchen.

Amber and Rafe were left alone in the living room where the fire had died and the only light came from a small lamp. The Cosmos Shield glittered.

Reaching out, she curved her hand over the rim, felt the weight of it as the magic that had been holding it in midair faded. Rafe was right, it wasn't heavy at all. "It's warm and…strong."

"Yeah."

She drew in a deep breath and let it out. "You did it. You really manifested it. If you got the shield, you should be able to find the knife."

He jerked straight, and his expression sharpened. "Wait. Wait. I did. I had the knife." His right hand flexed. "I had it for a minute in the game."

Then he widened his stance, settled into his balance, still frowning. Amber thought he was using the magical ability he'd developed to sense the energy of the knife.

His eyes lit, his whole face radiated a simple and heartfelt joy. "I brought it with me from the game, too." He blinked. "It's here in Denver." She only saw the gleam of his eyes before he grabbed her and twirled her around. "It's here! I don't know where it was before, but it's here!"

"Where?"

He set her on her feet. "Don't know. Somewhere."
Keeping one arm around her waist he rubbed his face
with his free hand. Amber heard the slight rasp of
bristles. Rafe shook his head. "Can't get it tonight.
But I'll trace it if I have to drive every damn street in
Denver."

An idea formed, but before she could say anything,
he swung her up in his arms. "Later. Tomorrow morning. Tonight is for us."

CHAPTER

20

RAFE WOKE AMBER UP FOR VIGOROUS predawn sex and a few minutes of cuddling before he left to "run the Circle with the dogs." His whole manner had become more cheerful at being able to act instead of wait. Since she couldn't go back to sleep, she got out of bed, stripped it and put on clean sheets and started laundry. The refrigerator was looking an empty white and the last of the chocolate in the pantry—pudding mix—had mysteriously disappeared.

Sizzitt the firesprite was nowhere to be found and Amber would have thought that she'd dreamed the small being except that the candles on the mantelpiece showed some use. The teakettle was still warm and sitting on a tile next to the range, so Rafe might have lit a burner for her to play in or something. A firesprite living in her stove! Magic.

quite the same type of Lightfolk, though Am-
sensed he was magic. Smoky dark shifted around
m as if he wore it like a garment. Bright twinkling
ights in a rainbow of colors sparkled through the fog.
Across from him was a large, thick-muscled man wearing gold…who had bull's horns and a broad nose and
didn't look human. *Gatekeeper.* The word rose whispery from Amber's most basic instincts to her brain.
Minotaur. Gatekeeper.

Eight Lightfolk, four couples, were being hugged
and held with the murmurs of goodbyes floating
to her. She watched as the short, stocky dwarf and
dwarfem separated themselves from the group and
marched hand-in-hand to the circle of green light.
Amber saw them nod to the men by the columns, pass
through to the center of the small circle, then vanish.

Another dwarven couple grunted and made noises
like the rattling of rocky gumballs falling through
a dispenser. Golden light flared around them. "The
old Earth royals have left through the dimensional
gate. We are the King and Queen of Earth, now,"
the dwarf said in a language that Amber heard and
understood with her mind, not her ears. She recalled
that the brownies had said some royals had left in the
fifth century.

The king straightened, sweeping his arms before
him and causing the chime of thick golden bracelets on
his wrists. The dwarfem laughed. She wore a woven
metal headdress with the strands ending in bells that
tinkled. The echo of the bracelets and bells flowed

The shield sat propped near the fireplace in the living room, an equally magical decoration.

Amber decided to abandon Rafe to the dogs and
Sizzitt and head to the grocery store. All the garages
were on an alley behind the houses so she could sneak
out without being seen by them. As far as she knew
he and the firesprite hadn't talked about driving.

When she got home from the store, she put a week's
worth of "wages" on the kitchen island holding the
fondue pot, including blocks ready to be melted. Since
the firesprite hadn't mentioned whether she preferred
milk or dark chocolate, Amber purchased both. She
didn't quite trust the brownies in the face of overwhelming temptation so she'd ringed the whole thing
with silver picture frames she'd had on hand. It was
true that silver was bad for the Lightfolk—major and
minor.

Rafe had left a boldly scrawled note on the dining
room table saying that he'd been invited to morning
classes at the lyceum and he and Sizzitt were gone for
the day.

And Conrad had called and wanted an update.

Conrad's check had cleared and she'd better damn
well do some work for him.

So Amber finished her chores, played with the puppies in the backyard, then left them to garden with
Tiro, who was working on her flower beds. She stuffed
herself with a large breakfast of protein, a three-egg
omelet with ham and three sorts of cheeses and a large
glass of milk. A couple of good meals and she would

The shield sat propped near the fireplace in the living room, an equally magical decoration.

Amber decided to abandon Rafe to the dogs and Sizzitt and head to the grocery store. All the garages were on an alley behind the houses so she could sneak out without being seen by them. As far as she knew he and the firesprite hadn't talked about driving.

When she got home from the store, she put a week's worth of "wages" on the kitchen island holding the fondue pot, including blocks ready to be melted. Since the firesprite hadn't mentioned whether she preferred milk or dark chocolate, Amber purchased both. She didn't quite trust the brownies in the face of overwhelming temptation so she'd ringed the whole thing with silver picture frames she'd had on hand. It was true that silver was bad for the Lightfolk—major and minor.

Rafe had left a boldly scrawled note on the dining room table saying that he'd been invited to morning classes at the lyceum and he and Sizzitt were gone for the day.

And Conrad had called and wanted an update.

Conrad's check had cleared and she'd better damn well do some work for him.

So Amber finished her chores, played with the puppies in the backyard, then left them to garden with Tiro, who was working on her flower beds. She stuffed herself with a large breakfast of protein, a three-egg omelet with ham and three sorts of cheeses and a large glass of milk. A couple of good meals and she would be ready to tackle the inception of Conrad's curse whenever it might be.

She, too, was becoming more aware of magic and the various sensations of each elemental energy. And as she moved Conrad's scroll back to the main area of her desk and unrolled it to the farthest end, anchoring it with paperweights, she had to admit it was a relief to consider Conrad's curse. It was just as difficult as Rafe's, and the man had been distraught, but it wasn't nearly as urgent as Rafe's death curse.

She spent the morning corresponding with an expert in medieval European history to whom she'd sent Conrad's information. He'd traced the line a couple of centuries farther back than she'd worked on for Conrad, but currently they were stuck, believing that there had been a name change.

So she unrolled the chart that she was penning for Conrad and set it atop the one the man had given her. It held his vibrations.

Another quick walk around the cul-de-sac and the moment had come. She took a small tray of beverages upstairs with her—water, apple juice and a good-size cup of coffee.

Amber felt the food and drink weigh her down, good for bringing her back to the present. She wasn't quite sure whether this would work, focusing her mind on the chart she'd made and linking with Conrad's time line and just following it where it led.

Surely the curse would be the greatest episode in the time line and her minor power would be drawn to that.

Since both Pavan and Vikos knew of the Cymblers, Lightfolk were most likely involved. So, deep breaths and clearing of her mind, and leaning over her desk and putting her hands on the charts, connecting with Conrad and his *family*.

All was different. Blackness crashed down on her, highlighted by a fountain of purple and gold sparks that faded, leaving her in a darkness she'd never experienced. A whirlwind spun her around, taking her breath, and she knew she was passing out. She was yanked to a stop and fell into a scene of eerie colors, with things, people—*Lightfolk*—outlined in neon auras.

It was night and the sweep of stars was bright and not quite the pattern she was used to. Very far back in time, then. Most of the place below her was shifting blue, with a small solid radiating brown. Set in the brown was a circle of columns made of a pale green light shooting into the sky. A minute passed as Amber realized that the blue was a lake, the brown an island and the green columns...simply magic.

There was a large mass of light that moved, and as it did, Amber noticed that it was a group of Lightfolk. Another blink or two and she saw the two guardians she'd met before, the elf Pavan and the dwarf Vikos. Both men didn't look younger, but their attitudes didn't have the same heaviness of experience that she'd felt when they'd visited her at home. They also appeared less...dense.

The closest couple of light-columns were flanked by two male beings. The nearest was a tall, thin man—

not quite the same type of Lightfolk, though Amber sensed he was magic. Smoky dark shifted around him as if he wore it like a garment. Bright twinkling lights in a rainbow of colors sparkled through the fog. Across from him was a large, thick-muscled man wearing gold...who had bull's horns and a broad nose and didn't look human. *Gatekeeper.* The word rose whispery from Amber's most basic instincts to her brain. Minotaur. Gatekeeper.

Eight Lightfolk, four couples, were being hugged and held with the murmurs of goodbyes floating to her. She watched as the short, stocky dwarf and dwarfem separated themselves from the group and marched hand-in-hand to the circle of green light. Amber saw them nod to the men by the columns, pass through to the center of the small circle, then vanish.

Another dwarven couple grunted and made noises like the rattling of rocky gumballs falling through a dispenser. Golden light flared around them. "The old Earth royals have left through the dimensional gate. We are the King and Queen of Earth, now," the dwarf said in a language that Amber heard and understood with her mind, not her ears. She recalled that the brownies had said some royals had left in the fifth century.

The king straightened, sweeping his arms before him and causing the chime of thick golden bracelets on his wrists. The dwarfem laughed. She wore a woven metal headdress with the strands ending in bells that tinkled. The echo of the bracelets and bells flowed

outward on a wave of musical magic that seemed to notify all Lightfolk that Earth power had changed.

Next a green-skinned man and woman linked arms. Their hair sparkled with droplets and they left seafoam in their wake as they walked through the grove and the gate.

She watched as elves more beautiful than belief glided through the air and into another place.

Each time there was a reaction to two left behind, a growing in stature and magic, a sending through the water or the air by the new kings and queens. And from the vibrations and reverberations, Amber sensed they were in what would become Italy.

Finally only the guardians and two couples remained, glowing deep lava red and orange. The King and Queen of Fire, djinns, and the couple who would soon become royal.

A man stepped from the shadows, a person who felt part human, whose magic was duller. The brightest woman cried out, stretched her arms toward him. The current King of Fire wrapped his arm around her waist. The lesser couple faded back from the trio, as did the guardians.

"I want my child to come with us! There is magic and time and energy enough to carry a babe," the Queen of Fire—the djinnfem—cried.

"No," said the human man wearing leather pants, a cloth shirt and long cape, cradling a bundle in a sheepskin. "She is my daughter, too, and she will stay here, on this planet with *me*." He didn't glow as brightly as the others. Definitely had human blood.

The red-toned man's thin upper lip lifted showing orange fire teeth. He spoke to the djinnfem. "She is only three-quarters Lightfolk. She should not leave this benighted place draining of magic for a realm richer in energy. She will not live as long as we. She will not appreciate her new world. Leave her with her father." The djinn turned the beautiful woman to face him and not the man and the baby. "Now we have wed, I will give you full-blooded Lightfolk children who will prosper in the world we go to. Not puling human-get." The infant had begun to cry.

Glancing over her shoulder at the man who held the tiny girl, the djinnfem's face showed lava tears flowing down her cheeks. "It should be *my* decision to make, whether I have her or not. Not *his*. Her father is not full-blooded Lightfolk. My decision."

"But it is not," the man said, and his tone was cool. "Your fellow queens and kings gave that decision to me and I choose to keep our child."

"I *love* her!" The queen wept.

"So you say. As you told me you loved me. But you don't," the human-Lightfolk man said. His expression turned fierce. "*I* love her."

The Fire King focused on his queen. "I have chosen you as my wife. You are Flashingsmoke now, Queen of Fire, strong in power and passion. Look to the future. Not the past." He took her hand, drew her to the center of the grove where rainbow waves of light shimmered like a soap bubble. "We'll go through the dimensional gate and to our new life. Forget her, she is his, and he is nothing. Our children will be rich in

magic and power and grace. His will die the human deaths."

But the queen wrenched away, ran back to the columns. "Give her to me, I beg you!" More lava tears hissed.

"No." The man cuddled the baby and stepped back.

The queen tossed her head of black and bronze ringlets. "Then I curse you, Cymbal Lore. You shall only have this one child. I *curse* you."

He rocked back on his heels

Her smile was cruel. "I curse you and your sons!"

"You would hurt our child's child!"

"Only males! Men with magic who would claim and take a babe from their mothers."

"And you don't think seeing her sons harmed will hurt her?" He spat on the ground. Bad move, it infuriated the queen more and her arm came up and her index finger pointed directly at him, streaming a current of magic Amber couldn't see but could feel.

"You shall lose your precious grandsons, males, soon after they are born. When you find them again, or their fathers find them again, the fathers will soon die. You take my daughter from me, and my chance to see her grow into her beauty. And I know you prize sons more than daughters. So sons shall be taken from your line."

The man's face went so expressionless it became scary. "You are djinnfem and fire and hurt yourself as you hurt me and our line. You let your temper reign with no thought to consequences. You demand what you want in the moment and will serve up grief to all, including yourself, to have that moment."

"Don't do this, Flashingsmoke," the other djinnfem said. "You tie this curse to yourself, you will always recall the grief you feel now. It will never fade. How will that work on your temper?"

"I care not for how she suffers," the human snapped. "I feel the curse upon me." He touched his daughter's cheek and looked stricken. "Upon us, to every tiny droplet of our humors." His head jerked up and his eyes seemed to burn. "What of the release? Each curse must have a release, a condition that must be met to break it."

The Fire Queen's smile got sharper, again she tossed her head. "The release is that you or one of the males of your line will bring his babe to me, at a dimensional gate, and offer the child to me in reparation for what I have lost."

Cymbal Lore sucked in a breath that held the weeping of the wind. "Magic is fading here. Who knows when there will be enough power gathered to form another gate?"

"Who knows?" the queen said and turned to her king, pressing herself against his side. He was frowning. "Let us go make those children of *ours*. I am done with this place."

"No, you aren't," Pavan the elf guardian said as she stepped through the gate. He shook his head, as did Vikos.

The new King and Queen of Fire blazed as power flowed to them, settled upon them—to the very last droplet of their humors—and sent crackling sparks showering high like fireworks, spreading over the sky and beyond. Fire Lightfolk followed a new royal couple.

Turning to the human, the queen said, "We are sorry for your curse, Cymbal Lore." She brushed her hand over the baby's head. "But I cannot lift the curse from this one. I am sorry."

"Time to go," said her consort. He inclined his head at Cymbal Lore. "It is never wise to mix Lightfolk and human blood."

The scene began to fade as if a gauze curtain misted before Amber. She felt the yank of the present and a rush of atmosphere compressed her lungs. The fall would be long and vicious, the landing hard.

A golden being appeared, held his hands out and she stopped. Flowing robes were gold, his hair shimmering blond, his skin tanned. His features were male perfection.

"Who?" The word was released on the merest breath, but echoed.

He smiled and it was charming and fun and tugged at her heart.

"Bilachoe," he said.

He flicked a hand and his magic slammed into her, toppling her end over end, lost like an untethered satellite in space. Fear swept through her in an icy tide. She must have been trembling but there was nothing to tremble against. Her breathing was harsh to her ears and fast, but not as quick as her stuttering heartbeat. Cold sweat beaded and slid grimly along her skin.

Bilachoe's brows arched. "Interesting, you have some tiny measure of magic." Again he smiled and again it was beautiful and pulled at her and she had to wrench her gaze away. Needed to close her eyes to escape him. Didn't dare.

"Do not help the cursed Davail, Cumulustre-get." One more brilliant smile. "Or I will peel the skin from your bones millimeter by millimeter."

The images he put in her head showed exactly that. How he'd done it to others.

Amber's gorge rose and she concentrated on forcing the vomit down.

"And I will do the same with Tiro, Pred and Hartha."

Now she saw him torturing a brownie—and a brownie-skin cover on a book of dark magic.

"And your dogs."

With the first raw slice of the boning knife along the side of a dog and the fur peeling back showing red and bloody muscle beneath, Amber screamed and screamed.

Pain wrapped around Amber's ankle like fiery whips and the scene and its neon colors vanished as she was jerked into the present. Then dog tongues rasped on her face and she writhed with pain, but she flung out her sensitized hands to grab them, hold them with hands that felt scraped raw by their fur. She let their wiggling bodies smash into her, gritted her teeth as her flesh and bones seemed pulverized. They were all right.

The hurt on her ankle went away. She didn't dare open her eyes.

"So you're back," Tiro said.

The puppies nudged her and she whimpered and they did the same, adding whines that screamed through her head like sirens. More sound pounded through her like earthquake vibrations, then stopped. Rafe yelled, "What's happened?"

"Lower your voice, boy, and don't touch her. She went far into the past." There was thudding and creaking. "Apparently to the Cymbal Lore curse."

"Conrad's curse? Hell. Amber, honey, how can I help?"

She managed to form a word on her lips, push air out to give it life. "Juice."

"Hartha!" Tiro snapped.

The scent of the browniefem came to Amber—newly turned earth.

Hartha tsked and Amber flinched at the sound. A tiny puff of breath from the woman. "That sensitive, is she? Hmm." The hum of three beehives drowned out other sounds. "I have a nice herbal tisane that might help." There was the thunder of two pops of displaced air, then the fragrance of sage. Amber grimaced and thought her face would crack and fall to the floor.

The air moved around her and Rafe was there with his natural scent overlaid with soap and shampoo. Back from his training at the lyceum. He slipped an arm behind her back and she groaned when he raised her; she didn't have the strength to lift her head. He grumbled and laid her back down, slid one arm under her neck, then the other under her back. She felt him, his concern, his tenderness, protectiveness. Slowly he brought her to a sitting position. She should open her eyes, but believed they would be hurt most by her sensitivity to things around her, maybe permanently, so she kept her eyelids down.

Rafe shifted until he was behind her, her head propped against his chest. A warm mug was placed against her lips. "Here, Amber honey, drink the good tea."

"Not good," she mumbled.

His chest trembled behind her but his laugh didn't emerge. "It has honey."

"Drink the damn tea," Tiro said. "Got brownie magic in it. We're of the Earth, and we can make healing potions."

That was more than she'd known before and her curiosity piqued. She wondered what brownie magic tasted like. When she opened her mouth, Rafe poured the brew ruthlessly down her throat.

It was a wonder she didn't choke, but Rafe had gauged the stream of liquid right. The drink tasted like sage, neither the brownie magic nor the honey cut that much. "I've closed the draperies over her bedroom windows," Hartha said. "You can take her in there." More movement around Amber, as if the brownies were as fretful as the dogs.

Rafe kicked the door closed behind them, then placed her gently on her bed, toed off his shoes and joined her, leaning on one elbow. He stroked her hair back from her face, kissed her lips. She felt like Sleeping Beauty or Snow White or something, not just Amber Sarga. A dribble of energy began to course through her, enough that she could turn her head and meet his eyes. He was beautiful.

Tears stung her eyes, dribbled down her temples. "Bilachoe was there."

"At the time Conrad was cursed?"

"No." Her lips cracked and salty blood welled, all too reminiscent of the images the evil one had planted in her brain. "He ambushed me."

"Did he hurt you?" Rafe sat up, tension infusing his muscles.

Amber managed to put a hand on her chest between her breasts and rub. That didn't make the sharp spiking of her heartbeat calm. "I don't think so. He threatened…if I broke your curse…torture me and the brownies…and the puppies." Her voice was low and raspy.

Rafe snarled, "All the better that I kill him, then." Rafe kissed her forehead. "And I don't want you to risk yourself or others by breaking my curse. Is that clear?" His eyes had turned dark sapphire and harder than the stone.

"Clear," she said, but if he needed her to break the curse so he could kill Bilachoe…she'd reconsider.

Rafe curved his hand around her face. "Where… when were you?"

Glad to change the subject, she said, "I have the story of Conrad's curse. It's very interesting."

He rolled from the bed to his feet, paced the width of the room at the bottom of her bed. "That's where and when you went? To the start of the curse on Conrad's family?"

"Yes, fifth-century Italy."

He circled the bed and sat next to her, enveloped her face with his hands. "We already know what needs to be done to break my curse, the Davail curse. Bilachoe laid the curse and I must kill him to break it. I don't want you to look at that scene. No need. You got that?"

"Yes." She frowned and was glad she had the energy to pucker the muscles. When she spoke her voice was stronger. "But your curse was invoked in the twelfth century. Seven centuries later."

"Don't care." His thumbs stroked her cheeks. "You aren't going that far back into time. No way. And—" he moved to lay down beside her, one of his hands went to the tab of her blouse and began unbuttoning "—neither of us are going back into that deadly game the elf loaded onto my tablet. The danger needs to be minimized for all of you."

She smiled. "All right." Sexual desire unfurled within her, warming her core, sending her more energy. She wanted this man. Pulling his shirt from his jeans, she slid her hands up his torso, lean and strong. His heart was beating as rapidly as hers. He leaned forward to kiss her. She opened her mouth so they could taste each other, connect deeply with each other even before sex.

Reassure each other that they were alive.

He drew back and all she could see was his dark blue eyes, his gaze fixed on hers. His hands slid down to link fingers with her. A shiver passed through her as she felt a circuit of energy between them open and cycle. Strong and steady and...lovely.

"I care for you," he said in an absolute tone.

"I care for you, too," she responded.

He squeezed her fingers. "We'll get through this together."

Then he closed his eyes and kissed her and she let her mouth cling to his and didn't call him on his lie.

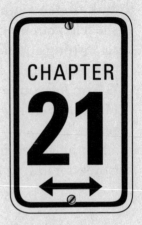

CHAPTER
21

HARTHA MADE DINNER THAT NIGHT. IT wasn't leftover corned beef and cabbage, which is what Amber usually ate after St. Patrick's Day. Of course, she'd had no leftovers.

The meal was a hearty beef stew, a pile of biscuits and side salads that included greens Amber didn't recognize. She thought that the Mistweaver brownies were there because Amber had chocolate in the house again, but they didn't say anything. Their noses had twitched—along with Tiro's—when they'd seen the chocolate near the fondue pot on the kitchen island. When Rafe and Sizzitt had returned, Amber had gathered the silver frames and let the firesprite set her own magical shields. Amber wasn't sure exactly what it was, but the air wavered like heat over concrete around the kitchen island.

While they ate, Sizzitt kept them company in the dining room fireplace.

Tiro slurped his last bite, burped and waved his china and utensils away to the open dishwasher in the kitchen, then said, "You manifested the Cosmos Shield."

Rafe stood and cleared his and Amber's bowls. "I did." He nodded toward the living room and the shield tilted away from the wall and rolled into the dining room. When he came back, he had bowls of chocolate pudding Amber had made. He set one in front of Amber at the large dining room table, three at Tiro's small brownie table and a little one close to the fire, where the pudding heated to liquid and rapidly vanished. The fire looked a little sluggish to Amber after the siphoning.

She applied herself to the pudding nearly as quickly as the brownies as Rafe picked up the shield and began doing tricks with it.

"I practiced stuff at the lyceum today. They had a little shield someone from the Society for Creative Anachronism brought in after I asked about them."

Amber raised her brows. She didn't think Rafe had ever heard of the SCA before today. "Don't you want some pudding?"

"I'm tired of chocolate," he said.

Tiro choked. Hartha and Pred and Amber stared at him. Rafe flipped the shield around some more, sent a slow smile to Amber. "I'll have dessert later."

He propped the shield against the wall again. "Not only did I manifest the shield, here. But I brought the knife to Denver somewhere. Amber's going to help me find it."

She nearly sagged in her chair at the thought of more magic. But if things worked out the way she thought, he'd be using his.

"How will we find it?" asked Tiro.

"Magic," Amber said.

Rafe appeared a little askance. He'd spent the day using his body and his mind in sport, as he was accustomed to.

"Hard going back and forth between mindsets?" Amber asked.

"Yeah. A little." He looked at the shield. "But that's sort of a link." His shoulders shifted. "I know it's there and it's mine—or rather a Davail's. Mine for now."

And the shadow of the death curse fell over the room.

"But I can get the Cosmos Dagger and learn to use it." Again his gaze focused on her.

"I'll be right back." Amber rose and went to her consultation room, pulled out the book of Denver maps from a bookcase, then opened a box and twined a chain around her fingers. By the time she returned the dining room table was not only cleared, but it also gleamed like it had been recently polished. Instead of the bowl with fruit as a centerpiece there was a stack of cork place mats that had been in a drawer in the pantry under a candle. Sizzitt sat on the wick.

"What do you have there?" Rafe asked.

She let the pendulum dangle from her fingers. One

end was a stone cut into an elongated pyramidical shape, the other had a bead of a different stone.

"Hmph," Tiro grunted as Rafe took a small step away. "If you can dowse with a divining rod, you can work a pendulum." Tiro grimaced. "More a work of air magic mixed with earth, than just earth, though."

"He has air. More air than earth inside him," Hartha contributed, joining her husband on the chair.

"First," Amber said, "why don't you close your eyes and try to *feel* in what direction the dagger might be and how far away?"

Looking doubtful, Rafe did, slowly turning in place until he faced southeast toward downtown Denver. Amber wasn't too surprised, and opened the book to the pages showing the offset grid of the oldest part of the city.

Rafe huffed a short breath, opened his eyes and pointed. "I followed Speer past Cherry Creek." He shrugged. "Then I lost the exact direction. Can't tell how far away."

"All right." Amber flipped over a few more pages, offered him the pendulum again. "Take it by the top and hold the pointed end over the map."

He grasped the bead with his forefinger and thumb warily.

"I know you're easier with fighting than with magic. But you're going to need both," she said. She was never more certain of anything. He put the pendulum over the map book and she stilled it.

With narrowed eyes and flexed jaw, he stared at the

map and the pendulum rock. It stayed motionless and he made a disgusted sound.

"Think of it as your stick," Amber said.

Rafe opened his fingers, reached into his pocket and said, "We should have done this in the first place." He smiled as he held the tiny rod.

Tiro said, "Yes, that has much more magic, and your magic."

Tiro's point was demonstrated when the map book's pages fluttered, then opened to a new section of Denver. Rafe's stick zoomed to a large gray building as if pulling his fingers, not being directed.

"What's that?" Rafe asked.

"The Museum of Nature & Science." She shook her head. "You manifested the knife in a museum. No doubt with top-of-the-line security. Nice going, champ." His dismissal of her pendulum still stung.

He raised his brows. "It's an old thing. It was probably drawn to other old things in Denver. Not a helluva lot of them."

"Somehow I don't think the objects in Jamestown, Virginia, are older than the dagger and the shield." She looked at Tiro. "Do you have any idea when they were made?"

Pred spoke up. "Made for Davails at the time when Lightfolk changed Davail bloodline. Gave Davails magic so they can kill evil bad ones."

Amber hesitated, walked over to the shield. "It looks older than that." Which wasn't true. It appeared as if it had been magicked into being the day before. "I mean, it seems like it might have been made at…the beginning of the universe." *That* was true and she felt herself flushing.

Pred sniffed and hopped down to join her. Ran his long, thin four-knuckled brownie fingers over the shield. "Time of Davail change."

"Humans call it the fifth century," Hartha affirmed.

So the Cymbler curse and the Davail change might have happened close to the same time. No wonder the men of those families seemed drawn together. Both were magical.

Amber left the shield, walked into the kitchen and poured herself a cup of coffee. She was pretty sure how Rafe would react at her next bit of information. Sipping her drink, she leaned on the wall with pocket doors that could close off the kitchen from the dining room and looked at her lover.

His virility and vitality blazed to her magical sight, as if all the many years of his life were compressed into these past months. Her heart clutched. He was becoming so dear after such a short amount of time. Maybe because they were going through this experience of learning about magic together. It would have been awfully lonely if she had no one to talk to. Unlike Jenni and Tamara, Amber didn't have a lot of Lightfolk blood, just a trace of elven and a gift that was more a curse.

Tiro was frowning at her. He was, as ever, of the opinion that she would lift Rafe's curse and age those many years of the rest of her life.

"...and we can go tomorrow morning to check out the museum, huh? I'm sure I'll know the dagger when

I see it, or feel it. It might not be in the museum at all, maybe just on the grounds." Rafe was there, taking her mug and stealing a swallow or two.

Amber cleared her throat, reached out and got her mug from Rafe. "The Denver Museum of Nature & Science opened a new exhibit yesterday." She inhaled, then let her breath out. "Pirates."

Rafe whooped and said, "Aarr!"

"It's aimed primarily at children." She tried to sound stern. But he picked her up and swung her around and she thought he was gaining strength, too. His magic was certainly leaking more from under the confining rune. Her mug tipped and fell from her grip.

And Hartha was there to catch any coffee that streamed from the cup, and Pred caught the mug, and Tiro crossed his arms. They all looked at her and Rafe with sad and brooding eyes.

She and Rafe arrived at the museum ready to view the pirates exhibit along with forty children and a few patient teachers. Since the exhibit was actually the salvage of a pirate ship, the first thing Amber saw as the escalator rose to the third floor was a large thing that looked like a meteorite with a trickle of water running over it. As a fountain it wasn't very good.

She went over to look at the hunk of iron, delaying their entrance until the children were all seated in the movie program. The mass was a concretion, objects from the ship becoming embedded in sand, rock and whatever else might be lying around on the ocean floor. After three hundred years, they'd all cemented together. Above the concretion were digital X-rays of items that had been discovered in the conglomeration…gold dust, pistol balls, coins. Most of the lump was a dense gray, hiding other treasures.

"The film's starting." Rafe hustled over, frowned at the lump of stuff, twined her fingers with his and took her away.

She and Rafe didn't do museums the same way. She was still in the first room, studying every artifact and reading information on the slave trade and the building of the ship, when he came back to her and muttered, "There isn't one knife in the exhibit."

"No?"

He rubbed the back of his neck. "The closest thing I saw was an iron spike and it's too small." He looked at a picture of a boat stacked with bodies—slaves—and then glanced away.

"The museum is a big place, and this exhibit is late seventeenth and early eighteenth century, certainly not having the oldest artifacts in the place."

"We passed a T-Rex on the way in," he grumbled. "That's plenty old." Then his face lightened with a smile and he patted his jacket over the pocket that held his small dowsing stick. "The big guy didn't do anything for me."

"You went through this place pretty fast, did you try—"

He lowered his voice. "The kids' energy messes me up. It's too volatile."

"Then why don't you actually look at the exhibit and the artifacts? I think it's fascinating so far."

Rafe grunted. "And this is just the slave part. The pirate stuff is better, they have mock-ups of one of the decks and the back cabin. Not to mention the dark room with water and lightning when the ship goes down." He shuddered. Then he angled to see the portraits of the pirate crew—all good-looking men of different races, an artist's conception of how the individuals might look. They appeared pretty damn romantic to Amber.

"Pirates," she said lowly, hopefully temptingly. "Arr. This is your best bet to get easy, accurate information on pirates for the rest of your—" She stopped. She'd actually forgotten.

They stared at each other. She narrowed her eyes, spoke even lower. "Your...disability...is being over-shadowed by your gift. At least to me." A knot in her stomach twisted tighter as she admitted to herself that *he*—his energy and magic and strength—was so much more overwhelming to her than the curse. Was it as deadly? She was sure of it, but she didn't sense it as much as she did the simple presence of her lover.

He angled and kissed her mouth, a fast press of lips, then those lips smiled. "It's getting lighter, isn't it? My *disability*." His brows went up as punctuation of his pleasure. He lifted his arm and flexed a biceps. "I'm training, feeling better." Again he patted his pocket. "In many ways."

"Go pay more attention. I bet that if you stood near the entrance, they'd let you get one of the kids' audio treasure-hunt deals."

"Yeah, yeah. The treasure looks good." Again he

glanced around and his shoulders twitched. "This slave stuff is hard, though."

"Very hard."

"Tell me my guys weren't into this."

"What?" she asked.

"You've seen my ancestry time line." He jutted his chin at a dated information board. "We came over to the new world pretty early. Tell me they didn't do this sort of thing."

She hadn't studied his time line, but had recognized a few prominent names in it and could give him a truth. "I'm not an expert in the slave trade, but I never heard the name Davail in connection with it, and I've done quite a few traces that have bumped up against it. Anytime I work for a black family, it's pretty much a given. But I'll send an email to one of my contacts to make sure."

"Appreciate it." His mouth went grim again. "We were too busy living with the curse. Felt too trapped by our own circumstances to want to trap others."

"That might be."

He lifted and dropped a shoulder, stared at her. "I suppose you're going to take your time here."

She *hated* being rushed in an exhibit. "Yes. But the Egyptian mummies are right down the hall and we passed the gems and minerals gallery when we came in, you can look through there, too. It's a pretty day. We'll walk around the building outside, just in case your lost item is there."

"Uh-uh." He touched her cheek with tenderness. "I can stick. Folks think I can't, but I can and I will."

"All right."

She read every plaque, looked at every object. The next time she caught up with him, he was hunkered in front of one of the cannons, peering down the muzzle. Now that she studied him, there appeared to be a pallor to his skin. He stood when she drew near, flipped a hand at the exhibit around her. "This didn't end well for anyone."

A woman gave them a dirty look as if she still hoped the pirates could escape doom.

"Shipwreck and lawless pirates," Amber said. "No way there could be a good ending."

Rafe took her fingers. "The historians make the case that there was more democracy and equal rights on the pirate ships."

"Uh-huh," Amber said. She stared at him, then shook her head. "No, I can't see your family as slave traders." She lifted her brows. "I could as pirates."

He laughed as she'd meant him to, and when they went to the next room, he had more of a swagger in his step. But her words were all too true. Most of the pirates were men with nothing to lose.

By the time they were in the last room and staring at more concretions in aquariums, she was feeling a little depressed. No good ending for anyone except the salvager and history buffs. And their trip had been a bust, too.

They spent most of the morning at the museum, and Rafe picked up a brochure that showed the floor plans. He bought some iron pyrite, fool's gold, for Amber as well as some fake doubloons for both of them and a book on the exhibit. They walked through the galleries and around the building until the wind came up and they returned to the car where Sizzitt was stretched on the dashboard, looking like a plastic figurine from an animated fantasy film. None of them talked on the way back, and Rafe dropped Amber off at home, then went on to the lyceum. Amber ran with the dogs, played with them, sent emails out on things she had to check, including Rafe's question about the slave trade and her own curiosity about pirates.

She spent some time reading information on the Third Crusade in the twelfth century from scholarly volumes she'd loaded on her own tablet, then took the dogs for a walk down to the Sensitive New Age Bean.

The pups loved hanging out on the sidewalk and watching other dogs walk by. And they were trained well enough to focus on her inside rather than every passing, waving tail.

As soon as she got her coffee and turned toward the inner rooms, she sensed it.

It was just a little curse.

A cough.

CHAPTER 22

THE COUGHING CAME FROM A YOUNG woman Amber had often seen studying at that round table, big books open and scattered around and stacked atop each other.

Another cough, this one deeper in the chest, and longer.

Amber sensed that if the cough wasn't taken care of, it would develop into something worse, something that could harm the girl for her entire life.

She should be in bed, not studying and abusing her body. Determination radiated from her.

Amber hesitated. But again there was a change for the worse in the balance. Right now the curse was small, but she felt it would become cumulative the more the girl fought it. And it was not a curse that had been laid with words and intent by someone with a lot of magic. That would make it easier to break.

Someone with a little gift had thought ill thoughts at the girl before her. Literally.

With a curse this small—minor with growing consequences—only her strongest bonds with others would be affected, the golden ones with the pups. Right now, thankfully, her connection with Rafe was in flux, sometimes strong, sometimes vanishingly thin. And the dogs were in close proximity, too. That added. She'd have to close those links down as much as possible so she took the greater hit.

She wasn't too surprised to see a small thread between herself and the girl...the medical student. Amber had spoken to her a couple of times, even shared a table when the coffee shop was packed. She didn't think the girl recalled her name, and Amber didn't remember hers, which was unusual because Amber liked knowing people and their names, whether she might have seen such names on any of her charts. But the student's escaped her. The bond she had with the young woman would help in lifting the curse, not harm. When the curse was lifted, there would be no backwash of aging to the student.

If Amber were going to break the curse, best do it quickly. It wouldn't cost her or the puppies much. Not enough to show.

And if she visualized her bonds with her dogs, as she'd learned to do much better in the last weeks, she could pinch it down to a thready mouse's whisker. Take most of the aging consequences herself.

She glanced around the coffee shop. No one was paying attention to her. She moved so she was blocked from the view of everyone except the coughing student, if she turned around. Amber set her mug of coffee down on a table and spread the fingers of both hands stiffly, reached for the little patch of mist floating in the girl's chest and yanked, quick and hard.

The mist stretched, thinned, snapped and vanished. A huge cough racked the girl.

Amber felt all the cells in her body sag a little, a draining of her vitality, a bit more energy that was gone forever. Then a feeling of euphoria welled through her, and a lightening of the atmosphere around her, of the girl's spirit, as the curse was broken and the shadow of it on her life lifted.

Going over to the student, Amber asked. "Are you all right?"

The young woman leaned back and wiped her sweatshirted arm across her beaded forehead, gave a soft groan. "Guess this will teach me to be more compassionate."

"What?" Amber asked.

With a weary smile, the student said, "I had a friend who was sick a whole semester and couldn't get her work done. I helped her, but wasn't nice about it." Another small smile that included a hint of self-disgust. "I really didn't get it."

"Get what?"

"That she could only do so much because she was sick."

"She was doing the best she could," Amber said.

Nodding, the young woman pulled out a tissue and honked into it. "Now I know."

A tingle started in the soles of Amber's feet, whisked up her whole body, and *she* knew. That had been the release for the curse. For the woman to understand what her friend was going through. Her sick friend had had a touch of magic to bind the girl.

"Are you still friends?" Amber asked.

"Not so much. She transferred out of state, is taking it easier at a less competitive school." A pause. "Better for her, I understand that now. Guess I'll email her an apology, though."

"Always good to stay in touch with true friends." But were the two of them that close? Not Amber's problem and she shouldn't interfere. She already had, and had used her major magic to break a curse, when just talking with the girl would have done that—hit the release point.

Hell. She rubbed her temples.

"I just can't do this," the girl said. Shaking her head, her bloodshot eyes went to the heap of books on the table. "All I see is spots. No way am I going to do well on that test." She thumped the big volumes shut. "I'll just have to crash and phone the prof and schedule a makeup."

"Someone will help you."

"Yeah, guess so. You have." She smiled up at Amber and this time it was unshadowed. Then she took a deep breath, let it out easily. "And I think I've turned the corner on this cough." She eyed the books with yearning. "I really wanted to master that material. No use pushing it, though."

"No," Amber said. She'd pushed it, as always. When if she'd waited...

"Thanks for stopping by," the girl said. "You made me see something I hadn't before."

Was that the curse-breaking power? Had Amber helped? She didn't know. Would never know.

The girl stood with a groan and loaded the books into her backpack, shook her own head. "I still like heavy texts. Maybe I'm addicted to the smell of high-lighter. See you."

"Yes," Amber said. She took a seat at the table and dropped her head in her hands. She'd helped. She should feel better about that. Instead she just questioned herself. Maybe she should become a counselor.

She didn't want to be a counselor.

The puppies were as frisky trotting home as when they'd come. Amber was wearier. She broke open her emergency stash of herbs and tea and made up drinks and a four-egg omelet using the herbs. She treated the dogs to their special wet food and fresh water. Smiled as they gobbled down their food.

Tiro tromped up the stairs and scowled at her. "I knew this would happen." He whistled to the pups, pointed to their beds. The dogs went to them and Amber reached into her pocket for treats to reward each of them. They crunched cheerfully, tails wagging. When they were done, Tiro waved a hand and they fell asleep.

"You broke a curse," he said flatly. "This was a stranger. How do you think you will resist helping the walking dead man, Rafe?"

Amber shuddered, then jutted her chin. "I'm learning new ways of breaking curses all the time. *Without* any help from you."

"Even with the dagger and the shield he won't kill Bilachoe. Maybe if he'd had more time to train, but he doesn't." Tiro's shrug had his shoulders rising all the way up to his ears. "Good thing you're the last of your line, I'll be free before I know it."

"I thought you were going to be nicer."

"You hurt those dogs."

"Not much. They didn't age any more than they would have if they'd stressed at a vet appointment." Her lips thinned and she scowled back at him. "Despite little help, I'm getting better at gauging bonds."

He snorted, angled his sharp chin upward. "You have four new gray hairs. Better use that rinse in your bathroom cabinet before loverboy comes back."

She flinched.

Tiro continued, "As for bonds. I don't think you know as much as you think." His lip curled and he looked her up and down. "You've picked up bonds with every Lightfolk you've touched since I've known you."

"Really?" That was interesting.

"You don't even know whether that's good or ill. Time for harsher measures," Tiro said, grabbing her hand. His was small and rock-hard. Darkness spun around her and cleared to night as her soles hit cobblestones.

"Where are we?" she asked.

"I transported you to the docks."

"Denver doesn't have docks."

Tiro grinned and it was a taunt more than anything else. "We aren't in Denver. Not even in the Americas." He dipped his fingers into a pants pocket and came up with a grubby-looking nutlike thing and shoved it into her hand.

"What's this?"

"Illusion and language spell. Temporary."

She sniffed it, smelled a little salt and a whole lot of dirt. But since she was curious, as always, she popped it into her mouth and chewed. Salty dirt, not terrible, but not good.

With a sweeping gesture, he indicated an inset doorway. The windows on each side of the door pulsed neon ads, probably for liquor.

Amber walked toward the door, and as she reached for the handle she saw her hand…looking old and wrinkled. She drew in a harsh breath and the scent of alcohol-saturated air. She was walking into a bar. She wasn't sure what was coming, but she reckoned it would be challenging, so she braced herself as she pulled the door open.

She stepped in to smoke and liquor.

And curses.

The place was alive with curses. Small ones, great ones. Ill wishes and generational curses. Curses that were actually layered upon a person.

Amber blinked and shook her head so she could see through the smoke. It was a small bar with shabby people sitting at the counter and in the three booths. Weary, hopeless despair hung as thick as the smoke.

"What is this place?"

"A bar where the cursed congregate," Tiro said. "Not many of these places. Bars might have one cursed soul, but not many."

Amber hadn't known that. She didn't spend much time in bars.

"I found this one especially for you."

At first no one paid any attention to her, and none of them noticed Tiro. The people might be magically cursed, but were too apathetic to strain to see magical beings. She was drawn to the center of the bar, felt magic under her feet. "What's this?" she murmured to Tiro.

He hopped onto the bar and sat, legs dangling, then grunted, "Special old sacred space."

She didn't ask sacred to what religion or culture. He wouldn't answer. Her gift seemed to lighten as if it were truly a sparkling magic she could use easily with no horrible consequences. If the burden of curses were also lightened here, no wonder people came and stayed.

Even with the nut the language was distant and garbled around her, but sounded Slavic. When the bartender spoke directly to her, the words seemed to hang outside her ear for a second, then pop as if through a barrier and into English. Tiro magicked a foreign bill onto the counter and a beer was served to her in a chipped pottery mug. Amber didn't actually touch it.

"Haven't seen you before," said a morose man with skin drooping on his face as if he'd been healthier and fatter. His curse was easy, the cure for it floated as a nearly tangible image before her.

"You don't look like you've been here long, either," Amber said. She meant to smile but a cackle emerged from her mouth. "I bet if you returned that thing you took, your hardships would go away."

He stared dark and long at her. "You think?"

"Yeah. I do." That, too, came out differently than she'd anticipated. With more force. The man wiped his hand over his mouth and nodded, turned and strode out of the door, his shoulders set with purpose.

Tiro snorted.

An old toothless man grabbed her hand and said, "I'd give anything to have me Phyl back."

Just like that, Amber *knew*. She saw the counter for his curse. Bending down and ignoring the guy's breath, she said, "You don't drink as much as you did, right?" The words changed from English to something else midflow.

"Nay. I drink not at all." He lifted a mug and sloshed the liquid around. The bite of peppermint came to Amber's nose.

"Tisane," he said. "It's hard to be around liquor, but it no longer tastes good t'me and I got me willpower." He tapped his temple with a gnarled finger. Then he looked around with a brooding gaze. "But these be m'friends. I don' know where else to go."

"Your lady had a little magic…"

"Always knew that."

"When she sent you away, she was thinking of the conditions of when you could come back."

The man's shaggy brows went up. "Eh?"

Amber licked her lips, then wished she hadn't as the taste of smoke and ashes and unhappiness lingered on her tongue. "She likes daisies? What if you brought her daisies and told her you loved her every day for a fortnight?"

His mouth moved soundlessly and his eyes filled. "Couldn't be so easy."

"No? Why don't you *try*." A wind of irritation whisked through her. She might be too soft, but at least she was *trying*. Trying to help herself and others. As soon as Rafe had accepted his curse, and heard of a way he might beat it, he'd set his mind on doing his best to break it. Neither one of them had given up. But here there was little hope and no attempt to change themselves or their circumstances.

She shouldn't judge. She'd been blessed, not cursed. She had no idea what these people had confronted. But she met the old man's eyes. "You have willpower? Show your Phyl. Go back to your wife and your life. Every day is new."

He shook his head, but shuffled from the place.

Tiro gargled and choked and she turned to see that he was so close it might even appear as if she were drinking the beer instead of him. He set the mug down with a clatter, his eyes narrow. "You used your curse breaking to *see* but not to lift. None of the others—"

"None of the others lived in Mystic Circle, had a lot of brownies for friends, did they?"

"None in such a place as Mystic Circle." He looked around the sad room, lip curling. "I don't see anyone else coming up to you for you to help. And those two that left. You think they'll follow through on their intentions?"

"I don't know, but I helped them, and the more I know about my gift, the more I can help. My ancestress studied our magic, too, didn't she? When I get her journals, I'll know more. Even if you don't help me."

"You can't tell me that you don't itch to remove every curse from every person in this place."

She lifted her brows. "Actually, I can." Her glance went to a dark corner. "A couple of these people are evil." She wouldn't say that they deserved their curses, but she didn't want to be in their company to see who had cursed them for what deeds.

"Let's go." Tiro's fingers went to her wrist. He still sounded grumpy, as if his lesson hadn't been fully appreciated.

The lesson Cumulustre had wanted his daughters to learn: not to cure others at the cost of draining themselves. Instead, Amber had begun to *see* the release of the curse when she looked at people. Another option for her.

She glanced at the door. She would really like to know if she'd at least helped the two she'd spoken to, but doubted Tiro would let her know.

"Don't you want to help more?" Tiro sneered. "Isn't there someone whose curse you feel compelled to break?"

Amber couldn't deny it. "Yes." She looked at a corner with a sad old woman who was drinking steadily. She'd driven her family away before she'd learned her lesson to be gentle with others and less selfish. The curse layering her was to be cutting and shrewish, see people only as they related to herself...until she lost her beauty, which her actions worked upon. Now she yearned for her children, but had no way to find them. This was a generational curse like Conrad's.

Amber had to set her feet solidly on the ground, make sure they didn't move so she wouldn't help the woman. If she helped the woman, she would drain herself and the puppies. The puppies and Rafe needed her. Her own self needed her to be more aware of the magic that she was using. *She* deserved to be considered first. If she helped the woman, she wouldn't recover in time to help Rafe if he needed it. Oh, she was pulled to the woman, to others who needed her, but... "I need to care for myself *first*. I am deserving of my own help and love."

Tiro stared at her. Then he grinned and wrapped his arms around one of her legs and they were gone from the bar and back home, carrying the odor of smoke and liquor and despair.

And hope—that she *was* learning what she should.

Then they'd arrived back at her beautiful clean and welcoming home, joyfully greeted by the puppies. She sank to the ground as they licked her and tumbled around her.

By the time Rafe returned, flush with triumph that his instructors had pronounced his progress "amazing," and detailing a couple of the fights, Amber was pretty much back to normal.

Sizzitt flew straight to the kitchen island and siphoned one of her bars up in a melted stream.

"She's not a big talker," Rafe said, cocking an eyebrow in the firesprite's direction. "And she really doesn't like me or humans." He shrugged.

Tiro stumped in and grunted, "Why should we like humans?"

"Why should we like brownies?" Rafe said.

"Brownies are useful," Amber said. They were fascinating, too, and so was the firesprite.

"We are beautiful," Pred said, appearing, along with Hartha. The smaller male brownie rubbed his hands and dirt scaled off them that Hartha vanished. "We are progressing well on the wheel of tunnels under Mystic Circle." Pred slanted Amber a glance and his nostrils flared. "There are wonderful smells coming from Tamara Thunderock's place, but she was not home and we can't go there unless we are invited."

"Why not?" Amber asked.

All of the brownies' ears rolled down to their heads. "The dwarves treated her badly."

That made no sense to Amber and she was about to ask more when Hartha summoned a wonderful-smelling dinner—chicken and dumplings and bread still warm from the oven.

"You do not have the dagger," Hartha said.

Rafe frowned. "No. I *know* it's in the museum, but I couldn't find it. Too much distortion from other stuff and the kids."

"Mystic Circle is mostly balanced energy that makes

working magic easier, and the neighborhood, too," Hartha said.

"I learned that," Rafe said. "I might have to take the big dowsing rod in, and I don't know how I'm going to do that. But I brought the brochure with the floor plans in case I can use the little dowsing stick like I did last night."

"I don't know how you're getting anything out of the museum. Unless you can draw it here?" Amber asked.

"Not going back into that game. It's dangerous," Rafe said.

Amber nearly choked on her food. "And just living here isn't?"

"Not in Mystic Circle," Tiro said. As usual, his dishes transferred into the dishwasher. He rose from his chair and stared at Rafe. "I like living here. You bought a house here, right?"

"Number two," Rafe said. He made a face. "The Fanciful House, the pink one."

"Your manhood would not be diminished by living in that house," Amber said. "And you can paint it."

"Huh," Rafe said.

"I'd like my chocolate dessert now," Pred said.

Amber looked at Hartha. "Chocolate isn't actually addicting to Lightfolk, is it?"

"No more than to humans," Hartha replied comfortably, taking care of the empty bowls. "We do not have access to it much. Soon we will not want it every day."

Pred sniffed.

"I have more pudding," Amber said, going to the refrigerator. She'd attached a silver chain around the handle.

"Good. I like pudding best," Pred said. "And we worked hard on tunneling today."

"Can I point out that that's illegal?" Amber said.

"We replaced your intake water pipes," Tiro said, once again sitting at his table, anticipating his pudding. "You should have better water pressure."

"Great!" Rafe said.

"Thank you," Amber said politely. They'd saved her thousands, not to mention the lack of mess and any worries about whether the pipes went under the blue spruce in her backyard. Making chocolate desserts for the brownies and keeping them in candy bars for the duration was cheap at the cost.

"Humans won't notice," Tiro said with disdain.

Amber plunked down the pudding before the brownies and put a bowl of mixed fruit before Rafe and herself, then nodded at the pamphlet with the museum floor plans unfolded on the table, and Rafe's computer tablet beside it. "You're sure you want to go back to the museum instead of into the game? Have you checked the game lately? Since you've already mastered what needed to be done, at least mostly?"

Rafe's spoon, with a hunk of melon, stopped on the way to his mouth. "No, I haven't." He glared at the computer. "I have problems touching that."

"Uh-huh," Amber said.

She drew it over to herself and turned it on. The screen showed a fading icon for *REAL* Fairies and

Dragons by Pavan. Rafe let out a sigh of relief, then leaned forward to peer at the tablet. "What's that?" He gestured with his spoon. Amber finished the blueberries she'd saved for last and looked at the computer. There appeared to be a new icon, faint, as if the computer application hadn't quite loaded.

"Something's there," she agreed. "Just not ready for you yet."

He grunted and sounded a lot like Tiro. Rafe pushed the computer away and held out his hand. His miniature divining rod, which had been in his jacket pocket on the clothes hook in the entryway, flew to his fingers. He moved a little, distributing his weight as if for a fight—or he was also developing a sense of how to use his personal magic. So much more fun than her curse breaking, with little in the way of cost but energy. She swallowed bitter envy.

Flipping the stick in his fingers, he smiled at her and she forced a smile back. "Yes, magic is a whole lot easier in Mystic Circle."

She stared at Rafe's computer. She actually *saw* little motes of magic vanish into it. Had Pavan modified it to run on that meld-magic stuff?

Now that she thought of it, she hadn't seen Rafe plug the pad in to charge since he'd been here, and it usually sat on the coffee table in the living room.

Rafe's chest expanded as he inhaled, a little line appeared between his brows, and he held his tiny dowsing rod over the map of the museum.

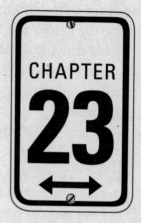

CHAPTER 23

AMBER STARED AT RAFE, WHO'D DEFINITELY gone crazy. "Break. Into. The. Museum."

"We just need to find the dagger." He gestured to the brochure with his miniature stick. "We have a map...a treasure map."

The idea of breaking into the museum made her sick. "This floor plan is general. We need exact blue-prints. Plans on how to avoid alarms—light and motion and weight and whatever."

Rafe made a disgusted noise and tapped the end of the rod against the paper. "The dagger isn't on the first floor." He flattened the pamphlet and held his small rod over the second floor. Again the stick swept the plan with no stop or hesitation. After a sharp breath, he shook out his arms, drank a sip of coffee, set the cup down and moved the paper again. His shoulders set and his eyes went out of focus. She could almost see him calling his magic, gathering the bit that seeped out from under the binding spell.

This time he went slower, following the path they'd done in person up the escalator to the third floor. The small stick halted and quivered right outside the pirate exhibition.

"What? What's here?" he asked, looking at her.

"It's the first concretion," Amber said. "I was reading the placards as you were following the school children into the small theater."

"That big conglomeration of stuff. Didn't it have X-rays, though?"

"Not all of it. The center was dark, so maybe you manifested the dagger right into it."

"Someplace very protected," Rafe said.

"That it is. Why couldn't it be on the grounds outside? I'm not sure how to do this." She waved a hand.

He set his stick down and caught her hand, gave her fingers a quick kiss. "I am. That dagger belongs to me. I can get it. With magic."

They crowded around the table. Rafe stood, Amber sat and the three brownies stood on chairs, watching him.

Rafe tapped the floor plan again. "This is where the Cosmos Dagger is. I think with all our magic, we can get it out."

But Pred and Hartha were shaking their heads.

"Think of it as a challenge!" Rafe cajoled.

"It is bad to go into big human buildings with scare-aways," Pred said.

"Scare-aways?"

He made a high, pulsing sound like an alarm system. "Oh."

Tiro snorted. "I'll go. You'll only need me and Sizzitt." His lip curled. "Amber can stay, as well as the Mistweaver brownies."

"I'm going with you," Amber said.

"I'd rather you didn't," Rafe said.

Amber stared at him. "You don't want me to come?"

His lips curved but his eyes were dark and serious. "Let's face it, breaking and entering is a crime. Especially museums with heavy alarm systems. I don't know how to do it. I'm thinking more of a smash-and-grab. I'd rather you aren't involved. You can post bail if I'm caught."

The Mistweaver brownies vanished without a word, leaving dust in the air and a hint of fear in the atmosphere.

She narrowed her eyes and pressed her lips together. "I don't think so." Tilting her head, she said, "You're sure you don't have any friends…."

"Conrad might have connections, but he's still in Eastern Europe and I don't want to talk to him about this. Too much explanation, and not on a cell phone or landlines."

As she held his gaze, she knew he was right. They'd gone on a journey together and far beyond the original project that she'd signed on for.

"All right. But I don't like it."

"You getting any bad feelings?"

She huffed. "I usually only get feelings about the past. No. You can't depend on me for premonitions."

Rafe sent her a look from under lowered brows. She matched his stare until he let a slow breath out. "If you insist on coming..."

"I do." She didn't want to, but she wouldn't let him go alone and she was sure she could help.

"You got any ideas?" he asked.

"For breaking into the museum? Nada." She shook her head. The very idea made her insides quake. She was a law-abiding person. She didn't even *like* caper movies.

"No pointers like you had about how to play Fairies and Dragons, or how to sense magic with a dowsing rod?" He twirled his stick in his fingers.

"Rafe, the game isn't real."

His face hardened briefly. "Felt real enough to me."

She shrugged.

"I *do* have an idea for the museum," he said.

She shifted in her seat. "We know nothing about its security or breaking in!"

"Nope. But I bet everything runs on electricity, even any backup systems. Sizzitt, you want to play with electricity in a big, big building?"

Sizzitt flashed in a streak of red, sat on the wick of the thick candle in the center of the table, flashing madly. "Yesss."

Rafe stared at her. "Can you cycle through electrical circuits and interrupt them?"

"Easssily!"

He raised an index finger at her. "Only interrupt all circuits for about, um—" he set his shoulders "—ten minutes? That will include the main electrical system and the backup." He glanced at Amber. "There's bound to be a backup, right?"

"Must be, and probably a separate generator, like you said, and the electricity is from solar panels."

"What?" Rafe blinked, grinned again. "It will be night."

Amber snorted.

"Tiro…" Rafe looked at him. Though the brownie appeared solid, his arms crossed on his chest, the tips of his ears quivered in interest. He'd already bought in to the scheme.

Rafe narrowed his eyes, as if not quite sure of the brownie. Amber kept her mouth shut. "Tiro, could you transport me to a large chunk of rock and sand and iron, here, and in complete darkness? Unlike all the other rocks in the museum, this one is being kept wet with a trickle of water. It's not submerged and it's not completely dry." Rafe tapped the map.

"I can feel such," Tiro said, jerking a nod. He raised his nose. "Darkness is not a problem in tunneling or transporting." Then he looked away. "But I can't transport you and me from here. We will have to be closer." His forehead wrinkled as he calculated. One shoulder rose and fell, then the other, and he spread his hands. "Can't transport you as far *there* as I could here in Mystic Circle. Maybe four blocks."

"Better to be close on site, then. Drive there. I'll need to release Sizzitt into one of the electrical lines going into the museum anyway," Rafe said.

Amber wetted her lips. "So Sizzitt can't run down, um, lines from here to the museum?"

"Yesss, I can!" Sizzitt said. For a moment fiery features appeared showing wild eyes and grin.

"She could take out all of Denver's electricity doing that," Rafe said.

"Yess!"

"Oh. I don't think that's a good idea," Amber said.

Sizzitt squashed down into a low, bright blue flame that Amber understood was irritation.

"Neither Sizzitt nor Tiro know Denver that well," Rafe said. "Not even as much as I do."

"So I guess I'll be driving." Amber frowned. "I think the best time to do this would be about 2:30 a.m. Do we know when end of shift is? I've read somewhere that it's best to hit a place then."

Rafe's brows rose. "No, we don't, and I don't think we should ask."

"There's plenty of traffic cameras between here and there, too," Amber said. "Maybe I should find a good route to minimize those."

"Amber," Rafe said quietly. "I want you to stay here."

"Nope. I'm your Denver expert."

"It'll be just a few minutes."

"If everything goes right. Everything doesn't go right in situations like these."

Rafe reached out and caressed her cheek. "It will be okay. What you need to remember is that we are taking *nothing* from the museum. I'm only retrieving an item I manifested inside the concretion."

"I don't get that," Amber said.

Rafe's turn to shrug. "Magic." He looked at the

shield. "Like that is." He walked over to the shield, set it at right angles to the wall. Brows lowered in concentration, he took the edge and to Amber's amazement, began moving the shield *into* the wall.

Her mouth dropped open.

With the shield about halfway in, Rafe began panting and sweat sheened his neck, hands and face. He released the shield.

Tiro walked up to the wall, then vanished inside it. Amber stifled an exclamation. Then Tiro was back nodding and rubbing his hands. "The molecules of the shield are between the spaces of the molecules of the wall. Well done."

"Ugh," said Amber, trying to picture that and not quite managing.

His mouth a flat line, Rafe wiped his hands on his jeans, then curved them around the edge of the shield and pulled it out of the wall, much more rapidly, turned the disk and leaned it back against the wall. He nodded to Amber gravely. "I can do this."

"In the complete dark, with guards patrolling? Don't you think the first thing they'll check is the special exhibit?"

A corner of Rafe's mouth lifted. "Don't know. I'd check the entrances first, myself."

"This is insane. We don't know anything about museum security."

"We don't have the time to learn. Quick and dirty, Amber." He smiled at Tiro and Sizzitt. "But I think we can do this. Take the electricity down. Transport to the concretion and hide in the shadows, pull out the dagger."

"Why can't you just manifest it from there to here?"

Rafe shrugged. "It's stuck." He frowned. "I think it got stuck when I manifested it from Chicago to Denver. My focus wavered or something, or maybe because we were in the game and not the real world."

Now Amber's arms were crossed over her breasts. "Crazy."

"Will you bail me out if we get caught?"

She closed her eyes. "Oh, my God. Even if you take out the electricity someone will call the cops. There's a police station near there."

"So we'll park at the farthest limit of Tiro's transporting skill. He'll take me there." Rafe zoomed his hand and whooshed. "Then back. Easy peasy."

"Oh, my God."

"Amber, honey. Honey, Amber…" His voice was low and caressing and he drew her up and into his arms. "It will work. What do you think, Sizzitt and Tiro?"

"What do I get for thiss?" asked Sizzitt.

"It will work," said Tiro. "We are Lightfolk. We do not accept human limitations."

Amber leaned against Rafe. His heart was thudding hard with excitement. She shook her head.

"Since this is going to be fun for you, Sizzitt, I don't think I should pay much."

"Two potss of chocolate a week, not one," she insisted.

"I should invest in a chocolate factory," Rafe grumbled. "Agreed, for seven months." He tensed as he said the words.

"Done!" said Sizzitt.

"We can do it tomorrow night," Rafe said. He looked at Sizzitt. "You can practice on the electricity here tomorrow." Then he gazed at Tiro. "Do you want to practice transporting? How much will it wear you out?"

Tiro shrugged. "I can transport you maybe four times."

"Good. We'll try once tomorrow."

With teeth gleaming in a smile, Tiro said, "Yes."

Amber didn't say again that she had a bad feeling about this. "We'll have to be careful."

Rafe's grin was quick and wide. He was enjoying the thought of the caper, already had an adrenaline rush going. "My middle name is 'careful.'"

"No, it isn't," Amber said at the same time as Tiro and Sizzitt.

Rafe raised his brows, smiling his pirate's smile again. "My middle name is Barakiel, the angel of good fortune."

She had nothing to refute those words but the curse and she didn't want to mention that. So she kissed him.

That night their lovemaking was urgent and panting and totally consuming.

Dawn had just sent light through her curtains when Rafe left the bed to run. Amber felt the mattress dip, then she slid back into sleep. A while later, the puppies bounded from the room and awakened her, still earlier than usual. Stretching her senses to follow her bonds with them, she found them quiet and in the kitchen, not eating. Their attention was fixed on something. Curious herself, she pulled on sweats and went downstairs to turn on the coffeemaker. She was on the second-floor landing when the rich smell of melted chocolate wafted to her nose. Smiling, Amber reckoned that the dogs were watching Sizzitt in the fondue pot. As Amber walked through the living room, sunlight hit the windows. She tiptoed through the dining room and stood on the threshold of the kitchen.

Sure enough, the dogs were sitting by the island, heads angled up. Amber could see the chocolate bubbling and boiling and—two?—glowing humanoid flames in the pot. She stared a few minutes before she realized they were mating. Then she couldn't tear herself away.

The dancing and melding and patterns formed were gorgeous. Not at all like random flames in a fire. She was mesmerized. And as she watched the two merge, there came a pop and spark and a minuscule white flare no larger than her pinky nail came into being.

Her throat closed in awe.

"Done! Good chocolate!" said a tiny voice. One of the flames shot away and three of the large bars of chocolate disappeared with it. The small white flame moved to the top of the larger yellow-orange one— Sizzitt.

"Get candless, big, sstupid human!" Sizzitt demanded. "The sspark and I need more food than thiss chocolate."

Amber ran to a cupboard in the pantry, got down her thickest candle with three wicks, set it in the curve of one arm and grabbed a few tea lights. She plunked them down on the island and arranged them.

Sizzitt and the white spark moved to the three-wicked candle, but the teeny white flare stayed attached to the larger flame. Zillions of questions buzzed in Amber's brain, but she didn't know enough about firesprites to understand what would be discourteous.

The front door slammed and a draft filtered through the house. Amber went to the island to block the air and Sizzitt stretched tall and laughed with crackles. "We are not sso weak to be blown out by open door air rush."

"Oh, excellent." Amber sighed as she saw the drying chocolate fondue and the caking in the pot. She reached toward the handle and stopped when she felt the bite of Sizzitt's flame.

"That iss *my* chocolate."

"I was going to clean—"

"We will usse every bit."

"All right."

"Something smells great," Rafe said. He walked in, bringing the odor of sweaty man. His T-shirt was stuck to him and his cutoff sweats unraveled even more along his thighs. Amber's pulse picked up.

"My chocolate," Sizzitt insisted.

"For sure," Rafe said and went to the coffeepot that had filled while Amber wasn't paying attention. He poured out a cup and leaned against the counter, savoring it. "So, Sizzitt, how went the mating?" He winked at Amber.

"I have a sspark," Sizzitt said. She withdrew an instant to show the bitty white flame. It wavered wildly and she expanded again.

"Cool," Rafe said. "I mean *hot*."

"I have done my duty," Sizzitt said. There was a fire snap. "It cosst me much."

"Three chocolate bars and a dip in the fondue pot," Amber said. She wondered if that was a fortune to the firesprite.

Rafe hid his smile behind his mug. "Yeah?"

Amber frowned at him.

"But my name iss no longer tainted. Family demandss much."

Rafe's eyes went distant. His mouth flattened. "Yes."

Amber let one of her questions tumble from her lips. "Can the spark survive on its own?"

"If ssomeone watchess it." A little pop that reminded Amber of a sniff. "Even a human might feed it. Better that fire Lightfolk help."

"Oh."

Clumping footsteps came from the basement stairs. Before Tiro put one foot farther than the last step, Sizzitt was there, hissing and flashing blue-white in his face. She'd left the spark alone on one of the tea lights. "You do *not* touch my chocolate! You do *not* touch my ssspark. If you do, I will tell Cumulusstre!"

Tiro flinched, hunched into his balance. His gaze slid to the kitchen island and the diminished stack of chocolate bars. His nostrils opened wide as he sniffed and turned his eyes toward the fondue pot. "Haven't touched your chocolate, have I? Won't. Won't harm the spark." He raised a palm outward. "By the first jewel."

Sizzitt flicked back to the tea light, gathered the spark, and blurred up to the wick on the large candle. Tiro shuffled along the far side of the room, lifted big eyes to Amber. "May I have some hot cocoa at least? Even that powdered stuff."

"Yes," Amber said and turned on the burner. There came a whispery "sssht" and the spark flew to the gas ring. Amber hesitated in putting the kettle on it.

Sizzitt added her flame to the fire. "I will heat water, then take the spark to the pilot light."

"All right," Amber said.

A mug with a huge heap of hot chocolate powder settled beside Tiro. "I can make it," he said. He jutted a chin at Rafe. "You stink."

Rafe raised his brows, went to the faucet and washed his mug, setting it to dry in the rack. "I would have thought that you'd be in a better mood after tunneling. Are you sure you want to go with us to the museum tonight?"

Tiro stamped his feet, his steps now sounding like rock grinding on rock, though he left no mark on the kitchen's wooden floor. "You can't do without me."

"Maybe not. Maybe I would contact Eight Corp again, or ask Tamara next door to do so." A green pasteboard card appeared in Rafe's hand and he flicked it with his thumb. "This is a nice magical artifact, loads of power. Bet I could write a message on it and send it to Pavan."

"He is very busy. He could not come."

"But someone might…"

"Wait, I remember," Amber said. "There's another brownie next door. One who's been disgraced, like Sizzitt. Sizzitt has found honor with us—" Amber waved a hand at the kitchen island and stack of chocolate "—and fortune. Maybe this other brownie could help clear his name by helping us."

"Break into the museum," Rafe murmured.

She tried not to think of that. She stuck out her chin. "Retrieve the Cosmos Dagger."

Tiro's mouth pursed. "The brownie serves the cat. You would have to get the cat's permission."

Amber slid her gaze to Rafe and saw he looked as if he felt odd, too. She continued smoothly, "I've often provided catnip for Chinook. I'm sure she might loan me her brownie for consideration, and he could have a good bounty, too."

Tiro shifted his feet and Amber saw a gleam in Rafe's eyes. They both knew they'd won.

"Maybe I want something more," Tiro said.

Rafe took up the negotiations. "Tell me."

CHAPTER
24

"I WANT TO LIVE HERE IN MYSTIC CIRCLE, with an uncursed human or two," Tiro said.

Now the amusement leached away. Amber felt her body's age and the curse shrouding Rafe. He nodded. "I've made a commitment to buy number two, the Fanciful House, and have feelers out to the owner of the Captain's house. I know my brother. If he came out here, he'd like the atmosphere and keep the house." Rafe paused. "He might be able to see you. In any event I can leave instructions that the place should not stand empty."

"A deal is made then," Tiro said, spitting on the floor and wiping it with his foot until it became a smear of mud. "I want more hot chocolate."

The kettle was hot and before Amber turned off the burner she checked on Sizzitt and the spark. Sizzitt shot from the flame to her three-wicked candle, nearly singeing Amber's eyebrows. Squinting, she could see a white glow in with the blue of the pilot.

"Sizzitt, I arranged for an early lesson at the lyceum." Rafe glanced at the kitchen clock. "In about forty-five minutes. Can you bodyguard me or should I cancel?"

"Sspark will be fine on pilot."

Amber said, "I'll be shopping." They were going through chocolate at an incredible rate. "What's the best kind of candle for spark?"

"Any will do."

"All right." Amber looked at the tea lights and the three-wick and decided that would be enough. Going over to Rafe, she pressed a kiss on his lips and took his hand. He smiled slowly. When they were near the stairs, she said, "How do you feel about shower sex?"

He picked her up and ran up the steps.

Later that morning, when Rafe and Sizzitt were practicing electrical interruption in her home, Amber drove to the museum and back. She checked on traffic cams and times. Not that there would be many people on the streets at 2:30 a.m., but more on a Friday night and early Saturday morning than a work-week night. Would that be better—more cars to blend in with? Or worse…slow them down? She didn't know.

Tiro accompanied her since he didn't know Denver and had never been to the City Park area. He hated the car. He crouched at the bottom of the passenger seat, holding a fluffy knit blanket that Amber recognized as being Jenni Weavers's that Hartha had provided.

Amber drove around City Park, where the museum and the zoo were located, and circled the drives and the parking lots a couple of times. Thankfully, they were full. Didn't security cameras work on a twenty-four-hour basis? Finally, Tiro gritted a "Let me out here." She stopped and noted they were at the end of a drive next to a streetlight. She got out as if to look at the flower bed. Tiro hopped out behind her, then sank, blanket and all, into the ground. Just before he disappeared, he said, "See you back at the house."

So, was he walking through the ground or what? She double-checked the area—no cameras in sight. Then she left, taking a circular route back home until she was sure they would be minimally tracked that night.

And Tiro and Sizzitt and Rafe were all cheerfully eating pieces of a three-layer chocolate cake when she returned. Rafe insisted that all would go smoothly. Amber just nodded and set every alarm in the house for 1:30 a.m.

Rafe was up first, and shut the dogs in his room. His gut was tight, but it wasn't telling him that something was dead wrong. Anticipation, yeah. Excitement, for sure. And finally doing something in the real world that might make a difference in his life, and the lives of his brother and that unknown cousin. The fencing practice was good, but it was just like mastering any other sport.

Magic, though, that was prime wild fun. The little tricks were nice, but this was the big one. Not just

breaking into the museum, but *manifesting* the dagger.
The dagger that could save his life.

He knew Amber worried, but as much as he lo—
Cared for her, she was a squishy. She wasn't used to
risking all to win all.

That was the only way he'd lived. Maybe he could
change...next year. That would be a challenge, too.

Amber drove the speed limit and took a route with
less traffic cameras on it than a direct one. She'd spent
fifteen minutes during the day artistically smearing
mud on her license plates. She wasn't a crime show
fan, but had picked up some stuff in her reading. She
only hoped the security outside the museum didn't
have infrared or something.

She parked, as they had planned, along the curve of
a drive near large trees bare of leaves, just outside of
the soft glare cast by a streetlight.

They got out. Rafe, with Sizzitt hovering near his
shoulder, and Amber closed the doors of the car with
soft *ker-chunks* that sounded as loud as shotgun explo-
sions. Or what she thought might be shotguns. She
didn't know those much, either.

Before her mind stopped dithering, Tiro was there,
rising out of the ground.

Rafe cupped his hands and Sizzitt settled between
his palms. "Remember, just the museum," Rafe said
in a tone that told Amber he'd been arguing with the
firesprite all day.

Sizzitt hissed anger.

Rafe lifted his hands as if throwing her and she sped

to the lightbulb on the post, went through the glass. A few instants later the lights went out. Not just at the museum, but those in the parking lot, too.

Holding out his hand for Tiro, Rafe nodded. "Let's do it."

Tiro clasped several of Rafe's fingers and they were gone before Amber could say "Good luck," or "Break a leg." She stared at the huge block of the museum in the dark.

Each second stretched long and agonizingly slow. Amber leaned against the car; they'd decided that Rafe would drive home—he was more likely to evade followers. She checked her palm computer for time about every five seconds. She tried to relax, but couldn't. Tried to soak up the quiet of the night, but even the slight breeze that crackled old autumn leaves sent alarm through her.

Wild scenarios exploded in her mind, leaving fragments of shrapnel. Sizzitt would blow out Denver's electrical grid and she and Rafe would both get caught and go to prison. Rafe would die there and she'd age rapidly as she lifted curses from everyone around her.

She began counting the fast and thudding beats of her heart.

The lights went out. With more of a swish than a pop, Tiro and Rafe were upstairs on the third floor outside the pirate exhibit. The brownie's grin was wide and his furry ears shook with excitement. He let go of Rafe's hand.

Voices called out, radios emitted static. Someone

was barking orders. The place was huge and the floors were open, so sound carried.

Even if Amber was right and the security force sent a man or two up to check out the special exhibit, Tiro had assured Rafe with brownie arrogance that they wouldn't be seen or heard or smelled or tasted.

Rafe resisted the urge to crack his knuckles. Tiro placed his hand on the concretion. It was wet and Rafe realized he was hearing the last trickle of water from the metal spout as it fell into the basin. The thing was also large and rough, it wouldn't take fingerprints.

Now it was his turn to use his magic.

He scraped every iota he had—he'd already discovered the entire amount he could access—and thought at the rock, focusing on it and not the movement and shouts echoing around him. He and Tiro were out of any path.

Manifest. He could hear the elf, Pavan, say the word and it, too, echoed, if only in Rafe's mind. He'd been watching the elf and could see those pale pink lips form the word. *Manifest.*

Something heavy shifted silently in the concretion. Yeah, the dagger was there. Pull? He tried. Footsteps marched along below. The escalators had stopped. He'd hear anyone come up, see the sweep of a flashlight. And, dammit, he'd lost the link to the knife with that little mind diversion.

Big breath in through the nose, quiet, count out an exhale through the mouth. *Manifest.* It was…there? He wished he'd paid attention to the concretion, the size and shape of it. Again, he lost the link.

"I can go have fun with the guards," Tiro offered.

"No."

Hurry up! That was Rafe's own nerves twanging through his head.

Hell. Breathe. Yesterday, he'd seen the shield go into the wall, the molecules between. So, *visualize.* Like he visualized a run, on snowboard or bike or motocross. Yes. Visualize the dagger. He'd dreamed of it all his life. There! There it was!

Almost as big as the concretion itself, and stuck with other objects.

Visualize magic fingers, an extension of his own, grasping it, pulling it out. Slowly, carefully.

"Heading up to the Phipp's special exhibit area now," a low voice reported.

"Still no signs of break-in, but police are on the way. In force," crackled a reply.

Hell!

Rafe was standing in the dark, ready to get caught, with a brownie hanging on to his jeans. This was almost as bad as in the game. Not quite as fun as he thought it would be. He was pumped with adrenaline, tipped on the edge of fight or flight response. Fight.

No!

Think back to the game and how he'd manifested the shield. He'd needed it.

Yes! That was the last key. *Need.* He needed the dagger. Now. It was his. Made for his line, the Davails. *It was his and he needed it so he could kill evil Dark ones, save those they'd harmed. Its purpose. His purpose.* Yes, sliding, sliding. Ignore the large round bright light stabbing up at an angle from the escalator. Trust Tiro to keep them in shadows. Only a big rock here, nothing of any value. Nothing easily stolen. Dude, go into the gallery and the exhibit, move on to the gold and the silver.

"All quiet. No activity. What's the power status?" the guard asked.

Rafe's blood was thundering in his ears. He was sweating and using a lot of magical energy. The dagger was sliding, sliding. Stuck.

The light flashed over him. He froze.

Need! I need the dagger. The beautiful Cosmos Dagger with blue universe and golden galaxies and stars. I need it. Its purpose and my purpose are one. It is mine! I need it now so I can go to my woman, my lover.

The hilt slipped into his hand with a burst of static electricity.

"What's that!" Running footsteps.

And they were out in the road, a few yards from the car and sweat was drying on his back and he could see Amber—sweet, serious Amber—waiting for him and he was grinning like an idiot and loping toward her.

He waggled the dagger for her to see. Tried to shift it. And found his fingers were clenched around the hilt and he couldn't let go.

What the fuck?

Rafe ran toward her, a wide grin on his face. His fingers were curved around the dagger. It looked a lot bigger than she'd expected. Tiro walked behind him, shoulders high, and scowling.

Tiro glanced back, yelled, "Evil guard attached to

dagger! Mist with eyes and teeth!" He vanished, and she didn't think it was to her house.

She could see it now, like a haze blotting out the museum. There *were* eyes, bright blue and scattered throughout the cloud. Winking with malevolence.

Rafe must have noted the horror on her face. He slowed to look back. He flinched and picked up speed, running too fast in the dark, depending on his natural balance. As he ran, she noticed a thin thread of black trailing like a line of flies from the hilt of the dagger extending from his fist to the shadowy menace.

"I'll drive," he yelled, heading toward the driver's side. As he reached for the handle he swore and opened his fingers, shook his hand. The knife remained against his palm. "Still stuck!"

He gripped the dagger, whirled and swept it across the line of mist. Even though it was sheathed, the air ripped with a high shriek. A fast exhale came from him. "It's gone for now, but I don't think it will take long…"

"Reforming as we speak," Amber said shakily. She jumped into the driver's seat and shoved open the passenger door for Rafe, started the car and drove to the lamppost where they were supposed to pick up Sizzitt.

"Sizzitt!" Rafe yelled. "Come help!"

The little flame reappeared in Amber's car lighter and the electricity of the museum blazed on, complete with alarms, behind them.

"Funzz!" Sizzitt crackled with laughter.

"Check out the evil guard—mist-with-eyes-and-teeth," Rafe said grimly. From the corner of her eye,

Amber saw his fingers flex open and closed around the knife that pointed down into the wheel well. Again he shook his hand. The knife remained.

Sizzitt scorched the ceiling fabric as she shot out of the car, then back. "Yess. Misst-with-eyess-and-teeth. Didn't ssee teeth yet."

"But they're there?" Amber's fingers clenched around the wheel. Her whole body was tense—she wanted to floor the car and zoom away. They were too close to the museum and would look guilty. She turned onto a street. It didn't appear like there were any roadblocks, thank heaven.

They hadn't gone through any doors. They'd stolen nothing. The guards would have reported that, she repeated the litany in her mind.

"Yess. It hass teeth. But it iss sslow and sstupid." Sizzitt sneered.

"No cops are following," Rafe said.

"Where iss Tiro?" asked Sizzitt.

"He left when he saw the mist," Amber said.

High fire-cracking-twigs laughter from Sizzitt, who flashed in and out of the lighter plug-in. Amber was sure the socket was ruined.

Heart in her throat, having to deliberately breathe, Amber drove and drove and drove. It should take less than a half hour to get home and they were hitting all the green lights.

But the mist-with-eyes-and-teeth still followed. The teeth gleamed white and dangerous and *many* in the rearview mirror.

Then she felt a bump and the car shot forward. "Shit."

"It's stretching a tentacle out to hit us," Rafe said.

The car slowed as if it were pulling something.

"And it looks like it's attached to the bumper," Rafe said. "But it's spreading out. Sizzitt, I know you hired on to guard me, but protect Amber first."

"Misst-with-eyess-and-teeth *nothing!*" Sizzitt shrieked. "I guard you, not Amber. Guard Rafe!"

Everything inside Amber went cold and hot and she found she was hyperventilating and steadied her breath again.

"We need to outrun it if we can. Get to Mystic Circle," Rafe said, as if Amber hadn't already figured that out. Did she dare speed? What happened if she got caught? The mist-with-eyes-and-teeth wouldn't care about cops, would it? Hurt them, too?

Another bump, this time lifting the car a foot and shooting it forward a few yards. Oh. Hell. No!

They hit the elevated portion of Speer Boulevard going thirty miles over the speed limit. And got bumped again. This time stronger, with more malice and intent. The evil thing was gaining, and learning, rapidly. Dread and panic zapped through her. The hair on the nape of her neck rose and her palms sweated. *Think!*

Another shove. Moving the car from the far right lane to the center. Good thing there weren't any other vehicles. Soon she wouldn't be able to stay on the street. Four lanes.

Buildings below. Then Park. River. Park. Highway!

Might survive going over the bridge to the river even with low water. The highway was always busy. Couldn't chance that.

She slowed. Rafe turned to stare at her but said nothing. The skin was tight on his face.

Then the car was airborne, speeding right over the guardrails, the median, the southbound lanes. Time slowed even as her heart pounded blood through her. She was dead. Rafe was dead. No need to worry about anything except how painful it would be and hope it was fast.

CHAPTER 25

THE STEERING WHEEL SEARED AMBER. SHE jerked her palms away. The seat belt burned a sash through her clothes. She turned her head to look at Rafe and the car was gone and she was falling and seeing flame eat it and the oil and gas ignite into a fireball and she curled fetal in the air and the fire ate at the mist, tangled together, fighting, consuming each other and Rafe yelled.

And she fell. And so did the fire and mist-with-eyes-and-teeth. Rafe's hands were on her. He shouted. His magic enveloped her and they slowed.

The car broke into tiny pieces.

The fireball and mist hit the water and spume and oily smoke sizzled and rose. And they died.

Sizzitt died. The bond between them ripped.

Amber plummeted. A few feet, jolted to the ground

atop Rafe and they rolled and he was up still yelling, did he not have to breathe? "Sizzitt!"

Her chest squeezed as she sucked air in and frozen fear broke around her and she was on grass by the riverbank. Hurting.

Pop. Pop.

Hartha was there. Pred.

Hartha's strong hands grabbed her arms. Amber's breath screamed out.

Hartha's face close. Only saw her face. Words slapped Amber's ears. "Spark is sputtering and dying. You must help! Pred will bring Rafe home."

Breath dragged in on darkness and shock and cold and Amber was home in her kitchen looking at the burners of her stove and a tiny streak of white in the blue. Barking came from upstairs where the pups were confined in Rafe's room.

"Help! Spark!" Hartha shouted.

Amber didn't know how.

"Search and link with a fire being!"

What? But her gift followed the demands. Her brain worked. A bond with the djinn who'd burned her, transported her. She *yanked* on the link.

Bellowing djinnman appeared in her kitchen. Hartha vanished. His face contorted with easy fury. "I will burn this place to the ground!"

Amber's dry lips cracked words. "Mystic Circle?" She stabbed her index finger at a burner. "Sizzitt died." That hurt. "Save Spark!"

He turned with inhuman grace, his predatory grin

seeming to linger in the air. "Little Spark small, good bite."

"Spark's life for chocolate on the island. You owe me for needlessly hurting me." Amber wasn't sure where the idea came from but it sounded good to her ringing ears.

He stretched and the fire in the burner rose high, the scent of rich chocolate filled the air along with wax and heated rock, and he was gone. Everything on the island was gone, too—chocolate, fondue pot, candles and all. The granite steamed.

"Amber Ssarga," said a high and tiny voice. Amber spun back to look at the stove.

The burner flame had diminished. Good. A firesprite larger than Sizzitt stood with Spark…in her arms?

"I wass called by djinn," the firesprite, female, said. "Sspark of the Csynder clan wass not well cared for."

"I'm sorry. I did the best I could."

The sprite's head bobbed. She seemed more defined than Sizzitt. More intelligent. Less selfish? Tears trickled down Amber's face as grief she hadn't expected flared within her. "There's a three-wicked candle on the dining room table." She swung an arm to point, realized she wasn't moving well. Shock? Adrenaline? The aftereffects of adrenaline and near death? She didn't know. The firesprite and Spark streaked from the kitchen into the dining room.

Amber swayed, bent her knees until she found her balance. That seemed to settle her brain in her skull, too. "I have a variety of candles. Let me get them."

"Besst would be handmade. Beesswax. Not big but long-burning with a sshort wick."

"There's a candle guy in the business district close by. I have some from him."

"I know thosse candless." There came pleasure and satisfaction in the firesprite's voice. "I vissit there ssometimess." A giggle like popping corn. "Closse to Mysstic Csircle and Jenni Weaverss, and balanced magic."

"Close to here," Amber said.

"Yess. All Lightfolk like Mysstic Csircle, major and minor."

Amber lifted one foot, then the other, got her body moving. She turned off the gas burner and walked to the pantry and the candle storage shelf. She took down a solid two-inch-tall and wide vanilla candle. When she reached the dining room the firesprite was standing on one of the wicks Sizzitt hadn't used, burning steadily, with Spark at the top of the flame, attached to the firesprite's "head."

A tiny "sst" came.

"Yes?" Amber asked.

"That wass Sspark," the firesprite said proudly.

"Wow." Amber was moving almost smoothly now. She set the candle near the larger one.

"You need a candle holder. To carry Sspark. It iss little and musst be watched. Sspark is lonely and could exstinguissh. Sspark iss too ssmall to ssurvive the disstances between candless in thiss housse. If Sspark iss with ssomeone not brownie, Sspark will be ssafe. Brownie is huge and earth-to-ssmother-fire and sscary."

"Oh. You aren't taking Spark with you?"

"Sspark hass bonded to thiss housse in Mysstic Csircle."

"Oh." Not to her mother, but to the place. Was that thoughtfulness or carelessness by Sizzitt? Amber didn't think the firesprite had anticipated dying, that guarding Rafe might be fatal. But she'd fulfilled her duty.

Loss. The first loss. Pain clawed at Amber's insides, all twisted because of the firesprite's death. Fear slicked Amber's gut. "I'll do my best by Spark." She hadn't known Sizzitt long, and hadn't considered the small being anything more than an acquaintance, but there was a hurt in her heart for the loss.

Amber limped into her study for a candle holder and a small trinket box. Spark was already on the new candle. Holding her breath, Amber lifted the candle and put it on the holder. Spark bent once, then remained steady. Opening the trinket box, Amber took out her largest "memory" ring, leaves of Black Hills gold in a large diamond shape, and slipped it on. She held up her hand. "This will remind me that I need to take Spark with me around the house."

"That iss good. All peopless of Mysstic Csircle are good."

Nice to know. Amber nodded dully. "I'll pay you for your trouble." She headed back to the refrigerator and the tall stack of large chocolate bars. When she turned to shout to the firesprite, she saw the tiny woman floating beside her.

"I like nutss in my chocolate."

"Almonds or peanuts?"

"Peanutss."

Amber slid a paper-wrapped bar from the middle of the stack, then wondered what to do with it. "The djinn took my fondue pot."

The firesprite beamed. "He sstill owess you. You gave him the chocolate but not the pot or the candless."

"That's right." Amber bludgeoned her mind. She was bruised and burned and Spark was safe, but what about Rafe? Fear shivered like an icy rain through her. Maybe it was the cold from the open refrigerator. Concentrate on the firesprite for now. "I have a little metal mixing bowl for your chocolate and you."

"I will vissit Sspark twice a day."

"Fine."

"Amber!" Rafe shouted.

Thank God! And he was still yelling.

The dogs went wild with barking again.

"In the kitchen," she called.

"Are you all right?" he shouted. He moved fast and was with her a few seconds after she answered, gripping her shoulders. She winced. She felt like she had a bad sunburn, at least on her shoulders. Weariness hovered over her like a storm cloud, soon to crash down.

He dropped his hands and shook his head. "Man, you're red."

"Guess so."

He reached into the fridge and snagged the milk,

dropping dirt with every move. Pred was there, too, staring at the inside of the refrigerator like it was the promised land.

Amber took three more bars and balanced a small glass saucer on the solid chocolate. "I have pudding." She'd made a triple batch.

She stared at Rafe. He was filthy. He shook his head and dirt fell from him. He grinned and pale lines appeared in his face as more caked soil dropped away.

"We took the scenic route," he said.

"The scenic route," Amber repeated. Soon her brain would be working on all cylinders, she hoped. That had her thoughts winging toward her…disintegrated… car. There were traffic cams on the lights along Speer. The crash had happened near the highway. Someone would have seen. Did anyone get the fireball on a phone camera? How long had the whole thing lasted, anyway?

"Pred and I transported in hops home," Rafe said. He smiled down at the small brownieman. "All the spots he knew between here and the Platte."

Pred folded his arms across his chest. "River is farthest Hartha and I go. Want pudding." But he didn't meet Amber's eyes and she thought he was lying.

Amber shut the fridge. Everyone moved and she went to the kitchen and prepared the new firesprite her treat. Amber peeled the paper off the bar, breaking it into pieces in the bowl and setting the bowl on the burner. The firesprite cackled with pleasure and dove in.

"You *are* all right," Rafe said.

"I think so." But she was beginning to yearn for a large tub of cool water.

"Better have Hartha check you out."

Just like that, Hartha was back. "How is Spark?"

Amber flinched, sped to the dining room. Spark was stretching and compacting, as if it were trying to gather enough magic to launch itself to the firesprite in the kitchen. "There now," Amber soothed. "We're here." She was tired but didn't know that she wanted to sit down. Hadn't the seat burned under her, too?

"Tssst," Spark said.

Hartha clucked and shook her head at Amber's charred and ragged clothes. "I have salve, and herbal burn-heal tea."

"Maybe something I could put in cool bath water?" Amber asked.

"Of course. I'll be right back."

Amber held out one of the chocolate bars to her. Hartha crossed her arms and frowned at Pred, then glanced back up at Amber, with eyes wide and her ears rotated back. "You should not think that we must be rewarded for everything we do. Friendship is not like that." She stared at the firesprite, then once again swung her gaze toward Pred. He shrank back a bit, but didn't take his stare off the chocolate.

"That's true," Amber said, and her words came slowly, slurring with tiredness. "But when friends help friends in a great way, tokens of gratitude can be offered." She wiggled the bar. Hartha took it and it disappeared.

The browniefem tilted her head back to stare at Amber. "I am your friend." Not a question.

"Yes, and I am your friend."

"Give Pred his pudding and the chocolate," Rafe said. He set the milk on the table, and tugged at a strand of Amber's hair. A clump came off in his fingers. "Ouch." He bent and feathered a kiss on her forehead. "Amber's had a rough night. She deserves quiet and a bath." His mouth curved. "You can leave the salve with me."

Amber looked him in the eyes and saw he was more revved than shocked. Of course. How many times had he cheated death over the years? This was just one more close call.

"You got the dagger," Pred said, staring at it in Rafe's fingers. "We helped."

"Sure did." He raised his hand and the dagger was still stuck to his palm. "I wonder—"

Then Tiro was there. "You're bonding with the Cosmos Dagger forged for the Davails after centuries of separation. Your bloodline has changed over the years."

"Bonding," Amber said. "Like superglue."

Rafe laughed and flung out his arms and the sheathed knife flew from his hand to the shield propped up by the living room fireplace as if it were magnetized. "I've got both items now." Triumph livened his tones.

"For sure," Amber echoed, then literally sagged with weariness.

Rafe's arm came around her upper back and she

whimpered with pain at the pressure. Hartha looked horrified, as though she'd lingered too long without helping Amber.

Amber gave Pred his pudding and a candy bar and Tiro a bar. Hartha vanished and was back with a steaming cup of tea that she put into Amber's hands. The outside of the mug was cold and Amber made a surprised sound. She drank a sip. Not too hot.

"I'll run your bath," Hartha said.

"Can you take care of the dogs? They're probably scratching the hell out of my door," Rafe said to Tiro. The brownie transported away and the pups quieted.

Holding his chocolate close, Pred hurried to Tiro's small café table with his pudding and candy, his small shoes leaving dirty prints on the floor. A spoon appeared in his hand and he shoveled the treat down.

"Thank you for helping us, Pred," Rafe said.

Pred paused and looked at them uncertainly, then his smile took up half his face. "Welcome." He sat back in the chair instead of hunched over. His small chest expanded with pride. "We did well." His glance darted to the dagger and the shield in the other room. "Very well. All of us."

"Yes," Rafe said. He swallowed hard. "Sizzitt died."

Pred shuddered. Hartha's shoulders lifted, framing her head, and her ears rolled down tight.

The new firesprite rose from the metal mixing bowl. Her voice was high yet even when she said, "Ssizzit honored her contract. Her name and tale will be renowned by her family. I will tell them. I will be back tomorrow." She flickered away.

Rafe's sad expression turned ironic. Amber couldn't help it, she sobbed.

"Finish your tea!" Hartha snapped.

Tears mixed with the liquid as Amber followed the order. The tisane didn't give her energy but her physical aches diminished. Her memory continued to flash images of her car exploding into a fireball, disintegrating. Of black mist and Sizzitt plunging into the water. Amber knew she'd dream of that for the rest of her life.

With a gentle finger, Rafe brushed a tear from her cheek. Her skin wasn't as sensitive, which was good because the tears had hurt.

"You're looking more pink instead of red," he said.

"Hartha is a very good healing brownie," Pred assured. "Made the tea and bath herbs quick and special just for Amber. Jenni never needs burn-heal."

"Because she's part djinn?" Rafe asked.

"Yes." Pred transported into the kitchen with his bowl, back to pick up his chocolate, then tilted his head. "I will help Tiro refinish your door upstairs. Glad you didn't die tonight, Rafe. Glad you didn't die tonight, Amber." He held out his hand to Hartha and the brownie woman took it and they vanished.

Amber leaned against Rafe. He smelled of sweat and dirt with a hint of green apples. "The caper's over and we did it."

He put both his arms around her, held her loosely and rubbed his cheek against her temple. "And it looks like we got away clean."

"I hope so. I don't think I'll report the loss of my car to my insurance, though."

"I'll get you a new one in the morning. I mean later this morning."

She was too tired to argue. "All right."

He tipped her chin up so their eyes met and she saw that magic still ran through him. "I have a chance now."

She didn't think he had a good one, but didn't say so, let her relief and happiness that he was alive and with her show instead, clamping her arms around him tightly. "I'm so glad we made it."

"Yeah." He trailed his lips across her cheek. "Wonder what a mist-with-eyes-and-teeth is."

"I'm just glad we didn't feel the teeth." Amber shuddered.

"Sizzitt died." And Rafe grabbed her close. She felt an inner tremor course through him, pass to her until they shook together.

Amber could scrounge up nothing more to say.

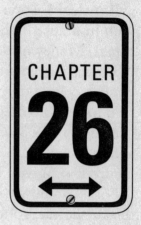

CHAPTER

26

THEIR LOVEMAKING THAT NIGHT WAS SLOW and gentle with an undertone of pure desperate need. They slept late, until eleven, then rose to be pampered by Hartha and Pred and Tiro with a good breakfast. The brownies seemed more cheerful, and Spark was strong and steady.

She cared for Rafe and the brownies and loved her dogs. And worried they might die like Sizzitt.

The news reported an electrical outage in central Denver and at the Denver Museum of Nature & Science, but commended the security staff and police for handling the threat. An inventory had been done and nothing was missing. A spokesman for the museum used his sound bite to pitch the wonders of the pirate exhibit.

Nothing was said about a fireball near Speer Boulevard and the highway. They'd gotten lucky with that.

Rafe had a newer model of her car delivered, along with insurance on his policy and title and registration papers. Money made a lot of things go faster.

Amber jogged with Rafe and the dogs around the circle a couple of times, knowing he held back, but he'd have more exercise when he went to the lyceum later. The more practice he could get in with the knife and the shield in the months before his birthday and a confrontation with Bilachoe, the better.

For a cooldown, the four of them walked around the cul-de-sac, Amber hand in hand with Rafe. This felt good and right. In her deepest heart, she wanted it forever.

More of her neighbors were in their yards and in a fit of enthusiasm, Amber began talking to them about a social get-together for everyone to meet Rafe, in a week, the next Saturday. Tamara offered to do most of the cooking and hold it in her larger backyard. Amber accepted, hoping that Jenni Weavers would be back by then.

So she was flushed and relaxed when they returned to the house, and even more at ease after shower sex.

After dressing in jeans and a blue shirt with three-quarter sleeves, she stopped in her office and booted up her computer. She'd been tracking down Rafe's distant cousin, who was also afflicted by the Davail curse, and thought she'd finally found him. He was descended from a third son who'd gone west with the trappers. The curse touched that family when the sons were close to the age of the men in Rafe's line, like some sort of oscillation.

Since the operating system software needed to be updated, she began that process and wandered downstairs to her consulting room where Rafe was scrutinizing the Cosmos Dagger and Shield.

She still hadn't gotten a good look at the knife, and Rafe was a little wary of touching it in case it clung to his hand as it had the night before.

They stood before the desk. The shield was awesome and the dagger was simply incredible. Holding her breath, she picked the knife up and felt a current of magic run through her fingers down to the soles of her feet, then bounce through her body to her head. She began trembling and Rafe put an arm around her. "Easy. It's not hurting you, is it?"

"No." She let herself sink into her balance. "Not exactly." Steady her hand. "It's just very powerful."

"I wasn't able to unsheathe it," Rafe said. "I figured if I put both hands on it, I'd be really stuck. Can you take the sheath off?"

She stamped her feet, hoping to rid herself of some energy and put the knife on the blotter just to show that she could, then lifted it again. Fingers curling over the grip, she took off the sheath with her left hand and put it down on the desk.

Unlike most knives she'd seen, the sheath was less gorgeous than the blade. The weapon itself was the length of Rafe's forearm and an elongated triangular shape, broad at the hilt and narrowing to a wicked point. Both edges were honed sharp. And the blade looked like the shield, blue with starbursts appearing and fading, but the edges were bright blue as if with flame or electricity. Beautiful and deadly.

"Wow," she said.

"Yeah," Rafe said. "It's light, too."

It hardly felt heavier than a good chef's knife.

There came a banging at the door and a loud *clunk*. The dogs raced from the kitchen to the door and hopped up and down, barking furiously. Amber glanced at the clock. "Postal carrier. I don't recall ordering anything heavy— Wait!" Her eyes widened. "I wonder if my ancestress's journals finally came."

"I'll go get them. Then you can study your books and I'll exercise with my weapons."

"In the backyard, without the dogs," Amber said.

"Yeah." At the door, Rafe ordered the dogs to sit. Amber turned to see the pups' butts hit the floor. He pointed at them. "Stay!" They wriggled but didn't leap to their feet or shoot out the door when he opened it. "Thanks!" he called in the direction of the carrier, and waved a hand before picking up a U.S. Post Office box and pulling the cardboard tab.

Just before he reached her and the desk, he seemed to stumble. The box fell, two books about eight by five inches and three inches thick fell out.

"Wha—" Amber stepped toward him.

Black smoke boiled from the box and filled the room. Stinking like rotting things, it pressed against her, sliding like grit over her skin.

Darkness fell. She saw nothing. She froze, afraid to move, not knowing where the others were. She saw nothing, could barely breathe, the dogs went crazy with hysterical barking. Rafe was yelling her name. Tiro was cursing like sharp rocks poking her eardrums. She was enveloped in black dust like a fog of coffee grounds. It hurt to breathe. She coughed.

No. Not fog. Blue eyes blinked. Mist-with-eyes-and-teeth!

This time she felt the teeth.

Sharp, snapping bites, eating her bare skin like acid. She screamed, her fingers tightened on the dagger and she brought it up and around, kept it close to her body and *slashed*. Again and again. The fog tore in swathes.

The edge of the shield and dagger sheath shredded the mist, too, wielded by a grim Rafe.

They fought.

Finally, the mist thinned, small holes turned into ragged patches, then portholes, then it was gone.

She was crying with pain and fear. Red and stinging bumps covered her arms, her neck and face. She opened her mouth wide, moaning each breath as her face swelled. Her fingers felt like sausages and she worried that her flesh would break her skin. Falling to her knees, she let the knife go. It slid into the sheath Rafe held. He dropped both shield and sheath on the desk.

"Hartha!" Rafe yelled. "Help!" He reached out an arm to hold Amber, then moved back. The dogs were circling a large pile of ashlike dust.

"Sit!" Rafe commanded, and they did.

The female brownie appeared, screeched like chalk on a blackboard, then held pale green stuff like seaweed in her hands. The next moment Amber's head and neck and arms were covered with cool and slimy compresses that soothed and numbed the sting.

"My God. Amber." Rafe's voice was thick. "What was that?"

"Mist-with-eyes-and-teeth," Tiro said. He kicked the dust heap and little pings and clatters came. To Amber's horror she saw small round objects, blue like the mist's eyes, roll from the pile. Bile swarmed up her throat and she forced it back, whimpering.

Rafe was there, sitting on the floor, his hands around her waist, pulling her back between his legs to lean against him.

"Mist eyes very valuable," Pred said matter-of-factly and gathered them up.

Amber could breathe through her nose again, so she shut her mouth and looked away until her roiling stomach steadied. The scent of burning sage made her glance back at the pile and she saw Hartha mixing the herb with the residue of the mist. Spark was dancing, a long and narrow yellow flame eating the sage leaves and dust.

"Came from the box," Pred said, and ripped the cardboard easily, adding it carefully to Spark's fire. The only thought that crossed Amber's stuttering mind was that she hoped the wooden floor would be all right. Hartha would probably stop Spark before it reached that.

"Attached to a book," Hartha said. She removed the drying seaweed from Amber and summoned more slimy fronds that Amber gratefully bent to have wrapped around her sores.

"But here in Mystic Circle we have balanced *good* Lightfolk magic," Pred said. "It could not live for long."

"Not to mention that Amber went after it with the Cosmos Dagger," Rafe said. He squeezed her middle. "Really good job." He kissed her head. "My heroine."

"Yes, the knife hurt it," Tiro said. "So did your shield and sheath."

"Tssst. Tssst. Ssst," contributed Spark. No one translated for Amber so she figured no one knew what the firesprite said, but its satisfied tone was evident.

"The mist headed for Amber," Rafe said.

Another warning. Since her lips were feeling nearly normal again, Amber spoke. "The journals are for me."

Tiro looked at the two fallen books, but didn't pick either up. "Pretty sure they are Tshilaba's. Look like hers."

"And the one that I have," Amber said, then decided not to talk much, she sounded odd—and scared—to her own ears.

"Booby-trapped," Rafe said grimly.

Tiro nodded. "Guess we know who. And he'll know that both his mists failed."

"Mists are minor," Pred whispered.

"That's right," Tiro said.

None of the brownies followed up with any listing of more major evils that might attack.

Hartha stripped Amber of her seaweed wrap and banished the old and replaced it with new. Then the browniefem was pressing the inevitable mug of healing tisane into Amber's hands. She sniffed. This time the herbal tea didn't smell good. All down ASAP, then. She guzzled. A sour taste coated her tongue, but her stomach settled. Her fingers were only a little swollen, her rings hadn't cut into her fingers, including the ring to remind her of Spark.

"Candle for Spark," she said.

Spark was larger than it had been this morning. Maybe it liked mist-with-eyes-and-teeth fuel. It seemed to skip over the floor, looking for every tiny mote of mist-dust.

Hartha handed Amber a candle. "Come on, Spark," she said.

The young firesprite hesitated, then flew a couple of feet to the wick.

"Good Spark!" Amber and Rafe said in unison. The dogs barked.

Rafe took the candle, stretched and put it on the desk.

"And good brownies," Amber continued. Her eyes watered. "I don't know what we'd do without you."

"That's for sure," Rafe said. He moved from behind Amber, stood and lifted her to her feet. "Thanks for the healing. How many more times do you need to do the kelp thing?"

Hartha's lips thinned. "Once or twice. We are lucky that evil magic does not like Mystic Circle." She jutted her chin at the desk chair and Rafe put Amber into it.

Once again the compresses were exchanged. This time Amber could smell the seaweed, and maybe a hint of Spark's vanilla candle. "The rotten stench is gone." She frowned. "I don't recall the mist smelling like that last night." Last night had smelled of oil and gas and fire.

Sniffing, Hartha nodded. "The mist began to die when brought into Mystic Circle."

"It was still too damn rough for Amber," Rafe said. He picked up the knife, pulled it from the sheath. Then he angled the dagger back and forth, letting light glint along each edge and across the blade.

Hitching a hip on the desk, he looked at the brownies. "This is only going to escalate, isn't it?"

Amber said, "Yes."

The brownies nodded. Spark hissed.

"The sooner I become competent with the dagger and the shield, the better." His jaw went hard, then he walked over and picked up the two leather volumes.

"Your hands!" Amber gasped. Swatches of seaweed fell from her face. Hartha tsked and replaced the seaweed on Amber's head and around her neck with new, wet plants.

"They're fine. No mist scum on the journals." He placed the two books side by side before her.

Then Hartha was there with a jar that she opened, scooping out green cream with glitter and rubbing the seaweed away from Amber's hands and the cream into them. As she did, Amber's own magic responded to the magical glitter, sparkling lavender. Amber wanted to lean back in her chair and give in to the sensual pleasure of having her hands rubbed, but she played it cool. She could feel the tea working inside her and the seaweed still soothed her hurts.

"Feeling better?" Rafe asked.

"Yes. Really, Hartha, I don't know what we'd do without you. Is there anything special I can get you?"

"Or I?" asked Rafe. "You patched me up a couple of times, too."

The small woman turned a deeper brown—from embarrassment? Amber thought so. Hartha shook her head. "No. We are well. You are keeping us company when Jenni is away."

"Ditto," Rafe said.

Amber sighed and decided to let ideas about how to reward the brownies sit in the back of her mind until she came up with something. "Will the cream hurt the leather book covers?" she asked.

"No," Hartha said.

Amber glanced at Rafe, then at Tiro. "I wonder if Tshilaba ever ran across the Davail curse."

Tiro crossed his arms and glowered. Rafe lifted his brows.

Shrugging, Amber flipped open the book and stared. The pages appeared to have been glued together and the center hollowed out. Her stomach sank. She made a noise and Rafe joined her.

Tendrils of gray fog floated, then cleared and she was looking down at a three-dimensional image of the torso of a handsome, sophisticated man. His hair was a wavy blond, his eyes blue, his tanned cheeks were sculpted and his chin had a cleft.

He looked at her, blinked, and a low and rolling laugh echoed through the room. The brownies vanished. The pups howled.

"Bilachoe," Amber whispered. She tried to close the book but the cover seemed stuck to the desk. Her other hand shot out to twine with Rafe's.

The man's head tilted forward as his laugh ended and he smirked. "I see my little surprise did some damage."

Amber's face and neck heated. Stupid to be embarrassed instead of panicked, but she was.

"Too bad you didn't die," the man continued. Oh, yeah, fear was rising. Amber flinched and stared. The image's mouth moved but none of the muscles in his cheeks or around his eyes did, a little like computer-animated people. Just...creepy.

Again Rafe took a corner of the desk and looked down. "Hey, Bilachoe."

A snarl came and went on the mouth. Now Amber thought the image rippled.

"The curse breaker and the death-cursed. You're together. How touching." Another smile. No, the image didn't ripple, the skin of the evil thing's face did, as if it didn't cover regular muscles, but—Amber thought hideously—a snake or two. She swallowed hard and some of her seaweed fell off and now it felt like protection. They weren't seeing the real evil, and he wasn't seeing her face, either. The dark cruelty in his eyes was focused on Rafe, Amber had been dismissed, as if he believed the threat of torture had cowed her.

Rafe showed his teeth. "I'm going to kill you."

Another laugh. This one didn't show human teeth, but sharp and jagged things that didn't belong in a human mouth and there was more gurgle to the sound.

Bilachoe had been human, right? He didn't seem like that now. But what decent human could drain others of their lives and their hope and their magic for his own benefit?

The polar opposite of her, Amber realized.

"That was easy," he said. "Because *I* cursed *you,* the curse itself constrained me from initiating personal combat."

Amber had been right, there had been a cost to Bilachoe for laying the curse, at least one weakness, and they hadn't known about it.

Bilachoe's torso minimized as a gray glove appeared, flew toward them. Amber jerked back. Rafe tensed but didn't move. The glove hit some barrier and fell.

"But since you threatened me, I am free of that constraint," Bilachoe said. "I challenge you to a duel."

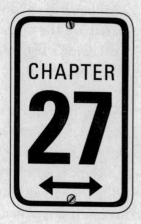

CHAPTER 27

RAFE'S HAND CLOSED OVER THE HILT OF the dagger. "A duel."

Bilachoe lifted his lip. "Don't you know the word? Didn't the *lyceum* you attend in that one-cow town teach you the history of the art you practice, child?"

Rafe's eyes flickered with calculation. His muscles, still tense, seemed to freeze and Amber knew why. Bilachoe knew where they were. He knew what Rafe was doing. And he had to know that Rafe had the shield and the dagger.

Amber tightened her fingers with Rafe's. "No."

Again Bilachoe smiled and now it appeared like a newscaster's. "Talk it over." He glanced down. "I'll give you two minutes. But know this, you can't win, Davail. During our fight your curse will draw all my attacks." Bilachoe threw back his head and laughed and wattles, red and black, showed under his chin.

Amber had to look away, but she knew what to ask. "What are the consequences if he doesn't meet you?"

Bilachoe's brows went up. "The man has issued a death threat. I have the right to defend myself...personally."

So he'd been bound not to touch Rafe. Send minions but not come himself. They hadn't known that. Amber's pulse picked up with fear and she bit her lips. The Dark one was right. They'd played into his hands.

She looked at Rafe. He met her eyes, squeezed her fingers. In his other hand he flashed the dagger at her. She knew that wouldn't be enough.

"I can't always stay in Mystic Circle. I need to train," he said.

"We could bring your teachers here...."

But he was shaking his head, then his eyes went distant. "Mystic Circle is a special place. I don't want it to turn into a prison for me."

"At least wait until Pavan and Vikos are available to help!"

"How could they help? Stand by and watch? This is *my* curse." His face—all those tiny muscles that Bilachoe didn't seem to have—hardened. "Bilachoe and his minions know where *we* live. He'd damn well want to hurt you...to hurt me. We aren't safe the minute we leave the cul-de-sac. I can't live like that."

"You *can*. You can live."

His smile was humorless. "Can I? With this guy waiting to ambush me?" He turned back to Bilachoe. "When can you be here?"

Bilachoe's eyebrows raised until they disappeared

and a bumpy forehead sloping steeply back showed in a pale shade of gray. Not too human. "There?"

Amber wondered if he was already in Denver. He could probably move instantly like other strongly magical folk.

"Forget I asked. We'll do this tomorrow night. I mean after midnight, early in the a.m. One a.m.," Rafe said. His brow lined as he thought. "Not in the city."

"Not in the city," Amber agreed. A place popped into her mind. She didn't know why, but it felt right. Or as right and blessed as a place could be. "Red Rocks."

"The amphitheater?" Rafe drew back in surprise.

She hadn't thought that far. It was March and there would be no shows. As far as she knew the only thing coming up would be the sunrise services Easter morning next month. She pulled over her laptop and accessed the page. Even if the park closed, what would keep magic out?

"Not the amphitheater. We don't want to ruin the place," Rafe said. He smiled at Bilachoe and said louder, "God knows what the *thing* has for blood."

A feral growl came from the image and once again it wavered.

Rafe scanned the map on Amber's laptop, and his tiny stick was in his fingers. "Yeah, Red Rocks feels good." He shot a glance to her, whispered, "Blessed. Sacred." The small divining rod swept over the map, then quivered at one point. "Red Rocks, Creation Rock, just north of the amphitheater, 1:00 a.m. See ya."

He yanked the cover of the book up, applying magic and muscle and closed it. He paced. "Yeah. This feels good."

It didn't to Amber. She felt scoured with fear and had to hold herself still to keep from trembling at the knowledge that she loved Rafe.

Tiro had been right all along.

She couldn't see him die. She knew what she had to do. She had to use her major power to break Rafe's curse before...or during...the fight. She would save her lover at the cost of herself.

From cold lips she said, "Not much time to prepare."

"That works for us, too." He drew her into his arms. "I'd bet he has more going on than we do." Her seaweed caked off, sticking to his shirt, skittering to the floor as she set her head against his neck. "Let's face it. No matter how hard I've trained, I'm still a human and he is...other."

The brownies popped in. They all looked sad and afraid. Hartha twisted her hands in her apron, Tiro twisted his hands in his cap and shot hot, angry glances at Amber.

Rafe went on. "And if Bilachoe's busy, he isn't sending minions after us, or coming himself today or tomorrow." Rafe gave them all a slashing grin. "Though I think I'll get there in plenty of time tomorrow, before sundown for sure."

Spending hours out of doors wouldn't faze him. "Make sure you pack out your trash."

"Yeah." He pushed the top of the laptop open flat, settled into his balance and closed his eyes, humming under his breath. Holding his stick loose between his fingers he checked the map again. Once more it stopped at Creation Rock. A breath filtered from his chest. He opened his eyes and nodded. "A lot of human energy there. *Good* human energy. I think I can tap into that." He returned to a previous page on the website. His eyes widened. "Next event is Easter. Sunrise."

"That's right," Amber said.

"Did I know that? I think I knew that," Rafe said. "Have Easter services been there for a long time?"

"I think before you and I were born."

"Good, that's good then." His shoulders moved. "I'm heading out. I need a good workout at a dojo and at the lyceum." He set the dagger down on the desk, placed his hand over the shield, smiled again. "It's vibrating. It's ready." He touched the knife with his index finger. "So is the dagger." Standing straight, he lifted his chin. "So am I. Get this over with when I'm at my peak. We'll make solid plans later today." He kissed her on the lips, swept his tongue over her mouth and she let him in. He probed, then withdrew, still smiling. Then he stretched and went into a kata pattern. "By God, it will be good to have this over with. One way or another."

Hartha choked. Pred and Tiro had tears in their eyes, too. He touched Hartha on her head. "Don't worry. I've got the shield and the dagger." He smiled again. "And magic." His gaze swung to Amber again, "And everything to live for." He waved, then, whistling, he went out the door, letting it slam behind him.

Amber and all the brownies watched. When he was gone, all of them turned to look at her, eyes huge and wet, ears trembling.

"Do any of you think he can beat Bilachoe in a duel, even with the Cosmos Dagger and Shield?" she asked.

All of them shook their heads. Spark made a little sputtering noise that sounded negative.

"You think he'll die?" Hard, hard to say those words.

They nodded. Spark spit.

Amber peeled the seaweed from her, met the brownie's stares.

"I love Rafe." Her lips turned down. "I still feel the need to help other cursed ones, but…"

"You learned the lesson that Cumulustre bound on your line," Tiro whispered.

Amber sighed and sank into the chair again. Her knees felt wobbly. "Don't drain yourself totally for others. To do so leaves you without resources for yourself, your family or to help anyone else." She jutted her chin. "But for Rafe, I'll do it. He isn't asking it of me." Her fingers had clenched into fists and she relaxed them. "It's mutual. Last night he wanted Sizzitt to protect me, not him. He'd lay down his life to defend me."

The brownies nodded.

She licked her lips. "So I'm going to break his curse."

Hartha was there, patting her leg. "Not before the duel. Only when he falls."

"Rafe has teeny chance of beating evil Darkfolk," Pred said doubtfully.

"Listen to Hartha," Tiro urged. He wasn't looking at Amber directly.

"All right. I should live through it," she said with more hope than belief, her smile a rictus on her face.

The brownies said nothing to that.

Amber's eyes stung so she scrubbed them. More kelp flaked. "I'd better prepare for the worst."

Once more the brownies nodded. She almost hated them.

That evening Rafe jogged with the pups around the cul-de-sac and thought of Amber. She wasn't what he was used to. He was accustomed to hard-bodied competitive women who lived and breathed sports like he did. Or groupies. Or party girls and models who might be in the same location to see and be seen.

Amber lived in Colorado and didn't own a pair of skis. He'd been through her basement and garage and storage rooms. Not one ski or snowshoe. There were hiking boots, packs and some gear so that was a relief. But she wasn't hard-bodied. Her muscles were toned, but not cut. He'd actually seen *aerobics* programs in her video library. She played with the dogs during breaks in her work and walked them a couple of times a day since he'd been with her, but he wouldn't say she was in top shape.

Her body was soft and she didn't seem competitive at all. Though she'd done damn well in that stupid game. She'd fought with her squishy character, and a couple of times when she was in her office, he'd loaded Fairies and Dragons on her laptop and seen that she played tough women—and men of a more hulking build than Rafe—who used their fists to fight monsters. But he didn't think she had the suppressed violence that would make her a success in the lyceum.

He was used to short affairs that burned hot and fast. That wasn't what he was getting with Amber. It was a short affair and damn hot. But Amber was a forever woman. He'd actually think about forever if he had it to give. As it was, he was holding back. He didn't want to be squishy emotionally or physically going into a fight to the death with evil. The thought made him snort and the dogs looked at him. He glanced around the circle. No one was out, as usual, so he let them off their leashes and shouted, *"Run!"*

So they all did.

Everyone was quiet during dinner and they didn't speak of the duel until Rafe brought it up.

Amber had spent the day getting ready for a change in her life.

Her will was made and filed with an attorney.

She'd found and rented and moved some stuff into a small bungalow a few blocks from Mystic Circle. Alternative living space for herself was a must. She couldn't bear to have Rafe return triumphant and realize that their time and chance for love had passed.

She might age even faster outside the cul-de-sac, be more prone to household accidents, but she didn't care.

She had her genealogy and her journals, even took a couple of jobs to keep her busy. She'd finished Conrad's family tree and shot it to him by email, as well as putting it up on the database that he'd used.

Of the new two journals, one was ruined beyond reading. The other gave a longer and more complete explanation on how to sever emotional bonds. Unfortunately, she'd need that.

This was the end of the line for the Cumulustre women. Finally. If it had been anyone else, even Conrad, she could have refused to break the curse. Soon Tiro would be free.

She was ready.

"I don't want you coming with me. You have to stay," Rafe said in the meanest, most demanding tone she'd heard from him. It might have worked if she hadn't known him so well. He wouldn't be a reluctant warrior, but he wouldn't be a harsh commander, either. More like a determined swashbuckler.

"I understand that," she said.

He stood and his chair fell and he caught it. Then he drew her up and held her close. His breath was warm against her ear, and he rubbed his cheek against her. "That's not a promise."

"I won't go with you," she said. "I have no intention of distracting you." She smiled and it was almost easy. She had a great tenderness for him, her lover. "You need all the focus you can get."

He swayed with her a little. "Thank you."

She didn't tell him that she'd follow him. Find a place to watch the duel. Be ready to break his curse if he needed her help. "I'll be praying." Also true.

"Okay." He sighed. "Okay." He drew back a little

and met her gaze. Yes, the reckless pirate was in his eyes. Ready to do or die. She was so afraid it was the latter, she couldn't breathe.

Curving his hand around her cheek, he said, "There'll be no reason for Bilachoe to go after you… if I don't make it."

No reason except the *thing* might like to eat her at the least, have fun torturing her. Make sure she wasn't around to break any more curses that might threaten him.

She'd told the brownies to stay in Mystic Circle and had gotten stares from their huge eyes as if she was crazy to think they'd leave when danger threatened.

"Okay." Rafe glanced at the brownies. "You're all staying here?"

"We must. Jenni and Aric are coming home soon," Hartha said.

"Soon?" Amber asked, hope swinging wildly high.

"A few days," Pred said.

"Oh."

Rafe waved that away. "Tiro?"

"I will stay with the dogs."

"Good."

Rafe ran through his plans and Amber watched his mobile face, his expansive gestures and ached.

She studied him.

She'd researched and worked and learned a lot in the past few weeks and now she shifted her vision to see the curse that enveloped her lover. She concentrated on the pattern, plucking a strand or two of the black and sticky webbing, looking for a good thread to pull that would unravel the whole thing with one good yank.

It took more than an hour, but finally she found one, marked it and readied it for use.

CHAPTER

28

THAT NIGHT AMBER DOZED ON AND OFF. Rafe would wake and want to love tenderly and then they'd sleep. She'd fear for him and need him and rouse him for fierce sex, then they'd tumble into sweet rapture and dark forgetfulness.

After they woke, she followed his lead and acted as if it were a normal morning. Then he went off for some last-minute training and Amber went upstairs.

With more despair than hope, she once again searched online for "Bilachoe." And she found a new, brief paragraph saying that he'd cursed a man and a fiery thought leaped from his forehead to the cursed one. Ever after, the demon had had a weakness in the forehead.

She didn't know who might have added such information—Pavan? But she was glad for it. She copied the item for Rafe.

Time to cut her emotional ties. On a curse this large, it might affect everyone she had more than a nodding acquaintance with. She couldn't risk harming them. She felt better about the method now that she'd read Tshilaba's journal.

Sinking into a meditative state, she let the faces of those she'd loved and helped, and who had loved and helped her, pass before her mind's eye. For the first time in years true images of her mother and aunt came to her and tears trickled down her face. The bonds to them had been cut cleanly by them, but the ends still throbbed with pain. Who or what was so important to them that they'd left her? She didn't know, and she'd never looked because she couldn't bear the revelation.

At least, if worse came to worst, she would leave no children. Friends to grieve, and Rafe—who would be free for the first time in his life and pursuing his dream—but no children. The dogs would transfer their love to Tiro or Rafe.

Rafe would be free of his curse. She could only imagine how a man like him, who treasured every moment of life, would revel in the delight of living. That thought had her mouth curving underneath the prickle of dried tears.

So she studied the bonds emanating from her, glowing with energy and power that flowed back and forth. First she looked at the pale ones, ranging from yellow to white human links. The tiniest were casual acquaintances—faces of people she knew to say "hi" to at the Sensitive New Age Bean. More surprising and stronger were her clients. She "touched" a pulsing one and "heard" a mother telling a story to her child—a story that Amber had provided with a family tree. She swallowed.

She visualized the bonds. Imagining cutting with a pair of scissors was too harsh. Instead she looked at the end of each bond, "magnified" them in her sight. Gently, gently, she frayed the end, making sure there wouldn't be a snap or a rebound.

Just before the last filament gave way, she said a blessing and sent a tiny surge of affection down the thread.

It took a while, but she felt peaceful as the smallest connections fell away.

Maybe she would live to make more.

Stronger still were the cords linking her and those whose curses she had broken.

Once again, she shredded and let the cords unravel with a blessing. This time she felt an emptiness and loneliness she didn't like.

She switched her "sight" from all the lovely human bonds, so many more than she'd expected, to the brightly colored threads to the Lightfolk.

The largest and strongest was to Jenni Weavers and it *did* look like woven embroidery floss of four merging colors of light: red-orange and gold and green-blue and blue-white, all equal. Wonderful. Amber gasped. Jenni had finished her own quest. Was happy and triumphant and celebrating…and in love.

If only the same could happen to Amber. Instead she sawed at the floss until it was down to two threads, then one, then Amber sent Jenni affection as it disintegrated. Jenni didn't seem to notice and Amber sniffed back incipient tears.

Amber's link to Tamara was smaller than Amber had imagined, which hurt a little before Amber realized that they hadn't had any in-depth conversations. Maybe in the future…

With a deep breath, she studied the other Lightfolk connections. Three large brownie bonds, she smiled as she saw they were chocolate-brown.

They knew she would be cutting the strands of friendship between them. This time Tiro would be free.

Hartha and Pred. She loved them. Hartha so calm and practical, Pred a jokester, not as strong.

Three fire bonds. She blinked. *Three?* More blinking as she studied the thickest. It was to Spark. Ah! Spark had been born in Amber's home, no wonder. The next was to the firesprite who tended Spark and the third small one was to the djinn who'd teleported Rafe and her from Eight Corp to the street.

A blue-violet-white thread ran to Pavan, the elf, who had shared in hospitality in her home, a thicker golden link to Vikos.

Everyone was right—Tiro and Cumulustre and Pavan. She'd brought whatever doom she had on herself.

But she also had the satisfaction of knowing that she'd saved lives. That was a real and untarnished legacy.

Slowly she unraveled the threads, let the magic linking them filter away in tiny bits of lavender glitter.

Now she hurt. But she wasn't done.

Her strongest bonds were to Rafe and the pups.

Oddly enough, the bond with Rafe was a deep and throbbing pink that didn't seem sexual. Love? She loved him, but didn't quite know how he felt about her. Caring, yes, but anything more?

And how many bonds would Rafe himself have? She sensed he'd have strong connections to his brother and uncle and Conrad. Maybe a myriad of thin, easily broken threads to acquaintances.

She shrugged and ceased studying that cable. Rafe, as the man whose curse she was breaking, would take no harm from her.

So she switched her inner sight to see the strong and unconditional love—pure silver—between Baxt and Zor and her. She loved them, no reason to deny it, and they loved her. Even as she contemplated the bonds, they were there, knocking her over as she sat, licking her face, and she held them and rubbed them.

Then Tiro stood at the threshold of the room with wrinkled face and sad eyes and called them to play outside.

She dreaded what came next. Her heart ached and her fingers clenched that she must cut her bond to the dogs. They certainly wouldn't survive what she was about to do. But they loved Hartha and Pred and Tiro…and Rafe. Rafe would care for them.

Is this how her mother and aunt felt? For an instant a flash of memory rose, of them both looking back at her from the taxi, tears running down their faces. No! She didn't want to recall that. She had to be strong.

This time she went to her bed and closed her eyes,

and took a long time to pick apart the threads, sending love down each portion.

When it was finally done, when she rose, she went out to the backyard and looked at the spears of tulips and grape hyacinths and daffodils poking through the earth. She wondered if she'd be here to see them bloom.

The dogs raced up to her and sniffed her, acting as if she were a stranger. Then they caught sight of Tiro gardening and ran away to play. She rubbed wetness from her face and turned away from them, cherishing the sound of their happy barks. She'd remember that forever.

With a sense of doom hanging over her, Amber finished her work on Rafe's family tree and uploaded it to the professional site as well as the one that most amateurs used, including his brother. She wasn't sure what Rafe had told his brother, but at least she'd explored and documented the Davail collateral line so someone else knew that the curse might pass to the distant cousin, the last of that line, before returning to Gabe again.

Not if she had anything to say about it. She loved Rafe and might be breaking his curse tonight.

If worse came to worst she had no idea how much she would age or how weak she would be.

She tried not to think about that.

Rafe rented a dual sport motorcycle—cycle and dirt bike—and rode to Red Rocks late in the afternoon.

He knew it was smart to check out the place before Bilachoe came, but he had to admit he didn't have the patience of some of the ex-military warriors he'd met. He'd walk around the park and keep his senses open, maybe even use his small stick to feel the different types of magic, but he didn't think Bilachoe would lay a trap. Still, it was a pretty spring day, no snow even at the higher elevation. There were a lot worse ways to spend an afternoon and evening than hiking in a great park. He found a good fold of rock to hide the cycle in, then went on foot.

Of course there were better places to spend what might be his last hours alive, too, like in Amber's bed. But he'd made do with a long and sexy kiss that had left him hard and Amber quivering. She'd clung for a moment, then, tears on her lashes, had given him a quick kiss and gone back inside her home. She had a superstition about watching someone drive out of sight, so she didn't. And he didn't look back, either.

The brownies had informed him and Amber that most Lightfolk couldn't transport to somewhere they'd never been, but they didn't know whether that applied to evil Dark ones.

They were under the impression that Bilachoe could. Rafe didn't know if brownie bladders were weak enough to let go in fear, but he had an idea that if they were, there would have been piss during the conversation.

Tiro told him that if a Lightfolk had a strong bond with someone—human or Lightfolk or other—that Lightfolk could transport to the person. Tiro had also

pointed out that Bilachoe and the Davails had been
linked by a death curse for centuries.

So the brownies were of the opinion that Bilachoe
would focus on Rafe like a missile and transport,
probably trying to take him out with the first blow.
And that would be at Bilachoe's timing. Maybe before
1:00 a.m. Mountain Time, maybe after, maybe in the
middle of the night.

For himself, Rafe had gotten a few bits of info from
the face-to-illusion meeting in the book. He was
pretty sure that the evil being wasn't at home in the
States and probably hadn't been west of Manhattan.

Scanning the dry, rough and totally magnificent
scenery around him, he felt down to his bones that it
would be an alien landscape for Bilachoe. Plains plants
were still dormant in their winter yellow and brown.
The huge and eerie shapes of red sandstone rock thrust
from the ground. Mysterious land and cultures unknown to the evil. One advantage to Rafe.

And from what Tiro and the other brownies knew
of the Dark, Bilachoe would be used to sending *minions* to do his dirty work.

This would be a hand-to-hand, or knife-to-knife,
or magic-blast-to-Cosmos-Dagger-and-Shield fight.
The hand-to-hand and the knife-to-knife he was prepared for as much as he could be. He'd practiced hard
at the dojo and with fencers at the lyceum. So he was
used to fighting and getting blows. He wondered how
fast Bilachoe was and the last time he might truly
have been hurt, fought while in pain. More advan-
tages for Rafe.

The magical nature of the duel would be strange. But maybe not as tough on Rafe as Bilachoe thought. When Rafe had awakened in the middle of the night from a bad dream, he'd reluctantly left Amber and padded down to the living room and his computer tablet. He'd checked the apps and found *REAL* Fairies and Dragons by Pavan nearly gone, and the new one now bright enough for him to read "Journey to Lightfolk Palaces."

That was intriguing and he'd recalled Pavan's words—that the Davail was supposed to show up at the Lightfolk palace on his thirty-third birthday for training to kill the evil Dark ones. The app was also heartening, as if the elf or the Lightfolk or whoever had loaded the program believed Rafe had a chance against Bilachoe.

Anyway, Rafe had sucked in a breath and sucked up his uneasiness at the first game and managed to bring back the Fairies and Dragons app. Then he'd spent two hours playing against magical monsters with his dagger and shield. Fireballs and icicles were thrown at him, radiation and pure magic blasted him, tumbling him head over ass. He limped, ached, and his wings were tattered when he finally flew to the Fairy Dome. There he stepped into the Fairy Ring and got healed, his exhaustion wiped away, his muscles eased and primed.

He didn't kid himself that Bilachoe would be as easy to defeat as the monsters in the game. But he had a weakness in his forehead, or so Amber reported.

The evil was Dark and powerful. But Rafe had hope

and a damn good future to live for and he would fight
to his last ounce of strength, his last drop of magic and
blood and energy.

There wasn't anyone on the park trails, the small
thread of cars had wound up to the trading post and
the amphitheater. So he saw no one and only heard the
wind and the birds and his own footfalls and soaked
up the sun and the scent of sagebrush. And his time
walking through the huge sandstone rocks settled him.
More, it turned off his mind like the best times before
a race and put him in another place. His own personal
quest.

But he knew what he was now. He knew the limitations that had been placed on his life and why. He
knew the curse and he would damn well break it. He'd
left long letters in his room at Amber's place, ready to
be mailed to his brother and Conrad if he failed.

Now he hiked and let the atmosphere of Red Rocks
work on him. He felt the magic, felt places that were
close to balanced elemental-magic-wise, due to Na-
tive American shamans. One was near Creation Rock
where he intended to fight.

Balanced elemental energy that he would be able
to use better than Bilachoe, who had taken the Dark
path. And there was all too human energy in the rock,
too. Energy of bands that had played, had created on
the stage, had given to the audience and been given
acclaim and applause back. An exchange of energy that
hummed in the huge monolith. He could use that, too,
just as he used it to summon the shield and dagger as
the sun set.

As the night wore on, Rafe tucked himself under an overhang that had gotten some sun and snoozed a little, his watch set to wake him at 10:00 p.m. so he could warm up and do some katas and practice exercises. The itchy feeling between his shoulder blades made him think that Bilachoe would come earlier than 1:00 a.m., but would make sure it was full dark in Denver. Might take him a while to get a fix on Rafe, enough that Rafe might sense a warning tug of magic.

Amber had a taxi drop her off at a house near Red Rocks at 10:00 p.m. She carried a large tote and was as ready as she could be. The night was dark, but the stars were brilliant and the moon waxing to the first quarter. Enough to see, in general. Like Rafe, she hadn't anticipated Bilachoe appearing before dark, but figured the Dark one would jump the gun. Also like Rafe she was dressed in layers and had her heavy parka on and a space blanket in her tote.

Unlike him, she was using the bond between them to locate where he was. He'd told her that he'd scout the whole park for the best magical energy.

She found him on the north side of Creation Rock that formed part of the amphitheater. Which was good because there was a parking lot where she could hide in the shadows and watch him. Since she loved him, she didn't need to be close to break his curse.

Marking a good place for her to wait, she left her tote blending in with the shadow of a boulder and walked the path to the gate where a limo would pick her up when all this was over and back. She needed to know the trail.

When she got back, she saw Rafe practicing. Earlier he'd told her with a quick grin that he planned to peak in his training tonight. Perfect.

She felt it was more like disaster.

Rafe's watch beeped, but he was already up. The sky was spectacular. It had been a long time since he'd seen the stars so close. And the temperature was dropping fast. It would freeze tonight, so he was glad he'd dressed warmly. Layers and leather. He stretched and bent and put on the shield and held the dagger loosely.

Then he moved slowly down the rock-studded incline to the area where he felt the best, where the magic was balanced most, though there was still more earth than water. Water was the least available here. The intervention of humans had helped. There were bathrooms and pipes near.

The massive rocks loomed over him, craggy black shadows against the night sky. In the distance Denver was a bright smear of lights. His heart and thoughts went to Amber, yearned for her. For this to be over and they could be together.

A hard tweak on his magic.

He caught his breath, tensed.

Attack!

A slam against his shield. Knocking him back. Hit! Hard!

Not by a body of flesh and blood. More like a steel skeleton.

He flipped and lit on stinging feet, panting, ready to fight. His dagger flamed blue and he thrust. Oh, yeah! It showed him the ragged outline of his enemy. And he could smell the guy. Enough to make a dude gag if a man had the breath.

He shot forward, bounced against a force field and staggered back.

Bilachoe waved a long staff. Electricity sizzled, shot to him.

Vanished into the shield with no trace.

Rafe panted, stared.

As Bilachoe stared at him.

The man's—thing's—robe had opened in the front, showing a glowing red skeleton. Head was a skull. Death's head. With flames as eyes. Bone fingers.

Truly a monster.

The lower jaw opened and high shrieking laughter knifed through Rafe.

Slow wave of the staff. Flames engulfed the skeleton, whipped the robe, didn't touch it.

Rafe jerked his shield and dagger in front of him and pressed forward. Inch by inch like against a strong wind. While the bastard laughed his ass off so hard he didn't use his tall, glowing staff with a nasty triple-bladed knife on the edge. A pike.

Geez, who used a *pike* nowadays?

Rafe hadn't practiced with pikes.

He drew on all his magic. Pushed *out!* Surged toward the Dark one, who wasn't dark but bright orange flames. Jabbed with the knife. Through the ribs. Nothing happened.

The pike hit his shield.

Pebbles rolled under his feet and he windmilled. There was a whoosh and then they weren't on the ground. They were atop the rock.

Need help! Emotion, not words.

Two silver disks shot from his pocket, spun toward Bilachoe. The silver dollars. Straight for Bilachoe's forehead.

The head lifted from the neck, *moved* out of the way.

Rafe rushed, got in a slash, was jammed back again. By magic.

And he knew.

A few days training wasn't enough to beat Bilachoe. Seven months training wouldn't have, either.

He didn't have much of a chance, but with luck and grit he might take the evil one with him. Maybe death would be quick. At least Amber wasn't here.

CHAPTER 29

WATCHING THE DUEL WAS PAINFUL. BILACHOE had more magic, but time and again Rafe evaded him, struck at the skeleton dancing in flame.

Amber prayed but it didn't seem like Rafe could win. He could take Bilachoe with him in death, but not win and live.

Flashing patterns hurt Amber's eyes. She couldn't look away.

Too afraid.

Though she trembled.

Rafe's curse was holding him back.

She'd hoped she wouldn't have to make the decision to save him and sacrifice herself. Had hoped beyond all reason that he'd have a chance against Bilachoe without her. Now it appeared that even if she broke the curse he might die.

Who knew how much the curse was limiting him? Was she so fatalistic that she wouldn't try?

She winced as Rafe ducked almost too slowly under the long whirl of Bilachoe's pike.

She wasn't fatalistic. She was optimistic, like Rafe. He wouldn't quit. She couldn't quit without knowing she'd done her best by him. She might fall, but she'd be fighting and she would damn well help Rafe win.

Her entire being focused on Rafe, she shot out her hands, even as Bilachoe's staff lit with lightning.

Now or never.

She *yanked* the gray shroud encasing Rafe as hard as she could. Her hands burned, scored by the curse. Her lungs seized. *More!* She gave it her all. The curse tore from him. Gone!

He blazed with light, the energy of his whole life ahead of him. With the brightness of all the lives that had been cut short before his. As she crumpled, the white-blue fireball that was Rafe surged toward the black flapping Bilachoe, who'd pivoted, his staff aiming at her!

Power—magic—engulfed Rafe. He used it. Flashed energy at the Dark beast, jabbed knife, shield, *everything*. His lunge carried him forward to the fallen evil. Bilachoe lay on his back, no simple skeleton now. The light still throbbing from Rafe in time with his heart showed a not-quite-human mangled face. Holes of nose—eaten by evil—and mouth open in surprise. Horrible fanged teeth.

And Rafe's tiny dowsing rod was jammed into the

monster's forehead. The stick flamed, too, cracking the skull and melting the guy's brain. Rafe swallowed and stepped away. Retreated even more when the stench rose. Back and back until a small fall of rocks near his feet let him know he was close to the edge.

He breathed shallowly, watching the robe flatten as the body beneath melted or fell into ash or something he really didn't want to consider. Didn't take as long as he'd expected. There was one small and oily-looking stream of fluid that dried rapidly, even before it reached the edge of the rock.

Creation Rock was now destruction rock. But the destruction of evil. What kind of mark—spiritually and physically—would that leave? Well, Easter was coming up. That should help, shouldn't it? And he'd let Pavan and Vikos know about it. Maybe they could move in a cleanup team or something.

Finally, when a breeze blew shreds of the robe Bilachoe had worn away and the scent of a cold spring night to Rafe's nose, he moved closer and toed the remnants of cloth and…stuff…. Cloth that fell apart when his boot touched it, knobby bits of gray and black that might have been bone. Rafe spit bile.

His miniature dowsing rod glowed neon pink like a plastic swizzle stick. He stared at it, but it had proved to be a formidable weapon and he didn't want to leave it. Gritting his teeth, he bent down and touched it with the top of his little finger. Not even static electricity. So he sheathed the dagger on his hip, picked up the stick and wiped it on his pants, then tucked it in his inner jacket pocket.

The moonlight was bright enough to show that the leather of his jacket was scraped and torn. Very much the worse for wear.

But the next deep breath he drew held nothing but the scents of a Colorado night and he whooped. He'd beaten Bilachoe! His curse was gone and the future was his. His and Amber's.

Yeah, he had to climb off the rock in the dark, but that was more of a challenge than a problem, and the descent would definitely eat up some of this amazing energy that had come out of nowhere and filled him. Manifested just at the right time. Luck. The angel of good fortune had been with him.

When Amber woke, the stars spun blurrily overhead. She blinked, but they didn't come into focus and as she drew in her first, shuddering breath she knew she'd aged many, many years.

The good news was she hadn't wet herself. The bad news was that she felt incredibly fragile, as if her bones themselves were thin. Panting, it took more than a few minutes to struggle to sit. Despite her long parka, she was cold, her hands and feet and especially her nose. She didn't seem to have enough energy even to shiver.

Her pocket computer beeped and she knew she had to get herself together to be picked up by the limo at the time she'd ordered it—2:30 a.m., and it was a half-mile walk to the gate closing the road. Easy for her before, but now? She didn't know.

When she shifted, the bones of her ass ground on dirt beneath her. She'd lost a lot of weight then, including muscle mass. Unsurprising since she'd used a lot of energy to break the curse. Given it all her juicy life force for years. Shouldn't have been so damn proud of her good butt.

At least she was thinking sharply. What would she have done if she'd lapsed into dementia?

She shuddered at the horror of that notion. She hadn't wanted to think of it, so she hadn't prepared. Another thing she hadn't managed well were her clothes. She hadn't taken that into consideration. They hung around her and looked too young for her age. Good thing her coat was something even her grand-mother would wear.

Decades might have passed for her body, but under an hour had transpired since the battle was fought. Her scarf gaped, letting in cold air. When she reached for the soft wool, she touched loose and wrinkled flesh and flinched.

Looking in the mirror was going to be bad.

Especially since she had no idea how the women of her family looked when they aged. Would her eyes be deep in sockets, or have puffy eyelids nearly covering them?

Her mouth dried and her jaw clenched. She had all her teeth. That was a plus.

Tilting her head back to look at the top of Creation Rock, she heard the tendons of her neck creak and felt a little pop. She froze, but there was no pain, so she didn't think she'd done any further damage to herself.

She saw nothing atop the rock. There were no little lumps of bodies. Then there came the gunning of a motorcycle, pretty much like the sound she'd heard when Rafe had taken off that afternoon. Since she didn't think Bilachoe would or could ride such a machine, Rafe was safe. Tears welled and flowed, overflowed her eyes in a rush. Her chest tight, pushing in and out with sobs, she pulled the wad of tissue from the coat pocket and mopped her face.

Moving slowly, she rolled onto her hands and knees, then rocked to her feet. Straightening as much as she could—and she hadn't suddenly developed osteoporosis, thank heaven—she stretched all her senses toward the rock to search for Bilachoe.

He was and wasn't there. As far as she could tell, bits of him were there but little flakes of him were blowing over the park and those were breaking down into smaller pieces. She didn't know where they'd all end up, but since he was dust and blowing away she didn't think he could come back from that.

All the evil that Bilachoe had caused, all the lives he'd cut short, had worked on him alive or dead or both. The curse he'd made had claimed him. He'd gone down to Rafe and her and to *good*.

And the more she stood in the cold wind, the more it sapped her. So she'd better start putting one foot in front of the other and moving. Her breath came shallowly, sharply cold, sliding down to chill her inside. She wobbled on her feet. Her tears had left frozen lines on her cheeks. She dug in her bag for a small but bright flashlight. The time was nearing 2:00 a.m. and the only lights around were the few lights in the park, the distant city lights.

Her bag was heavier than she'd expected, and she moved slower than she'd thought and on the long walk on the uneven trail, adrenaline kept her company as she feared for her balance.

And that she wouldn't make the rendezvous in time. But her cell worked and she held it in her hand like the lifeline it was.

She made it to the gate ten minutes before the limo arrived to take her to her new home and a life she hadn't really wanted. Aching to her bones and weary, she fell asleep and didn't wake until they pulled up before the bungalow.

The chauffeur held her door open. As she creaked out, he set his hand under her elbow and gently boosted. With no show of impatience he matched her shuffling steps to the door of the house she'd rented and helped her up the two steps. Amber was panting. She didn't know how strong her body was, or could become, but she'd work at it. Later. Tomorrow. If she didn't die from exhaustion in the night.

"Is someone waiting up for you, ma'am?" the man asked, glancing at the porch light and a glimmer coming from between the curtains. Amber had left a small light on.

"My daughter-in-law," she lied, then added, "though she might have fallen asleep." Amber sighed. "She's a heavy sleeper." Taking her key from an outside pocket of her purse, one key on a light keychain, she stabbed at the keyhole.

"Allow me." The driver took the key from her fingers and slipped it smoothly into the lock. Amber watched the tendons and muscles flex in his strong brown hand as he turned the key and opened the door. Beautiful. Worthy of envy.

He shoved the door open to a small but welcoming entryway painted a soft yellow. "There you are, home."

"Yes," Amber said. Her voice cracked. She opened the main compartment of her purse and fumbled to pull out her wallet.

His hand covered hers. "Everything's been taken care of, ma'am. You enjoy your night now."

She glanced up at his equally beautiful face and said, "Thank you—you, too." She managed a smile. "Sweet dreams."

"Thank you. Take care now." Then he pulled the door shut after her and left her alone.

The house didn't smell like home, but it wasn't bad—clean with a touch of magic, a hint of mango. Amber wobbled three steps to the living room and let her purse fall on the sofa. She wanted to drop there, too, but if she did, she wouldn't get up again and bed was a better idea.

Still as she shuffled along toward the bedroom, a gleam in the kitchen caught her eye. Did she have a night-light there? She didn't know, but it pulled her, the fragrance of magic.

Step by slow step she made it to the threshold and found that she hadn't lied, after all.

Spark shimmered in the glass bowl of a peachy-orange candle, mango.

"Spark," Amber said faintly.

Spark straightened and there was the outline of a humanoid being, slightly triangular, shoulders wider than the rest.

"I am Ssargass," he said.

She crumpled. Again. Then crawled from the kitchen to the bedroom and heaved herself onto the mattress and slept.

Rafe zoomed through the night, feeling the absolute freedom of a future stretching out years for him. Magic and pure triumph sizzled through him. Oh, yeah! The curse was effing gone. Gone, gone, gone! He sent the bike up and down hills, hit a hundred on a couple of straightaways. After a while the frenetic energy slowed into an easy rhythm and he headed toward Amber and home.

He took the cul-de-sac at nearly a forty-five-degree angle. Twice. Then he stopped and parked the bike and swaggered through the door with his shield on his arm, the dagger sheathed on his thigh and twirling his little stick in his fingers. He was ready for the rest of his life. With Amber.

Though the light was on in the living room like it had been when he'd gone out on St. Pat's, Amber hadn't waited up for him. That hurt and he rubbed his chest.

The place was too quiet. A chill sank into him. He strode through the first floor and noted Amber's laptop was gone and there was no Spark in the kitchen.

More and more a bad feeling pressed in on him. He left the silent kitchen, noted that Tiro's door was closed, as usual. Then he realized he was still holding his shield and rod as if to fight the anxiety that was buzzing around him like gnats. He set them on the dining room table and moved back to the entryway.

"Amber!" he yelled, then, "Baxt! Zor!"

Loud barking sounded through the house. The dogs were in his room again. He took the stairs fast and opened his door. Here was a small light, too, and the welcoming mass of the dogs pressing against him, licking his hands, giving him rubs as if he was their favorite person—Amber—and not the new and interesting guy who played with them...Rafe.

"Yeah, yeah." He petted the dogs briskly, glancing around. Seemed the same as when he'd left. His stuff was still there and that was good. His key to the front door had worked.

"Amber!" he yelled again.

"She's gone," Tiro said. The brownie stood at the top of the stairs. He didn't look like he usually did. His expression was off and so was his color.

"Gone?" Pure shock had Rafe stiffening his suddenly weak knees.

"You think you broke that curse yourself? Were able to kill such a one as Bilachoe?" Tiro snorted.

Rafe narrowed his eyes. "What are you saying?"

"That Amber broke the curse and paid the price."

"What?!" Fear crawled in his belly, eating at him. "Is she hurt? She's not..." His jaw clenched, he struggled to find his link with Amber. It was there! "I would have known if she was dead. How hurt is she?"

Tiro didn't meet his eyes. "Not hurt exactly. She's well and in good health."

Rafe got the idea that there was a load of qualifications to that statement. "Tell me."

"I am sworn not to," the brownie said, ears dipping.

"Why aren't you with her?" Rafe demanded.

"I am bound to serve her and she refused to have me. She wanted me to stay here with you." He stomped around the landing, rumbled his words like pebbles hitting concrete. "Only that stupid young fire-sprite is with her. Spark."

Rafe glared at the brownie, then sat on the floor and let the dogs bump him as he held them. That felt good, at least. "We both know that even magic has loopholes." When he thought about Amber saving him, he tasted bitter bile. But he couldn't deny that he'd have been dead if she hadn't. "Damn squishy," he muttered, and let Baxt lick his face.

Tiro stood as still as a garden gnome, not looking at all as cheerful.

Rafe prompted, "Loopholes? What happened to Amber and where can I find her?"

Tiro snapped, "You've always known the cost to Amber, from the very beginning. Think about it." The brownie vanished but not until he'd looked significantly at Rafe's computer tablet on the dining room table.

Rafe spent the rest of the night in Amber's bed. He liked the scent of it, being able to think she was with him. Why the hell had she left?

Maybe she didn't want to be with him.

The hell she didn't. She loved him. Had to. He'd known that and now she'd proven it. She'd saved his life at a cost to herself.

Dammit.

Rafe tabbed through every damn thing on his tablet. Every email, every report, every weblink. He scoured the game "Journey to Lightfolk Palaces" for clues, but there was no info. Finally, computer still in hand, sleep swallowed him.

Amber woke up stiff and sore and in a room that didn't smell right.

As she moved, she caught sight of her wrinkled hands and subsided.

She needed to go check herself out in a mirror, but that seemed too hard. Yet she couldn't go forward with her life without knowing the bottom line.

Peeling off her clothes, she noted that her body didn't look as terrible as she'd imagined, and she reminded herself that she still had her teeth and no osteoporosis. She also figured that if she'd been in better shape, she would have lost less muscle mass. That had her thinking of Rafe and she knew however many years she'd lost, it had been worth it to preserve his life.

The bathroom was next door and a large mirror ran above the double sink.

She steeled herself and slowly faced her reflection....

CHAPTER 30

AMBER GASPED AND HER VEINED HAND went to her saggy throat. Her hair was white, of course, her face lined but...soft. She'd had plenty of elderly clients and was a pretty good judge of age. She wasn't in her seventies. Not even in her eighties. She had to be in her nineties. No wonder she was so frail.

Meantime, her heart rate had picked up and was spurting through her and rushing in her ears. She hung on to the counter and breathed slowly and steadily. If she managed to survive this panic attack it would prove her heart was in pretty good working order, too.

"Hello, Amber!" Sargas—her namesake—flicked onto a scented candle.

She blinked until the dark spotting her vision cleared. Still leaning against the counter, she took a tumbler and shakily held it under water for a drink.

After she'd slaked the dryness in her throat, she replied, "Hello, Sargas."

"The big fire in the ssky hass come!"

"The sun's up."

"Yess! I would like to go out and ssit in the yellow-white."

"You want to sit in the sunshine."

"Yess."

Amber sent a jaundiced gaze to the bathtub. She wasn't sure if she got in it whether she'd get out. There were no handles in the enclosure at all. Something she hadn't thought mattered.

Her life had changed. Time to get used to it.

"Let me get dressed and some coffee and we'll sit in the sun." She remained cold. She'd bundle up but go out onto the front porch and sit with Sargas. The last friend of her old life.

Rafe woke up groggy, then grief caved in on him. Amber was gone.

He groaned and doggy breath hit him as Zor leaned down and licked his eyebrows while Baxt pawed Rafe's feet. Staggering to the shower, he flung off clothes as he went, then heard his watch alarm chime that it was a half hour before his morning training lesson. He hesitated.

His curse was gone. As he did a full body stretch, he could *feel* it gone. The fight with Bilachoe was over and won. His muscles moved easily, and he was in great shape.

Next up was presenting himself at a Lightfolk palace on his thirty-third birthday.

No, next up was finding Amber.

He wasn't going to run, or fence or practice martial arts until that was done. And he still wanted to know how she was.

So he canceled his sessions. After the shower and while he ate breakfast, he continued to scan his computer for the information Tiro had said was there. The brownie wasn't talking and only sent him significant looks. His eyes stung with the strain, like they'd been rolled in dirt. His butt hurt from sitting too long.

Eventually the sunshine and the dogs lured him outside and around the circle a couple of times. Then it was back into the house until he had exhausted every last scrap of a document on his tablet.

Hands stacked behind his head, Rafe lay on Amber's bed, hurting and feeling empty. The pups had joined him, sniffing around the room as if the scents were new, then lying down beside him. Treating him as if he was their most important person, not Amber. That slipped nasty cold down his spine.

He went over everything he knew about Amber from the first words Conrad had said about her to the report, to the look in her eyes and the way her body felt soft against his when she kissed him goodbye.

The *D*s were hitting him. Dread and desperation and doom. Now and again they'd snuck up on him in nightmares and he'd close them out. That was about how short his life might be. Now they were all about Amber.

After listening to the dogs snore, he shook his head. He still didn't get it. He grabbed his cell from the bedside table and phoned Ace Investigations and left a message for them to trace Amber as soon as possible, no expense spared.

The first couple of days, as she painfully learned her limitations, were the worst.

She ordered in groceries, and more—two walkers, one with a seat and a bag, and two canes, a regular one and one of those with four little feet, a quad cane. She'd always been sure of her balance, but thought she had an inner ear problem. Her hearing wasn't what she thought it should be.

Eventually she'd have to go to a doctor and get an exam. That would be interesting and fun. Somehow she'd have to make a new identity. Hmm. She had contacts in the genealogical community that might put her in touch with someone.

A lot of people had disappeared and reappeared with new names over the centuries.

She took several photos of herself until she was satisfied with the best of a bad lot, and emailed a friend of a friend of an acquaintance with the request for new documentation for her grandmother. It went surprisingly easily, with many of the papers emailed to her and the rest to be couriered. It hadn't been inexpensive, but not as tough as she thought—not as difficult as it would have been for a younger person. She wouldn't be getting a driver's license but an identity card.

And looking at her bank accounts, she realized she

had plenty of money to live even a wealthy lifestyle for the rest of her life...and she finally realized what her mother and aunt had done.

They'd been pulled by some sort of dreadful curse, but they had also ensured that whatever family survived—themselves and Amber or just Amber—would have enough wealth to live well for generations.

As much as she hated it, she was learning to adapt to her new life.

Her new identity papers, for Opal Sarga, came the third day...followed shortly by Rafe.

Ace Investigations took longer to find information about Amber than Rafe wanted, but when he returned from running the next morning he got an email that his purchase of number two Mystic Circle had been approved. They could close on the deal in a month if he was still of a mind to buy the house. He wanted the house, any property he could get here in Mystic Circle. And he thought it was best to keep the places out of Eight Corp's hands. Though he wasn't sure whether he wanted to move into number two or not. He sat and stared at the email screen. A month.

A month ago he was still in denial of his curse and magic. He was the old Rafe, involved in sports competitions and living each moment of his short life to the limit.

Now he was a new man, ready to claim his magic and the rest of his life. All because of Amber. He loved her, couldn't imagine life without her. Next month?

No, he wasn't ready to contemplate next month, not even next week, not even tomorrow, without Amber.

He was going to her.

Though it was only six blocks to Amber's new place—or the place she'd rented for Opal Sarga—Rafe drove. He had a huge bouquet of mixed flowers, a bottle of champagne and a box of two dozen of her favorite cookies.

Tucking the champagne and flowers under his arm, he knocked on the door. No one came. There wasn't even the sound of steps inside.

He wouldn't give up. They had all of their lives in front of them. "Amber, come out. I know you're in there!"

This time he pounded...then he sensed movement behind the door.

It opened slowly, revealing a very old woman, leaning on a cane. She didn't open the screen door. "There is no Amber here."

He didn't have much experience with the elderly, but he summoned up his best smile and offered the box of cookies. He could get more from Tamara. "I know Amber Sarga rented this place for you. Where can I find her?"

"Amber isn't here. She's gone, beyond where you can find her."

His body knew before his mind, the way she smelled, held herself, phrased her words. His insides seized in anger and pain and denial. A cry ripped from him, reverberating inside and out. He dropped everything and the champagne shattered on the concrete porch with an explosion that rattled his brain. He reeled back until he hit a square brick pillar.

"No!"

Her head tilted in a way he'd loved, but the face was not that of the woman he loved.

The heart was. The spirit was. Being in her company would be the same, if nothing else. "Amber?" His throat was dry. He coughed and it scraped through him. "Amber, honey?"

She just stared at him with dark and melancholy eyes.

"This was— You changed because—" He couldn't put it into words. Doing that would make it real.

"Breaking curses ages me," she said in a too calm tone. She should be raging. "It always has."

No, he didn't want to think of that. But he just stared at her thin body, her white hair, the way she leaned heavily on the cane in her hand.

"No."

"Yes." Her voice quavered, then her spine straightened and her eyes turned fierce. "I paid the price and I was glad to do that. But I don't want you in my life, Rafe. I'd like you to remember me as I was *then* rather than as I am now. Please go. Fast."

"I love you." It was true. The heart and spirit and soul of her still called to him.

Her smile was wobbly. "Don't be absurd."

"Don't tell me what I feel. I love you. I still want to be with you." He ground the true words out.

"You have an active life," she said. "A quest to go on, and great evil to defeat." She kept her voice steady.

"I can't join you on that. Please leave me in peace, Rafe. Don't come back." She closed the door in his face.

His guts had twisted and were frozen and bathed in acid inside him. His eyes went blind. He moved, hit a step and lost his balance, and fell and hit the ground and rolled and came up to his feet and began walking away, hunched over.

He couldn't think, could only move through the haze of loss and grief. Finally came to himself as he realized some animal was whimpering with pain and he should find it, tend to it. Then he understood it was himself and stopped. Instead of the moans, there was roaring in his ears.

Hands braced on knees, he panted until the cold sweat that covered him began to dry and itch. Slowly he straightened, belly still tight and pitching acid. His vision cleared from dull white. If he moved, he'd lose his breakfast.

As he'd already lost his lover.

No! Loopholes. There had to be loopholes. But frantic anxiety at the back of his brain mocked him. Sure, there had been loopholes in his curse. Kill Bilachoe. Which he couldn't have done.

Jaw tightening, he shoved the thought aside, looked around him. He was lost.

No. He just didn't know where he was. The area still looked generally familiar. He knew the alphabetical grid in this part of town.

As he breathed heavily, Rafe knew that any Dark

monster could have taken him down a hundred times by now.

And he also knew he wouldn't have cared. He felt shattered inside, all of the jagged pieces of himself, his love for Amber, slicing at him. He didn't know how he functioned.

A burning line of heat came over his heart—the dowsing stick. He pulled it from his inner jacket pocket.

It felt good in his fingers. As if somehow he could fix everything.

He had to act as if he could. Vertebra by vertebra he stood tall. His hand holding the stick fell to his side. "Home," he said. It was Mystic Circle and Amber's house, and the tiny rod pressed him westward and south. Fine. He'd explore every loophole to help Amber until he was dead.

Rafe hadn't driven away, but he was gone. Amber had folded onto the couch until she sensed he was out of the neighborhood. The smell of champagne seeped to her. So she levered herself up and opened the door and looked at the shattered bits of bottle and battered, beautiful blossoms, and a box of Tamara's baked goods on its side. Where were brownies when you needed them?

She'd sent Tiro away. Maybe she could reconsider.

Then Sargas was there. *I can fixs!* He zoomed through the screen door, thankfully not burning a hole in it. The firesprite flashed along the droplets and stream of champagne until he came to the puddle, then sucked it up. Even as she wondered whether alcohol affected the sprite, all traces of dampness were gone...and the dark green of the bottle had melted and merged into the concrete floor of the porch. A rather pretty effect but a little unexplainable and Amber couldn't help but think of the brownies again.

Sargas flickered near the pastry box. "Chocolate insside," he said, with a slight mournful note in his sizzle. He couldn't get in the box without torching it.

The color of Tamara's label showed Amber that cookies were inside. She hadn't lost her sweet tooth. With measured steps and motions she picked the box up and took it inside, giving Sargas a double-fudge chocolate chip cookie and returning for the flowers. She'd keep them until they died, as her former life had died, as Rafe's love for her would die.

He'd leave Denver soon enough. Before she went into assisted living.

"Pavan!" Rafe yelled, visualizing the elf, sending all his magic out into a call. "I need you here! Pavan!" He scrabbled for his computer tablet in the midst of the books on the coffee table and clicked it on, stabbed at the program "Journey to Lightfolk Palaces," thought of the elf again and yelled, "Pavan!"

A column of blue-violet sparkles appeared in the dim living room, then solidified into the elf guardian. The dude actually looked tired. Rafe stared. "Sorry for my impatience."

Pavan grimaced. A staff appeared in his hand and he leaned on it. Rafe gestured to the big, soft chair.

"Please, sit." He kept himself from shifting his feet or pacing until the guy sat. "Can I get you some cocoa or something?"

The elf leaned back, closing his eyes. "Brandy would be good."

"Okay." Rafe went to the cabinet that held Amber's liquor and sorted through it. Yep, she had an excellent label of brandy. When he pulled it out, Tiro was there with a snifter that appeared too delicate to be glass. Something an elf would drink out of, Rafe supposed. He took the cup with a nod to the small man.

"The brownie is agitated, too," Pavan said. His eyes were still closed and he appeared nearly boneless in the chair. Rich magic—air-elemental-magic—emanated from him in small swirls of light. Rafe figured the elf could still move fast and deadly if he wanted, and when his hand closed around the snifter Rafe offered, he was sure of that.

"What has happened?" Pavan asked after taking a sip of the liquor.

"Bilachoe is dead."

Pavan opened his eyes. His mouth curved faintly. "Excellent." Another sip. "You killed him?"

"Sort of." Rafe grimaced. "Amber Sarga broke my curse. That and one of my weapons did it."

Pavan's brows went up. He stared at Tiro. "You didn't stop her." He didn't wait for an answer and snorted. "No one could ever stop those women of Cumulustre's line. I hope Cumulustre didn't die from this." Pavan's tone was as sharp as Rafe's dagger. The elf glanced at Tiro, who cringed. "She's still alive, otherwise you wouldn't be here." Then Pavan turned his bright blue stare on Rafe. "You're right. Your curse is gone. You can fulfill your destiny, the destiny of *your* line."

There was silence as Pavan's eyes went distant and he drank his brandy. With discreet gestures, Tiro pointed to the kitchen, mimed eating. Rafe recalled that dark chocolate went well with brandy. He went and got a candy bar and even put it on a plate.

With a nod of thanks, Pavan set down his drink on a table, bit into the chocolate, then turned his attention back to Rafe. "You called me thrice. What do you need?"

Rafe straightened his shoulders, glanced at the elf's eyes, then focused on his mouth so he wouldn't be snared by the elf's power. "Amber aged. I want that fixed."

"Fixed," Pavan said in a voice that seemed to freeze the air between them.

"Yes."

"You dare to bargain with me?" Frosty amusement.

"No. No bargain. A request." Rafe swallowed. "I'll do what needs to be done."

A slight sigh came from the elf and there was something about it that let Rafe's muscles ease.

"I think you already have," Pavan murmured. "Done enough. Though you will be expected at a Lightfolk palace on your thirty-third birthday."

Rafe nodded, focused on the pale pink lips. "I'll be there." He took a breath. "I'd like Cumulustre to be notified that his last descendant needs him to release his binding."

"You know nothing of this matter." The icy shards of words were back, aimed at his chest, and, dammit, stabbing toward his fast-beating heart.

"I know something," Rafe contradicted. "But not all. I'd like Cumulustre notified that Amber needs him."

The scent of ozone came, lightning sizzled in the fireplace, igniting the logs, thunder rolled throughout the house and the dogs howled. Tiro crawled under the afghan on the love seat where he was sitting and behind a pillow. Rafe was battered by the air in the room. He swayed and sank into his balance but he didn't fall.

"I will consider it," Pavan snapped and left, brandy snifter and drink, chocolate and plate and all.

Rafe grinned in relief, rolled his shoulders. "That went well."

Tiro laughed hysterically.

At the end of the day, Amber knew she had to tie up the last knot. So she called Tiro. She was propped in bed, with Sargas glimmering on the bedside candle. Even though the pilot light in the oven was better for him, he'd wanted to stay with her.

She looked at the brownie. "You were right, all along." She strove to keep the bitterness out of her voice.

Instead of a sneer or a smirk, he lowered his head, but Amber gasped as she saw brownish tears fall to the rug. "I did not want this. I never wanted this," Tiro said, nearly a sob.

Amber reached for a chocolate candy nugget and offered it to him. He shook his head in denial.

"Age and death happen to us all." She smiled and felt her face fold into lines. "It's not so bad. And you can be sure that I've learned my lesson. Too late, perhaps, but it's done. And now you are free. Go to Cumulustre and tell him."

The brownie ran forward and hopped onto her bed, hugging her and getting snot on her nightgown. That didn't matter much, either. She patted his head. "It's fine, Tiro." Her own voice was creakier than she cared for. "You did your best and you *did* help me."

He lifted his head and his eyes were huge, his split pupils nearly round. "You helped a lot of people." His sniff was loud and wet. "So did all your line."

Amber smiled. "That's not too bad a heritage."

"No."

"And Rafe is fine?" she asked lightly.

"He hurts and is angry."

She held out the rest of the bag of nuggets. "Here you are. I release you from your binding. Go to Cumulustre now."

Tiro peeked at her. "He will be angry with you."

Amber laughed, spread her arms wide. She'd learned acceptance of limitations more now than ever before. "What would he do to an old woman? Let him fuss."

Tiro took the chocolate. "I will tell Cumulustre. He will be angry, but I don't care. I am staying with Rafe at Mystic Circle." The brownie vanished.

And once more she was alone.

CHAPTER

31

THE NEXT DAY A KNOCK CAME AT AMBER'S door and startled her from a doze. She turned to see out the front window, but her body didn't twist well, especially not with a laptop on her knees. She set it aside, missing the heat—she was often cold, now—and groaned to her feet. She grabbed the quad cane she was no longer too proud to use and thumped the three feet to the doorway. The diamond-paned glass in the door showed an exquisite face and silver hair. Pavan, the elf.

She opened the door and stood holding the handle.

"So the Cumulustre line is finally dying, without learning their lesson," he said.

Not even rudimentary courtesy this time. Fine with her. "I learned my lesson fine, and my ancestresses probably did, too." Amber was glad her teeth were still strong, she bared them in an angry grin. "And this Cumulustre, this *Sarga,* ensured that the Davail line lived, a bloodline you seem to believe is important but which the Lightfolk did not safeguard. So don't tell me that I didn't help. That I didn't give you a result that you Lightfolk wanted."

His lips lost their curl. "We lost track of the Davail bloodline. Furthermore we were bound not to interfere."

Amber shrugged. "That's your story. I was able to track that bloodline easily enough."

"It's the truth, and you used computers and modern technology that wasn't available to us."

"Don't tell me you couldn't have found him by tracing his magic."

"A lot of humans have elven magic."

"A lot of bloodlines are specifically *engineered?* That must make a difference."

His voice hardened. "And here's another truth. *Your* ancestors lost track of Cumulustre. And every single time you broke a curse and aged yourselves, *you hurt him, too.* You think a binding only goes one way? He would not survive another one of your kind."

"No." Her hand trembled to her chest.

"Truth." The word literally rang like a silver bell. "My friend Cumulustre is nearly as bad off as you are."

"Oh, no."

Pavan angled his chin. "Do you want to continue to speak of this out here?"

"No." She stepped away from the door and took the cane, moved slowly into the kitchen. "What do you want to drink?"

"So gracious," he mocked.

"You're in." She turned on the burner under the kettle. "What do you want?"

"I recently visited Rafe."

The mug she'd had in her hand fell a few inches to the counter, rolled off and shattered on the tile floor. She just stared at the mess, thinking how long it would take her to clean it, not wanting to think of Rafe and her shattered relationship and heart.

"How is he?" she asked. Her voice sounded thin to her own ears.

"Not well." With a gesture, Pavan reversed the damage of the cup until it was whole and sitting next to the kettle.

"Sick!"

"Not physically." An unamused smile came and went on the elf's face. "He is in as good condition as ever. Mentally, he is stunned and not thinking well. Emotionally, he is wounded and bleeding."

"I am sorry for that," she whispered. Blindly, she reached for the hot chocolate mix and dumped teaspoons of it in both cups.

"He did not ask for you to save him. You made that decision without advising him or his input."

Sargas came to sit on the burner fire and flared outward to Pavan. The elf's eyes widened and he stepped back.

"Amber iss a good persson."

One side of Pavan's mouth lifted in a charming smile. "A protector?"

"Yes. Thank you, Sargas."

"Sargas," Pavan murmured. "He took your name."

"Yes. And what you said about me making the decision about Rafe without talking to him is true. I love...loved...him. I saw him about to die during that duel. A duel no one else observed, helped us with. I saved him and I paid the price." She lifted her chin defiantly, but didn't look the elf in his eyes. She wouldn't let him bespell her. Then she felt the wetness of tears traveling down the creases of her cheeks and had to stop a sob of mortification. Fumbling in her apron pocket, she pulled out a tissue and wiped up. "I had learned my lesson, believe me, but I could not let Rafe die." She shrugged, feeling the weight of his scrutiny.

"Perhaps I do believe you."

The kettle whistled. She lifted it. It wasn't full. It only had enough water for a couple of mugs of hot chocolate. Gritting her teeth, she forced her hand to be steady as she poured. The scent of chocolate rose and it was comforting.

Pavan twirled his finger in the air and the water and cocoa mixed. Amber stirred her own with a spoon. She drank and it was good, warming her stomach.

"Rafe asked me to contact Cumulustre that he may break the binding on you and restore your youth."

Now her stomach clenched. She was too afraid to hope. Had given that up. So she drank and when she could, she said, "But the binding works both ways and Cumulustre is harmed."

Pavan nodded. "He might or might not have the power and the magic to allay or reverse his original spell."

She looked him in the eyes. It hardly mattered

whether Pavan caught her in a spell or not. "I under-stand. And I understand that you might not want to tell him of Rafe's request. I made my choice, and I would do the same again. You do as you believe right."

The elf drank down the hot chocolate, waved and his mug was clean. He took a stride back from her and for the first time, she saw respect in his eyes.

He bowed. To her. "Your courage is more than I thought." Then he was gone.

Amber snorted. "The foolhardiness of my bloodline was never in question. Only our intelligence."

Even two days later it was becoming harder to get out of bed in the morning. The few jobs she had didn't seem to hold her interest. She tired easily and was cold nearly all the time. Staying in bed was lovely.

Sargas flickered onto the bedside wick. He spent the nights on one of the pilot lights in the stove, and was moving around the smaller bungalow more eas-ily. Amber had candles evenly spaced throughout the house.

"The big flame iss in the ssky!" Sargas said excitedly. He loved watching the sun come up.

Amber missed her eastern bedroom window. The front of the house still faced east, but her tiny bedroom was on the north side off the living-dining room. She'd also determined that she'd moved too far from the business district. The walk there and back was beyond her. So she was more isolated and she didn't like that.

"Get up and look at the ssky ball!" Sargas said.

She smiled. Her tiny cheerleader. And there was something about today that she'd been anticipating. She didn't recall what, but she'd check her computer calendar during breakfast.

So she dressed in sweats and added an apron and sweater. When she consulted her calendar her omelet turned cold and rubbery in her mouth. It had been a week ago she and Rafe had received the journals, the duel challenge had been sent. And she'd organized a get-together with everyone on the cul-de-sac to meet Rafe. She'd been so proud and happy then. So sure somehow they could defeat Bilachoe in the next few months.

And she was tired again. But there was work. When she finished these two cases, she'd leave this place for assisted living. Maybe she'd take a senior cruise.

Sargas shimmered happily in his candle bowl on the breakfast table. No, scratch the cruise.

She was washing her dishes and looking out the window at the dry and pitiful backyard when a silver streak cut the blue sky, hit the center of her yard with a smacking, lightning crackle and formed into an elf.

The smallest elf she'd ever seen.

A young elf, no more than a boy of about seven or eight.

Her skin goose-bumped as she got a bad feeling. He came up to her back door and banged on it with a small fist.

She went through the back porch and opened it. They stared at each other and her mouth dried.

He sighed and shook his head. His manner and his

eyes weren't that of a child. He offered a fine-boned small hand. "Cumulustre."

"So you, uh, became younger as we aged?"

"Correct."

Amber bit her lip. She knew to the depth of her bones then something none of her ancestresses had. While they'd been hurting themselves, they'd hurt this elf, deeply, consistently. They'd been so wrong.

"Amber Sarga." She took his hand and there was a sweet connection there, like coming home. She told herself it was only elven magic. "Come in."

Her ultimate ancestor studied her with eyes the color of the sky. "I think you should come out. When was the last time you left that abode?"

"Yesterday afternoon." She'd sat on the front porch and talked to the neighbors when they'd walked by and introduced themselves.

His head tilted, showing a pointed chin. He must have been a beautiful man. With a sweeping gesture, he indicated the backyard that was mostly dried and cracked dirt with a touch of green. "This place doesn't hold any indications of you."

She hadn't been out in the back. It had been too depressing, and she didn't have the strength to garden, nor the will to change someone else's place into her own vision.

"Pavan visited me," Cumulustre said. A brief, sour smile. "I don't often go among my people in my condition."

"I'm sorry."

He snorted. "Pavan informed me that you were in

trouble." A couple of beats of ironic silence this time. "As if I didn't know. He said that your lover, a *Davail,* requested that I break the geas, the binding I laid upon your bloodline."

Hope ached through every cell, must have filtered from her eyes. She wanted to curl up with the pain but would not do so before this arrogant elf, one of her ultimate forebears. Still, she had to swallow to gather enough spit to speak, and wet her lips before the words would issue with aged whisperiness. "You could do that? Reverse our problems?"

The boy nodded, face impassive but storms moving in his eyes. "Now I can. It would have been difficult even two weeks ago. Nearly impossible."

She kept her spine straight. "I would have chanced it."

His lips thinned and he jerked a nod. "So would have I. It would have been a touchy business to see if the siphoning of age from you to me would have killed us both or only one of us."

Amber reckoned she might have been the one.

"But now I have a much better chance."

"How?"

He smiled and his lips curved boyishly, though his gaze remained older than hers by centuries. "Like this." He set his palms inward and about two feet apart, curving his fingers. As she watched a shimmer began in the air, then formed into a thin bubble. At first it was iridescent, then the skin of it took on a faint hint of blue. His hands moved to the bottom of the sphere, cradling it. Then he pushed it up into the air.

The bubble rose fast, vanished against the blue sky quickly.

Cumulustre grinned at her. "We will see what it captures."

"Captures?"

"You aren't aware of what went on these past three months with Jindesfarne Mistweaver?"

"No." She huffed. "I've just started learning about the Lightfolk in the past couple of weeks."

Cumulustre examined her. "I can see that." He hummed a couple of bars of music that Amber strained her ears to listen to, then said, "There is more magic in the world. Bubbles of pure magic recently rose from the core of the planet. Most of them popped and released magic throughout the world. I hope to find and capture a small one that will provide me with enough energy to reverse the binding I placed on your family and myself."

"Wow," was all Amber found to say.

"Again, this would not have been possible even a fortnight ago." A smile that made him inhumanly beautiful appeared on his face. "I have been keeping track of one or two bubbles." He glanced at her with a lifted silver brow. "If you want more detailed information, you should consult Jindesfarne Mistweaver Emberdrake, who lived next to you in Mystic Circle. Or Eight Corp, which is managing the melding of Lightfolk magic and human science."

"I heard about that melding. Visited Eight Corp." She rubbed her arm where the djinn had burnt it.

The elf's lips firmed and she thought she saw lightning flash in his eyes, making them blue-white, then dark, then the standard bright blue. "I will ensure that you are welcome there."

Had he read her thoughts? Maybe. "Thank you," she said. Then she finally remembered her manners. "Would you like something to drink?"

Again he smiled like a boy. "I hear you have a good way with chocolate."

"I'll get us some cocoa," she said, grateful to go back inside the house. She needed her thick coat. He didn't follow her in and that was a relief, too. She poured pure chocolate syrup into cold milk and zapped two drinks in the microwave, and was back in the yard with Cumulustre in under five minutes. She liked being with him.

He took a mug from her, and drank from it, closed his eyes and sighed. "Very good."

"Thank you." She drank her own. It wasn't the best she'd ever made, but it would do.

"I am not sure how much to tell you of the Lightfolk now," he said.

"Or my magic?"

"You've been told as much as you should be about that." When he replied his voice almost grated and his anger and disappointment resurged. Amber wished she had kept her mouth shut. He looked away from her, at the dry yard that was mostly cracked dirt.

She scalded her tongue on the damn chocolate.

A minute passed. Two. She drank and the atmosphere around her was infused with air magic simply due to Cumulustre's presence. Her senses sharpened.

She followed his gaze to the west, toward Mystic Circle, and thought she could hear the exuberant voices of Tamara and Jenni setting up the party she'd organized to welcome Rafe to the neighborhood. Tears pressed hard behind her eyes.

She cleared her throat and glanced sideways at Cumulustre. "Do you know if Rafe got to buy the Fanciful House in Mystic Circle?"

"He did."

"Thank you."

The elf's expression was austere. Then his nostrils widened, his head tilted back as he looked into the sky and the man's pure relief was the scent of lilacs in the air.

Every breath they took was one of excitement and anticipation. She actually heard his breath hitch, saw his hands tremble around his mug. He yearned for his age as much as she wanted her youth.

Soon she saw what he had. His blue-tinged bubble descended and within it was a smaller bubble swirling with color. As it came down, Amber saw that the colors were a mixture of those she associated with elemental magic. She flinched as she saw that most was fire-orange and red, but there was a good deal of white-blue-violet that was air, and a thick streak of the gold for earth. The least amount were a few tendrils of blue-green water.

Cumulustre held out his hands and his bubble lit on them.

"What is it?" Amber breathed, afraid she might pop one or more of the bubbles and that could be really bad.

Cumulustre smiled and it was the first carefree one Amber had seen. Lovely. "Pure magic, given to us with grace by this planet, the Earth. With this energy and magic, I should be able to free the binding spell from us."

The bubble and the magic seething inside was hypnotic, even more than Rafe's shield and dagger. Her hopes glittered and swirled and changed with it, sometimes great and wondrous, sometimes aching in her tight chest beyond belief. She might get her life back! Tears trailed down her cheeks.

"I think we may need some help. Do you agree to ask for some?"

"Yes."

"Pavan? Tiro?" Cumulustre whispered.

A moment later the elf guardian and the formerly grumpy brownie appeared. He saw Amber and tears spurted from his eyes. She tottered to him. "Shhh. Shhh. It's going to be okay."

Tiro flung himself on her and wiped his face on her apron. His arms around her legs were strong. And wonderful. Friends. Bonds between old friends could spring up so quickly. Then he abandoned her to walk slowly over to Cumulustre, who wasn't that much taller than the brownie, maybe eight inches. Tiro took off his felt cap and squeezed it in his hands, his ears drooped. "I failed you," he said, his breath hitching.

"No. You served me and my line well."

"I could not stop them from throwing their lives away."

"They did help people," Cumulustre said with distinct unenthusiasm. He looked at Amber. "In my anger when I made the binding on my first daughter and cut myself off from my line, I didn't know that I was affected by my geas, too. The only way to break the binding on us both was for you Cumulustre women to learn your lesson."

"Amber...Amber had learned." Tiro blinked big eyes up at the boy elf. "Truly. But she loved the Davail." Tiro sniffed long and hard. "She could not turn away from his death curse."

"Still flawed," Amber said.

"We shall see," Cumulustre said. "If you are, this spell won't work. I wish to lift the binding because it is no longer needed. If you had not continued to break curses, it would have fallen away by itself, but now the magical binding must sense that you *have* learned not to drain yourself for others. To put saving yourself and your energies first. The spell will make allowances for true love, but will probe your heart and your mind to know that what I wanted for my bloodline, strong women who know their own worth, is within you."

"All right."

"If Pavan and Tiro and I and you, yourself, Amber, are wrong, both you and I are doomed."

She held herself proudly, sent a glance to each one of them. "We are not wrong."

"It will take blood, mine and yours," Cumulustre said.

"Fine."

He pushed up his sleeve and held out his arm. A sharply pointed knife appeared in Pavan's hand, gleamed in the sun. The older elf sliced Cumulustre's wrist and his blood was like mercury, quicksilver. Fascinating. Pavan slit a vein at her wrist and deep red blood turned scarlet.

Cumulustre took her hand and set his bloody arm against hers. Their blood mingled and the natural bond twined thick and fast between them, like a cable of sparkling blue-white, blood-red. Huge. She *felt* him, Cumulustre, and he was kin. Her throat closed. *Kin,* as she hadn't had in twenty years.

The bubble broke and the energy whipped out, and Amber was blinded by a flash. Then she was frozen. To her mind's eye, it looked like her body was coated with clear plastic, then it *broke open.* Inside were glowing stars in a foggy mass, all bound with a golden net. The ends of the net were in her red-throbbing heart-star and her white mind-star. Not quite like a curse.

She felt a tug at the cord and again she was inside, not out. The cord constricted—more, it slid like probes into her mind and heart, yanked at her as if testing. All the times she'd broken curses flickered before her—sickness, emotional wounds, true love being shunted aside. The moment in the bar crystallized, her own words rolled through her. "I need to care for myself *first.* I am deserving of my own help and love." Her feelings of inadequacy, she understood now, were because she'd been abandoned. Her mother and aunt had not loved her enough to stay, so she had to show people, *everyone,* she was good by helping others at the cost of herself. Not to mention that she *did* want to help people. But she had to put herself first.

The golden net unraveled. She had time for a breath of magic-rich air or two before she was locked in agony. It felt like a strainer was going up her, cutting her into patterned pieces, checking every cell. Her feet went through the sieve and were minced, her bones sliced up her legs. When it reached her womb she began a long scream, thought it might be echoed by the sound of delicate glass breaking. Breaking. She was breaking, her flesh gobbets, and now her heart, her scream went on and on, her very last breath. Her mind dimmed and she would have passed out if she hadn't somehow had a bright and sparkling fizz to lean against and gain energy, a small and solid presence that held her still and steady. Love that felt familiar to her. A tiny flame she could focus upon.

And it was done.

CHAPTER 32

SHE LAY ON THE DIRT, PANTING. SOMEONE else was, too. "Thank you, from both of us," said a weary, musical voice. "You may go."

"Glad to," said a strained, equally musical one, and a rumble grumble grunt that might come from a brownie.

When the pain subsided and she got enough breath, she lifted a weak hand to her eyes. Her fingertips felt crust gluing her lashes to her cheeks. She rubbed them and looked up and deep blue sky greeted her. The most beautiful thing she'd ever seen.

She felt heavier. Not just in muscle mass, but in her emotions, her heart, her mind. But who wouldn't after something like that? She got one elbow under her, propped up on it, and found herself looking at a gorgeous naked male elf. Who stirred no emotion in her.

Cumulustre. *Then* emotions slammed into her. Kin. Loving kin who had held her and helped her through the ordeal, along with the absent Pavan and Tiro.

Me, too! came a tiny voice in her mind.

Sargas. *Yes, you, too,* she sent mentally.

The elf grunted and sat up, and between blinks he was clothed in fluid white stuff that looked like armor. Then he stood with inhuman grace and glided over to her, offering a hand.

"It worked!" She took his hand and rose easily, her muscles moving smoothly. She saw her hands, the skin was tight and pretty and she couldn't stop a gulp of tearful relief.

Cumulustre squeezed her fingers and dropped them, stepping back to study her. Faint frown lines creasing his brow. "I can see that you have learned other ways to break curses beyond the major one. Interesting." He paused, flashed a brilliant smile. "Well done."

She stood tall, lifted her chin. "My gift has grown." Perhaps it would have always evolved to what she had now—options to use her major magic. She didn't know. But she'd definitely learned her lesson. "I've grown."

"I can see that…daughter."

Pleasure flushed through her, heating her cheeks. "Thank you, sire."

Another hesitation as he studied her head to foot, then he said, "Unlike most elves, I have no other bloodlines." His mouth turned sour. "I didn't have the vitality to beget them after the binding was in place."

Amber started to snap at him but was forestalled by his raised hand.

"My foolishness as well as your foremother's." Grief passed over his face and Amber thought that however long he'd lived, the loss remained fresh, a consequence of longevity. Once again he focused on her face. "I can see her in the shape of your eyes, even after all these generations."

They stared at each other. Amber only saw a beautiful elf, not much older than she.

"I have heard that your home is in Mystic Circle." He glanced in that direction as if he might be able to see through six blocks.

"Yes."

"And you have a lover, perhaps a mate."

Anxiety twisted her stomach. How much of what she'd told Rafe was true? That they'd only loved because of the desperate circumstances. She loved him, would always love him, but what about his feelings? "Perhaps," she said, and shifted her balance.

Cumulustre chuckled. "And I can see that you are impatient to see him. I, too, am impatient…to see the next generation."

The heat that had subsided on her cheeks rose again, just as hot. Cumulustre's smile was sly, his eyes half-lidded. "Go seduce him."

"No magic!" she snapped, found her palm pressing against her heart. "I couldn't bear it if you influenced his love with magic and it faded—the magic and the love."

Lifting one brow, the elf said, "There is always

magic between a man and a maid." Now his eyes turned bright laser-blue and snagged her and she knew she'd been wrong to look in them directly. He could do anything with her.

His voice was equally mesmerizing. "I see that you love him truly and for a lifetime. I see that the bond between you was forged by such circumstances and under the effect of the awakening of your magic that it was strong."

Was being the significant word. Though the fact that Rafe had stayed and asked for help gave her hope that what they had could grow stronger.

Cumulustre glanced away, releasing her from his thrall. "I will visit you in Mystic Circle in the future." His whole expression went to glowing happiness. "Now I must mend my own ties with my kind, visit my own friends who have grieved not to see me these many years." After a flourishing bow, he disappeared.

Amber was filled with energy and hope and the need to claim Rafe as soon as possible. She didn't know how long he might grieve for her, but was sure it wasn't going to be years. She could only hope that he hadn't already moved on.

She ran to the back porch and got her large suitcase, threw her clothes and her laptop and the few other things—a mug, candles—she'd brought or purchased into this new life with her.

"Sargas?"

"I am here," he said, flaming long on his three-wick

candle. He shot toward her, streaked around her and back to his wick. "You are harder."

Her muscles felt firm and strong. "Not as squishy, for sure. Can you call the firesprite who helped transport you here to take you back to my home in Mystic Circle?"

"Yesss." He sparkled orange and red. Excitement and joy? "I love Mysstic Csircle!"

"Me, too. I'm sure there will be enough chocolate there to pay her off." Amber frowned. "I had ingredients for a chocolate pie. I can't see Rafe making that. As long as we have milk, we should be good." Her lips turned down. "Though I'd like candied violets. Maybe the brownies will make them for us."

"We do not ussually get to eat flowerss." Sargas sounded intrigued.

"All right, promise her a chocolate pie of her own, with violets. If not today, then tomorrow. I can do that myself if need be." Even if she had to buy violet plants for the blooms. She glanced out the backyard. No violets here. Dandelions were beginning to poke out yellow heads. The only hint of green in the dry yard.

She turned away from the window at a hiss, only to see the firesprite and Sargas merge and flash out of sight.

And she was left alone in this house.

Panic rose to coat her throat. It was, really, a very nice house. But it had been a place of despair for her. She never wanted to come back. So get all that she could cram in the wheeled suitcase and leave. The small amount of food in the refrigerator and any mess could be taken care of by a cleaning service or brownies. Someone *else*.

She did a quick scan for stuff, tidied as she went, left the canes and the walkers in the back porch. Double-checked that she had all her documents, electronics and books. The suitcase wasn't organized, very helter-skelter, but she shut it and zipped it anyway, and headed for the front door. She locked it behind her and bumped down the steps to the sidewalk. She wanted to leave the key in a bush or the mailbox or under a rock or flowerpot. That wouldn't be responsible. So she shoved it into the outer pocket of the suitcase and began rolling it away, nearly trotting. It felt *good* to run. She didn't care about the stares she was getting from a neighbor or two. She was *outta there*.

She didn't look back.

"Spark has returned," Tiro said.

Rafe grunted. He was in his usual position during the time he wasn't training. His spine was curved into the pillows of the living room couch, feet on the coffee table, deep in the game of "Journey to the Lightfolk Palaces" on his tablet computer. It was fully as realistic as the despised Fairies and Dragons that he'd been glad to see fade from his app screen.

The program was more of an adventure quest set on an Earth dotted with towns instead of great human cities. He had to sense magic and follow streams of it. On the map, Mystic Circle was a gorgeous whirlpool of balanced magic, as was the area surrounding it—

Denver. Another deep well of it showed a few miles away from the cul-de-sac where he thought Eight Corp was. Though the company was considered a Lightfolk Royal Holding, it was not marked with the symbol that showed a "palace." Rafe had actually read the instructions of the game.

He'd journeyed hundreds of miles and thought he found an Earth palace near Yellowstone National Park. Tiro would not confirm nor deny. The Mistweaver brownies were busy taking care of Jenni Mistweaver Emberdrake and her new husband, Aric Paramon, who'd arrived unexpectedly.

Rafe had actually thought he'd seen them come out of a tree in the park in the middle of the cul-de-sac during one of his dawn runs. Whatever was going on at the house next door, it was taking up a lot of time and brownie service and magic. He and Tiro were living on take-out from restaurants a few blocks away and Rafe's scrambled eggs.

Though Rafe had felt a shudder go through him as more magic swept out from next door—balanced magic that made everything around him sharper, as if he'd looked through a blurred camera lens. The cul-de-sac was more vibrant and the trees and lawn seemed to bud into spring overnight.

Anyway, the brownies weren't talking. They weren't even coming by to mooch the stack of chocolate bars that remained in the cupboard.

In the game, Rafe had hesitated at the "door" of the earth palace. Despite his acquaintance with Vikos, he didn't feel an earth palace was where he wanted to present himself on his thirty-third birthday. To show that he'd won the Cosmos Dagger. To be taught by Lightfolk warriors to fight and kill Dark ones. He wanted an air palace, and he would find one.

So much for the magical part of his life. On the human front, he'd spent hours on the phone with his brother Gabe and his uncle.

Both of them had felt it when the curse had been broken. Gabe said it was as if a backpack loaded with rocks had fallen away. He'd called Rafe and though Rafe hadn't told him the whole story yet, Rafe figured it would only be a matter of time.

Gabe had agreed with the purchase of number two Mystic Circle and would be coming to check out the rest of the neighborhood in a month or so for real estate investments. He hadn't lost any time confessing to Cynthia and the wedding was set for Thanksgiving week.

Rafe's uncle had been a little cooler, but the distance between them was being bridged.

Conrad had called. They'd spoken in near-code about what had happened. Conrad was interested but distracted. He'd taken an apartment in a small city close to where Marta was living. She'd agreed to meet with him. For once, Rafe didn't feel negative toward her. Magic was in his life and had changed him. Who was to say that magic wasn't working on Conrad and Marta, too?

And he understood how his friend ached for a lost love. Rafe damn well hurt.

"I said that Spark is back." Tiro actually hopped

onto Rafe's calves and stood staring down at him, hands on hips. He was heavier than he looked. Rafe didn't think he could move his legs and his feet were going numb fast.

"Spark's back." Fear shot through Rafe, he sat up. "Amber isn't—" He shut his imagination down, couldn't say the words. His heart beat loudly in his ears from the throb of dread.

"Spark says his name is Sargas."

Rafe blinked. "Spark, Sargas is a *he?*"

"He has determined his sex."

"Oh." Rafe tried to move. Couldn't because of the pressure on his ankles. He had one pissed-off brownie. "Ow."

There were thumps outside like a large beast. Rafe stiffened. No evil could come into the Circle, now or ever. That he knew.

Swishing across the wooden porch. The knocker slammed.

Tiro's face blazed happiness and he disappeared. "Come *on!*" he yelled at Rafe.

Rafe jolted to his feet, winced at the needles of returning blood. He lurched from the living room to the entryway. Tiro was by the door, hopping up and down with thumps that seemed to echo through the house like a heartbeat.

Opening the door, he saw a beautiful woman who made his breath stop and his own heart stutter. She looked like Amber's younger sister.

No.

Not. Sister.

"Amber?"

She wet her lips. He remembered Amber doing that. Her golden-brown eyes were and weren't the same. They were bright and clear, but held a wealth of experience. He pulled her in, into the house, into his arms. Against him.

She smelled right. But, hell, she was younger than he. And a serious woman with expectations. He didn't mess with young women with expectations.

Her mouth was on his and he tasted *her*. His Amber, his woman. Oh, yeah, he did mess with younger, serious women. She wasn't getting away from him again. Ever.

He drew away, stroked her cheek. The texture of her skin was different. Her body appeared a little less lush, too. Something to look forward to, her filling out more. And he knew she'd make a lovely old woman. He wanted to see every single change. "Mine," he said. Grabbed at a passing thought. "Love you. Marry me."

"Yes. I love you, too. Oh, yes, I'll marry you!"

He picked her up and cradled her in his arms and knew that he had all that he ever wanted.

Rafe's arms around her had tears leaking from her eyes again. This time of joy. He hadn't left! He wanted her and she wanted him. So badly.

But she met Tiro's eyes as he hopped through the stair rails to the floor of the entryway. "Thank you. For coming to me, and your help this morning. You are free."

He turned the deep brown of embarrassed brownie. "I like my room. I want to stay here."

"Of course." She looked up at Rafe, "Fine with you?"

"Yeah, yeah. Sure. Good job, Tiro," Rafe said. Amber got the impression that he had no idea of the conversation or what he'd said.

With a pop, Tiro disappeared.

"We're alone, right?" Rafe asked.

"Where are the dogs?"

"You don't really want to see the dogs right now, do you?" His panting breath was close to her face and she smelled apples and mint and coffee. He had a good hold on her, but was running up the stairs.

"No, the pups can wait until later." They didn't remember her anyway.

"They're out back." He took a deep breath, barely able to believe he had her in his arms. "God, *Amber.*"

Rafe shoved the door to her bedroom open with his shoulder. She saw that he'd slept there and hadn't made the bed. He tossed her through the air and she landed with a laugh.

He was ripping his clothes off as he followed her. As he pounced.

And the feel of his hard and strong body against her own, her firm flesh, was nearly more than she could bear. She helped him with his shirt, his jeans. And then they were kissing and touching, and petting and stroking and driving each other close to climax. Just with hands on taut, flushed and heated skin.

He rolled over her, joined with her and she reveled in the way her body undulated under his, arched, strove to ecstasy with his. Her lover. Her fiancé. Her man, proving that she was all woman and his.

They peaked together, moaned each other's name and held each other tightly.

She looked at him, his face rough with stubble, his eyes dilated from sex but focused on her. He slipped a hand around her nape and brought her close, nibbled on her lips, probed her mouth with his tongue, then withdrew. "You. Your taste is almost the same. Almost but not quite. But it is you." His muscular arms clamped her so close she could barely breathe, but she wanted that, wanted this connection, this *bond* with him.

"Yes, it's me. At my real age. Cumulustre came by this morning and we were able to reverse the aging process. He—"

But Rafe kissed her again. "Later. We can discuss all that later." He moved and she realized he was ready to love again. "My Amber."

"My Rafe."

They held on to each other, kept their eyes on each other as they moved together and shattered together and were remade.

This time he rolled and scooted until their sides touched, all the while linking fingers with her. She waited until love fog cleared from her mind, and she was breathing less raggedly before saying, "You stayed."

"Yeah. It hurt to stay, but I thought it would hurt worse to leave." His mouth twisted. "I couldn't leave, but I didn't do much. Worked out at the dojo. Trained at the lyceum. Played the new game Pavan gave me. Didn't do much at all. I couldn't believe the changes in my life. That my future was spread before me, but you weren't in it." He stroked her hair. "I asked Pavan to fix your age problem."

"He told me. It was touch and go."

Rafe closed his eyes, gathered her close again. "I don't think I want to face that right now. Later when I'm sure that you won't vanish."

Amber scrutinized Rafe and suppressed her worry. He didn't appear in great shape. Oh, his muscles were fine, but he'd lost weight and there were new lines in his face. And not just from his duel with Bilachoe, though that had marked him. The loss of her had hurt him.

She closed her eyes, cherishing their closeness. They held each other for a couple of minutes in blissful silence. Then their lips molded together in another kiss that had renewed passion flooding through her.

Rafe flopped back against the pillows. "Wow."

"Yes." She stroked his hair back from his forehead.

"You broke my curse." He lifted her hand and kissed her palm. "Now we're together for the rest of our lives."

Unspeakable happiness filled her until she could barely breathe. She loved him and his love for her shone brilliantly in his eyes so that she had to glance down at their joined hands.

"Yes. Whatever we decide to do. Whether it's journeying to a Lightfolk palace or helping your cousin or someday having a child—"

"A kid? I don't want, can't have—" He stopped, knowledge dawned in his eyes. "A child. A son. I can have a son. A son I can watch grow. A first son who won't die before his thirty-third birthday." Rafe looked dazed.

"That's right. Whatever we do, I want you to know that I am determined to help."

"You've always been."

"That's right. I haven't changed in that, but I know my limitations."

"You aren't going to be breaking any more curses, are you?" he asked warily. "No more death curses—" his voice came husky, he looked away from her and swallowed "—or really bad curses like Conrad's?"

"No. I have other options." She set her mouth. "Even if I hadn't, I understand that not caring for myself means that I don't have as much energy to help as I might. I've grown." She lifted up to meet his eyes. "I know that no matter how hard you try there are some things you can't change...and I have to accept life as it is."

Her palm computer left in the pile of her clothes trilled an alarm and she frowned.

"What's that?" Rafe asked.

A glow of pure happiness suffused her. "The party. Time to go to the party."

"What party?"

"The get-together at Tamara's that I organized last week on our walk." Amber rolled from her bed to her feet, loving the feel of her muscles moving well. Rafe tugged at her hand. "I'd rather stay in bed."

"Let's go let you meet your neighbors."

"I've got my whole life to live," he said.

Again he tugged and she grinned at him. "And I've got my balance." She leaned down and kissed him. "Welcome to Mystic Circle."

★ ★ ★ ★ ★

*What happens when magic affects
a wholly human woman?
What do the royals have in mind for her?
Come back to find out!*

ACKNOWLEDGMENTS

For more information on Red Rocks:
http://www.redrocksonline.com.

For information on the architectural styles of Denver: *Denver, The City Beautiful* by Thomas J. Noel and Barbara S. Norgren published by Historic Denver, Inc., Denver, Colorado, 1987; Leonard Leonard & Associates: *www.leonardleonard.com/neighborhoods/styles.shtml.*

Research also took me to the Denver Museum of Nature & Science and the exhibit of the Whydah, *www.whydah.org.*

Thanks to them for their answers about concretions, knives and swords. Thanks also to the National Geographic Society for sponsoring the exhibit.

More thanks to the National Weather Service Advanced Hydrolic Prediction Service for water levels of the Platte in March, Google maps for closeups of the area I traveled twice a day on the bus when I had the day job, and the Colorado Victorian Bed and Breakfast Inns.

Most of the houses on Mystic Circle are within walking distance of me, though all can be found in Denver except the Castle, which is more imaginary, though there are castlelike homes. I'll have photos of the houses on my blog, *http://www.robindowens.blogspot.com*, pics of Amber and Rafe as they appear in Fairies and Dragons, and some cut scenes on my website, *http://www.robindowens.com.*

As for the people who live in the nine houses of

Mystic Circle...they will arrive as their friends and family are written about...or, like Kiri Palger, whose heroine is Jenni Weavers, they'll be drawn to the place....

And please remember—and share with your friends—that illegal downloads of books hurt the author. If you enjoy and respect our work, please buy an authorized copy. Thank you for supporting us.

Follow your heart and magic will come,

Robin D. Owens

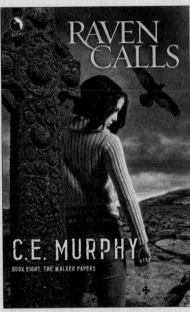

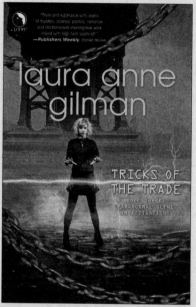

There's more to Kaylin Neya than meets the eye....
New York Times bestselling author

MICHELLE SAGARA

is back with the latest volume in her
darkly magical *Chronicles of Elantra* series!

Seven corpses are discovered in the streets of a Dragon's
fief. All identical, down to their clothing. Kaylin Neya is
assigned to discover who they were, who killed them—
and why. Is the evil lurking at the borders of Elantra
preparing to cross over?

CAST IN RUIN

Available now.